Maya Angelou
" The Heart
of a woman"

THE
DAY
THE
MUSIC
DIED

THE DAY THE

A NOVEL BY

A KENT CARROLL BOOK

MUSIC DIED

Joseph C. Smith

Grove Press, Inc./New York

First Edition 1981
First Printing 1981
ISBN: 0-394-51951-5
Grove Press ISBN: 0-8021-0208-5
Library of Congress Catalog Card Number: 80-8914

Manufactured in the United States of America

Distributed by Random House, Inc., New York

GROVE PRESS, INC., 196 West Houston Street, New York, N.Y. 10014

To John and David
And their sons

ACKNOWLEDGMENTS

If you would like to discover in what esteem you are held by your friends, I would suggest you mention to them that the reason you have not been around lately is because you have been hard at work on your first novel. You would be, I assure you, surprised by their various responses; and, like me, most grateful to those who unhesitatingly offered encouragement and assistance.

And so, in the order of their appearances between the lines of the pages that will follow, I would like to express my gratitude to Evelyn Griffith, who was the first to read my words and declare them literate; to Doreen Lowe, who spent many hours in the University of Hawaii Library researching my material; to Bob Hein, whose insight into human frailty prevented a traumatic personal experience from interrupting my work; to Betty Sakamoto and Leonard Lovewell, for their immediate support and unflagging interest; and to my good friends Shell Hanson and Ben Almasin, who somehow managed to listen patiently while I recited to them my most brilliant passages—which I would, of course, later delete.

I would also like to add a special thanks to Doris Strother, for her generosity and understanding in helping me prepare the manuscript; to Kent Carroll, my editor at Grove Press, whose letters and phone calls always seemed to arrive at exactly the right time; to my former wife and dear friend, Thora; and, finally, to Bobby Smith, who taught me most of what I know and feel about music.

All history is but a romance, unless it is studied as an example.

—*Croly*

PROLOGUE

Looking back upon these early years, the 1950's, even in the surrealistic glare of all that has happened since, it would be easy to assume that anyone of reasonable intelligence might have predicted the changes the music would bring. But that would be an unfair assumption to make. After all, it wasn't as though somebody suddenly discovered something new. The music had been around from the beginning, and for many Americans it was already an embarrassment, a blunt reminder of misshapen attitudes and unspeakable cruelties placed upon one race of men by another, and for the ultimate benefit of neither.

Yet, to say that the music evolved solely from human suffering would be inaccurate, for its roots lay more in faith than unhappiness, and its massive appeal to young people, as well as the antipathy it generated in their elders, came from its great, penetrating humor— humor being the foundation upon which the entertainment industry was built.

For many, involvement began casually. Thoughts were not of cultural heritages, but of profits, and there was no idea of the awesome power about to be unleashed. The early rhythm and blues artists did, however, recognize the power of the music and its potential for good or evil, and many of them—Faye Adams, Clyde McPhatter and Sam Cook, among others—sought the approval of their ministers and peers before they would take it from the church and perform it in public dancehalls and nightclubs. They realized that while it appeared to be simple and repetitive, it contained a pulse that could touch the human spirit at its most primordial level. It was music that could be easily packaged and merchandised, but not easily understood. And certainly, in the years that followed, many of the people who profited from it most, were the ones who least understood it.

BOOK ONE

One man's word is no man's word; we should quietly hear both sides.

—*Goethe*

HOLLYWOOD
JUNE 1956

There are rare people who seem to have success from the beginning, almost as though the world had been poised in anticipation of their arrival, and Mark Donovan was one of those few. As if to emphasize that point, he had been less than an hour old, barely powdered and diapered, before the first photographers were taking his picture.

Having been greeted so warmly, and treated, for the most part, with the same deference ever since, he could have very easily decided to forgo the rigors of accomplishment, settled back on his laurels, such as they were, and waited for destiny to peel him a grape. The fact that he did not do so spoke well for his character, and the intervening years had seen him mature into a bright young man, properly educated and eager to assume whatever responsibilities his emerging position in the affairs of business might offer.

Good Irish stock had also given him a physical attractiveness beyond usual proportions. He stood a fraction over six feet tall, with a strong face accented by intelligent blue eyes and topped by a thick shock of hair burnished to a dark copper by the California sun.

There are some, of course, who would not attach much importance to such physical attributes, nor did he. Nevertheless, studies have proved fairly conclusively that a young man who attains a height of six feet and possesses engaging looks and, incidentally, financial independence, is likely to be more easily dissuaded from the drudgery of corporate insecurity than a young man of similar age who attains a height of, say, five feet and who possesses unattractive features and less than two hundred dollars in the bank.

So, from the beginning, Mark Donovan had a lifetime skating pass. But strangely enough, the thought of using it had seldom occurred to him.

Now, it was a little past eight-thirty A.M. in the late spring of 1956 when he pulled out of the driveway of his Malibu beach cottage and made a right turn onto Pacific Coast Highway. The car he was driving, a bright red Corvette convertible, had arrived four days earlier, a birthday present from his father and mother, Peter and May Donovan. Peter Donovan was finishing a movie in Spain, his seventy-third lead role in a feature film. And as usual, as she had been for the past twenty-seven years, May Donovan was at his side.

Despite the gift, however, it had been a rather hollow birthday for Mark. The Donovans were a close-knit family, and birthdays were always special occasions. This year, not only were Mark's parents away in Europe, but also his younger sister, Helen, had recently married and was living in New York, awaiting the birth of her first child.

The note Mark had found stuck on the steering wheel the morning the car had been delivered was typical of his mother. She had probably had it flown in from Europe with the rushes of the movie his dad was making, and delivered to his house by studio messenger. It was written in her familiar scrawl:

My dearest Mark,

How sad the business has become that we must go traipsing halfway around the world to make a film.

Your Aunt Helen has made beautiful costumes, as usual, for this "epic," and Uncle Jim has come up with some kind of gadget to blow your dear old dad to smithereens in the last scene. Positively ghastly!

Talked with your sister yesterday. She is doing well, with no complications. She said you must call her, since she can never seem to catch up with you.

The car was your father's idea. I never would have chosen something so obviously unsafe. So, dear, before you decide to go dragging along the highway, please remember that the pain I experienced bringing you into this world would be infinitesimal compared to the anguish I would feel if you should leave it before I do.

Love,
Mother

P.S. Darling, please go by the house as soon as you can and see that Emma and Will are taking care of things. They are getting old and Emma has a tendency to let garbage pile up in the kitchen.

At the bottom of the note, Peter Donovan had scribbled:

Happy Birthday, Son. Max Geary phoned me from New York a couple of days ago. I think he has a hell of a surprise for you!

Mark had reached Sunset Boulevard. He was in the left-turn lane, waiting for the light to change, when two teenage girls in bathing suits pulled alongside him. The pretty brunette behind the wheel looked over at him and squealed. He never knew how to react when that happened, as it often did. His resemblance to his father was remarkable, at least the Peter Donovan whose old movies were seen several times a month on the late show, and he never knew if the adulation was for his father or himself.

The girl in the passenger seat, a freckle-faced redhead of thirteen, peered across at him. She smiled as seductively as the braces on her teeth would allow, then turned their car radio to full volume. Fats Domino's voice suddenly blared across at Mark:

> *You know I love, yes I do . . .*
> *And I'm savin' all my lovin' jes' for you . . .*

Immediately the cars behind him started honking. He smiled at the girls, waved, and made his turn. By the time he reached the familiar UCLA turnoff, the sun had fully broken through the early-morning clouds and he could see the first traces of the day's smog against the mountains to his left. He noticed himself still humming the song, and he smiled as he recalled the night he'd met Fats.

It had happened during his junior year of college, after a night game at the Coliseum. He and a few of his teammates had walked the mile or so through the black neighborhood to the nightclub on South Broadway where Domino was performing. The line waiting to get in had stretched halfway around the block, but the doorman had spotted them in their UCLA jackets and sneaked them in without paying. The dance hall was so packed, they couldn't find seats, but since none of them drank much, they were happy to spend the night hanging over the bandstand railing, kibitzing with Fats and bobbing in time to the music. It was good music. There was no way anybody could listen to it and keep still.

At the end of the night, somebody must have told Domino who they were, because he had come out of his dressing room and allowed his picture to be taken with them. Mark still had the picture put away somewhere, of himself and his teammates posing on either side of the chubby little black entertainer all decked out in a bright pink suit with a towel around his neck.

Later, as they were walking back to their cars, a mild argument had flared up between the two black team members and the rest of them. The black guys were angry because Domino and B. B. King and Johnny Ace and the other big r&b stars could get their records played only on a few small radio stations, while the big white stars were copying their records and making a lot more money—like, for example, Buddy Morrow, who had copied Jimmy Forrest's record of "Night Train" and was playing places like the Hollywood Palladium, while Forrest was still stuck doing one-nighters and small clubs, still trying to make ends meet.

It was something Mark had never thought about until then.

And now, thinking back to that night—except for the argument, of course—touched him with nostalgia. He had always enjoyed listening to music when he was younger, maybe even more than he had realized at the time. Even when he was a kid, when his folks had bought season tickets to the Greek Theater and his father would take the whole family out for dinner and then see Chevalier or Garland. He could still remember those nights, his father driving through Griffith Park with the top down and people in passing cars gawking and smiling and waving at them. And later, when he reached college, he and his friends would drive down to the Lighthouse in Hermosa Beach on weekends to see Shorty Rogers and Stan Levy and some of the other ex-Kenton sidemen who had left the band to go out on their own. But he'd never thought much about it at the time, he'd just been having fun, and it hadn't mattered what kind of music it was: jazz, r&b, pop, all kinds—just so it was good.

He was now approaching the Beverly Hills Hotel. The driver of a white Jaguar going the other way honked at him, and he recognized the man as a family friend, a writer who had worked on several of his father's movies. A moment later, Barbara Stanwyck, making a right turn out of the hotel driveway, saw him and waved.

He continued along, enjoying the feel of the car and the warmth of the sun on his face. He had driven this hallowed ground of Beverly Hills a thousand times before. He knew every turn in the road, and many of the famous people who lived inside these majestic pastel mansions. He had always taken it for granted before, his good life. But this morning, maybe because the people he loved most were in distant, scattered parts of the world, he thought about how safe and unencumbered his life had always been.

He wasn't lucky simply because he was the son of a movie star. He had never been spoiled; May Donovan had seen to that. He was lucky because his whole life had been spent among some of the most enlightened, most successful people in the world. And not merely the publicly successful, but the dedicated, creative people who were unknown outside of their professions, who quietly went about their daily tasks of holding the world together.

And now, at twenty-four, he was just beginning to understand why his parents had raised him so carefully, had tried so hard to

18 ·

instill in him the very best values that their world of success had to offer. They had been relentless in their determination to teach him sound values. From the time he could remember, they had explained to him that it wasn't who you were or what you owned that determined the ultimate quality of your life, but the depth of your character. They had never wavered from that belief, and nothing had underlined their feelings more than the way they approached the matter of race. Around the Donovan house a person was first judged by how decent a human being he was, then by how well he did whatever it was he did.

Mark could still remember his mother placing a glass in his little five-year-old fingers, telling him, "Now, Mark, you take this drink over to the piano and you *be sure* to put it *in* Mr. Tatum's hands, because he has trouble with his eyes and he doesn't see very well."

And he could remember a few years later, during one of his parents' parties, standing beside the piano while Louis Armstrong played and sang "Sleepy Time Down South." And when Mark had voiced surprise that Armstrong, a trumpet player, could play the piano so well, Armstrong had laughed that gravelly laugh of his and said, "Son, I was *married* to a piano player, didn't you know that?"

Black actors and actresses, like Dooley Wilson and Hattie McDaniel, had also visited the house on occasion. Nor did the Donovans confine their invitations to show people. The year before Dr. Bunche had been awarded the Nobel Prize, he had personally come by the house to talk to Mark about attending UCLA, just as he himself had done. The school chancellor knew both Ralph Bunche and the Donovans, and he had requested Bunche to do so because he felt that Mark would be the type of student-athlete to inspire other, less-motivated students. At the time, Mark had been considering Stanford, but Dr. Bunche's talk with him had helped to change his mind.

Even now, Dr. Bunche still attended occasional informal dinners at the house sometimes, to remain until late in the evening to share his vast political knowledge with May and Peter Donovan and their friends.

There was a phrase Mark's mother used to describe people: *form and substance*. According to her, there were only four kinds of people in the world: people of form, people of substance, people of neither form nor substance, and people who "labor in the vineyard of life," as she liked to put it, to acquire both form *and* substance. By her definition, a man of form and substance was a man with a desire to be proficient at his calling, who respected the obligation of trying to be the person he led others to believe he was.

Mark's parents had taught him that a man of substance was not prejudiced. Logically, he had no reason to be if he was proficient at his craft. He could achieve success on his own merits without impeding the progress of others.

Having been taught to think in such a manner, Mark now found himself becoming increasingly impatient with many of his professional colleagues. Too many of them were people of very little form and no apparent substance, reluctant to put forth the necessary effort to pull their own weight. And prejudice was only one of the devices they used to advance themselves beyond their abilities.

It further annoyed him that they took it for granted he thought as they did, in the process allowing themselves to assume that he had received his executive position with the company as a gift from Max Geary. Anyone who did think that, of course, didn't know Geary. Max Geary wouldn't hire his *own* son at ITRC if he was unqualified for the job. But even worse, a great many people, particularly in sales and promotion, seemed to resent Mark *more* after they learned how well he had prepared himself for his position, as though his education was a betrayal of their trust in how the system was supposed to work.

It was a twisted logic he was confronting daily, and finding more and more difficulty in unraveling. He knew that he should not waste time trying to do so, for his best strategy lay in scaling the corporate ladder as quickly as possible, because at the top he would be in a stronger position to exert influence upon the attitudes of those around him.

He checked his watch as he crossed Vine Street. Traffic had slowed him a bit. It was now twenty minutes past nine. The meeting was scheduled for ten, but since Geary always flew in on a company plane, executives were forewarned to make themselves available a half-hour earlier.

He reached his street, made a right turn toward Santa Monica Boulevard, and pulled into the ITRC parking lot.

The building that housed the West Coast division of the International Transcription and Recording Corporation resembled a large, slightly run-down warehouse. Like almost everything else about the company, aesthetics were secondary to function.

A reception area and two recording studios comprised most of the first floor. One of the studios was standard size, about forty feet square. The other was huge, capable of holding as many as one hundred musicians, and was used primarily for recording movie soundtracks and symphony orchestras.

The second floor consisted of several smaller studios used for remixing and editing, plus storage areas and the offices of a few minor administrative and clerical people. The offices of the company's junior executives were on the third floor, and on the top floor were the offices of all senior West Coast ITRC executives, a small twelve-chair conference room, and a three-room suite, generally unoccupied, there for the use of any ranking company official who came in from the East Coast or the Far East and needed it for a few days to conduct business in California.

What would normally have been the front of the building was a half-block west, on Gower Street. It had no entrances, planned so there would be a minimum of people walking in off the street. Any walking in off the street was done three thousand miles away, at the seventy-eight-story International Transcription and Recording Corporation Building on Thirty-ninth Street in New York City.

But occasionally, of course, ambitious young artists and/or promoters did wander in with audition tapes or completed masters in an effort to be signed by the company. When they did, they were informed by a very polite, very pretty redhead named Sandy that no decisions of that nature were made through the West Coast offices, which was true, and that she would be very happy to forward the material to New York—which she did, religiously. And which, at least in the two years Mark had worked there, always came back with the same answer: no.

The reason being, ITRC already had three hundred and forty-five artists under contract, including seven different symphony conductors. It controlled the recording careers of some of the most popular, most honored, most culturally influential, and—until recently—most salable artists in the world. Any new artist who was signed to the company almost certainly had to go through the elaborate filtering process of acquiring top-quality management, prior media exposure, and the multitude of other factors that entered into the making of a prestige recording artist.

The company had first opened its doors for business on June 15, 1912, in New Brunswick, New Jersey, with its founder, Maxwell P. Geary, receiving the personal handshake and good wishes of Thomas A. Edison. The photograph taken on that estimable occasion, restored and enlarged, held a place of honor in the foyer of ITRC's main office building in New York.

Over the years, the company had applied for and received slightly in excess of twelve hundred patents. The first of these, issued in July 1912, was for a tiny gear that stabilized the turning of the cylinder that held recorded sound. The most recent patent, applied for in May 1956, was also for a small gear, a tiny piece of machinery that ensured the detonation of a nuclear warhead within one-four-thousandth of a second of the instant it was programmed to go off.

The history of ITRC was, in a sense, a capsulized history of America itself: Maxwell Geary had been a glassmaker in Dresden prior to immigrating to America at the turn of the century and settling in New Brunswick. He was not only a skilled craftsman but also a lover of fine music, and a tinkerer, as well. In the course of experimenting with his old Edison Talking Machine, he created several inventions that helped to improve the then-unsophisticated quality of recorded music. His inventions brought him to the attention of Thomas Edison himself, and after being loosely associated with Edison for a few years, Geary had entered business on his own, forming ITRC with capital amounting to less than a thousand dollars.

But it was his son who had brought the company to prominence. After graduating from Rutgers, Maxwell Junior had taken advanced courses in electrical engineering at MIT, before convincing his father to expand into the business of manufacturing radios. Almost immediately, ITRC radios became the capstone of the industry, outselling such established lines as Philco, Emerson, and Crosley. Thereafter, the company had flourished.

At the inception of World War II, ITRC entered into the manufacture of weapons and by war's end was firmly entrenched in the Fortune 500, where it had remained ever since. Now, after the Korean conflict, the company was in the process of divesting itself of government contracts, to concentrate on the manufacture of inexpensive mass-produced stereos and television components.

But even though ITRC, with all of its varied divisions, had evolved into a huge conglomerate over the past forty-four years, its prestige product had always been mechanically reproduced music.

The total revenue from sales of ITRC recordings during the previous fiscal year had amounted to more than twenty-seven million dollars, enough to classify the company among the "big five" major recording companies, although still accounting for less than half of ITRC's total income for that year. Impressive as that amount appeared, however, the current year's figures represented a sharp decline in sales; total sales for the prior fiscal year, ending June 15, 1955, had been in the area of thirty-nine million dollars. Now, in one year, the total sales of ITRC recordings had declined by almost one-third.

New York, needless to say, was not happy.

Mark studied the sky as he alighted from the car. The only clouds were in the direction from which he had just come, west, and after deciding that the possibilities for rain were remote, he left the top down and entered the building.

" 'Morning, Mr. Donovan."

"Good morning, Sandy. Has Mr. Geary arrived yet?"

"No, sir . . . but Mr. Dibley called from Burbank about ten minutes ago to say that the plane will be on time and the meeting will begin as scheduled."

Mark nodded his thanks and continued to the elevator. His office was a two-room suite on the third floor. The sign on the door read:

M. DONOVAN

ASSISTANT GENERAL MGR.

MARKETING

WEST COAST DIVISION

As he entered, he noted that he was still without a secretary. Barbara Ellis, the pretty, efficient black girl who had been with him since he began with the company, had left to become a June bride, and since Mark's typing left much to be desired, he had been calling downstairs for a temporary replacement whenever his workload required. But he hadn't needed a full-time secretary for the past month. Most of that time had been taken up with traveling to the company's Western offices, with trying to pacify ITRC distributors concerned about the rapid decline in the company's sales.

Their sales had dropped because the record business had changed radically with the new popularity of rock music, r&b, and even some country-and-western releases. Consumer buying patterns were being reshaped, and every distributor Mark spoke with in his travels was disgruntled at the company's inability to ship competitive products. Things had become so bad that a few were even threatening to pull out of their agreements with ITRC and go into independent distribution.

And since ITRC was the same as any other large corporation, the easiest way to tell when changes were in progress was by the attitudes of the company's secretaries. They seemed to know weeks ahead when something significant was about to happen. Moreover, they all had their favorite executives whom they tried to protect in the corporate infighting, and since Mark was by far the most eligible bachelor in the organization, they looked after his interests especially closely. Lately, their attitudes toward him had been solicitous to the point of embarrassing him.

Then, of course, there had been Peter Donovan's note . . .

Mark was at his desk, chewing on the unlit pipe he affected to make himself look older in corporate meetings, his desk phone buzzed.

Cameron Dibley's secretary said, "Mr. Donovan, Mr. Geary is in the building, and the meeting will be as scheduled."

He glanced through the papers in front of him one more time, making a last-minute check of the facts he intended to present to Max Geary and the other men. Then he grinned and tossed the pipe into the wastebasket beside his desk.

At one minute before ten, Mark pushed open the door to the fourth-floor conference room and saw Max Geary sitting alone at the head of the conference table.

Max was an old and respected friend of the Donovan family. His friendship with Peter Donovan stretched back more than thirty years. He had been present at Mark's christening, and he loved the younger man almost as much as he had loved his own son, Maxwell III, who had been lost at Guadalcanal.

Geary was engrossed in the papers before him when he heard the door open. He glanced up quickly, saw Mark, and jumped to his feet, extending his hand. "Mark, my boy! Good to see you."

Mark beamed at Geary's reception. He had always held Max Geary a bit in awe, this thin, energetic man with the thick mane of white hair who had been an adviser to every President since Calvin Coolidge and whose picture had appeared on the covers of *Time, Look, Life, Fortune, Newsweek,* and every other magazine of importance so many times that everyone but his secretary and *Who's Who* had long since lost count.

Mark offered his hand. Geary, grasping it firmly, pulled Mark to him and gave him a quick, fatherly hug. "How are you, son?"

"I'm fine, Uncle Max. How've you been?"

"Listen, while I'm thinking of it"—Geary nodded affirmatively to Mark's question—'I saw your dad a few days ago. He's fine, looking great, sends his love. And your mother! Christ—May Donovan is still the prettiest woman who ever lived! They said to tell you they should be home in a month or so. They're going to take a little motor trip through Italy and France as soon as Pete winds up the picture. To relax a little, you know? And your mother said to tell you to stay home once in a while. I guess she's tried to call you a few times. . . ."

"Yes, I know. I got a note from her on my birthday—oh, I want to thank you for the present, too."

"Don't thank me," Geary said quickly. "You have to thank your

Aunt Glemmie for that. I haven't picked out a present in twenty years. What was it, cufflinks again?"

"Yes, gold." Mark smiled. "And I can use them, too." He hesitated an instant. "How is she, Uncle Max? Any better?"

Geary's face immediately became somber. "We don't know yet, son. Right now it's tests, tests . . . and more tests." He forced a smile. "You ought to call her. I know she'd be pleased to hear from you."

"I will, I promise."

"Good! Now as I was saying," he waved Mark to a seat and resumed his own at the head of the table, "I just got back from Europe, stopped in New York long enough to sit in on a couple of meetings, then flew right out here. I'd talked to Pete last week, trying to convince him to take the job of spokesman for the new line of stereos coming out next year. Finally talked him into it, so I figured what the hell I hadn't seen the old bastard for two or three years, I might as well fly over there and take him the contracts myself." He laughed at Mark's surprised expression. "I don't know why he didn't mention it to you. It's a good contract, three years at a hundred and a half per."

"He wrote that he'd talked to you, but he didn't mention representing the company." He shrugged. "But you know Dad, he never talks about money."

"I don't blame him," Geary kidded. "If I had his money, I wouldn't worry about it either."

They hadn't seen each other for several months and found many things to talk about. Several minutes later the door opened a crack and Cameron Dibley, Mark's boss, peeked in. There were two other men in the hallway behind. Mark guessed that Dibley and Max would have already spent a few minutes alone together. Now, at Geary's nod, Dibley stepped inside and the other two men followed him to seats at the table. Mark studied their faces, trying to anticipate the subject of the meeting.

Dibley sat on Mark's immediate right. A long-time vice-president of the company, he was an affable, efficient Englishman who still maintained a trace of the accent he had brought across the Atlantic forty years before. It was his primary responsibility to see to it that instructions from New York were carried out as expeditiously as possible.

Mark had never seen the other two men before, although he did recognize one of them, Robert Stermis, from a recent profile in Business Week. He knew that Stermis was a graduate of Harvard Business School, the brilliant head of Stermis and Associates, a marketing-research and motivational-buying firm based in Boston. Tall, thin, with a receding hairline, Stermis appeared to be in his mid-thirties.

The other man, shorter and darker, was introduced to Mark as Gino Turicotti, from ITRC's division of corporate planning. His unaffected, abrupt manner of moving and speaking reminded Mark a little of Max Geary himself. Turicotti took a seat across the table from Mark, on Geary's left, lit a cigarette, and joined the other men in waiting for Geary to begin.

Geary looked at them for a moment, his face expressionless as he marshaled his thoughts. When he spoke, there was an edge to his voice, a trace of near-anger. He was no longer Mark's "Uncle Max." He was Maxwell P. Geary, Junior, president and chairman of the board of the International Transcription and Recording Corporation, a publicly held company that had grossed in excess of seventy million during its previous fiscal year.

"As you gentlemen already know," Geary began, "ITRC's record division has suffered an *atrocious* year, the most rapid decline in sales in the history of the company, 32.8 percent in one year. We've finally had to face facts, and so a few months ago we put Bob Stermis' company to work finding out just what the hell is happening. He brought in his findings two weeks ago. I want you to hear them." He glanced at Stermis. "Bob, bring them up-to-date. . . ."

Stermis removed some papers from the folder on the table in front of him, studied them momentarily, cleared his throat, and began:

"Well, the first thing we discovered was—to our surprise, I might add—apparently nobody, no company has ever undertaken a complete independent study of the record industry before. And since we did not have time to make a comprehensive study ourselves, all we can offer at this time are what amount to rough estimates and, hopefully, educated guesses.

"As close as we have been able to determine, the entire gross of the phonograph-record industry for the 1955 calendar year totaled somewhere in the vicinity of two hundred and eighty million dollars. ITRC was able to acquire sales totaling only 11.2 percent of that market, and of course there was an even further decline in sales during the first five months of this calendar year. We estimate that in years past ITRC has accounted for as much as 20 percent of the total estimated accumulated sales of the entire industry in one calendar year. As we continued to delve, we began to uncover some surprising facts. I use the word 'facts' advisedly, of course.

"One, in the immediately preceding eighteen- to twenty-four-month period prior to the date our study was begun, the record industry had undergone what can only be described as a complete upheaval, and now the spectrum which covers what was previously termed 'pop' music has been widened considerably. It now includes what was formerly called 'race' music, which is to say, music performed by colored artists and aimed primarily, although not exclusively, toward the colored market; and what was formerly called 'country-and-western' or 'hillbilly' music, which was aimed primarily, although not always, toward the generally low-income Southern white market.

"Our second 'fact' can only be considered a trend at the present time, as we have no way of determining if it will continue, or for how long. But for the first time in the history of the American record industry, more than half of the total sales are being obtained by small companies—companies that began operations within the past five years with capitalization of less than one hundred thousand dollars.

"We have no way of determining how many of these companies have entered business in the past few years, or even within the last year, since many of them have not even sought business licenses. We do feel safe in concluding, however, that the majority of the sales which have been lost by your company and the other major labels have been absorbed by these small companies.

"Our third 'fact' should not be surprising to you. As record men, it must be obvious to you by now what a tremendous impact colored artists, musicians, and songwriters have made on the recent market. Again, we must admit that our surveys were necessarily cursory, but from talking with independent distributors, radio people, and other groups in related parts of the industry, we would estimate that for the past calendar year, colored artists have accounted for a *minimum* of 25 percent, perhaps even as much as 40 percent, of the industry's total sales. In previous years that figure would have amounted to a *maximum* of 15 percent.

"Also, we must refer briefly to what are called in your business 'cover' records. As you know, these recordings, made by established white artists, copying the arrangements and general 'sound' of colored records, have been a stabilizing factor in maintaining salable products for the major manufacturers such as ITRC. But as you are too well aware, small manufacturers have brought numerous suits against ITRC and other major manufacturers, calling into question the legalities of duplicating arrangements without permission. There is some question of copyright infringement involved, and this matter is now in the federal courts. In our recommendations we have taken a stand against cover records, obviously not on a moral basis, because that is not our concern, but rather because we have concluded that they are, at best, merely a temporary stopgap action against the thrust of the types of records being made by smaller companies. For example, we have concluded that most of the sales accumulated by ITRC through the use of cover records have been because of superior distribution and merchandising procedures rather than because of the public's preference for the cover records themselves. . . ."

The four men were listening intently—Turicotti furiously puffing a cigarette; Dibley sitting erect, nodding occasionally; Mark leaning forward, alert to every word; and Geary impassively tapping his fingers against the arm of his chair.

"The last 'fact,' " Stermis continued, "may well prove to be the most significant of all. It concerns a definite drop in the age of the average pop-music purchaser. During the past calendar year we estimated the average age of buyers to have been fifteen years, seven months. But during the first five months of this year, that buyer's age appears to have dropped almost another *full year*. That trend is so pronounced that we hesitate even to label it merely a trend; we feel it presages a permanent change in the market. If that proves to be correct, it will necessitate an entirely different merchandising and promotional setup for ITRC and the other major manufacturers. What it will mean, in fact, is that the entire record industry will be entering into a completely new era, the era of the very young, extremely responsive consumer. . . ."

Stermis continued his report for another twenty minutes, before Mark, briefly, presented his own findings and conclusions. They coincided almost exactly with the information Stermis had presented. When Mark had finished, Geary resumed control of the meeting.

"Okay, those are the problems. You can see what we've done. We've sat around while the whole business ran off and left us. We've been too fat for too long. We've diversified into government contracts, research and development, television components, and we've damn near forgotten that the business of recorded music was one of the main things that got us here in the first place. However, we haven't been fast asleep. We put Bob here to work on it six months ago, and at the same time requested recommendations from Planning." He glanced at Turicotti. "Gino?"

Turicotti stabbed out his cigarette and opened the folder in front of him. He sounded more like the foreman of a construction gang than a businessman. "Okay, fellas, here's what we've got. First of all, a record division that's so goddamned bulky and unmanageable, half the time nobody has the slightest idea who's doing what.

"Now, this is going to sound pretty callous, I know, but we've got *at least* a hundred acts we've got to get rid of in the next couple of years. We're saddled with a stable full of prestige artists whose records we can't *give* away. We've got twenty-eight artists on guarantees of fifty grand or more per year . . ."

He paused a moment to let that sink in.

". . . and we've got promotion people who have been with us so long they check in for work in the morning and go straight to the golf course or the coffee shop"—he made a face—"or back home to bed. We've got twenty-four syndicated *International Transcription Hour* radio shows in small- and medium-market cities, some of which have been on the air since the twenties, which don't sell half enough records to pay for their costs. I'll tell you one thing, if we haven't been asleep at the wheel, we've damn sure gone through a hell of a lot of stop signs."

The men chuckled wryly as Turicotti pulled a mimeographed sheet from the file in front of him and jabbed at it with a stubby forefinger. "I want you to listen to this. This says everything. Listen . . . On March 12 of last year, according to the most reliable trade journal we have, six of the top-ten records were r-and-b covers. Think about that, *six* of them! I want you to listen to this:

"Number one, 'Sincerely,' a McGuire Sisters cover of an r-and-b hit by the Moonglows. Number three—"

"That's Alan Freed's group," Mark interjected. "He's pretty powerful right now."

"All I know," Turicotti said disgustedly, trying to head off any more interruptions, "it's not one of *ours*. Now, listen . . . Number three, 'Tweedlee Dee,' a Georgia Gibbs cover of an r-and-b hit by Lavern Baker. Number five, 'Kokomo,' a Perry Como cover of an r-and-b record by somebody named Gene and Eunice. Number seven, 'Hearts of Stone.' Here the Fontaine Sisters covered a group called the Jewels. Number eight, 'Earth Angel,' the Crew—"

"Well, that's all fine and dandy," Dibley interrupted in his precise, dignified voice, looking across the table at Turicotti, "and your point is well taken, but I don't think—"

"No"—Turicotti extended his palm for silence—"I wanna make this point. This was over a year ago, and it's *still* going on. You see, the problem is, everybody in our business thinks this is just gonna blow away, this rock-'n'-roll thing. Well, it's not—not before we go broke, anyhow—it's a fact of life. We have a different market out there now, and they're dictating to *us* what they want to hear, so we'd better pay attention if we want to stay in business. Now, where was I? . . . Oh, yeah—number ten, 'Kokomo' again, by the Crewcuts again. There's a group with two records in the top ten, and I doubt if anybody in this room's even heard of them."

"They're a Canadian group," Mark said. "I understand we had a chance at them but turned them down."

"Thanks," Turicotti growled. "I didn't know that. You just made my day." He replaced the paper in the folder and gave it a firm slap with the palm of his hand. "Six cover records in the top ten, and not one of them ours. We can't even *cover* a hit. We're even turning down artists who *can* cover hits. And we're sitting around on our butts, a day late and a dollar short, trying to convince ourselves that we're one of the biggies—cheez!" He shook his head disgustedly.

"So where do we go from here?" Mark asked quietly.

"Well, for one thing," Turicotti said, "Calkins is out."

Mark and Cameron Dibley were visibly surprised. E. V. Calkins had been president of the record division of ITRC for more than a quarter-century. His gray-haired, distinguished manner of communicating company policies was ITRC's public image.

"He simply refuses to change his general approach to the record business," Geary interjected, more for the benefit of Cameron Dibley than for anyone else at the table, aware that Dibley and Calkins had been close friends for many years. "And don't worry, we're not telling tales out of school, Calkins has been notified. His resignation will be on my desk when I get back to New York. And he's going to walk away with close to a half-million in treasury stock, plus a pension of forty-two thousand a year, so let's not worry about E. V. Calkins."

Dibley nodded, smiled a little mandatory smile, and said nothing. He wondered what else was coming.

"So, as of August 1," Max Geary announced, "the new president of ITRC Records will be Gino Turicotti."

Again the shock registered on Dibley's face. Why? Why, with all the experience and knowledge in the New York record office, did Max Geary pull somebody out of Planning to head the entire record division? Max must be losing his bloody mind!

Mark had liked Gino Turicotti from the moment he met him. Now, as Turicotti impulsively leaned over and gave Cameron Dibley's shoulder a reassuring pat, Mark liked the man even better.

"Listen," Turicotti said, to all of them, but mainly to Dibley, "nobody in this company respects E. V. Calkins more than I do. He's done as much for ITRC as any one man could, but he simply cannot face facts. He's like damn near everybody in Records, unable to accept the fact that this business is in the process of doing a complete turnaround. Let me give you guys an example:

"A couple of months ago a guy got arrested in Philadelphia for extortion. They caught him strong-arming one-stop owners into putting his label's crap on their jukeboxes. You think that's an isolated case? Well, let me tell you something, he's just one of a kind. The whole goddamn business is getting to be like that. It's being overrun by a bunch of animals with no respect for traditional, ethical ways of doing business. And while we've been sitting around trying to convince ourselves we're still a major label, these guys have been out there clawing and scratching, trying to get their records played and sold any way they can."

He paused a moment, again directing his attention to the folder on the table in front of him. "Because of that"—he looked at Mark—"we in Planning have made some pretty drastic recommendations, which were just approved at a special board meeting last Friday. Here's the deal: we're creating an entirely new label, to be called Champ Records . . ."

Cameron Dibley winced.

". . . and we're putting Mark in charge of it."

"But, my word, *Champ* Records?" Dibley made the name sound absurd. "Surely Planning can come up with a more . . . ah, suitable name than *Champ* Records?"

Turicotti chuckled but ignored him. He continued to direct his words to Mark. "Now, I don't want to mislead you, kid, it's going to be strictly rhythm and blues—Mickey Mouse all the way. And we're only going to capitalize it at one hundred grand, out of which will come your salary, office expenses, help, the whole shot, including recording and pressing costs." He paused to light a cigarette while he studied Mark's expression. "What's the matter, you look stunned—don't you think you can handle it?"

Mark *was* stunned. A whole new label? With him running it? So that was what the note from his dad was about. Well, his dad hadn't been kidding, Max Geary did have a surprise for him. He looked around the table at the faces of the men, not knowing what to say. "Why me?" he finally asked.

"A fair question," Turicotti said. "We chose you for a number of reasons. In the first place, you've got the education." He briefly consulted Mark's file. "You've got a master's in marketing, you're young, and like Stermis said a minute ago, it seems the business is turning more and more in the direction of the young buyer. You've been with us for a couple of years now and you've done everything we've asked of you and done it well. So why not you?"

"I think I could understand better if you'd tell me a little more about the label," Mark said, still in a mild state of shock.

"Okay, like I said, it's going to be operated almost entirely independent of ITRC, completely different merchandising setup and everything. We've chosen thirty-nine independent distributors, most of whom we've already talked to about handling the line." He pulled a typewritten sheet from the folder and handed it to Mark. "Now, as you can see there, we're going rhythm and blues because, as Stermis also told us a few minutes ago, colored artists seem to be wielding the most influence in the present market. Also, r-and-b sessions are generally less expensive."

Mark studied the paper. He had a million questions to ask but didn't know where to begin. "Hmmm"—he wished he'd brought his pipe with him—"you say it's going to be capitalized independently. Why? Will it be a secret that ITRC's money is behind it?"

"No, no—how the hell can you keep something like that secret? We're just not going to exploit the fact, that's all. Anybody who wants to can find out where the money came from, but I doubt if more than a handful of people in the business really care. Let me see . . . how can I best explain it to you?"

He stabbed his cigarette into the ashtray and ran his hand over his face a few times, trying to frame his thoughts. "Okay, look at it this way . . . we're using the same principle a scientist uses when he tags a deer. He wants to know where that animal goes, what it does when it gets there. You see, one of the things we've had to face in Planning is that our merchandising channels are all screwed up, completely outdated. For the past twenty-five years all we've had to do to release a new record has simply been to mail it out to radio stations across the country, then send a promo man around a few days later as follow-up to make sure it got there in one piece. We've got thirty-two hundred stations on our list. Now, from what we can determine, half . . . no, two-thirds of those stations make no substantial contributions whatsoever to our record sales. In most areas, the people who are actually buying most of the available product are only listening to one or two stations. Those stations have become damn near impossible for us to crack. So we mail them a couple of records, so what? So they throw them in the trash or wait until they get enough to send to a home for unwed mothers. Whatever they've been doing, it's a cinch they haven't been playing them on the air enough to do us very much good."

"What kind of sales figures do you project for this new label?"

"Frankly, we don't care. A hundred thou is not going to hurt us at all. If you can make the label pay, so much the better, but you won't be under any pressure at all. You're gonna be there to fulfill a vital function for us, which is to get information we don't have access to now. Everyone in marketing, sales, and promotion will be watching Champ, and hopefully, after you get it moving, we can solve some of the mysteries about independent distribution. We want to know where the bottlenecks are, what stations are most effective in which markets, what dj's are approachable, and if not, why not.

"Another thing is, you're gonna buy us time while we change personnel all over the country. Some people are gonna be retired, a hell of a lot are gonna get fired. We're also gonna open up a publishing house for our record division, which we've never had before. To put it bluntly, we're gonna have to change our whole image into—"

"Let me wrap this up, Gino," Max Geary interrupted. "Mark, Cam—I'm going to give you two a quick look at the whole picture. We're in trouble—I'm sure you both know that by now. How bad, I can't say. But as you know, we've already divested ourselves of most of our government contracts, and you both probably know, too, we took a bath doing it. You've watched our stock drop during the past year, and I'm sure you've heard the scuttlebutt about the proxy fight going on in New York since the beginning of the year. On top of all that, we've already got more than twenty million invested in Japan for our new line of stereos, and we're committed to a hell of a lot more. The reason we've made such a tremendous commitment is that, as of the first of the year, we officially stop pressing 78's. From there on it's going to be only 45's and albums. All of us, all the majors, are firmly committed to that change in product.

"But in the meantime, I'll tell you frankly, we're faced with one hell of a cash-flow problem. We divested our government contracts and reinvested in Japan with the idea that the record end would take care of us. Now, instead of the record end holding us up as we had planned, it's threatening to blow us out of the ballgame. Not only can we not give our product away, but as Gino said, we're precommitted to millions in advances to artists who are, for all practical purposes, obsolete."

Geary looked at the dejected faces around him and mustered a small smile of encouragement. "Now, wait a minute, you guys, we're not ready to go into a Chapter Eleven, not yet, not by a damn sight. We've still got a lot going for us. Picture this: if we're successful in convincing the public to buy 45's and albums, and by that I mean all the majors, we're no longer talking about a three-hundred-million-dollar-a-year pie, we're talking about an eventual *billion*-dollar-a-year pie. And that's worth breaking our backs for, because then the record end will no longer be a twenty-seven-million-dollar-a-year enterprise, we'll be cutting off a hundred-million-dollar-a-year chunk—"

"And that's where I come in," Turicotti interrupted, "because nobody's gonna be *offering* us pieces of that pie. We're gonna have to get out there with a sharp knife just like everybody else. And it's gonna take hard-nosed, aggressive management to pull it off."

There was a few seconds of silence, before Geary spoke again. "Now you've got the picture—not all of it, but enough to see that we've got our work cut out for us for the next few years. Any questions?" He paused. There were none. "Okay, good, let's wrap this thing up. An hour after I leave here, I'll be on my way to Japan. And the sooner I leave, the sooner I can get back to New York. This meeting"—he smiled and he tapped his pen on the edge of the table three times—"is hereby adjourned."

Dibley, Stermis, and Geary began chatting informally, as Mark sat there trying to let it all sink in. "Where do I start?" he asked Turicotti.

"You've got a week to tie up your business here. Cameron will decide who your replacement will be. As of next Monday morning, Planning will have sent you a complete set of guidelines, channels. The main thing is, we don't want Champ connected with the ITRC 'good-music' image, so you'll have to find outside offices."

"What about production procedures?"

"You'll have to determine your own."

"Artists? Arrangers?"

"That's up to you, too. If we had a few decent artists or a few halfway knowledgeable production people, we wouldn't have to set up the Champ thing in the first place. Do it any way you want, it's your baby." He gathered his papers and stuck them back in his attaché case. "I'll be back from Japan in ten days. I'll spend some time with you then, going over what you've done up to that point, making suggestions."

The men filed toward the door, shaking Mark's hand and wishing him luck. Max Geary was the last to leave. He gave Mark's shoulder a squeeze. "Don't worry about it, son. Just do the best you can with it and you'll do all right. We know that, that's why we chose you."

"Well, all I *can* do is the best I can," Mark said.

"Seems to me I heard those exact words before—about thirty years ago, standing on a train platform at Penn Station."

"From whom?"

"Oh," Geary chuckled, "from some joker who'd just signed a seventy-five-dollar-a-week contract and thought he was going to come out here and set the movie business on its ear."

NASHVILLE
JUNE 1956

Carl Clinger was a thorough and organized man, and six weeks of inquiries and more than fifteen hundred dollars' worth of private-detective fees had proven to his complete satisfaction that the four men he had chosen to be his partners were among the most perceptive and discreet of all those presently engaged in the business of making and selling country music.

He was so engrossed in trying to assimilate and memorize the last-minute information he had compiled about their personal finances and private lives that when the phone rang, it took him a few seconds to figure out where the sound was coming from.

He rummaged around under the pile of papers on the desk and found the receiver. It was Lonnie. He had just picked up Willard Jefferson at the airport. He would deliver Jefferson to his hotel, pick up Tommy Lee, and be there in an hour. The meeting would begin a half-hour after that.

Satisfied, Carl replaced the receiver and carefully began to separate the mound of papers in front of him into four smaller stacks. Pausing every now and then to recheck a bit of information, he placed each stack into a separate manila envelope. Each envelope had a name on it. Buddy Jepstone. Red Leach. Robert Blandings. Willard Jefferson.

He had spoken with the men in the past few days, and each of them had given him a verbal promise to invest in the company: twelve hundred and fifty shares, at one hundred dollars per share. One-half payable upon subscription, the other half, or fraction thereof, callable at any time after thirty days' notice.

A quarter-million liquid, another quarter in the oven, plus the four-to-one current ratio he had allowed to accumulate over the past few months, plus another hundred thousand in short-term bonds that would mature in less than ninety days.

He was ready to do some tall dealing, and four hundred thousand should put him right up there with the big boys.

He placed the four envelopes into the large leather briefcase at his feet. Before making absolutely certain it was locked, he extracted a sheaf of legal-size notepaper—corporation papers, financial statements, stock offerings—and thumbed through them to make sure they were all there in the order in which he intended to present them.

Everything was ready.

He had started to work immediately upon arising. Now, still barefoot and in his bathrobe, he stood and stretched to his full five-six height, yawned, and ran his fingers through his oily black hair. As he padded to the bathroom to begin dressing, his eyes automatically swept around the thirty-five-dollar-a-day suite, double-checking that everything was in order.

He had rented the suite to impress the men. It was certainly more impressive than his little office down at the warehouse, and they could discuss things here in privacy.

And if he knew Red Leach, they were going to need all the privacy they could get.

Twenty minutes later, he was showered and shaved, dressed casually, except for his shoes. He always wore expensive shoes. These were Stacy-Adams, cost him thirty-eight dollars a pair. Good shoes always gave him an added bit of confidence. They were the one thing that made him feel like he had really left Gaston County for good.

He wanted a cup of coffee. But coffee made him sweat, and he didn't want to appear nervous when they got there, so he satisfied himself by going into the small kitchen and pouring himself a glass of ice water.

He came back, sat on the arm of the sofa, and stared out the window across the parking lot three stories below, empty except for his own black Cadillac sedan.

As he watched the heat waves roll across the rich, sun-baked Tennessee soil a few miles south of downtown Nashville, it occurred to him that not once in the last ten years had he ever taken the time to sit down and reflect on his life, where he had come from, or how he got to where he was. Now, as he thought about it, he was moved to let out a self-satisfied little chuckle. He shook his head once, gave a sigh of self-admiration, and said to the empty room, "Boy, you sure *have* come a long way."

And he had. He certainly had. . . .

Carl Aaron Clinger, thirty-two, was born on a little ten acre sharecropping farm in Gaston County, Tennessee, within view of the Mississippi state line. Rednecked and dirt-poor, he joined the Navy in 1942 at eighteen. He spent three years seeing all the action a man could put up with and not drown himself from pissing in his pants.

He was in San Diego waiting to get out, when he met Barbara Jean Pratt, Chief Petty Officer Pratt's daughter. Her mother had sent her out from Nashville to visit her father as a graduation present. The first time Carl saw her she was eighteen, and country pretty. He was twenty-two. Never knew what she saw in him, he had hillbilly scrawled all over his scraggly ass. But she must have seen something, because two weeks after he spotted her coming out of the officers' mess with her father, he popped her cherry in the backseat of his old thirty-six Plymouth on the way home from a party in National City.

They had spent most of their time together after that. It was 1946. The war hadn't long been over, and thousands of men were going back into civilian life, most of them with better qualifications than his for earning a living.

He had barely made it through the eighth grade, and he had no idea what he was going to do with himself once he got out.

He had no family. He had been in boot camp for only two weeks when his mother died of a heart attack from trying to work that ten acre clump of clay all by herself. His only brother, Skip, had stepped on a mine in Salerno. His sister, Maylene, the last anybody had heard, was whoring up around the shipyards in Alameda. And nobody had seen the old man since Carl was a kid.

So the only thing Carl knew for sure was that he had no reason to go back to Gaston County.

One night, as he and Bobbie Jean were sitting in Balboa Park, talking about getting married, she mentioned to him that old man Pratt had said something about the Navy offering a "civilian reentry program." Even though Carl was sensitive about his lack of education, Bobbie Jean talked him into taking what they called "aptitude tests."

He took three days of tests. They were something! Reading. Counting. Trying to fit little pieces of wood together. Names of people he had never heard of. Interviews with "vocational counselors."

At the end he was pretty sure he wasn't suited for a thing, except maybe moving to Detroit and trying to get a job on an assembly line.

A week after the tests were over, he got called in for a final interview. His counselor was a smart little man named Weinstein. After Weinstein had spent about ten minutes telling Carl all the things they'd found out he couldn't do, he'd made a couple of suggestions: "You've got two basic choices. You can try to find some kind of job as an unskilled laborer while you try to get a high-school diploma, and use the Bill later to get more education, maybe trade school. Or—and this might surprise you—you could try to get into sales work.

"Our tests show that even though you haven't had much education, you seem to be bright and ambitious. And you're not afraid of people—that's the main thing." The surprise must have shown on Carl's face. "You never know"—Weinstein had laughed—"you might make a good salesman. I don't know if you know it or not, but some salesmen make more money than doctors and lawyers. What the hell, at the worst you get to wear a clean shirt every day."

Strangely enough, Carl had felt pretty good when he left the interview. The more he thought about it, the more he decided there were a lot worse things he could do to earn a living than wear a clean shirt every day and make money by convincing people to buy what he wanted them to buy.

He made his first sales pitch that night, to Bobbie Jean. She was a little undecided at first, but by the time he got through explaining to her what the counselor had told him about some salesmen making more money than doctors and lawyers, he had sold her.

They started going around to the public libraries, borrowing what books they could find on how to be a good salesman. When they ran out of library books, they combed the bookstores downtown.

There wasn't anything for Carl to do at the base but make up his bunk in the mornings, so he'd do a lot of studying during the day. And every night he and Bobbie Jean would go downtown to the same little coffee shop on First and Broadway, sit in the back booth, drink coffee, and study salesmanship books until the place closed at midnight.

They were sitting there one night in March of forty-six when he proposed to her.

They talked it over and decided there wasn't much point in trying to have a big wedding. Carl had no family to speak of, and Bobbie Jean's mother, Louella, and old man Pratt had been divorced for years and couldn't stand the sight of each other, so a big wedding would be a waste of time. After he had proposed to Bobbie Jean, he talked to Mrs. Pratt long distance several times. She made him feel she wouldn't interfere in his and Bobbie Jean's life if they wanted to come and live with her for a while. Also, Bobbie Jean was very close to her younger brother, Lonnell and had promised that after she visited her father she would come back home and help put Lonnie through law school.

They got married the day Carl was discharged and headed for Nashville the same night.

It was the best ten days of Carl's life before or since. The first day out, about ten miles the other side of Flagstaff, he took a good long look at Bobbie Jean sitting next to him in the car, her reddish-blond hair flying in the mountain air and her green eyes flashing as she chattered on about their future together. It was the first time he realized that he really did love her, and he knew then that he was willing to spend the rest of his life working hard to make things as easy for her as he could.

Two nights later, in a grubby three-dollar-a-night motel room a few miles east of Amarillo, as Bobbie Jean lay on her back feeling Carl pump his seed into her—the seed that would eventually turn out to be their daughter, Lucinda—she realized, in the limited wisdom of her eighteen years, that she loved him, too, more than she had thought it possible to love anybody.

They spent the rest of the trip exploring each other's minds and bodies, and the more they explored, the more they rejoiced in what they had found. By the time their mud-splattered old Plymouth chugged through the Nashville city limits, their future together, at least in their own minds, was already a reality.

Bobbie Jean had little trouble finding work. She got a job almost immediately as a clerk at the First National Bank of Nashville.

It took Carl a little longer, almost a month of answering ads, before he found something that looked promising—a job at I. V. Ware's appliance store and record distributorship on Hermitage Avenue. His job was to take orders from stores for the records handled by Ware, as well as to try to get new records played on radio stations. His territory was the entire state of Tennessee, and the top half of Arkansas and Mississippi.

Mr. Ware wouldn't put Carl on percentage at first, saying that the only thing his other salesmen had ever done was hang around hotel lobbies all day getting drunk and the gin mills at night, trying to pick up the girls who came to the country-music dances.

They finally settled on a salary of seventy-five dollars a week, plus fifty dollars a week more for traveling and hotel expenses.

But if there had ever been such a thing as a born salesman, Carl was it. He was bright, innovative, and hungry—especially hungry—and was soon selling more records than I. V. Ware had imagined possible.

The way Carl did it was simple: he was the first record promoter in that part of the country to service the dj's. Up until Carl Clinger started bringing his records around for them to play, nobody had ever thought enough of the country-music dj's to bring them coffee and doughnuts, or sit around and talk with them half the lonely night, or slip them a twenty-dollar bill on the way out. But Carl did, and they showed their appreciation by constantly playing his records, sometimes until the grooves were all but worn out on the brittle old 78's.

Carl was smart enough to know that he had discovered a good thing, but after his first swing around the territory, he was also smart enough to realize he didn't know a damn thing about the record business. So, three weeks later, when he got back home to Nashville, he set about rectifying that problem.

First he wrote for a five-year subscription to *Cashbox* magazine, the music-business trade journal. Then he bought a twelve-volume set of *The Complete Salesman*. He made them his two-part Bible.

The salesmanship books stressed "always go an extra mile," and by the time he made the second swing through his territory a month later, he was bringing not only coffee and doughnuts and twenty-dollar bills but also sour mash and promises of paid-up motel rooms complete with tender young hookers—for those dj's who were lucky enough to be heard by a fairly large audience and who promised to play his records for a couple of weeks after he had left the area.

When he got back to Nashville the second time and showed I. V. Ware the orders he had taken, Ware immediately raised his salary twenty-five dollars a week, plus a commission of eight percent.

In the meantime, true to her word, Louella Pratt had not given him and Bobbie Jean a minute's problem. To the contrary, Mrs. Pratt was a godsend for them, company for Bobbie Jean during the long months before the baby was born, when Carl had to spend most of his time out on the road promoting records.

By the time Lucinda was born, Carl had traded the scruffy old Plymouth for a brand-new, two-tone blue straight-backed Pontiac coupé.

Now he was making his rounds in style. Like the salesmanship books said, going the "extra mile" paid off in tangible dividends.

There is, in the record business, what is referred to as "scuttlebutt," a network of rumors and gossip that is faster and more effective in spreading news than the most efficient big-city newspaper. Now the scuttlebutt began to mention Carl Clinger's name. The word was out that Ware's record distributorship in Nashville had become, because of this hotshot new salesman, the hottest distributorship in the country-music business. And not only was Ware selling an asspocket full of records, he was also paying the manufacturers on time, which was unheard-of.

It wasn't long before other manufacturers began to knock on I. V. Ware's door.

Despite the fact that Ware had been in business since the early thirties, when Carl first went to work for the company it distributed for only one fairly large independent manufacturer, plus seven small, underfinanced labels that could scrape up barely enough money for an occasional release. Two years and four top-ten country hits later, I. V. Ware was distributing the products of two more major independent country-music manufacturers, as well as fourteen other fairly solvent smaller manufacturers that could generally come up with the money to press enough records to meet whatever demands Carl might create for their products.

Still, the chances are that nobody would have ever heard of Clinger, other than a few people in the country-music record business, except that exactly two years, ten months, twenty-one days, three hours, and thirty-seven minutes after he was hired by I. V. Ware, he got the break of his life.

It happened one Tuesday afternoon. Ware was eating his lunch at his desk in his cluttered little office in the back of his new warehouse on Linden Boulevard, talking long-distance to the biggest independent record man in the country-music business, when he got excited and choked to death on a chicken bone.

It was a tribute to Carl's understanding of the principles of aggressive salesmanship, as well as his grasp of the priorities of the music business, that less than an hour after Mr. Ware was pronounced dead at the scene, Carl was on the phone to Houston, convincing their biggest supplier, Willard Jefferson, that Ware's distributorship would, indeed, remain open for business, bigger and better than ever. Under another name, of course. And it would be operated with "dynamic new innovations," a phrase Carl had picked up from *The Complete Salesman*.

Carl and Bobbie Jean stayed up all that night, making plans to buy the company. Mr. Ware had been very closemouthed about his affairs, and they had only a vague idea of the volume the company was doing. About four A.M. they went down to the warehouse and went through the files. As close as they could determine, the business was earning somewhere between twenty-five and twenty-eight hundred dollars a month, including the sale of appliances, with extremely good possibilities for growth.

Even though Bobbie Jean was pregnant again at the time, and

the added expenses of hospital bills and the pressing need for a home of their own had to be considered, they decided to buy it.

At six A.M. they were on the phone. They borrowed five thousand dollars from Chief Petty Officer Pratt, and seventy-five hundred more from Louella Pratt. To that was added the three thousand dollars they had saved toward their home, which gave them a little over fifteen thousand dollars to work with.

By noon they had secured loan approval of five thousand dollars from Bobbie Jean's bank, and by one o'clock that afternoon Carl was sitting in attorney Robert Blandings' office on the fourth floor of the Mortgage and Trust Building, listening to advice on the best way to cut a few corners.

Bob Blandings had handled I. V. Ware's legal affairs for years—what little work there had been—and he knew that Ware had not left a will. He also knew that Ware's widow, Elvira, now living in a rest home on the West Side, incapacitated from a series of strokes brought on by acute alcoholism, was in no condition to make any decisions regarding disposal of the business. Blandings thought Ware had a daughter up North somewhere, Detroit or Chicago. He wasn't sure about that, but he could find out.

Six days later, a few hours after the corpse of I. V. Ware had been safely interred in Rosedale Cemetery, Mrs. Harleen Ware Cummings was seated in front of the same desk at which her father had come to his sudden demise, very carefully signing two certified checks, each for ten thousand dollars. One was made out to her personally; the other was made out for deposit in a newly created trust account, to be administered by Robert M. Blandings, which would provide for all of Elvira Ware's needs at the rest home for the remainder of her natural life.

Carl already had the sign painted: NEW SOUTH DISTRIBUTORS. It went up later that afternoon.

By now Carl had learned his profession well, but one thing that cannot be learned from salesmanship books is timing. A man cannot be taught to look at the calendar of his life and arrange to be in the right place at the right time.

Nevertheless, from that day in August 1877 when Thomas Edison struck a needle to a piece of tinfoil, until the day I. V. Ware changed his mind at the last minute and ordered fried chicken instead of his usual cheeseburger, there had not been a more opportune time than the spring of 1949 to enter the business of selling mechanically reproduced music, nor a better place for it than Nashville, Tennessee, USA.

The funny thing was, Carl didn't really care that much for music.

Unlike a lot of "down-home good ole boys," he had never tried to do any picking and singing, which worked in his favor, because he didn't give a damn about the artistic merits of his products. He simply thought of phonograph records as something to sell, and if I. V. Ware had been engaged in the selling of toilet seats and the same opportunity had come up, Carl would have been motivated to purchase the company with the same dispatch.

And, as he had promised Willard Jefferson, he did have a few "dynamic new ideas" he wanted to try out. One of them, "guaranteed sales," eventually changed the entire structure of the music business.

The plan was simple:

After Carl had secured promises of extensive airplay for a new record by the dj's of a particular area, he would go into the surrounding stores and talk the buyers into stocking large numbers of the new release. He would then "guarantee" the sales of the record in the event it did not sell, by promising to pay out of his own pocket the difference between the amount sold and whatever was left on the shelf after a three-month period. In effect, he would pay for shelf time by buying the record back at retail prices.

Like all good sales gimmicks, the plan was practically foolproof. There was almost no way he could lose. He would study *Cashbox* and choose only a record that had proved its salability in other, smaller markets. By the time he placed it in the stores in larger cities, including Nashville, the dj's—who were becoming increasingly indebted to him—would already be blasting the record over the air, informing their listeners that it was a "red-hot," "can't-miss" piece of country wax.

New South Distributors doubled sales within a year.

Two years from the day Harleen Ware Cummings got on the train to go back to Detroit, the company was grossing over eight thousand dollars a month.

Two years later the broadcasting license for one of the mid-South's most powerful radio stations became available. The station was owned by State Senator Montague Richardson, who was using it to give himself free advertisements in his campaign to become a congressman. One of his opponents reported him to the FCC and he had to divest himself of it immediately. It was a clear-channel fifty-thousand-watt station whose license allowed it to broadcast from sundown to sunup. The asking price was two hundred thousand dollars, but Richardson was in no position to wait, and Bob Blandings negotiated him down to one hundred and twenty-five thousand, cash. Blandings, who had uncovered the deal, invested thirty-five thousand dollars of his own money. Then he talked one of his clients, Red Leach, the "grand old man" of country music, into putting up an equal amount. Carl put up fifty-five thousand and retained the largest portion of ownership shares.

The station, which had been floundering, became an immediate success, mainly because its new owners erected a two-hundred-foot transmitter about fifty feet from the Mississippi River. The transmitter signal was doubled because of its close proximity to the water, and on a clear night it could be picked up all the way from Bakersfield, California, to Augusta, Maine. If it was illegal, nobody ever said anything about it.

Carl hired a dumpy little dropout from the state university in Knoxville to broadcast the entire shift. Her name was Millicent Michaelson. She called herself "Millie the kitten." She had two things to recommend her, a low, throaty voice, and an insatiable appetite for anything having to do with sex.

Millie became the darling of the truckers. When she offered to send them a copy of whatever record she was playing, together with an autographed picture of herself in "something comfortable," country-record sales began to increase dramatically.

A year after Carl, Blandings, and Leach purchased the station, it was making money like a private mint. Millie Michaelson was earning, legally and under the table, close to fifty thousand dollars a year, and Carl was invited to go to New York to receive a plaque from the Music Manufacturers and Retailers of America as "The man who has done the most to gain acceptance and respect for country-and-western music throughout America."

It wasn't too long after that that Carl met Tommy Lee Whitaker.

Carl was sitting at his desk one morning when his secretary ushered in a tall redheaded kid with a "master" he wanted Carl to hear. The kid looked like a hobo, but he was likable. He thought Carl could place it with one of the companies New South Distributors was handling records for. Carl listened to the dub; it sounded fine to him. He promised Tommy Lee he would do whatever he could.

That same morning, Bobbie Jean's brother, Lonnie, dropped by. The three of them went to lunch. By the time lunch was over, Lonnie and Tommy Lee had talked Carl into starting his own label, Carousel Records, and putting Tommy Lee in charge of production.

The record Tommy Lee brought in became a hit. It stayed on the top-ten country-music charts for seventeen weeks. It even crawled inside the top forty on the pop charts for two or three weeks, but it was a bit too "country" to make much impression there.

It finally wound up selling more than two hundred thousand copies. The artist, Tommy Lee's cousin on his father's side, Bobby Joe Whitaker, was destined to become the biggest thing in country music until Elvis came along.

For Carl, Tommy Lee Whitaker turned out to be a treasure. Within a year of the day he first set foot in Carl's office, he had produced two more top-ten country hits for his cousin Bobby Joe, plus another nice-sized country hit for a cute, pop-sounding blond named Sarah Tindall.

And so, ten years after he had been discharged from the Navy, two children and three businesses later, Carl Clinger was well on his way to becoming a millionaire. He had earned the right to indulge in a little self-admiration, for he certainly had come a long way, in time and distance, from the ignorant young hillbilly who had sat in Balboa Park with his girlfriend pondering his future.

Now, as he perched there on the edge of the sofa tapping his signet ring against a forgotten half-empty glass of warm water, he saw a two-year-old convertible turn into the parking lot, and watched as Lonnie and Tommy Lee got out and started toward the front of the building.

He shook his head in anger. He had told Tommy Lee to wear a shirt and tie so he would look older when Carl presented him to the investors as the man who would be in charge of producing the records their money would be riding on. Tommy Lee had worn a shirt and tie, all right. He had also put on a sport coat that was about two sizes too small for him, a pair of dirty blue jeans, and scuffed-up tennis shoes.

He looked about fourteen years old.

Carl shook his head again, this time more in exasperation than anger, before he slowly got to his feet and started across the room to open the door for them.

CHICAGO
JUNE 1956

At the same time that Carl Clinger was crossing the room to open the door for Lonnie and Tommy Lee, five hundred and forty-four miles to the north, Monroe Wilcox was driving his dark green Buick Roadmaster through the flooded intersection of Sixty-third Street and Cottage Grove Avenue, on his way to a meeting with the most powerful black gangster in the city of Chicago.

As he slowly steered the car through the heavy late-afternoon thunderstorm, he ran over in his mind the things he had heard about the Green brothers, trying to separate what might be truth from what he knew must be no more than accumulated street talk.

Originally, there were three brothers, Ted, Marvis, and Leon. They came up quickly. One year Marvis was running numbers up and down South Parkway, Leon was running a floating crap game between the Morrison Hotel, the back of the Regal Theater, and the basement of the Savoy Ballroom, and Ted was running the "jenny" and the "pigeon drop" out of the downtown bus depots and train stations.

The next year they were banking the Southside policy wheel with their own money.

Right after the war, the story went, the year the Italians and the Jews were killing each other off for control of the national wire services, the Green brothers had very coolly past-posted the Chicago bookies out of more than a half-million dollars.

The con, according to street gossip, had been Ted's idea. It took him more than two years to set it up.

He sent Leon out West, to Bay Meadows, Santa Anita, anywhere the horses were running. At the same time, he had Marvis covering the tracks on the East Coast, Belmont Park, Pimlico, wherever.

Ted had several phone lines on his desk, with a hustler on each one, stationed as close to a bookie as he could get. Leon or Marvis would call him long distance before a race began, watch it, and give

Ted the results. Ted would then immediately relay it to a hustler, who would go running into his bookie's, looking stupid and waving his money around.

Likely as not, the bookie would take the bet. The hustler would sit around awhile, looking at the racing form, pretending to wait for the results. As soon as the winner was confirmed, he would act surprised, get his money, maybe bet a little on the next race—although he had no idea which horse would win—and split.

Each hustler got to keep half of whatever he conned his bookie out of.

The Green brothers ran the scam for more than a year. They had everybody they could trust working for them, from janitors and domestics to schoolteachers and insurance salesmen, anybody who was a regular horse player and had been playing the same bookie for a while.

The con was run so smoothly that nobody caught on, although a few of the big boys out in Cicero did get a little suspicious once or twice. But it never crossed their minds that the whole thing had been put together by some "stupid goddamned niggers" down on the Southside.

Then, after the Green brothers got their bank together, the Italians and Jews woke up one morning to find their entire Southside policy wheel stolen from them.

It didn't take them long to learn who was behind it, and that it was their own money that had financed the takeover. Naturally, they were pissed, and they immediately jumped on the phone to New Orleans and offered contracts to four of the meanest, nigger-hatingest hit men they could buy, to come to Chicago and blow the Green brothers away.

The hit men came into town quietly, and played dead for about a week, trying to lull the Greens. Then they caught Marvis coming out of his old lady's pad one afternoon. They shot him in broad daylight, point-blank, cut him almost in half with two sawed-off shotguns. This made them cocky, and they swaggered through the Southside ghetto, pretending to be cops, asking for Ted and Leon. Which was a mistake.

They were never seen again, but two days after they hit Marvis, a black Chrysler sedan was found parked in front of an expensive Lake Shore address. There was a brown paper sack on the front seat. Inside it, wrapped in pink butcher paper, were the bloody stumps of four Caucasian right hands.

The war lasted four months. Eleven people were murdered—four blacks and seven more whites, all within the confines of the Southside ghetto.

When it was over, Ted and Leon Green, and their street people, were cutting up a pot the Justice Department estimated at somewhere between $250,000 and $300,000 per week.

That was the Ted Green that Monroe was on his way to see now.

The rain had slackened by the time he turned off Sixty-third onto Loomis Avenue. He drove slowly, leaning across the seat, peering out the passenger window, until he found the number he was looking for.

The house, a nondescript two-story frame building, didn't impress him. What did impress him were the bars he could see guarding every window, upstairs and down.

He backed the big car neatly into a parking space next to a fire hydrant, reached behind the seat for his attaché case, and slid across. Just as his feet hit the pavement, there was a mighty rumble, and a jagged blue-white bolt streaked across the ominous-looking Chicago sky. He jammed his stingy-brim hat farther down on his head, pulled his raincoat tighter around his small frame, and sprinted across the sidewalk. The iron gate was unlocked. He pushed it open and took the steps two at a time, jabbed the bell once, twice, three times.

The man who opened the door didn't impress him, either. He looked to be in his late forties, early fifties. He was almost completely gray-haired, thin, stood about half a head taller than Monroe, maybe five-ten. He was in house slippers, and wore a blue-and-white-striped silk bathrobe, with a lavender sport shirt underneath, buttoned all the way up to his neck.

Monroe studied the man's sharp features, the smooth jet-black skin, and immediately pegged him for one of those *geechees* from North Carolina. *Notorious niggers.* Play games with them and they will be very happy to cut you a brand-new asshole.

The man's eyes automatically swept around the street, settled on Monroe. "You Wilcox?" he asked. His voice had a slight lilt to it, almost West Indian. Monroe nodded, and the man motioned him inside, into a dimly lit foyer. He hung Monroe's dripping hat and raincoat on a mahogany clothes tree and made a sign for Monroe to follow him. They passed the doorway to a large living room furnished completely in white—rug, couch, tables, everything—and went up a flight of stairs to a small corner room that had been made into an office.

"I'm Ted Green," the man said, closing the door and sticking out his hand. "You want something to drink? Coffee? Beer?"

Monroe shook his head.

"Listen, little brother"—there was a hint of a smile on Green's face—"you gonna come up here and ask me to let you have some of my money, you better be ready to sit and talk a spell."

"Okay," Monroe said, "gimme a RC."

While Green was behind the small bar in one corner of the room pouring their drinks, Monroe looked over the office. There was a large mirror embedded in the wall to his left. He had a feeling he was being watched.

Green handed him a glass, opened a bottle of Atlas Prager for himself, and settled into the swivel chair behind the desk. He looked Monroe over carefully for a few seconds without speaking, like a good con man sizing up a mark. "Okay, little brother," he finally spoke, "I checked you out. You seem like a sharp little nigger on the way up. What you got in mind?"

Monroe took a sip of his RC and cleared his throat. "You know anything about the music business?" he asked.

"Umm-hmm. Yeah, I know a little bit," Green said.

"In that case, you probably know I just wrote and produced the number-one record in the country."

"Yeah, I know that too," Green said.

Monroe felt a flicker of irritation at the man's condescending manner. He leaned forward in the seat and raised his voice a fraction. "Then you know I ain't no poor-butt nigger, right?"

"Never said you was." Green was playing with him.

"Dig," Monroe said, pissed, "if you know I didn't come up here to fuck around and waste your time, let's knock off the shit and talk like grown folks, okay?"

Ted Green was not accustomed to talk like that. He leaned over and extracted a cigar from the humidor on a corner of the desk, tore the cellophane free, and slowly ran his tongue up and down the shaft, never taking his eyes off Monroe's face. He lit it carefully, took a sip of his beer, and leaned back in the chair and blew a cloud of smoke at the ceiling. The con man had disappeared. The toughest black gangster in Chicago was talking now. "Okay, little brother," he said quietly, "suppose you tell me why you think I ought to give you a hundred thousand dollars?"

"If you already checked me out," Monroe said, "you know I own a little record store on Indiana Avenue, Monroe's Record Rack?" Green nodded. "It ain't much," Monroe continued. "I make a bill and a half a week off it, two at the most. Walking-around money, you know, chump change. But I also got a label, Big City Records,

• 49

that I had for a couple of years now. I put out a few things on it before, but I never had the bread to really take care of business like I wanted to. But I think I'm ready to get serious with it now."

"Why now?" Green asked.

"Well, I been fucking around with music for the last two or three years, ever since I came back from Korea. I wrote some r-and-b tunes, did pretty well. All the time, I was learning the business, you know what I mean? Now that I got the number-one record in the country, I'm sure that I *know* what I'm doing. I ain't guessing no more, and I'm getting ready to deal."

"Yeah, I can dig that, little brother." Green nodded. "But what makes you think them Jews are gonna *let* you deal?"

"That's where you come in." Monroe took another sip of his RC. "See, big money eats up little money in business, just like in a poker game. And I know if I try to go into business, especially the record business, without enough bread to back my play, them mother-fuckers are gonna stomp me into the dust. But if I got enough money, where I don't have to be running scared all the time . . ." He jabbed the air with the middle finger of his right hand.

"Yeah, you got that right," Green said. He thought for a moment. "Lemme ask you something. How'd you get that record out that you got out now?"

"Well, like I said, I got this little jive-assed company. And I had a few things out on it that got a little airplay, so I got a reputation in the neighborhood. Somebody turned me onto a group of young nig-gers that just graduated from DuSable, called themselves the Tru-tones. The group itself wasn't too heavy, but the lead, a boy named Dave Washington, had a damned good tenor voice. They auditioned for me, and I thought they had a chance. I worked with them a little while, picking out tunes for them, tightening their harmony, stuff like that, and took them into the studio. The session cost me about four hundred bucks. But the record came out so good, I didn't even try to hustle it. I put it out on my own label, here and in Detroit and Cleveland. That's called 'testing the market,' you know?" Green nodded, interested. "And the next thing I know, I'm getting some pretty nice orders, ten, twelve thousand a pop."

"Umm-hmmm . . ." Green said, puffing his cigar.

"So, naturally, I shipped the records out, figuring I could pay for more pressings as the bread came in from the distributors."

"But you never got paid, right?"

"Naw, I didn't get paid." Monroe's laugh was embarrassed. "I just kept getting telegrams to send out more records."

Green laughed. "You wasn't *that* big a fool, was you?"

"Shit, I didn't have enough money to press no more records anyhow. So I jumped on a plane to New York with the telegrams, went around to a few companies, and sold the master. You know what I mean by 'master'?"

"Yeah, I can figure that out," Green said.

"Anyhow, I sold the master to a company called Chartmaker Records. They put it out, and it shot on up to number one."

"You get any front money?"

"Yeah, six thousand, plus a twelve-percent royalty contract."

"You get it in writing?"

Monroe scowled at Green. Green got the message. "Don't get mad, little brother," he said. "You'd be surprised at how many niggers ain't got sense enough to get nothing down in writing." Monroe grunted, acknowledging the apology. "You got to pay the group out of that twelve percent?" Green asked.

"Yeah, three percent."

"How much you think the record's sold so far?"

Monroe sipped his RC thoughtfully. "Well, this is the second week it's been number one. It's just breaking good. I would say . . . a quarter-million so far."

Green leaned farther back in his seat and puffed his cigar. "Umm-hmmm . . ." he figured, ". . . so we already talking about thirty grand, right?"

"Thirty grand that's *owed* me so far," Monroe corrected.

"Why you say it like that?" Green asked sarcastically. "You don't think they gonna short-count you, do you?"

"Shit, I *know* they gonna short-count me, man. By the time they get through adding up them phony returns, charging me for promotion records that ain't never been sent out, breakage, all that bullshit, I'll be lucky to come out with half of what's owed me."

"Umm-hmmm. . . ." Green sipped his beer. "Who owns that company?"

"A Jew named Saul Goldman runs it. But I don't know if it's all his money."

"You still got them little niggers, the, uh, Tru-tones, under contract to you?"

"Naw, I had to give them to Chartmaker for three years, to make the deal. But I held on to the publishing."

"And you still have the say-so about what their next records are gonna be?"

"Oh, yeah, I'm still producing them."

"How about management?"

"Yeah, I got that too."

"Umm-hmm." Green nodded his head slowly, new respect for the little man across the desk creeping into his eyes. "You a smart little nigger, all right." He got up and stuck his hands into the pockets of his robe and paced the room for a few moments without speaking. Finally he gave a little grunt, sat back down at his desk, relit his cigar, and smiled. "You know something, little brother? I won a lot of money off you."

The statement came off the wall. Monroe was startled.

"What you mean?"

"You used to fight, didn't you?"

"Yeah, seven or eight years ago."

"Didn't you used to fight them Tuesday-night amateur fights at the Savoy?"

"Yeah?"

"Featherweight, right?" Monroe nodded. "Yeah!" Green snapped his fingers. "I thought that was you when you walked in. You was a tough little monkey, all right." He smiled. "How come you didn't turn pro?"

"I could of turned pro," Monroe's somber little face grew even more serious. "I had some offers. And I didn't mind the training none. Shit, I was *always* in shape." He couldn't keep the pride out of his voice. "But I used to go down to the gym and see cats like Johnny Bratton and Beau Jack, niggers who could *fight*, man! They were winning and still getting the shit beat out of them, you know what I mean? And they weren't getting no money. The white man was getting all the money. All they were getting was a little notoriety, you know. I figured, fuck that!"

"Well, one thing's for sure." Green shook his head slowly, as if he were dealing with a retarded child. "You didn't fight long enough to get your brains scrambled. How come you want to get in the record business? The rottenest paddy motherfuckers in the *world* run the record business, you know that."

"I want to make some money," Monroe said simply.

"Listen," Green's voice turned cold, his eyes bored into Monroe's, "that's just what the average dumb nigger would say. And I would have thrown the average nigger out of here five minutes ago. Now, I asked you a straight question, give me a straight answer."

"I'm sorry, man," Monroe said, neither contrite nor apologetic, just being honest. "I wasn't trying to shine you on. I just, uh, never put it in words before. I mean, *I* know why. I just ain't never tried to explain it to nobody before."

Green puffed his cigar. "Try now," he said.

Monroe swallowed the last of his RC. He put the glass down on the floor beside his chair and squeezed his nose and sniffed the way fighters do when it's time to get down to real business. He sensed that Ted Green was just about to make up his mind.

As Monroe tried to frame his answer, Green sat across from him and studied him carefully. He knew people. His whole life had been built on understanding people, checking out the larceny in their hearts, and taking advantage of it. But Monroe seemed to be without guile. He didn't appear to have that certain kind of fear, that lack of confidence, that made him want something for nothing. Green had seen a few people like him. Not many, because there weren't many, but a few. Champions. They had that look about them. If you knock them down a hundred times, you still better be ready for the hundred and first, or they'd find a way to beat you.

"Okay," Monroe finally got his head together, "I'll tell you why I want to get in the record business, and I mean the *real* record business, where the money and the power is: because I'm tired of being shit on, and pissed on, and stomped on, and taken advantage of for things I ain't never been taught.

"I spent my whole life hustling and scuffling, trying to keep some rags on my ass, some beans on my table. I ain't never had time to sit down and learn nothing that's gonna really make me some money, you know? But there's one thing I do know better than any white man in the world, and that's my music, the music of my people. I know it better than any white man who ever lived. Business, politics, technical shit—that's all his turf. But music—that's my turf. I got him covered any way he goes when it comes to colored folk's music."

A faraway look came into his eyes, as if he were looking through some invisible curtains that allowed him to see, at the same time, into both the future and the past. "See, before, when the white man was stealing the colored man's music—dixieland, swing music, jazz— he wasn't really stealing all that much. He wasn't stealing the music so much as a way of *doing* the music, you know what I mean? He could lie and jive himself that it wasn't really our music, because by the time he got through fucking it up, it wasn't. It wasn't no real imitation of us.

"But now he's getting ready to steal the real colored folk's music. He's getting ready to steal the colored man's soul. He can call it rock 'n' roll, or whatever he wants, but it's just our church music. It's our rhythm and our timing, the feeling in our hearts." He nodded his head confidently. "And I got the number-one record in the whole country, right now, *today*, because I know how to put that music down on a record better than anybody, so people can hear it and dig it—"

"That ain't nothing," Green interrupted. "A lot of niggers know that music. I was raised up on the same kind of music myself."

"Yeah, but see, there's a hell of a difference between you and me and the average nigger out there on them streets," Monroe said. "The average cat on the streets wants to be loved by the white man. He ain't never gonna get into nothing, because he don't want to make the white man mad. Man, I don't give a fuck about being loved by the white man, I want him to *respect* me! Now, he might love me because I'm nice, but he ain't gonna respect me unless I'm strong."

"Yeah, you got that right," Green said. "Go on."

"Listen, ever since I was a kid I've been studying him, just like he's been studying me. He's been trying to take advantage of me every way he could, giving me as little as he could, making as much off me as he could. He calls that 'business.' Now I got him over a barrel. I got something he wants, bad. My music. That's my business, and I'm going to give him as little as I can and make as much money off him as I can. I ain't gonna give it to him, or sell it to him cheap just so he'll pat me on the head and tell me what a nice little nigger I am."

"Well, if you ain't gonna give it to him, and you ain't gonna sell it to him, what *are* you gonna do?" Green asked.

"I'm going to *ignore* him," Monroe said, "for the next five years, at least." He leaned forward in the seat, his eyes shining like little black marbles. "See, the first thing he's got to do is come up with a 'King.' He can't do a goddamned thing until he gets his King. He had the 'King of Jazz,' who couldn't play no jazz, remember? And he had the 'King of Swing,' that cats like Millinder, or Kirk, or Erskine Hawkins could of blown off the stage anytime of the day or night, anywhere."

"Well, now he's got that hillbilly from Tennessee, the one with the sideburns, the one that does all that ass-shaking," Green said.

"Yeah, but that dude's just clowning," Monroe said. "They can't take him serious. They got to have somebody they can take halfway serious, as far as music is concerned, so they can put him on top, call him the 'King,' and make it seem like he's better than all the niggers, you dig?"

"I still say that silly-looking motherfucker is the one they gonna call the 'King,'" Green said, absorbed in Monroe's theories.

"Okay, so he becomes the 'King of Rock and Roll.' That's obvious bullshit. It's still gonna take the white man another five years to learn how to imitate our music so it don't sound like no joke. And even after that, he's still got to come back to us to get some more soul."

"What you mean?"

"Dig," Monroe said "Rock 'n' roll is like a mule. It's big and strong, but it can't make itself over, you know? You got to go back to a horse and a jackass to make another mule. And you got to go back to jazz and the blues to make some more rock, because rock 'n' roll ain't really music, it's just imitation music."

"Umm-hmmm . . ." Green said, chewing his cigar, nodding, taking it all in.

"Now, understand this," Monroe said heatedly, "I ain't no motherfucking fool! I know the white man has got to come out on top. He's got the radio, the television. He can fuck around with people's minds, especially kids', and make them buy damn near anything he wants them to. And eventually he's gonna be able to convince them that the imitation is better than the real thing. But until he can finish conning them, they are gonna decide for themselves what they want to buy. And as long as they decide for themselves, I'm gonna sell a *whole* lot of records."

"Umm-hmm . . ." Green said.

"Now, I know the motherfucker is gonna throw everything at me he can, to keep me from making it. But he needs me a hell of a lot more than I need him, at least right now. Later on, when he don't need me, he'll tell me right quick to kiss his ass. But right now he's got to come to me, to get my knowledge. So I ain't going to him to ask him for a goddamned thing. I'm gonna cut my own records. Put them out on my own label. I'm gonna publish all my own tunes. Control my own artists. I ain't gonna deal with nothing personally but the colored market. Colored dj's, colored record stores. I got to go through white distributors right now, because there ain't no colored ones. But if I get big enough, I'm even gonna set up some colored distributors. And if I'm gonna do all that, I'll need some big money, some grand-theft money."

He stopped talking and leaned back in his chair. The two men stared at each other for a full minute, not saying a word. Green was still nodding his head, trying to digest everything Monroe had told him. He extracted the soggy cigar from between his teeth, crumpled it, and threw it into the wastebasket next to the desk. He got to his feet, still not speaking, and went to the bar again. This time, instead of getting himself another beer, he dropped a few ice cubes into a water glass and poured in four fingers of Ambassador 25. He swirled the glass around absentmindedly. He kept on swirling the glass, grunting to himself every now and then, until sweat began to form on the outside of the glass and run between his fingers. He took a sip and gave Monroe a little salute. "You serious, ain't you, little brother?" he asked quietly.

"Serious as a goddamned heart attack," Monroe said. "You think you can let me have the money?"

"Well, I got the money. The money ain't no problem. The point is, can we work something out?"

"What you got in mind?"

"Well, let me say this. I got the money, but I ain't *supposed* to have the money, you know what I mean? The government's on my ass like stink on shit. That's why I live in this neighborhood, why I drive a Catalina instead of a De Ville. I'm watched all the time. Therefore, I cannot *legally* go into business with you. If I do, the first thing the tax man's gonna ask me is, where did I come up with a hundred grand from, you know what I mean?"

Monroe nodded.

"But I can back you," Green said. "I can stand for whatever you need. I like what you said about not going to the white man with your hat in your hand. So I can back you, and it don't necessarily have to stop at no hundred grand, neither. If you need more, I got more."

Monroe took a deep breath and exhaled very slowly, trying to get control of himself. He had it, baby! All the backing he needed. And he hadn't been lying to Ted Green. He could make it, if he just had somebody to stand behind him. But as happy as he was, he knew he wouldn't feel comfortable trying to express his gratitude, so he just nodded once and asked, "How about some juice if I need it?"

"What you mean? Muscle?" Green's face hardened immediately.

"Yeah. I mean, suppose I start putting out records and my distributors don't pay me? Suppose some paddies walk into my office one day and tell me I can't do no more business? Suppose they say I've got some partners I don't want?"

"Umm-hmmm . . ." Green said, pulling a fresh cigar from the humidor and going through the long, slow process of getting it lit. "Let me say something to you, little brother," he finally said, choosing his words with obvious care. "Niggers are just a little drop in a big bucket. Now, down here in the colored neighborhood, I am *The Man*. Nothing happens that I don't say can happen, at least to colored folks. Anybody come into my territory and start fucking around, they got trouble's mammy.

"But once I get out of this neighborhood, I'm just another nigger.

I ain't really got shit to say about shit. I got to deal with them paddy motherfuckers like they say deal, because I am in their territory. So if something goes down and I can help you, I will. If I can't, I'll tell you, and you just have to do the best you can."

"Okay," Monroe said, nodding. "I can dig that, I appreciate you not trying to feed me a lot of crap. But how we gonna work out the money?"

"That ain't no problem," Green said. "I cover you. You come to me when you need money. Tell me what you need it for. I ain't saying that to put strings on it. I'm saying that's part of the deal because I don't want to see you get your ass in no crack, with me or nobody else. I'll back your play for five years, or until you get your nuts out of the dust, whichever comes first. You start getting on your feet, we sit down and talk about how you can pay me back."

Monroe thought about that for a moment. It wasn't what he had in mind, but he could live with it. At least he had something to fall back on if he hit some rough times. "All right, I'll go for it," he said. "But suppose I can't pay you back at the end of five years? Suppose I just blow your money?"

Green puffed his cigar and stared at Monroe in silence, turning something over in his mind. When he answered, his voice was quiet, as if he were about to reveal a side of himself he would have preferred never to show. "Don't think I'm no fucking trick, now, little brother," he said. "I have niggers asking me for money every day of my life. Most of them are no-account dreaming niggers. You ain't. You already made a little something out of yourself.

"The average nigger in your position, with a little store and the biggest record in the country, and about to come into a little money, would be downtown right now, picking out a new Cadillac. You ain't. You ain't out there showing off, hanging around the Sutherland and Roberts Show Lounge, letting all the jive-time niggers fill your head with shit. You're sitting down here, with me, with somebody that can help you get on your feet for good. I like that. I got to respect that.

"So I ain't gonna hold you to nothing you can't do. I know how hard it's gonna be for you to do what you got in mind. And I know there's a damn good chance that you ain't gonna be able to pull it off, too. All I ask is that you work hard and do the best you can. You run up against a wall, where you can't go no farther, come see me and I'll bail you out." He took a big slug of his drink, swallowed it slowly, and fixed Monroe with a glare that he could feel in the roots of his hair. "Just remember"—his voice cut through the air like an icicle—"I'm a hustler, and I know every play in the game. You try to bullshit me, cheat me, or deal me off the bottom of the deck, you *will* wind up on the wash-rack at the Southside Funeral Parlor, getting your motherfucking face scrubbed with Rinso, you dig?"

Monroe nodded almost imperceptibly.

"Okay." Green stood. "I got to run down the hall and talk to somebody. I don't have to, you understand, it's just a formality. When I get back, we'll go over this whole thing again, to make sure we don't have no misunderstandings later." He opened the door. "You want something else to drink. Another RC?"

"Yeah," Monroe said, "I don't mind if I do."

"Help yourself," Green said, stepping into the hall. "You're family now."

NEW YORK
JUNE 1956

A long time before, in the fifth-grade coatroom at Crescent Heights Grammar School in Los Angeles, a ten-year-old named Marty Pitowsky was running the straight scoop down to a new kid who had just transferred in. In the process, Marty mentioned another kid by the name of Paulie Schultz. The new kid said he hadn't met him yet.

"Well, you'll know him when you see him," Marty said, about to give the all-time perfect description of Paulie. "As soon as he says hello, you'll get this overpowering urge to kick his ass."

And the new kid had answered immediately. "Oh! *Him.*"

Now, eight years later, the urge was, if anything, even more overpowering in those who had the distinct misfortune of making the acquaintance of Paulie Schultz.

It wasn't simply because Paulie was so abrasive and obnoxious. It was because he was so totally oblivious of the fact and because overconfidence ran out of him like shit out of a diarrhetic elephant.

Take today, for example.

Here he was, on the Monday following his high-school graduation, eighteen years old, standing in front of Jack Dempsey's Restaurant on Forty-ninth and Broadway, looking at the charts in the new *Cashbox* magazine—and angry because the first record he ever produced was only number ninety-seven in the country.

It never occurred to him that, since he had been hanging around recording studios for only a few months and had a no-more-than-rudimentary idea what he was doing, he should be grateful to have a record anywhere on the charts. Neither did it occur to him that, since he had stolen the tune *and* the arrangement almost intact from an old Gatemouth Jackson r&b record, he should be grateful to be here at all, instead of in a courtroom.

Paulie had been in New York for little more than an hour. The airport limo had dropped him off at Forty-second and Broadway twenty minutes before. In the time it took him to walk up to Forty-ninth Street, he had sized up the town. He could already see it was overrated. He was convinced he would have it completely figured out in six months.

Paulie closed *Cashbox*, picked up his two-suiter, and started walking again past the Turf where all the music-business people congregated, and left toward Seventh Avenue. He entered an office building about a half-block down. The director inside gave him the number he was looking for, and he took the rickety iron-gate elevator to the fourth floor. Down the hall, another left, and he was standing in front of his uncle's office.

The sign on the door read "Chartmaker Records."

He pushed the door open and entered a dingy two-room suite. The floor was uncarpeted, covered with a faded black-and-white-checkerboard tile. The only furnishings were an ancient file cabinet, three chrome-legged chairs, and a steel desk.

The woman behind the desk, a nervous-looking brunette in her late twenties, was just about to roll another invoice into her Underwood when she looked up and saw Paulie standing over her.

"I wanna see Mr. Goldman," Paulie demanded in his whiny voice.

"I'm sorry, Mr. Goldman's busy." The woman pointed to the door behind her. Paulie could hear a man's voice on the other side, shouting at somebody on the phone. "He's not accepting any appointments at all today," she said. "You wanna make an appointment for some other time?"

"Do me a favor," Paulie said impatiently, "tell Saul his nephew from California is here."

"Oh, you must be Paul Schultz!" The woman was surprisingly pretty when she smiled. "I'm sorry, I didn't mean to be rude. But we've got the number-one record, you know, and I'm so busy I don't know if I'm coming or going." She offered her hand. "Hi! I'm Tracey."

"Forget it," Paulie said, ignoring her hand. "I'll tell him myself."

As Paulie strutted around her desk, Tracey Burnstein fought an overpowering urge to put her foot up his ass.

The inner office was furnished as shabbily as the one Paulie had just left. There was a torn naugahyde couch directly behind the door, with a broken left front leg. A rusted ashtray teetered beside it. Two filing cabinets leaned against the far wall in an inverted V. Next to them was a large scarred desk piled high with invoices, trade magazines, and radio survey charts.

The man behind the desk was Saul Goldman, Paulie's mother's brother. He was a squat, balding man in his late forties. He had removed his suit coat and was in a short-sleeved white shirt and a flowered print tie loosened at the collar. The hand holding the phone he was shouting into sported a diamond pinkie ring that Paulie judged to be at least ten carats.

Without interrupting his tirade, Goldman waved Paulie to the couch. Paulie sat there a moment, listening, before it became obvious to him that his uncle was arguing with a distributor, threatening to pull the Chartmaker line if the man didn't order more records.

A distasteful expression crossed Paulie's face as he watched his uncle. He thought about the last time he had seen Goldman, five years before, in Los Angeles, at Paulie's bar mitzvah. He hadn't liked his uncle then, and he could tell right away he wasn't going to like him now. As far as Paulie was concerned, Saul Goldman was a big-mouthed, no-talent shlemiel. A clown who barely managed to hang on to his business from year to year by peddling the worst crap anybody ever heard.

What Paulie did not know, because his mother and his other older relatives had always been too ashamed to mention, was that Saul Goldman was *not* a clown. He had spent his early manhood on the fringes of the old Murder Inc. gang in Brooklyn, hijacking whiskey trucks for Dutch Schultz and organizing the docks for Louie Buchalter.

Another thing Paulie did not know about his uncle was that Goldman, in partnership with two other men from the old days, owned close to eleven hundred jukeboxes scattered throughout New York, Connecticut, and New Jersey.

No, even though he looked like a fool, Saul Goldman was definitely not a fool. He was a very tough, astute businessman who happened to find himself in a business for which he had no aptitude. He couldn't even clap his hands in time to the music he put out on his label. He had gone into the record business only because he owned a piece of all those boxes, and being a manufacturer gave him a chance to put on a silk shirt and a silk tie and take some hundred-dollar-a-night hooker over to the Copa, or to the Town and Country in Brooklyn and be treated like a minor big shot by some of the wise guys.

Goldman finally finished coercing his distributor into ordering another ten thousand records. He slammed the receiver down, glanced at Paulie, and immediately began dialing another number. "Good to see you again, kid. How are you? How are things on the Coast? How's your mother?"

By the time Goldman got through asking the questions, his new party had come on the wire. He launched into another tirade, using the same threatening tactics.

Paulie didn't bother to answer. He just sat there staring at his uncle, the distasteful expression on his face growing progressively more pronounced. How come, he asked himself, we don't *sell* anything? We always *peddle* our stuff, like whoever we're doing business with is too goddamned stupid to make up their own minds.

Goldman slammed the phone down again. "Y'see," he said, reading Paulie's mind, "the trouble with distributors is, they're fucking lazy! They wait for you to hand them a hit record on a silver platter. Then they sit around on their *tocheses*, bragging to their *shvitser* buddies, and waiting for fucking orders to come in! Lemme tell you something, kid, in this business you can't wait! When you got it in the grooves, you gotta *move*, you know what I mean?"

"Yeah, yeah," Paulie said.

Goldman lit a cigar and yelled out the door for Tracey to inform any callers that he was in conference. "All right, kid," he addressed himself to Paulie, "the first thing I wanna know is, why didn't you give me a shot at that record you cut out on the Coast?"

"I didn't have time," Paulie said.

"What do you mean, you didn't have time? For one phone call?"

"Like you said," Paulie mocked his uncle, "when you got it in the grooves, you gotta *move*."

"Do me a favor, kid?" Goldman rasped around his cigar. "Can the crap, huh?"

"Okay, you really wanna know? I'll tell you."

"Tell me," Goldman said.

"Because you got a shit company, Saul."

Goldman almost choked on his cigar. For a moment he forgot he was talking to his sister's kid. "Why, you little half-baked cocksu . . ." He struggled to control his temper. "What the hell are you talking about? I got the number-one record in the whole goddamn country! I ain't got a shit company, *you* got a shit brain!"

Paulie was enjoying the flush of anger that had colored his uncle's bald spot crimson. "Aw, f'Chrissakes, Saul, knock it off, huh? You ain't been on the charts for three years, and you just lucked into this record. You couldn't cut a goddamn hit if your life depended on it."

"Jesus! *Jeesus!*" Goldman threw his hands in the air and wheeled his chair around to face the window. "Will you listen to this bullshit!" he shrieked at a pile of garbage in the alley below. "I can't believe this bullshit!"

"Aw, for crying out loud, Saul, will you knock it off?" Paulie's whine as good as said his uncle was purposely giving him a hard time. "The reason I'm here is to help you."

Saul Goldman slowly swung his chair back around to face his nephew. The expression on his face turned from anger to disbelief. He had an overwhelming urge to kick Paulie's ass. If this wasn't his sister Hannah's kid, God help him. He would be halfway down the elevator shaft by now.

"Now, lemme get this straight," Goldman said, making a final effort to control his temper. "You cut one little bullshit record. The goddamn thing ain't even in the top twenty yet—if it's ever gonna get there, which I sincerely doubt—and you come strolling in from the Coast, into *my* office, which has been here for better than ten years, and tell me I got a shit company. You are here to 'help' me, huh? Are you crazy? How the hell are you gonna help *me*?"

"Okay," Paulie sighed, "so you got the number-one record in the country. So what? You didn't cut it, did you?"

"No," Goldman said sarcastically, "I was sitting here in the office one day, jacking off, and the goddamn record just flew in the window and hit me in the goddamn head! What the hell do you mean I didn't cut the record myself? You're goddamn right I cut the record myself!"

"Saul," Paulie said quietly, "you're a fucking liar. A colored guy named Monroe Wilcox cut the record in Chicago damn near a year ago. He tried to sell it on his own label, but he ran out of money. He brought the record in to you, already recorded, mixed, and mastered. Now, let's knock off the shit. If I'm going to be working with you, don't try to bullshit me around, understand?"

Goldman decided, for the moment, not to pursue who had actually recorded the record, because Paulie had said something else he absolutely could not let go by.

"I'd better straighten you out right now, kid," Goldman said, a trickle of spit drooling from the crack in his cigar. "There is no way you are gonna be working *with* me. In fact, the way this conversation's going, there is very little chance you are even going to be working *for* me.

"Now, listen. Your mother called me and asked would I, as a personal favor to her, take you in and teach you the business. She told me what to expect, that you have a tendency to act like a little prick sometimes. But underneath, according to her, you are really a good-hearted little cocksucker. Well, lemme tell you something. You are a pain in the ass, and I'm just about to haul your butt out to La Guardia and personally put you on the plane back to California. Have you got that?"

Paulie returned his uncle's stare for a few seconds, satisfied. He knew one thing: once you let a guy know you're not going to let him shove you around, he's got to be grateful when you throw him a crumb. "Okay, Saul," he said half-contritely, throwing his uncle a crumb. "I didn't mean to piss you off. When I said you had a shit company, I didn't mean the company itself was bad. I only meant that you don't know what the fuck *you're* doing."

Goldman stared at his nephew, trying to figure out what the hell kind of an apology that was.

"You see, Saul," Paulie continued, lying, "I like you. I've always liked you. Even though you don't know a goddamn thing about music, you got a pretty fair head for business, you know what I mean?"

"Now, wait a fucking minute—" Goldman began.

"No," Paulie interrupted, "let me finish. You see, the music business is changing. There's a new kind of sound coming in, what I call 'the colored sound . . .' "

What *he* calls the colored sound, Goldman thought. Dammit, I would give my left nut to kick this pompous little son of a bitch's ass!

". . . and I understand this new music. I've been listening to it since I was a kid—"

"You're *still* a goddamned kid!" Goldman bellowed.

"—and I know what other kids my age want to hear. I'm going to be frank with you, Saul," Paulie said immodestly, "when it comes to understanding colored music, I'm a genius. I gotta admit it, I'm a fucking genius—you know what I mean?"

"No, I don't know what you mean!" Goldman's temper was gone. "The only thing I know about you is that you are ten pounds of shit in a two-dollar toaster. You been in the record business fifteen fucking minutes, and already you're a goddamn genius! I get the feeling after you been in the business another half-hour, we're gonna all have to stand in line to kiss your ass! Now, lemme tell you one goddamn thing—"

The buzzer on his desk sounded.

"No calls!" he yelled through the slightly open door.

"I think this one might be important," Tracey called back.

Goldman snatched the receiver off the hook. He listened a minute, and immediately started in on a distributor in Florida who claimed that the majority of records in a shipment of seven thousand 45's had arrived warped and unfit for merchandising.

While Goldman ranted, Paulie leaned back against the couch and thought about why he was such a genius when it came to colored music.

He had four hundred and seventy-one reasons. In his closet at his mother's house on Genesee Avenue in Los Angeles, four hundred and seventy-one rhythm-and-blues 78's were carefully packed and ready for shipping. Enough material to cut rock-'n'-roll hits for the next ten years. He couldn't miss. The record he had on the charts now, "Good Easy Loving," was proof of that. He had cleaned up the words a little, changed a couple of chords, and look at the son of a bitch.

Funny how things changed. When he was a kid, he used to hate his mother for making him take those goddamn piano lessons. Then, in junior high, he had to take up the goddamned flute. The *flute*, f'Chrissakes!

But it had started to pay off when he'd wandered into that recording studio on Fairfax last winter, when he was trying to find a job for Christmas vacation.

It seemed so easy it only took him a couple of days before he was in the control booth making suggestions.

Then Ruby, the black woman who cleaned up for his old lady a couple of times a week, happened to mention that she had a garage full of old records at her new place. And since she was a Christian lady, and her house was consecrated to the Lord, she had no intention of keeping that sinful devil music around.

So he had volunteered to take them off her hands. All these jerks around the studio were staying up half the night trying to write songs that sounded colored, and old Ruby turns him on to damn near every r&b hit that was ever made. It was like finding money!

Goldman was off the phone. He chewed his cigar in resigned anger. Sweat had beaded up on his bald spot. He looked tired. "Christ" he shook his head, "these goddamn distributors are always trying to steal from you. Now take this son-of-a-bitch."

"See," Paulie interjected quickly, "that's exactly what I been telling you. You got a pretty good head for business, and I got so many ideas they're about to bust my head open. I can cut twenty hits for you, Saul. No bullshit, twenty goddamn hits. All you've got to do is sell them, you know what I mean?"

Goldman nodded his head catercornered, neither yes nor no. Paulie could see his uncle beginning to weaken.

"Lemme ask you something?" Paulie asked quickly. "Who's got production rights to the Tru-tones, you or Wilcox?"

Goldman started to lie, but figured his nephew would probably find out soon enough. "Wilcox," he said.

"Yeah, that's what I thought." Paulie shook his head in disappointment. "How about publishing—has he got that, too?"

"Yeah," Goldman said, "I let him have that, too. I ain't got no source of material for his kind of artists, you know."

"Lemme ask you something else," Paulie said. "When is the group gonna be in town again?"

"I've got their itinerary here somewhere . . ." Goldman shuffled through the papers on his desk. "Oh, yeah, here it is . . . lemme see. They're in South Carolina now, tonight, Aiken. They're working their way north, doing one-nighters for the next couple of weeks . . ." He flipped to another page. "They open at the Apollo Theater here in town in about three, three and a half weeks." He dropped the paper on his desk and looked up at his nephew. "Why?"

"Okay," Paulie said, thinking hard, "when is Wilcox supposed to record them again?"

"Lemme see . . ." Goldman consulted the Tru-tones' itinerary once again. "They've got a week off after they finish the Apollo. Then they open at the Regal in Chicago. I guess Wilcox is planning on recording them during that week." He dropped the paper back on the desk. "Why?"

"When is he supposed to give you the master on the follow-up?"

"Before the end of the month."

"This month?"

"Next month."

"He ain't gonna have time. He won't see them until the last week of next month."

"Well, we ain't got a contract for that specific date. We just agreed to that orally."

"So you got a verbal contract—"

"Yeah."

"—which don't mean a goddamn thing in court."

"Now, wait a goddamn minute!"

"No, no"—Paulie raised his palm quickly—"I was just thinking out loud."

"Oh, yeah? Well, you're just about to think me into a lawsuit."

"At least gimme a chance to tell you what I'm thinking before you panic," Paulie said, leaning back against the couch, beginning to tuck his uncle into his hip pocket. "I've got this tune I wrote, see? It'd be the perfect follow-up to the hit they've got out now." Goldman gave a slight nod. "Now, lemme ask you one more thing," Paulie continued. "What's a good two-track studio in town?"

Goldman thought for a minute, still not understanding what his nephew was getting at. "Well . . . there's Bell, up in the Great Northern, on Fifty-seventh. They've got a two-track in there."

"Okay!" Paulie snapped his fingers. It really wasn't as spontaneous as he made it look, since he had been thinking about it all night on the flight from Los Angeles. "Here's what we're gonna do." He leaned forward on the couch and lowered his voice conspiratorially. "In the next couple of weeks I'll go into the studio and cut the track for a follow-up. When they get here, you lay a couple of grand on them and we'll run them in and put the voices on before they go to Chicago. Then, while Wilcox is fucking around trying to get another release together, we'll put the record out, promote the hell out of it, you know what I mean?"

Goldman looked at his nephew with a little more respect, but declined. "Naw, kid, that's a damn good idea, I have to admit, but I don't think—"

"Why not?" Paulie interrupted.

"Well, in the first place, I got an iron-clad contract with Wilcox that says he's gonna be producing the group as long as they're on the label."

"No problem," Paulie said confidently. "When the time comes, we just tell Wilcox that the distributors were crying for a new release on the group, and we knew he couldn't get his together in time."

"Oh, sure," Goldman said sarcastically. "Wilcox is really gonna go for that, ain't he?"

"So fucking what?" Paulie snorted. "What's he gonna do, sue?"

"Aw, I ain't worried about that. Wilcox is a fucking pussy. He ain't got two quarters to rub together. The thing is, I've always tried to run a legit operation here, you know what I mean?"

"I should of brought a fucking shovel," Paulie said.

"No, no," Goldman persisted, "things like that get out in the business, you know?"

"So what kind of contract you got with him?"

"Twelve percent."

"So you're gonna sit there and tell me you're gonna *pay* him twelve percent? Your ass!"

"Well, no . . . I mean, hell no, I ain't gonna pay the whole twelve! I got to take out for returns, breakage, all that stuff, you know?"

"Tell me about it," Paulie said.

"Okay, okay." Goldman threw up his hands. It angered him, having to ask his nephew for advice, but it looked like he had a pretty good business head on him. "But I still got a publishing agreement with him, you know?" he said, making a last stand against the greed that was causing his pocket to itch.

"No problem," Paulie said. "Just tell him that he can't expect to get publishing on the tune if he didn't write it. That's just simple business, right?"

Goldman chewed his cigar and thought about that for a minute. "You never met Wilcox, did you?" he asked.

Paulie shook his head disdainfully.

"Come to think of it, he ain't like the average colored boy. He's got a little *chutzpah*. He ain't gonna lay down and whine like the average one of them."

"Well, hell, if you're scared of him—"

"Jeeesus!" Goldman blew up again. "I'm sitting here trying my best to hold an intelligent fucking conversation with you, and all you're giving me is bullshit!"

"All right! All right! If it comes to a showdown, offer him his regular twelve-percent contract and tell him you'll split the publishing with him. And of course, we hold on to the copyright."

"I don't know, kid . . ." Goldman was tentative.

"Aw, f'Chrissakes, Saul!" Now it was Paulie's turn to blow up. "The reason he gave you the goddamn master in the first place was because he didn't have the money to sell it himself. If it comes down to a lawsuit, he's got to file it in New York, right? I know goddamn well you ain't gonna pay him a dime of the royalties on this record he's got with us now, not until the first of the year. Well, if you don't pay him, where the hell's he gonna get the money to come in here and take you to court? And make it clear to him, if he gives you any shit, you ain't never gonna pay him the goddamn money. And say by some chance he does come up with the money to sue you, we can fuck around for two or three years and settle out of court ten cents on the dollar, right?" Goldman nodded. "So what's the goddamn problem?"

Goldman thought about it. Paulie was right. He knew Wilcox needed the money. He was surprised he hadn't called already, bugging him for an advance against royalties. "You sure you got the tune?" he asked Paulie.

"Saul, I've got the fucking tune," Paulie said, thinking he'd better call his mother as soon as he could and tell her to get those records to him immediately.

"Okay, okay," Goldman said, "lemme kick it around for a couple of days."

Paulie knew his uncle had already made up his mind. "Okay, and while you're kicking that around, let's kick around a couple of other things, too."

"Like what?"

"Like money. What kind of deal are we gonna have?"

"You mean, ah, between you and me, huh?" Goldman hedged. Actually, he had been thinking of a deal before Paulie arrived, something akin to room and board and a couple of bucks a week while the kid worked as a flunky in the business. But the little son of a bitch was so goddamn arrogant, Goldman was afraid to offer it to him. "Listen, f'Chrissakes, don't worry about money. Let *me* worry about money. I'm your uncle, I'll take care of you."

"Okay, I'll tell you what we'll do," Paulie said, ignoring the feeble attempt at a con. "We'll split fifty-fifty, half, right down the middle."

"Fine, fine," Goldman said, "and I can use my half to buy a set of matching dunce caps, right?"

Paulie allowed a hint of a smile to touch his lips, which for him was the same as becoming hysterical. "I'm not buying your bullshit and you're not buying mine. So let's make a deal, okay?"

Jeeesus! Goldman thought. This kid was something! Once again he deferred to his nephew. "So what have you got in mind?"

"First, lemme ask you a question. How many artists have you got on the label now?"

"I only got four acts now." Goldman sounded a little sheepish. "I've been cutting back, paring down, trying to anticipate new trends in the market, you know what I mean?"

Oh, Christ, Paulie thought. "So who've you got?"

"Well . . ." Goldman began, lowering his voice, trying to impress his nephew, "I've got Marge Bowlen."

"Who?"

"Marge Bowlen. Don't tell me you never heard of Marge Bowlen?"

"Who the fuck is Marge Bowlen?"

"*Marge Bowlen*, goddammit! Hell of a looker. She's at the Four Hundred Lounge in Atlantic City right now. She's gonna be the next Margaret Whiting."

Oh, Christ, Paulie thought, mentally crossing her off. "Who else you got?"

"Well, I got Sammy Patucci. Just signed him to a seven-year contract."

"Sammy Patucci, huh? Okay, who is Sammy Patucci? The next Tony Bennett?"

"No, no, no!" Goldman looked at his nephew in exasperation. "He's an accordion player. Hell of an accordion player! He's gonna be another Dick Contino. Hell, he's gonna be *bigger* than Dick Contino, take my word for it."

"Okay, I'll take your word for it," Paulie said, shaking his head. "Who else you got?"

"Well, of course I still got the Banjo Serenaders. Just signed them to a new contract, too."

"Oh!" Paulie rolled his eyes at the ceiling. "How the hell could I forget the Banjo Serenaders?"

"Y'see, kid"—Goldman missed the sarcasm, thought he saw the chance to regain the upper hand in the conversation—"that's exactly why your mother wants me to take you in and teach you the business. You don't know a goddamn thing about the business. I had a million-selling record on the Serenaders a couple of years ago. They're the hottest banjo group in the fucking country. Just getting ready to go into Vegas. Television. The whole shot."

"Great," Paulie said, "just great. Now, don't tell me, lemme guess the fourth act? The Tru-tones, right?"

"Right."

"Saul, there is no doubt about it, you've got the shittiest fucking label in the business."

"All right, goddammit, that does it! You little stinking, dried-up—"

"Okay! Okay! Okay! Okay . . ." Paulie had to shout his uncle down for a full minute. Goldman finally sat there in silence, his bald spot the color of a sour beet, spit drooling down his unlit, chewed-up cigar.

"Okay, I got the deal," Paulie announced.

"What's the deal?" Goldman looked like he wanted to go to the bathroom.

"This is the deal. You keep Marge Bowlen, Sammy Patucci, and the Banjo Serenaders. Record them yourself. Keep all the profits, you know what I mean?" Goldman nodded, smiling a little. "And we'll put up a new company for me, a production thing, just for the acts I produce. Call it, say, S&G Productions. No, what the hell, call it G&S Productions. We'll put up a new publishing house, too. G&S Music. I make the records, you sell them. We go half. I don't even want a salary, just half of what we make. Plus, you give me a free hand in production."

"In other words, I spend my money and only get half the gravy. What the hell kind of a deal is that?"

"Well, you got a chance. You can either go for it, or you can sit there and slowly lose your ass while everybody is out buying rock-'n'-roll music and you're trying to produce the next Margaret Whiting."

Saul Goldman was not a stupid man. He looked at his skinny little, pimply-faced nephew for a long time, mulling it over, trying to make up his mind. He knew most rock-'n'-roll sessions didn't cost much money, a few hundred at the most. Most of them were bootlegged, which is to say, non-union. He also knew that the only reason he had been able to sell any records at all lately, except for the master Wilcox brought in, was that he owned a piece of all those boxes. The only markets he could sell Marge Bowlen and Sammy Patucci in was the Northeast. And, Christ, even with the boxes he hadn't been able to do much with them lately. And the Serenaders were dead. The dj's never even took their stuff out of the mailing envelopes anymore. . . . He must have listened to that goddamn Tru-tone record at least a hundred times, trying to figure out what made it sell. It sounded like shit to him, a bunch of niggers howling, that's all. The business was changing so goddamn fast nowadays. . . . His publishing company wasn't doing much. He couldn't get airplay, so he wasn't making much performance money. He wasn't selling sheet music. Nobody was recording his tunes on other labels, so he wasn't earning mechanicals. . . . Suppose this little prick really did know what he was doing? His record was selling, wasn't it? And it was on a nothing little company. If the company had some decent distribution, the record would probably be doing better than it was. What the hell? With this Tru-tone hit out he could afford to drop twenty grand, especially since Paulie had decided to forego a salary. He could keep an eye on the little cocksucker so he didn't piss money down the drain on session costs. Yeah, fuck it, he'd go for the deal.

"Listen, kid," he said to Paulie, "you're my nephew. I'll tell you what I'm gonna do. I'm gonna give this a good, long look. Really think about it. Of course, you understand, I ain't about to give up no fifty fucking percent of the profits, but I'll make you a good, fair offer—*if* I decide to go with the deal."

Goddammit! Paulie thought. I knew I should of asked for more! Like my own publishing company. "Half or no deal," he said.

"Listen, don't worry about it, kid. Deals like this take time, you know? We've got a lot of things to go over, lotta plans to make. And right now I gotta get back on the horn and wake these fucking distributors up. So why don't you get settled, relax the rest of the day. Look at the sights, maybe think about what kind of a deal we can come up with if I decide to set up this production thing."

"I already told you the fucking deal," Paulie said.

"Okay, okay, no problem." Goldman changed the subject. "You got any idea where you're gonna be staying?"

"How would I know?" Paulie shrugged. "I just got here."

"Okay. . ." Goldman thought for a moment. Before Paulie arrived he had just about decided to let the kid stay with him, until he got settled in. But, Jesus, Rachel already thought his family was shit. If he brought this one home . . . Christ, he hated to think what would happen. He had the place up in the West Seventies, where he took the broads from time to time. He could let the kid stay there for a couple of weeks. No sweat there, he had to go down to Atlantic City to see Marge for the next couple of weekends anyhow.

"Okay," he said, writing out an address for Paulie, "you can stay here for a little while. Remember, I said a *little* while, so don't get too goddamn comfortable. Take the rest of the day to get settled in. I got something important to do tonight, otherwise I'd take you out to see your aunt, but we can do that tomorrow. I usually get here about nine, so make it early."

"Yeah, okay," Paulie said, looking around the room. "But if I'm a little late getting in, don't worry about it. I think I might start checking out some new offices. This place is a fucking embarrassment. We've got the number-one record in the country, you know? We shouldn't have to do business in a place like this." He plucked a piece of stuffing out of the torn spot on the arm of the couch and clucked his tongue in disgust. "Yeah, Saul, this is a goddamn shame."

Goldman's face was expressionless; he just looked at his nephew. He was too tired to hassle the point. He felt like he had just gone fifteen rounds with Marciano. "Yeah, okay, kid." He sighed, stubbing his wet cigar in the ashtray, fishing around in the top drawer for the bottle of medicine he kept there. "I'll see you tomorrow."

"Saul . . ." Paulie stood up, smiling, extending his hand, ignoring the loud *clomp* the couch made as the broken front leg gave way. "I can already see it's gonna be a real pleasure working with you."

Goldman smiled a weak smile and reluctantly shook his nephew's limp hand. He watched Paulie strut through the door, heard the outer-office door slam a couple of seconds later.

He mumbled something under his breath, shook two pills from the bottle, stuck them under his tongue, and reached for the phone.

NASHVILLE
JUNE 1956

The pungent odor of uncapped I. W. Harper and stale cigar smoke hung in the room like a foul-smelling cloud.

Tommy Lee Whitaker sat in the straight-backed chair by the door, bored, tugging at the tight collar of his overstarched white shirt, trying to figure out why Carl had wanted him to sit there through the whole meeting.

He knew that the men were supposed to look him over, to decide if they wanted him to stay on as the head producer for Carousel after Carl moved the company out to California.

Well, they had looked him over, all right. Twice. Once when they first got there, and once again an hour ago, when they sent him downstairs for some more ice. The rest of the time, as far as they were concerned, he could have been a stick of furniture.

When the meeting first started, Blandings, the pompous lawyer with the manner of a backwoods country preacher, had appointed himself in charge of things. But nobody had paid much attention, so after the first half-hour all he had done was wipe his glasses on his tie and tell them how sorry they would be later if they didn't listen to him now.

And Willard Jefferson, the slightly hunchbacked old man from Texas, who looked like a turtle and thought he knew everything there was to know about the record business, kept hawking and spitting into the coffeecup on the floor next to the couch, and reminding everybody that they had to be careful about "cornflakes of int'rest."

They had been going back and forth over the same old shit for better than two hours now, and it was no wonder Tommy Lee could feel his concentration fighting a losing battle. Half the time he didn't even know what they were talking about.

True, there was a lot of money involved—a half-million dollars, to be exact—so there were a lot of problems to work out. But Tommy

Lee understood, after sitting there all that time, the biggest problem they had to work out was Red Leach.

Whiskey-voiced Red Leach, the "grand old man" of country music, was an institution in that part of the country. He had been half lit up when he got there, and drinking steadily ever since. And every time it looked like Carl and the others were about to come to some kind of an understanding, Leach would drop in his two cents' worth and stir up some more debate.

Tommy Lee's butt was beginning to hurt again.

He tipped his chair back against the wall, for what seemed like the fiftieth time, and tried to make himself more comfortable. He lit another cigarette, but his mouth was already so dry and the room was so smoky, he could barely taste it. He took a couple of puffs and irritatedly stuffed it out in the ashtray on the desk beside him.

And peeked around the lamp to see how Lonnie was holding up.

Lonnie Pratt, Carl's overweight brother-in-law, was sitting across the room from Tommy Lee. He didn't look like he was holding up too well. He tired easily from hauling all that extra weight around, and now he was slumped down on the end of his spine with his pudgy fingers laced together across his bulging stomach. He had his legs sprawled out on the floor in front of him, his pants legs hiked up above his black-and-white argyle socks.

He looked like a dozing Porky Pig.

Lonnie and Tommy Lee had become pretty good friends after Carl put up the money to start Carousel. Lonnie had already passed the bar, although nobody would ever know it to talk to him. He acted as if his only ambition in life was to run errands for Carl. But he wasn't as dumb as he appeared, and he had helped Blandings put this deal together.

According to what Lonnie had told Tommy Lee, Carl already had almost enough money to swing the deal without any investors at all, and what he didn't have, he could borrow from the banks. What he really wanted from Leach, Jefferson, and Jepstone was not their money so much as access to the radio stations they controlled.

That was why Carl had been putting up with so much nonsense from Red Leach during this meeting. Not counting the radio station he owned with Carl and Blandings, Leach owned four or five stations scattered around the mid-South. He was crucial to the deal because he could almost break a country record in Tennessee and Kentucky all by himself.

And Willard Jefferson, when it came to behind-the-scenes action, was even more powerful than Red Leach. Not only was Jefferson the biggest booking agent in the Southwest, he also owned a string of radio and television stations that stretched from Arizona to eastern Louisiana, including two in important markets, Galveston and Austin. It was known by country artists that anybody who worked for Willard Jefferson, anybody he liked, was almost assured of having at least a regional hit record in the towns where his stations were strong.

But Red Leach and Willard Jefferson combined couldn't touch Buddy Jepstone.

Tommy Lee had never seen a real movie star before, and it felt strange even being in the same room with Buddy Jepstone. The first few times Jepstone had spoken, Tommy Lee had automatically glanced over to see if the television was on. He couldn't help it. Jepstone's light baritone drawl was almost as familiar to Tommy Lee as his own father's voice. When he was a kid, he'd spent half his life *being* Buddy Jepstone. He'd owned a Buddy Jepstone gun-and-holster set, a Buddy Jepstone rifle, Buddy Jepstone comic books. Anything that Buddy Jepstone had put his name on, little Tommy Lee Whitaker from Bessemer, Alabama, had wheedled his folks into buying.

The only thing that disappointed Tommy Lee about Jepstone was that Jepstone was so small. He barely came up to Tommy Lee's shoulder. But even so, Jepstone dominated the whole room, and without saying or doing much at all—just sitting there on the end of the couch, chewing on his five-dollar cigar, and nodding a little every once in a while when somebody said something to him that made a little sense.

Carl had checked Jepstone out very thoroughly, before asking Willard Jefferson, who booked Jepstone on rodeos and state fairs, to introduce them. As far as anybody could determine, Jepstone was worth more than thirty million dollars. He owned just about everything a man could own, including radio stations in Los Angeles, Houston, Chicago, New York, and Washington, D.C.

And Carl knew, if he could convince Jepstone to come in on the deal, everybody else would follow—and Carousel records would stand an excellent chance of becoming the biggest country/pop label in the history of the music business.

But with all that riding on the deal, Tommy Lee still had to admit that Carl wasn't pandering to anybody. He was talking to Jepstone and the others like he didn't care who they were, like he was the one doing *them* a favor. That came as no surprise, though; everybody in the music business knew that Carl Clinger could sell a tambourine to the pope.

Tommy Lee's mind was suddenly snapped back to attention by

the change that had come over the room. It looked as if Buddy Jepstone was about to make his decision.

". . . wrap this thing up if we can," he was saying. "I've got to catch a plane out of here tonight. Some of you boys been hemming and hawing so much"—he smiled at Willard Jefferson at the other end of the couch—"I get the feeling that y'all are scared to put your money on the table.

"Now . . ." He waited for the chuckles to subside. "Let's see if we can't put this thing in a nutshell. I don't think we need to go over the financial part again. Anybody who ain't got that part right by now don't have no business being here. But as I understand it, Carl, the main reason you want to get some new money into your company is because you think that country music is about ready for a change. You think it's time to take it on over into the pop field. Make it more classy. Violins instead of fiddles. Choirs in the back singing, that sort of stuff. And to do that like you want to, you're going to have to move your whole operation on out to Hollywood, so people won't be apt to think of Carousel as just another little country-music record company, right?"

"Wait a minute, now," Willard Jefferson interjected. "Let me put in right here that I, for one, don't think that a move like that is completely necessary at this time."

"No, I can see Carl's point," Jepstone said. "There ain't nothing wrong with California, it's been good to me. And there's a damn sight more money in California than there is in Tennessee, can't nobody argue about that."

"Hell, if that's the case, if Nashville ain't good enough for him, why don't he move the goddamn company on up to New York?" Red Leach said angrily. "There's a damn sight more money up there than there is in California, and that'll give them New York Jews a chance to—"

"Goddammit, Red, shut up!" Jepstone shouted in exasperation. "You been talking ever since you sat down, and you ain't got to no point yet." He wasn't quite as angry as he sounded. It was easy to see that he and Red had been good friends for a long time, but it was also easy to see that Leach could get on Jepstone's nerves.

Leach sat back a little farther in his overstuffed chair, his expression more sullen than angry.

"Let's get on with it," Blandings said huffily.

"There's just one or two more things I want to get straight with you on, Carl," Jepstone continued, ignoring Blandings, as he had been doing throughout the meeting. "First, you say you're going to put your brother-in-law there"—he waved his cigar absentmindedly at Lonnie—"in charge of handling all the legal work. Contracts, collecting from deadbeats, stuff like that."

"Well, of course, Bob here is going to be handling the real important things," Carl explained. "He's more experienced, but I think it's important to have somebody in the office who can take care of legal business on a day-to-day basis. And Lonnie can represent me on things that ain't important enough to take up my time personally."

Jepstone glanced over at Lonnie slumped down in the chair, and didn't look too impressed. "Umm-hmm," he said unenthusiastically. "Now, second, you're gonna put the kid here"—he waved his cigar at Tommy Lee—"in charge of making the majority of the records. Don't you think he's a mite young to be handling all that responsibility?"

"Well, now, you got to understand," Carl began, looking at Tommy Lee and wondering why he didn't sit up straighter in the chair and try to act a little older, "Tommy Lee ain't going to be the musical director of the label. We're going to have to hire somebody a little older for that, somebody who can read music and arrange for fiddles, somebody who knows the ins and outs of studio work out there. What Tommy Lee is going to be in charge of, basically, is working with the artists, picking out tunes, getting schedules together."

"But he *does* look a mite young," Jepstone persisted.

"Let me remind you of something now," Carl said. "Tommy Lee's done already got me four top-ten country records in less than two years, so I've got to vouch for him. He don't look like too much sitting over there slouched down like that, but he knows what he's doing around a studio. And don't forget, I'm going to be there every day, watching him, with my foot up his behind if need be."

"Well, if I'm going to put my faith in you," Jepstone said, taking a sip of whiskey and puffing his cigar thoughtfully, "I guess I'm going to have to put my faith in the people you think are right for the job." He thought a little longer before he continued, obviously choosing his words with care. "Let me put my cards on the table, Carl. You must look all right to me, otherwise I wouldn't be here. You've put two or three nice little businesses together, and the people in the music industry think highly of you. You've already got yourself a nice little record company, and I can see why you think it's time to step things up some. I tried a lot of new things in motion pictures twenty years ago, when I was your age, things that everybody was quick to tell me couldn't be done. But I did them, and it worked out fine for me and those that went along with me. You got some damn good ideas, and it don't take a whole lot of intelligence to see where, if they're handled right, with enough money behind them, they might work out.

"But"—his eyes narrowed—"there is one thing that I ain't too sure about. I don't mean to offend you none, Carl, but I'm going to have to state my piece. Two or three times you brought up the subject of coloreds, how you intend to record them and put them out on the company. I'm just not too sure I would feel right about putting my money behind all that coon-shouting music." He heard a little stirring of agreement around him. "I ain't just being prejudiced, now, although I'm from the South just like the rest of y'all, and I have to admit that I am prejudiced some. But I'm dead set against it from the standpoint of good solid business, too—"

"Business my ass!" Red Leach slammed his empty glass and leaped to his feet, glad that somebody besides himself finally had the gumption to bring up the race issue. "This ain't got a damned thing to do with business, this is just the difference between right and wrong."

Jepstone started to say something else, but changed his mind and leaned back against the couch. He had known Red Leach long enough to know that when Red made up his mind to talk, there wasn't anything or anybody that could shut him up.

Red had the floor now—finally.

He stood there in the center of the small room, wobbling drunkenly in his hand-tooled cowboy boots, the anger in his red-rimmed eyes backed up by the convictions of twenty-five years in the country-music record business.

"Now, y'all listen to me, and listen good!" he said angrily. "I ain't gonna say this but once, and if we can't come to some kind of an understanding, I'm gonna get the hell out of here and go on about my business! Now, listen! I ain't got no intentions whatsoever of taking the hard-earned money that I have sweated for most of my grown-up life, and using it to make some money for a bunch of goddamn niggers who ain't gonna do nothing with it but buy Cadillacs, straighten their hair, get drunk, and chase around after white women! Y'all can call that progress if you want, but that ain't progress to me! That cuts across my grain, and I'd take every penny I've got and throw it in the goddamn Mississippi River before I'd use it for that! Now, that, gentlemen, is all I got to say about the goddamn matter!"

Satisfied that he had made his point, he sat back down and poured himself a stiff shot of I. W. Harper.

The room was absolutely quiet. Everybody was waiting for Carl to answer.

Carl ran his fingers through his hair and sighed. He knew he had made a mistake. Like Jepstone said, the subject of race had come up two or three times before in the meeting, and each time Carl had let it pass, thinking it wouldn't be too important to the men once he had shown them what he intended to do with the company over the long haul. But he had to face it: Red Leach had voiced the feeling of every man in the room. Leach and the others were four of the pillars of the country-music establishment. They had been doing things the same way ever since Jimmy Davis had put down his guitar and gone to sit in the Louisiana governor's mansion. To their way of thinking, country music—and country-music money—didn't have a thing to do with blacks.

He understood how they thought. Anybody who had been born in Gaston County, Tennessee, couldn't help but understand them. They had been trash, come up from nothing. They had been helped a little along the way, but mostly they had done it on their own, just like him. Their fear was the same as his fear—not that somebody might be strong enough to come along and take their money and their respect away from them, but that they might, through their own lack of education and insight, be stupid enough to throw it away themselves.

That was enough thinking. Now it was time to dance with the gal he'd brought to the party. Selling. He was a salesman, and he had to convince them that he was right. And he knew just how to go about it. There was a little trick he'd learned years ago in *The Complete Salesman.* He had used it successfully at least a hundred times in the past. It was called "Retreat, Turn, and Advance."

He downed his drink in one gulp and set the glass firmly on the table beside him, letting his eyes settle on Red Leach, but careful to keep any hint of anger out of his voice. "You're absolutely right, Red," he said, and just as the older man began to relax in triumph, added, ". . . *most of the time.* But this time you're wrong, and I'm gonna tell you why."

Carl had knocked Red's guard down, and he was about to show why he was the number-one salesman in the music industry. He pretended to address Leach, but he was really talking to Jepstone, because Jepstone was the key to the whole deal.

"You see, Red," he began, "you ain't really in the record business no more, you're in the radio and the publishing business more than anything else. I'm in the record business. I get my money from one place, you get yours from a different place altogether, except for mechanicals, of course.

"You notice how your artists' royalties are getting smaller and smaller? That's because the record business is changing. People are starting to get away from that old-time gitfiddle music. They want something new, something that's gonna make them get up and shake their behinds a little. Fed, the record business is changing every day, and those folks who are too set in their ways to change with it are going to get left at the gate."

Leach started to say something, but Jepstone quickly raised his palm to quiet him. He wanted to hear what Carl was saying.

"Listen to me, now," Carl continued. "Red, Buddy, all y'all, listen to me. Them niggers y'all are so worried about are already buying Cadillacs and getting drunk and sleeping with white women. I'm out there every day, pushing records, checking sales, and I *know* how much money them niggers are making. They're making more goddamn money than a fat man can piss on!

"The trouble with you boys is that you done got in a rut. When you look in the trades to see what's selling, you don't get your heads past the country-music pages. If you'd look a little further you'd see that damn near every week some nigger on one of them little Jew companies has got the number-one record in the country. And the number two, three, four, five, and six, too, half the time. Hit records by niggers are outselling country-music hits by as much as two, three, and sometimes *four* to one. That fat little nigger boy from New Orleans is selling a half-million or more records on every release. They say it's a million. Well, it ain't no million, but it's still a damn sight more records than I sell on one release. I'm a lucky son of a bitch if I sell a third that many records, and I've got a damn good little country-music label!"

The men sipped their drinks, listening hard. Surprisingly enough, nobody more so than Red.

"A while back," Carl continued, "when I first started promoting records, they used to call coon-shouting 'race music.' Now they call it 'rhythm and blues.' But it don't matter what they call it, it's still the same thing. And it still must be what most of the people want to buy, because they're buying it. Now, let's quit bullshitting ourselves about that. Facts are facts!"

He paused a moment to let what he had just said sink in, before letting his voice drop to a confidential whisper.

"But there's a good side and a bad side to everything, ain't there? And the good side to this is that most niggers can't get recorded on nothing but little no-account companies. The majors ain't gonna sign too many of them. They got their quotas, you all know that. And whatever niggers they do sign up, the chances are they ain't gonna give them no worthwhile promotion, ain't that right?"

The men nodded in agreement. All except Leach, who was just now moving over to the middle of the fence.

"Okay, let's take it a little bit further," Carl continued, specifically addressing Leach. "Most of the time niggers don't even get their royalties from them little fly-by-night companies. They don't know how to go about getting their performance money from their songwriting, and they ain't got enough juice to collect their mechanicals from nobody. On top of that, they ain't got no source of capital they can go to to get in business for themselves. The few that try, most of the time, can't get a damn bit of decent airplay." He stared at Leach and feigned exasperation. "Now, goddammit, Red, even you have got to agree with that!"

"I reckon that's true," Leach admitted grudgingly.

Carl could feel the mood of the room beginning to shift back to him. And being the salesman that he was, he could not be satisfied until Red Leach was his staunchest ally. He focused his attention on Leach, momentarily ignoring Jefferson, Blandings, and Jepstone.

"You see, Red, I didn't just wake up one morning and decide to put niggers on my company. I gave it a lot of thought. And one of the things I thought about, like I said, is that most of the records by niggers that make any noise at all are put out on them little no-account companies first. Most of them little operations ain't got a pot nor a window, let alone enough money to press and ship no worthwhile amount of records. So what they generally do is test the market first, put them out in one or two places to find out if they've got something that's gonna sell. And most of the time they wind up selling the master to a bigger company with better distribution. One of the reasons I want a nice-sized little kitty in back of us is because we're gonna be picking up a lot of masters from them little companies."

He paused a beat to see how the "us" and "we" went over. It passed—which was a sure buying sign.

"Some of them masters are naturally gonna happen to be by niggers," he continued. "I can't help that, and neither can you—it's a situation that happens to exist in the music business at the present time. But even if we don't like it, we might as well take advantage of it, ain't that right?"

The men continued to nod for a few seconds after he had stopped talking, which was one of the surest buying signs of all.

He relaxed and looked around the room. Even Tommy Lee had become alert. He was now sitting straight up in his chair, instinctively aware that what Carl was saying somehow held the key to his own future.

Once again the Complete Salesman, Carl motioned for Lonnie to fix him another drink. He sipped it leisurely. The sale had been made. All he had to do now was begin his close.

"I don't want to sound like no blowhard," he resumed, "but y'all know I was the country-music 'Man of the Year' again last year. So I'm sure y'all trust my opinion about what's good and what ain't good in the record business." They gave him the nods he wanted. "Well, let me tell you boys something I've learned in the ten years I've been in this business. Listen. If you want to make money, you've got to go with the flow. Now, that's worth repeating, ain't it? *If you want to make money, you've got to go with the flow.*"

He smiled and sipped his drink. "Hell, I sell a lot of records by niggers, out of the store and off the radio. That money sits as good in my pocket as any other money I've ever made in my life. But I don't do nothing to *break* them records. I ain't about to gamble my air time and my listeners' tastes on no new record anyhow, if I can help it. Especially not by no niggers, I ain't. I just tell my girl to play them *after* they get on the regional charts in the trades or after a few people have called in and asked for them.

"Now, I'm gonna say this last thing and then I believe we can put this matter to rest once and for all. This is what I intend to do, what I will call my 'corporate policy.' First of all, we don't buy nothing off the streets from no nigger would-be producers. I don't give a damn how good we think it is, we don't buy it from them direct. We make them go through a respectable white businessman. Second, we don't do no business with nigger-owned companies if we can help it, be it publishing, recording, or management. Make them go through a white man.

"If we pick up a master that happens to be by a nigger, our standard contract will be for that master and *one* follow-up release. The follow-up is just to sop up any gravy that may be left on the plate. And you boys know as well as I do that the way the pop market is getting to be these days, the chances of a new artist, 'specially a nigger, getting two hits in a row is mighty slim, unless he's got one hell of a lot of promotion behind him." He sipped the last of his drink. "Now, before I get off this subject, anybody got any questions?"

The men looked around at each other with satisfaction, smiling, shaking their heads in unison. They were convinced; what Carl said sounded perfectly logical and fair to them. He had obviously given the matter a good deal of thought.

"*Well*, now," Red Leach said expansively, breaking the temporary silence and pouring himself a generous shot of whiskey, "I believe we can have a little drink to 'corporate policy,' can't we, boys?"

"Well, let's drink up and get on with it," Blandings said briskly, trying to use the newly relaxed atmosphere in the room to assume control of the meeting. "We still have a lot of serious matters left to discuss."

"I beg to differ with you, couns'lor," Red Leach said, looking down at the empty bucket beside his chair. "The only *serious* problem we got right now is that we seem to have run out of ice."

To get to the ice machine, Tommy Lee had to go all the way downstairs, across the lobby, down a little hallway, out the back door, across the parking lot, slide through a little gap in the fence, and walk all the way to the back of the gas station next door.

Now, as he stood there in the fading late-afternoon sunlight, dropping quarters into the machine, he was debating with himself whether or not he should take a chance and call Sarah's house again.

He'd tried to call her the last time he came downstairs for ice, which was—he looked at his watch—an hour and twenty-five minutes ago, and she still wasn't back. And he didn't want to call again, because the last person he wanted to talk to right now was her roommate, Millie Michaelson. The last time he'd called, he could tell that Millie was in bed with somebody, which wasn't anything special. Millie was generally in bed with somebody every time he called or went over there to pick up Sarah.

But he was genuinely worried about Sarah now.

She had phoned him Saturday afternoon from Shreveport and said she was leaving for Nashville right after the show that night. That was three days ago. A lot of things could happen in five-hundred-and-some-odd miles, especially if Bobby Joe or one of those fools in his band got drunk and tried to cut off some time.

She had left a little more than three weeks ago, when her record was just starting to break, to pick up Bobby Joe's tour in Donley County, Texas. Willard Jefferson's office had booked her on about twenty one-nighters all across the state. Tommy Lee didn't want to see her go, but he couldn't try to hold her back, either. After all, a hit record is a hit record.

But he hadn't had any idea at all he was going to miss her this much. There wasn't any sense in lying to himself, he was in love.

He had already asked her to marry him, but that was before the record came out and turned into a hit. She hadn't said no, she had just kind of passed it off, saying she had to think about it some. But he was going to ask her again, soon as she returned. With the royalties from her song due soon, along with the royalties from the flip side of Bobby Joe's new hit record, he would soon be coming into a fair amount of money. And the way the meeting was going upstairs, Carl would be moving the company out to California fast, which meant his salary would probably be going up, too. So he could afford to get married and take care of a wife now.

He could already see it. . . .

Moving to Hollywood. Married to Sarah and living in one of those houses you see in the movies, stuck on the side of a mountain, with a big swimming pool in the backyard. He could see himself kissing Sarah good-bye in the mornings, driving to work in a good-looking drop-top, a pocket full of goddamn money. Carl had already said he was going to put the Carousel office as close to the corner of Hollywood and Vine as he could get, and Tommy Lee could picture himself driving down Hollywood Boulevard. Pulling into his own parking space and walking to his office, all the little secretaries making it known that they would like to give him some tang. And he could see Sarah riding with him some evenings, on their way to one of those high-class Hollywood recording studios. And he'd cut another hit on her, and when they got through they'd go to one of those expensive Hollywood restaurants, and he'd be sitting there eating a steak, and Rock Hudson or John Wayne or somebody like that would be sitting at the next table, looking at him and waving hello.

Hell, it could happen. This was Nineteen Fifty Six. Anything could happen. He'd just spent two hours sitting in the same room with Buddy Jepstone, hadn't he?

Over by the gas pumps, somebody slammed the hood down on a car and brought Tommy Lee back to where he was. He yanked the plastic bag out of the machine, slit it with his pocketknife, and dumped the ice into the bucket.

No, he decided, there wasn't any sense in calling Sarah's house again. He'd just go back upstairs and hope the meeting ended soon. When it did, he'd go over there and wait for her. If necessary, he could always crawl up on the swing in the backyard and go to sleep. Millie didn't finish at the station until sunup, and Sarah should be home long before then.

He had to smile at himself as he slid through the fence to get back to the hotel parking lot: it was a damn shame to be that much in love.

He was halfway across the lobby when he heard a familiar voice.

"Tommy Lee! What the hell you doing here, boy?"

Tommy Lee was shocked to see red-haired, red-faced Goose Halsey coming out of the hotel coffee shop, picking his teeth and grinning.

"What am *I* doing here?" Tommy Lee asked. "You mean what are *you* doing here, that's what I want to know. When did you all get back?"

"Me and Alvin got in about four o'clock this afternoon. Left N'Orleans bout nine this morning, driving Bobby Joe's wagon, hauling ass."

"Did Sarah and Bobby Joe come back with you all?"

"Naw, shit, the last time I saw them was Saturday night, backstage at the *Hayride*. Bobby Joe was drunk out of his goddamn mind, as usual, and some disc jockey had Sarah hemmed up in a corner with a mike stuck down her throat." He looked down at the ice bucket in Tommy Lee's hand. "What *are* you doing here? A party upstairs or something?"

"No, I'm here for the meeting. Carl's getting ready to move the company out to Hollywood, and he's got some people upstairs who are gonna put in some money."

"Yeah, seems like I heard Bobby Joe or somebody talking about that. Who's up there? Anybody I know?"

"Damn right. Buddy Jepstone."

Goose let out a rebel yell that made two old men in a far corner of the lobby watching television jump straight up in their seats. "Buddy Jepstone! You're a goddamn liar!"

"I ain't shitting," Tommy Lee said. "He's up there right this minute, big as life."

"No shit? Buddy Jepstone . . ." Goose was awestruck. "I wonder if there's any way you can get me in to meet him?"

"No, I don't think so. They're talking some pretty big business up there now. In fact, I'd better run this ice on back up before it melts. Where can I call you later? I want to talk to you."

"Wait a minute now," Goose said quickly, grabbing Tommy Lee's arm. "I got something I want to show you."

"What?"

"I got a new car."

"Oh, yeah?" Tommy Lee was impressed. "What kind?"

"I don't want to tell you, man, I want to *show* it to you. I just got it today. That's why I busted ass getting back to town, to sign the papers before the office closed. Why don't you run that ice on upstairs and come back down? I got a little rip in the car. You can help me celebrate."

"No, I'd better not, Carl might not like it. Where're you gonna be later? I'll call you."

"Aw, man, bullshit! You're supposed to be a big-time executive, ain't you? Hell, just go on back up there and give them the ice and tell Carl you got some business to 'tend to and you'll be back in a few minutes, that's all."

Tommy Lee stood there hesitating, trying to make up his mind.

"Go on, now," Goose urged. "I'll be right here when you get back."

Tommy Lee was back downstairs in a few minutes. He followed Goose down the short hallway to the parking lot in back.

"Well, what you think?" Goose asked, raring back on his heels with his hands folded behind him, like a proud father looking at his newborn son.

Tommy Lee looked at the sleek Cadillac convertible parked by the back door with the top down. It was brand-new, a rich-looking midnight blue, with whitewall tires and white leather upholstery. He walked around to the front and looked at the shiny grille, went around to the other side and noted the letters GH in neat gold script on the passenger door, continued on around the back, and not knowing what else to do, kicked the tires, then came back to where Goose was standing by the driver's side.

"It's a bitch," he said.

Goose rocked back and forth on his heels a few more times, nodding in agreement. "It's a bitch, ain't it?" he asked, like the thought had just occurred to him.

"How much it cost you?"

"About fifty-five."

"How much you still owe?"

"About eighteen hundred. I traded my Ninety-eight in before we left in March, and I been sending money home on it every week."

"That ain't much at all," Tommy Lee said, doing a little calculating of his own. "It's worth it."

"Hop in, I'll run you around the block."

"No, I'd better not. They look like they ain't gonna be too much longer upstairs. Carl's already got them looking at the corporation papers, and soon as they sign, they're gonna be through, and I'd better be there to say good-bye."

"Well, you got time to have a little drink, ain't you? I got some Granddad."

Tommy Lee thought a minute. Everybody upstairs was already half-drunk, including Carl. Even Lonnie was drinking now, so he knew they wouldn't notice any liquor on his breath when he got back.

"Okay," he said, going back around to the passenger side, "but I ain't got too long."

They got in. Goose flipped on the ignition key so the radio would play, and reached in the glove compartment and pulled out a pint of whiskey and two paper cups.

"Shit, man, you must be expecting company." Tommy Lee laughed, taking the half-full cup.

"Man, I got a brand-new car and a hundred dollars in my pocket that I don't owe nobody yet. You *know* I'm gonna be expecting company before this night's over."

They drank, not knowing what to say next. They weren't really close friends. Goose was almost thirty. He was from down in Texas somewhere and had been running up and down the road with different country bands for about ten years. And by the time Tommy Lee met him, Goose had already played bass on so many country hits, and traveled with so many big-name country groups, Tommy Lee was a little nervous around him.

"Listen, while I'm thinking about it," Goose said, reading Tommy Lee's mind, "you got any sessions coming up?"

"How long you in town for?"

"Shit, I don't know. I ain't talked to nobody yet. Probably about two, three weeks."

"You going back out with Bobby Joe?"

Goose took a slug of his drink and cleared his throat noisily. "Man, I don't know about Bobby Joe. That sum'bitch's crazy! He almost got me killed two or three times." He took another drink. "Ain't he some kin to you?"

"Yeah, he's my daddy's brother's boy. But we ain't that close. I'm from Bessemer, just below Birmingham, and he's from down by Butler County. And he's a little older than me, too." He flipped a cigarette out of the pack on the dashboard, lit it, and took a drink. "How'd he almost get you killed?"

"Well, see, first of all, you got to understand Bobby Joe. He don't care about nothing, you know what I mean? The only thing he wants to do is get drunk, or drop some pills, and find some pussy. I mean, that's *all* he cares about. Like, we're playing this dance in Lubbock, which ain't too far from my home, so I know how mean them sum'bitches are down there. And I'm up on stage playing, right? All of a sudden I hear this commotion off to the side of the bandstand. I look over, and there's four or five guys got Bobby Joe penned up in a corner. This one ole boy's already got his blade out, getting ready to cut Bobby Joe's fool head off and stick it up his behind."

"No shit? How come?"

"Bobby Joe's over there drunk. Been fooling around at their table all night, and snuck and offered this cowboy's wife a hundred dollars to go out in the station wagon with him."

"Aw, *fuuuck*," Tommy Lee said in disgust.

"Yeah, that's what I mean. I been out there on the road long enough to know you don't do that kind of stuff."

"I ain't been out there at all, and I know better than that."

"Yeah, that's why I said I don't know if I'm gonna go back out with Bobby Joe again. He pays good money, and I was getting extra for leading the band. But, shit, I got a brand-new car. I got to live long enough to wear it out." He poured himself another drink. "But that don't have nothing to do with recording. That's why I asked you if you got some dates for me while I'm here in town. I'll record with Bobby Joe or anybody else that's going to pay me some money."

"Yeah, well"—Tommy Lee held his cup out, and Goose poured him another drink—"things are kind of up in the air right now. Carl's been getting ready to move to California since the first of the year, so we're behind. I wrote a couple of new tunes for Bobby Joe, and I'll probably take him on in the studio as soon as he gets back, if he ain't back now, but I ain't got no idea when that's gonna be. We ain't recorded nobody for over a month. The last date I cut was on Sarah just before she left to go join up with you all."

"You cut Sarah, too? I knew she was on the label, but I didn't know you recorded her yourself. Did you cut that thing she's got out now?"

"Yeah, I recorded that with her about six or seven months ago."

"No shit! I didn't know that. That's a damn good record, man, a *damn* good record. It's already top-ten, ain't it?"

"Number four this week, number ninety-one on the pop charts."

"Whose tune is it?"

"Mine."

"You're a goddamn liar!"

"No, I ain't. It's mine. I wrote it."

"You wrote that tune, Tommy Lee? Shit, we got to have another drink to that!" Goose poured a little more Granddad into Tommy Lee's cup, which was only down an inch or so. "Drink up, man. You gonna make some money off that song. I heard it this morning before I left N'Orleans. Some pop gal's already covered it. Patti Page or one of them gals like that. And me and Alvin heard it again this afternoon, by Sarah, just before we hit Franklin." He slapped the steering wheel. "You gonna be driving one of these before long, boy."

"I'm gonna get me one as soon as I get out to Hollywood. I damn near got the money now, but I ain't quite twenty-one yet. Soon as I get old enough to put it in my own name, I'm gonna get Carl—"

"Goddamn!" Goose interrupted, suddenly reaching for the volume knob on the radio. "Ain't that a bitch! We're sitting here talking about it, and it comes in right over the radio."

He turned the volume up, not quite as far as it would go, but almost.

The four-bar introduction was just ending, and Sarah Tindall's delicate alto voice floated into the car. She didn't have a voice of power or range, but it was warm and intimate-sounding. And she had good pitch. Her pitch was usually right in the middle of the note, which made her easy to listen to.

Tommy Lee leaned his head back against the seat and looked up at the sky. It was getting on to dusk now. The day was cooling off. And the way the record sounded—the sweet, pretty way Sarah was singing—she could have been right there in the car, sitting next to him with her head on his shoulder.

His mind was made up. He was going to ask her to marry him as soon as he saw her. Anything was better than walking around feeling like your right hand was missing.

"Boy, that is some kind of a pretty record," Goose said admiringly when the record was over, leaning across the steering wheel to turn the volume down. "I heard it before, like I told you, played it on the stage every night for two or three weeks, but I never listened to it good. You should be right proud of yourself, Tommy Lee."

"Thank you," Tommy Lee said, trying to sound as modest as he could. "She's got a right pretty little voice, don't she?"

"Hmmm," Goose said, dragging off his cigarette and shaking his head wryly. "To listen to her sing like that, all sweet and innocent, you'd never think she could fuck like a brood mare."

Tommy Lee felt a stab somewhere back in his stomach, a feeling he had never experienced before, like somebody had stuck a knife in him and yanked it out so quick that all he could feel was the emptiness in the center of the wound.

He didn't want to hear any more. But he was sitting there with a paper cup half-full of whiskey, and didn't know how to suddenly leave.

"Takes a mighty smart man to figure out a woman sometimes," he said lamely, trying to hide the shiver in his voice.

"You ain't in love with her or nothing like that, are you, Tommy Lee?" Goose's reaction to Tommy Lee's words was surprisingly perceptive. "I mean, I wouldn't have said nothing like that if I thought—"

"In love? With Sarah? Shhhit, man, you must be kidding!" The way Goose had put the question, Tommy Lee didn't know what else he could say. He couldn't lie and say he hadn't been seeing her. He had taken her to all of Bobby Joe's sessions with him, and damn near everybody in Nashville had seen them together at one time or another. "I mean, I have dipped my wick in her a couple of times," he continued, "but I never got serious. Shit, I ain't that crazy."

"You sure now?" Goose's face showed genuine concern. "I wouldn't want to say nothing to hurt your feelings, you know that."

"About Sarah? Man, you can't hurt my feelings by telling me nothing about Sarah. She's a friend, that's all. I've known her for a couple of years. Picked her up hitchhiking summer before last, ten or twelve miles outside of Fayette, Alabama. She had been living with some old moonshiner. She was scared of him, trying to get away. She wasn't nothing but trash. Dirty, didn't have no place to go, no family or nothing."

The harsh words immediately made him feel guilty, disloyal to her.

"I mean, I don't *dislike* her," he added quickly, "I ain't trying to say that. But she ain't nothing special to me, neither."

He took a big slug of his whiskey, trying to finish it before Goose got to whatever it was he was working up to tell him.

"Well, that's good," Goose said, letting out a sigh of relief, "because that gal is something. Boy, she is *something!*"

Tommy Lee finished his drink and started to set the cup on the dashboard, but Goose had already uncapped the bottle and plucked the cup out of his hand. "Here, let me pour you a short one. I got to tell you this before you go."

"No, I'd better get back on upstairs. Where you gonna be? I'll call you later on. . . ."

"This ain't gonna take but a minute," Goose said, handing him the cup. "Drink up, this is the damnedest thing you ever heard. I been playing music for better than ten years now, but I ain't never had nothing happen to me like what I'm about to tell you."

Tommy Lee put the drink to his lips and looked at Goose in the fading sunlight. He felt himself reaching for the door handle, to get the hell out of there, but Goose was already talking.

". . . last Friday night, and we're finishing up the tour in Beaumont. Bobby Joe and Sarah got to be in Shreveport the next morning to rehearse for the *Hayride*, to push their new records. They ain't gonna use our band on the radio, they got their own boys, so the tour's over for us.

"In the meantime, Bobby Joe's done met this rich ole boy from Port Arthur, who's got a home down there right on the water. At the most, Arthur ain't but an hour's ride from where we are, that time of night, so we pile on out there, the whole show and half the people in the dance hall. Party our asses off! Food! Man, you can't believe what kind of a spread they laid out for us! All kinds of whiskey. And

90 ·

dope! Anything you want to smoke or swallow, they got. And there must of been gals for every one of us. I don't mean no crocodiles, neither, I mean some of the prettiest, long-leggedest tang you ever laid eyes on.

"So we get to picking and singing and running back out there in the little house where they keep the boats, smoking dope and getting pissy-eyed. Best goddamned party I ever been to!

"Well, about three or four that morning, Bobby Joe and Sarah have got to leave to go into Shreveport to get ready to rehearse for the show that night. Bobby Joe's so fucked up he can't drive hisself, and like a fool I volunteer to run him on up there. Alvin says he'll ride on up with us to keep me company. And Milton Henry, the rhythm player, done wasted the whole evening with this married gal from Beaumont who wasn't getting up off of nothing, so naturally he's mad. So he says, fuck it, he ain't never seen the *Hayride* before and he'll ride on up there with us. And you know Greg and T.R. and Billy Jim Sykes. Shit, you show them ole boys some pussy, you got to turn a shotgun on them to get them away. So they ain't coming with us. They talk Bobby Joe into letting them keep the wagon until Sunday morning, when they can drive up there and meet us. So anyhow, the five of us pile into Bobby Joe's Cad. I'm driving. Alvin's in the seat next to me, Milton's in the back behind me, Sarah's sitting in the middle of the backseat, and Bobby Joe's sitting where he always sits, in the backseat on the passenger side. You got the picture so far?"

"I think so," Tommy Lee said, wishing he didn't. And wishing the whiskey in his stomach wasn't churning around so much.

"Okay. Now, before I go any further, I got to tell you what's been happening all this time, ever since Sarah joined up with us. You know Bobby Joe, he thinks he's a big star and all that shit. And he can't stand to be around no gal he can't get next to, 'specially no gal as pretty as Sarah. So he's been sweet-talking her and buying her presents ever since she got there. But she ain't having nothing to do with him, not like he wants, anyhow. All the same, she's been going off somewhere with a different guy damn near every night, in every town we played, you know what I mean? So we all know she had to be giving up something, and it was pissing Bobby Joe off.

"So anyhow, we're leaving Port Arthur, going into Shreveport. I'm driving. Alvin's asleep in the seat next to me. Soon as we get going a little, I can hear Bobby Joe back there trying to sweet-talk Sarah. But I ain't paying no attention, he's been doing that right along and it ain't got him noplace yet. We get up around Newton and I start hearing this commotion coming from back there. I sneak a look over my shoulder and I see Sarah and Bobby Joe all locked up together, kissing, and Milton playing like he's asleep in the seat right behind me. I know Milton ain't asleep 'cause he's trying to snore, and I roomed with him enough to know that he don't never snore.

"I keep driving. A few miles later, I hear this sound coming from the backseat, like a little kitty mewing. I know what it is. I don't *believe* it, but I know what it is. I sneak another look, and sure enough, Sarah's done hiked her dress up and she's sitting straddle-legged on Bobby Joe, giving him about all he can handle."

"Ain't that a bitch," Tommy Lee said, taking another drink, trying to sound like it didn't matter to him. He could feel his hands shaking a little, but he knew if Goose was driving, there was a damn good chance that he didn't see all that he thought he saw.

"No, that ain't the whole story," Goose went on. "I mean, I been traveling on the road long enough to know that that's gonna happen every now and then, 'specially with Bobby Joe. The gals fall all over theirselves trying to get at him. But let me tell you what happened next.

"I'm still driving, see? And a few miles later I hear some real snoring. I look back there again, and it's Bobby Joe this time. And he's out. He ain't fooling none, he's really out. He drinks so much and drops so many pills, you know, it's a wonder he ain't killed hisself before now. Anyhow, we get to that little stretch of road up by San Augustine, close to the Louisiana line, and I start hearing the same little mewing noise. I say to myself, shit, now I *know* this ain't happening. But it's right behind my head this time, like, a foot from my ear. And you know Milton always was jealous of Bobby Joe, so I know he's done made up his mind he's gonna lay it to Sarah long enough to make her forget all about Bobby Joe. Pretty soon that little mewing noise stops, and she's groaning and carrying on, and they're back there going like a house afire.

"By the time we get to the bridge going into Logansport, getting ready to cross over into Louisiana, it's quiet again. I take another look. Sarah's done got off of Milton's lap and she's sitting there between him and Bobby Joe with her head on Bobby Joe's shoulder, asleep. And Milton's just staring out the window.

"So, I don't say nothing, I just pull off to the side of the road. Milton don't say nothing, neither. He just opens the back door and gets out and gets in the front behind the wheel. I get in back next to her. I sit there for a few miles I don't generally cotton to no bloody seconds, let alone no sloppy thirds. But I had been fooling around with this ole gal at the party down in Arthur, and just about the time she was ready, I got to stop and drive Bobby Joe and them up to Shreveport, so I wasn't in no shape to begin with.

"So anyhow, Milton's driving, and the sun's just starting to come up, and I know I better make my move. So I reach over for Sarah. Now, I'm gonna tell you the truth, if she had of said no, my feelings wouldn't of been that hurt. And the truth is, I ain't been on no goddamn gangbang since I was thirteen or fourteen, living back home in Midland. I guess I'm kind of ashamed of myself now, but the truth is, I had been listening to that shit for more'n a hundred miles. And the gal is pretty, ain't no mistaking that. She's one of the prettiest little things I've ever seen.

"So I reach over there for her, figuring I'm gonna have to kiss her and play with her a little bit, and wondering how I'm gonna keep my hand from getting all wet. But you know what she did? She just climbed up over me straddle-legged, and waited for me to get my pants open. Then she come down on me and put her head on my shoulder and started making that little mewing noise. We stayed like that all the way into Wallace, a little ways before you get to Shreveport."

Tommy Lee sat there in silence, holding the empty paper cup in his hand, staring at the radio.

"But I'm gonna tell you something, Tommy Lee," Goose said, flipping his cigarette over the side of the car into the parking lot. "It makes me feel sad to think about it. It was like it didn't have nothing to do with sex, none of it. That sounds crazy, don't it? I mean, I'm riding along the highway giving her all I got, and she's crawled up on my lap like a little girl. Like screwing me and Milton and Bobby Joe didn't mean that much to her at all, like all that she really cared about was somebody holding her and paying some attention to her. Sounds foolish, don't it?"

Tommy Lee had crumpled the empty paper cup in his hand. He kept staring at the radio in silence, listening to the song that was playing:

> *I walk forty-seven miles of barb wire,*
> *I use a cobra snake for a necktie,*
> *I got a brand-new house on the roadside,*
> *Made from rattlesnake hide.*
> *I got a brand-new chimney made up on top,*
> *Made out of a human skull,*
> *Now come on take a walk with me, Arlene*
> *And tell me*

> *Who do you love?*
> *Who do you love?*
> *Tombstone hand and a graveyard mind*
> *I'm just twenty-two and I don't mind dying*
> *Who do you love? . . .*

"No," he said, reaching for the door handle, "that don't sound foolish at all."

HOLLYWOOD
JULY 1956

About all that Mark Donovan had time to accomplish in the ten days that Gino Turicotti was in Japan with Max Geary was select an office, begin comparing furniture prices, and start sending out a few feelers for talent. And read and reread the set of guidelines that had been forwarded to him by ITRC's corporate-planning division in New York.

The small, three-room suite he chose was on the fifth floor of an eight-story building in the 6300 block of Sunset Boulevard, in a part of "old Hollywood" that was fast becoming a row of underfinanced, fact-buck record companies. There were five other small labels in the same building, and Champ Records, with its nugatory title blended right in.

At first, the whole Champ idea had seemed a ridiculous and pointless waste of time and money to Mark. But Turicotti, on his return from Japan and prior to continuing on to New York to assume the presidency of ITRC Records, spent the better part of a day with Mark and convinced him of the absolute necessity of forming the stepchild, subsidiary label.

As Turicotti had explained, for a company as large and well established as ITRC to lose almost a third of its record sales in one twelve-month period had not only decreased the company's immediate cash flow and operating ratio to an alarming level but also contributed to the overall trauma the entertainment industry was undergoing as a result of the sudden popularity of rock-'n'-roll music.

ITRC's classical-music division, which it termed its Gold Label Series, was a permanent liability to the company. Not once in its forty-year existence had it ever been able to pay for itself. Its costs were assumed by the pop-music division.

Also, ITRC provided financial backing for at least one Broadway show per season, more when the pop division's profits from the previous fiscal year allowed.

Then, too, in the postwar years, with the decline of the major motion-picture studios and the advent of television as a major entertainment force, film production had fallen more and more into the hands of independent producers. In many cases, they had to provide for their own financing. ITRC had invested heavily in motion-picture production during the past decade, resulting in profits from film rentals and movie soundtracks; but even more important, this had afforded the company the opportunity to sign new artists, who were assured of extensive media exposure.

Then, of course, there were the publishers.

The major music publishers of America had been sleeping in the same bed with ITRC for more than two generations, and they were not about to allow ITRC to desert them and their huge catalogs of standards without bringing to bear all the pressure they could generate.

And finally—and most important—there were the stockholders.

ITRC stockholders had grown fat and spoiled over the years. Not once since 1926, when the company had offered its first public shares, had ITRC failed to declare a dividend at the appointed time.

Now the stockholders were putting Max Geary and the other officers of the corporation in a totally untenable position. On the one hand, they demanded that the company continue an uninterrupted return of profits. And on the other, they demanded that the company withstand the market pressures that were resulting from the phenomenal public acceptance of this new rock-'n'-roll sound, this peculiar and undignified hybrid of black and hillbilly music.

As a consequence, all that ITRC could do at present was dip one tentative toe into the raging pop-music whirlpool and quietly try to determine which way the current was going to flow.

Turicotti explained to Mark his reason for accepting the responsibilities of heading one of the largest recording companies in the world without benefit of prior experience in the day-to-day record business: nobody else in New York was capable of taking the job at face value. Everyone, it seemed, had all sorts of preconceived ideas as to how things *should* be done, instead of accepting the fact that the changes now taking place in the business were pervasive. Whether anyone liked it or not, it appeared that the way records were now being marketed was the only way they would continue to be sold for as far into the future as could be predicted.

Turicotti then said something that surprised Mark. According to him, Max Geary liked the new music—found it a welcome change from the staid old Tin Pan Alley ditties, more vibrant, more in touch with everyday people and everyday life. Geary also felt that rock-

'n'-roll music had already contributed to a permanent change in the buying public's musical tastes—and the majority of ITRC's future album sales could conceivably result, not from traditional pop artists, but from the presently maligned rock-'n'-roll musicians and singers.

For the present, however, nobody in the company was buying Geary's theories, not the officers, not any of the old-line employees, not even Gino Turicotti. But Geary was the boss, the general. And he had decreed that Mark Donovan should carry the company's black-and-gold colors into the interdictive rhythm-and-blues market, find the areas of susceptibility, and send word back as to where ITRC should eventually place its resources.

A few days after Turicotti left for New York, Barbara Ellis, the young black woman who had been Mark's secretary from his first days with the company, informed personnel that she was ready to return to work.

The guidelines set down by New York had specifically stated that Mark was not to hire from within the organization, preferring that Champ maintain as little identity with the parent company as possible. Nevertheless, he was able to maneuver and hire her immediately.

In the two years that Barbara had worked for Mark, they had never entered into a formal boss-employee relationship. They had become friends. Barbara had always been amused at the fuss Mark created among the secretaries and other female employees of ITRC, and although she and Mark were about the same age, her relationship with him bordered on the maternal. She thought of him as an unusually sensitive man, if a little naive when it came to corporate manipulations, and she was very protective of what she deemed his best interests.

So after she had been back for about a week, and acquired most of the equipment and supplies she needed to get things operating smoothly, it seemed quite natural for him to rest on a corner of her desk one afternoon, share a coffee break with her, and admit that he was having problems getting Champ Records under way.

"What's the first thing we need?" she asked, getting right to the point.

He had already given the question considerable thought. "Well, I've never been involved in production before. We probably need a music director more than anything else."

"Now, that's funny." She laughed. "Everybody in the world thinks he knows what makes a hit record. They've even got little kids on television trying to pick hits. And you sit there and admit that you don't know what to do. I'll say one thing for you, you sure don't have any ego problems."

"So what's the next step for a nice kid like me?"

"Hmmm." She sipped her coffee and thought a moment. "Claude," she mentioned her new husband, "has a cousin who plays really good piano. And he plays on a lot of record sessions, too. I'll call him tonight when I get home and see if he knows somebody."

She made several phone calls from home that night and learned that there were five or six moderately successful rhythm-and-blues companies operating in the Los Angeles area. They had entered business during or shortly after the war, they controlled some of the most popular artists in the traditional r&b market, and they were consistently doing business of upward of a half-million dollars a year.

One man, she learned, was primarily responsible for the hits recorded on the West Coast by those companies. His name was Sam Crockett, known in the business as "Crying Sam."

Crockett had been a saxophone player with a number of big-name black swing bands before the war. And after coming out of the service, getting married, and not wanting to travel any longer, he had drifted into the local, non-union r&b recording scene. After a while, he had discovered that there was a good chance he would wind up leading most of the sessions he was called on to play. On most of them he was the only musician who could read and write music.

Before joining Jimmy Lunceford's band in 1933, he had received a fairly decent musical education at a little black college in Florida. But after he had started recording, he realized that his skills were limited, so he enrolled in a local conservatory and studied arranging, theory, and harmony. Most of his record dates didn't require that knowledge. But when they did, he was prepared.

Sam Crockett sounded like just the man Mark was looking for. Barbara arranged an appointment for the next day.

Promptly at two o'clock in the afternoon, Barbara ushered in a dour little black man with close-cropped kinky gray hair and the sharp features of a dark-skinned Indian. His eyes held such a sad expression, Mark didn't wonder at the nickname "Crying Sam."

Mark shook his hand and offered him a seat. "I'm glad you could make it so soon," he said, a little unsure of himself, perhaps about to hire someone who knew more about his job than he did.

"When your secretary called me last night, she made it sound like a matter of life and death," Crockett said.

"It's not *that* serious." Mark laughed. "Just crucial."

Crockett frowned. "You look familiar. Do I know you?"

"No, I don't think so," Mark said, and explained who his father was.

Sam Crockett's sad eyes lighted in a dazzling smile. "You Pete Donovan's boy?" He leaned across the desk and offered his hand again. This time his grasp was friendlier, less reserved. "He's a hell of a nice guy. How's he doing?"

"Do you know Dad?" Mark didn't know why he was surprised; half the people he met knew and liked his father. "Where do you know him from?"

"Oh, I don't really know him. I haven't seen him for years, except in the movies. But back in the thirties they used to have a big nightclub out in Culver City, called the Cotton Club. We used to play there all the time when I was with Lunceford, and all the big movie stars used to come in. That's where I met your dad and . . ." Crockett was about to say "your ma, too," but remembering how often movie stars married and divorced, he changed it to, ". . . he really was a nice guy. Down-to-earth. The kind of guy, even if you don't know him, you *feel* like you do. He still like that?"

"I don't think my dad'll ever change," Mark said, a touch of pride in his voice.

The ice was broken. The conversation immediately became comfortable, and before long Crockett was entertaining Mark with stories about his prewar big-band days.

Sitting there talking with Crockett fascinated Mark. After two years in the record business, and now the head of a completely independent subsidiary label, he still had never done more than pass casual remarks with a professional musician.

"Well, now, I know you didn't invite me up here just to hear me run off at the mouth," Crockett said after they had been talking awhile. "You got somebody you want me to do a little arranging behind, or what?"

"There may be a little more to it than that, Sam. . . .Let me ask you a couple of questions, okay?"

"Go 'head on."

"Barbara told me you're in charge of most of the r&b sessions around town, is that right?"

"Well, I don't know if you could rightly say 'in charge.' Most of them little sessions ain't got but four or five men on them, you know. And half the musicians can't read nohow."

"What exactly is it you do, then?"

Crockett was quiet for a moment. "Now that I think about it"—a little smile crossed his face—"I guess you could say I am in charge. I call the guys. Sometimes I pick out the tunes. If there's any horn parts, I write them out. All that stuff."

Mark hesitated before asking the next question, not wanting to put Crockett on the spot. "Have you ever cut any hits?"

"Oh . . ." Sam thought for a minute. "Probably about twenty-five or thirty."

Mark had been leaning back in his chair, relaxed, enjoying the conversation, his calf hooked over a corner of the desk. But the number "twenty-five" made him bolt upright, disbelief showing on his face. "What?"

"At least twenty-five," Sam said matter-of-factly, shrugging his shoulders. "Maybe more than that. I don't know, I ain't never counted them up."

From the way Crockett repeated the statement, Mark knew he wasn't lying, at least not intentionally. But twenty-five hit records, for God's sake! It was unbelievable that a man with Sam Crockett's credentials would be floating around the city just waiting for someone to call him to arrange a session.

"Sam, you've got to be kidding," Mark said.

"No, I ain't. I ain't kidding at all," Crockett said, and immediately began to reel off some titles, and the r&b artists who had recorded them.

Mark was unfamiliar with most of the songs, except those that had been "covered" by larger companies, using white artists. "You mean, you did all the original dates on those tunes?" he asked.

"Yeah. Wrote some of them, too."

"Which ones?" Mark asked.

Again Crockett ran off a few titles, most of them unfamiliar to Mark, until the last. The last song had been a million-seller, recorded on one of the major labels by a popular young homosexual movie star. Mark remembered the tune, a simple r&b-type ditty, with a refrain that was repeated throughout the record by a chorus of black girls in the background. Until he'd spoken with Sam, he hadn't even known that the popular version was a cover record.

"I don't want to mislead you none," Crockett interrupted Mark's thoughts. "I didn't write it by myself. I wrote it with the boy that recorded it." He mentioned a vaguely familiar r&b singer whose name Mark had seen on the tail end of the pop charts a few times. "Him and me sat down at my house and wrote it the night before the date. He had just come off the road and didn't have all his songs picked, so we wrote that thing. Didn't have no idea it was gonna be that big a hit, though. It was just supposed to be a backup."

"Did you get label credit?" Mark asked, making a mental note to tell Barbara to pick up the record. He would have bet that Crockett was telling the truth, but, still, he didn't want to get conned the first time out.

"Oh, yeah, I got credit," Sam said quickly, "me and the boy I wrote it with. 'Course, the man who owns the company put his name on it, too, like he does with every tune that he puts out, even though he don't have nothing at all to do with the writing."

Mark nodded, thinking. "Sam, just out of curiosity, let me ask you something. How much, how many copies, would you say an average r&b record sells?"

"Ain't no telling, ain't no telling," Crockett said, shaking his head emphatically. "I get statements from them little companies all the time, but I know they ain't right. Biggest statement I ever got was on that record, and it wasn't for but 228,000. Which I know was a lie. It had to do at least twice that much."

"Well, what would you guess an average r&b record sells?"

"That would be hard to say," Sam hedged again, "since I don't feel I ever got no honest statement. But I'd say, oh, about a quarter-million to three hundred thousand."

Mark shook his head in astonishment at his own lack of knowledge. It was hard to believe that he had been in the music business for two years and was still so uninformed about what was going on. For an instant he felt a flush of insecurity, again wondering why Max Geary and Gino Turicotti had chosen him for this job.

But they probably didn't know some of the things Sam Crockett was telling him, either.

He had looked at his budget again earlier in the day, in anticipation of this meeting, and he knew he couldn't begin to offer Crockett what he was worth. But he knew Crockett was the man he needed. He had to give it a try.

"Do you want to work for me, Sam?" He felt foolish as soon as the words were out of his mouth. Of course Crockett didn't want to work for him, not at the prices he could pay.

"What do you mean by 'work for you'?" Crockett was wary. "You mean, you want me to do some arranging for you?"

"I mean, I want you to work for Champ Records, full-time. Handle all the sessions, sign artists, hire musicians, choose songs. Everything."

The look on Sam Crockett's fifty-year-old face was a silent indictment of the record business he had labored in for the past decade. It had never crossed his mind that he would be offered a job by a legitimate record company.

Mark took Crockett's expression for a lack of enthusiasm rather than the disbelief it mirrored. "Of course, I can't pay you what you're worth," he added quickly. "I can only afford two hundred a week."

Crockett opened his mouth to accept. But Mark, afraid that Crockett was going to say no, continued talking.

"And I'll tell you what else I can do. I'll pay you a penny a record for every copy that we sell. That's in addition to your salary. Plus, leader's fee on every session, on top of your arranging fee. You can play on any outside sessions you want, as long as it doesn't interfere with your job here. But I would prefer that you don't do any outside arranging as long as you're working for us, if that's all right with you?" He hadn't meant for the last statement to sound like a question.

"You serious?" Crockett asked in disbelief.

"You're not under contract to anybody else, are you?"

Contract? Crockett thought. This young white fellow was going to hire him as an a&r man and give him a bonafide contract, too? He'd never thought that would happen. "No, I ain't under contract to nobody," he said, trying to hide his excitement. Then he figured maybe he'd better apply a little pressure, so he added ominously, "Yet."

"Good," Mark said, relieved. "I'll have one drawn up the first thing Monday morning. It will be for one year, with two one-year options. I should tell you in advance, though, that I have no idea how long we'll be here. It may be a year, it may be longer. But the job is yours for as long as we're in business, Sam."

Crockett studied the open, handsome young face across the desk from him. Damned if he didn't like this young fellow. Naturally, he wasn't going to jump right up and trust him completely. White men had cheated him too many times for that. But there was something about this boy that just made you like him. He'd check him out good, test him a couple of times. And if he was really as straight as he seemed to be, old Sam would do all he could to see that Champ made a little money.

"When do you want me to start?" he asked.

"How about Monday morning?"

"I'll be here."

"Fine," Mark said. "Now, before you go, let me run over a couple of things with you. How about artists and material? Have you got anything I can hear right away?"

"Oh, yeah," Sam said, happy to be through talking money. "I always got kids calling me up, wanting me to help them get with a label. And I've got a couple of tunes I ain't recorded yet. And I know a few good songwriters, too. I think I can get things moving pretty quick."

"How about publishing? Are the tunes open, you think?"

"I know mine are. I figure you can probably work something out with them other writers."

"Good. Did you see the door to the left of Barbara as you came in?" Crockett nodded. "Okay, that will be your office. I know you'll need a piano and a tape recorder, and a desk and some filing cabinets. Tell you what you do, just make out a list over the weekend and give it to Barbara when you come in Monday, and we'll have everything for you as soon as possible, okay?"

"You got a deal."

"I guess that's it, then," Mark said, rising, putting out his hand. "I think we're going to do all right, Sam."

Crockett shook Mark's hand firmly. He looked ten years younger as he headed for the door. Not having to get out there and hustle and scuffle for gigs puts a little extra spring in a man's step.

Barbara came in a few seconds later. "Well," she asked, "what do you think?"

"Oh, I think he's going to work out fine," Mark said, and added, "I think I'm pretty smart to have you for a secretary. Thank you, Barbara."

"My pleasure, Mr. Donovan," she said, making a small curtsy. "Just don't forget who your friends are when you get to be a big shot and have all those peons throwing themselves at your feet."

Mark laughed. " 'Modest expression is a beautiful setting to the diamond of talent and genius,' as Seneca used to say."

"Forget I brought it up," she said.

CHICAGO
AUGUST 1956

Maudie Perkins was four years younger than Monroe Wilcox, but even at twenty-three she looked more like a child than a woman. She stood a fraction under five feet tall, weighed less than a hundred pounds. She had clear mulatto skin with a few freckles sprinkled across the bridge of her small nose, and curly reddish-brown hair that clung to the sides of her face, making a delicate frame for the soft, wide mouth that always seemed, at least to Monroe, to be turned up in a smile.

Until three or four months ago, he had never taken her seriously. He had always thought of her as a kid—understandably so, because she and his younger sister, Carleen, were friends from kindergarten days. Maudie was the little kid who used to hang around the house with Carleen, playing with dolls and jacks or jumping "double-dutch" rope in the backyard.

Once, when he was twelve or thirteen, and Maudie was eight or nine, he was lying on the living-room floor reading a book about Joe Louis, when Maudie came up behind him, kissed him on the cheek, and told him she loved him and one day was going to marry him. He wasn't too hip to being kissed by one of his little sister's snot-nosed friends, and he had popped her on the butt so hard his hand stung for the next ten minutes.

Then, when he was eighteen or nineteen, after he had started fighting, she and Carleen used to come to all his matches. She was there at his last fight, the one that made him decide not to turn pro.

The match was held at a basement athletic club on North Clark Street on the near Northside, the kind of place where the officials let the contest continue until the fighters punch themselves senseless.

His opponent was a Puerto Rican boy from the Westside. The Puerto Rican must have started boxing when he was three years old.

In the last round, the third round, the Puerto Rican tried to put Monroe away. They stood in the center of the ring, toe-to-toe, two sons of the ghetto and the barrio, trying to win the fifty dollars that would be slipped under the table to whoever was lucky enough to survive. There were only fifteen or twenty seconds left in the fight when the Puerto Rican went down. After he was counted out, they took him out of the ring on a stretcher, straight to Cook County Hospital.

Monroe himself had to be helped out of the ring. He was downstairs in the smelly little dressing cubicle, stretched out on a rubbing table, when Maudie burst in. She was still a kid then, maybe first year of high school. She ran over to the table and took Monroe's face in her hands and stroked it and kissed it, huge tears streaming down her face. She kept repeating, over and over, how much she loved him, until the fat Italian who ran the club dragged her away and shoved her out the door.

Monroe joined the Marines the next week.

By the time he was discharged, Maudie had married some would-be-cute hustler with a heavy distaste for honest work, who was giving her fifty kinds of hell. Monroe saw her only once or twice during the time she was married. Then, after she cut her husband loose and started hanging around with Carleen again, he saw her all the time.

But even though she had been married and had turned into a righteous little fox, Monroe still thought of her as a kid. He probably always would have, if she and Carleen hadn't gotten together to change his mind.

One night he invited them up to his flat to fix a late snack and listen to some records. He was just getting over the flu, so he went to bed early, leaving them still sitting at the kitchen table, talking.

Actually, they weren't just talking; what they were doing was scheming.

When he woke up the next morning, Maudie was lying in bed next to him, naked. She was staring at him with almost no expression, except for maybe a slight glint of determination just the way a woman would look at the man she loves, and has known and trusted all her life.

That was the morning she became his woman, and the way it happened was so uncool, whenever they thought about it they couldn't help but laugh. Maudie called it the "most pitiful rap" she had ever heard.

Monroe could still remember the conversation: "What you doing here, girl?"

"Waiting for you to wake up."

"Okay, I'm awake. Now what?"

"What you mean, now what?"

"I mean, you must of seen me wake up a hundred times. It ain't no big thing. How come you laying there with your clothes off like that?"

"You ain't that dumb. You know why I'm laying here like this."

"You mean . . ." Ha! Ha! Ha! You want me to . . . Ha! Ha! Ha! . . ."

"Don't make fun of me, nigger!"

"Aw, Maudie, I ain't making fun of you, but you're just like a little sister to me. I couldn't, uh, uh . . . do that with you. . . ."

"Well, I may be just *like* your little sister, but I *ain't* your little sister. I've been in love with you ever since you were running around in short pants with your ashy knees showing, cheating at marbles!"

"Shit, I don't believe that. We used to fight like cats and dogs. Still do, for that matter. Now, get up from here and put your clothes on before I spank your little ass."

"I'm in love with you, Roe."

"You're serious, ain't you?"

"Yes."

"Okay, I'm gonna cut your little jive program right in half. If you been in love with me all this time, how come you married that no-count nigger while I was in the war?"

" 'Cause you were always sending pictures of you and them ugly Chinese girls. Always had your arms around two or three of them at a time, like you really thought you were hot shit."

"That didn't mean nothing, all the guys used to do that. It wasn't nothing happening. They weren't nothing but whores. Just someplace to hang out while their daddies and boyfriends were loading up their guns for us. Anyhow, that shows how dumb you are, they weren't Chinese, they were Korean."

"I don't care if they were *nigger*nese! You shouldn't have been hanging on them, hugging them like that."

"Yeah, well, that ain't got nothing to do with *now*. I still wouldn't feel right doing it with you. That would be just like making it with Carleen. Hell, I wouldn't know where to start."

"Okay, nigger, if you're that dumb, I'll *show* you where to start. First, you put one hand here. Like this . . . see? Then you rub it. Like this . . . see? Then we kiss. . . . Like that, see? Then you . . . ummm . . . Damn! Okay, now we can forget about all that little-sister talk."

They had made love, and Maudie's firm little body had fitted itself to Monroe's small frame like it had been created for him.

Later, in the months that had passed since that morning, Monroe discovered it was easy to love someone you've known all your life. It was certainly easier than trying to find love with some babe you picked up at a party, who was forever trying to run those little silly street games on you. And you didn't have to change. You could go right on being yourself.

And Maudie wasn't merely pretty, she was in control of her life. She had started attending classes at the University of Chicago after her marriage broke up. Now she had less than a year to go before she received her degree in sociology. They hadn't talked it over yet, but they both knew as soon as she finished school, and as soon as he got his record company moving, they would get married.

They might make it, too.

He kept finding out new things he liked about her, things he had never noticed in all the time he had known her. Like, how well she could cook. And how she kept herself and her surroundings spotlessly clean.

And as for Maudie, she really had loved Monroe for as long as she could remember, and she was intelligent enough, and sensitive enough, to see and understand the relentless energy and ambition that drove him to try to make something of himself.

It had been a busy two months for Monroe since his first meeting with Ted Green. Between running his record store, putting together a new record of the Tru-tones, and trying to get his record company in working order—signing artists, choosing songs, lining up distributors he felt he could trust, or who would condescend to do business with a black businessman—his personal life had deteriorated to zero.

So today, on this hot Saturday afternoon in August, he was standing at the counter in the Rite-way Cleaners on Fifty-fifth and Cottage Grove, where Maudie worked part-time. He had been hanging around there for ten or fifteen minutes, talking, enjoying her company, and making plans for the two of them to attend church together the next morning.

He was just getting ready to go back to his store to relieve Carleen. Maudie was in the rear of the shop, bagging his clothes, and he had his back to the counter, was facing the door, idly checking the babes as they strolled down Cottage Grove in their lightweight summer dresses . . .

. . . *when the record came over the radio.* . . .

He didn't pay any attention at first. But as the music and the voices touched his consciousness, he slowly turned around and stared at the little portable radio sitting there by the cash register.

The loose, slighty out-of-tune harmony could have belonged to any one of fifty little black background groups. But the lead voice sounded familiar. If he hadn't known better, he would have sworn it was Dave Washington.

He listened carefully, leaning forward a bit, unconsciously nodding his head in time to the driving gospel beat.

Just as the record ended, Maudie came back with his clothes. She was saying something to him, and he quickly leaned across the counter and put his finger to her lips, shaking his head for her to be quiet.

"... *the down sound that's going around* ..." Al Baxter, Chicago's number-one black disc jockey, was saying, "... *yeah, folks* ... *it's the Tru-tones* ... *a fine record by a fine group* ... *home boys, from right here in Chicago* ... *back with another hit* ... '*Going Down Slow.*'"

Monroe's eyes turned to slits, the anger and shock on his face so intense that Maudie let out an involuntary gasp. "You all right, Roe?"

"Gimme the phone!" She automatically reached under the counter, still staring at him, wondering what had shaken him so. "Better gimme the book, too," he added.

She put them both on the counter and watched in silence as he hurriedly flipped through the thick directory. He found the number he wanted, dialed it, waited a few seconds. Busy. He swore softly and looked at his watch. Twenty after three. He knew Baxter went off the air at four o'clock. The best thing to do would be to drive over to the Westside and try to catch him before he left the studio.

"You okay, honey?" Maudie asked again, concerned.

His hands were shaking so much from the sudden anger and shock, when he pulled the money out of his pocket to pay her, change flew all over the floor. He didn't even glance down at it. "I ain't okay yet," he said, snatching his clothes off the rack, hurrying toward the door, "but you can bet your fine little ass I'm gonna *be* okay!"

Outside, he sprinted the half-block to where his Roadmaster was parked. Goddammit! Some silly bastard had double-parked a pearl-gray DeVille at a thirty-degree angle to his car, blocking him in.

He tried the door to the Cad. It was locked.

He ran back to his own car, unlocked the trunk, tossed his clothes inside, and slammed it shut. The window on the driver's side of his car was open. He reached in and impatiently began honking the horn, looking around the street to see if anybody was coming to let him out. Nobody did. He stood there for a minute, honking the horn, trying to decide if he should break the window on the Cad and release the brake. If he did, he would still have to push the goddamn thing out into traffic—and maybe kill the nigger whoever owned it, if the son of a bitch saw him doing it.

He knew he had seen the car before, seen it at least a dozen times. A pearl-gray coupé with leopard-skin seats. Goddammit, who owned that car?

He kept thinking. A picture popped into his mind. He had it! That pimp, Smiley!

He thought a little longer. Where would a pimp with a pearl-gray Cadillac be on a hot Saturday afternoon in Chicago?

Only one place, getting his hair fried!

His eyes quickly covered the street. Sure enough, about three-quarters of a block away, on the other side, was a barbershop. He ducked through traffic and sprinted down the block. There were several customers inside. He spotted his man immediately in the second chair, wearing a lavender shirt with white lace trim and matching lavender pants. It was Smiley, all right. He must have parked there right after Monroe went in the cleaner's, because the barber was already combing the hot yellow straightening cream through his hair, and Smiley was already beginning to sweat.

Monroe hurried over to him. "Is that your hog double-parked down the street, man?" he asked, trying to keep the anger out of his voice.

Smiley tilted his head to the side, threw Monroe a laid-back look. "Yeah, little brother, that's me, all right. What about it?"

"Move it. I got to get out."

The pimp smiled, keeping his cool, showing off the row of gold-framed front teeth that gave him his nickname. "I ain't moving nothing right now, little brother. Can't you see the man's already got the shit on my head?"

"Then gimme the keys, I'll move it."

Smiley must have been holding court for the other customers before Monroe came in, because he included the whole room in his disdainful drawl. "Dig this motherfucker, men. . . .This motherfucker must think I'm crazy. He's gonna walk in here like he's in a big hurry, and just like *that*"—he snapped his fingers, showing off a large diamond ring—"just like that, I'm gonna hand him the keys to a seven-thousand-dollar car." The customers laughed appreciatively. Even the barber had to grin at that. Smiley turned back to Monroe. "You got to come up with a better game than that, little brother." He started to laugh again.

Most of the laugh was still in Smiley's throat when Monroe

yanked him out of the chair so violently that one pointed patent-leather shoe caught in the footrest of the barber chair, and he wound up sprawled across the floor in a wide-angle U, with Monroe holding him up by his shirtfront.

"Now, motherfucker, you want to play, but I got business to 'tend to!" Monroe's face was about a half-inch away from the tip of Smiley's nose. "I ain't gonna tell you but one more time, *stop fucking around and move your goddamn car!*"

Smiley started to say something, to try to save a little face, but the look in Monroe's eyes stopped him in time. He nodded and let Monroe finish pulling him to his feet. They went out the door, Smiley wearing the pinstriped bib sprinkled with flecks of yellow processing cream, hobbling on the foot that had caught in the chair.

By the time they got to the cars, Monroe could tell that the straightening cream was starting to heat up Smiley's scalp, because Smiley didn't say a word. He just jumped in his car and backed it up as fast as he could.

Monroe pulled out, tires screaming, heading north on Cottage Grove.

He glanced at his watch again. He had lost seven or eight minutes fucking around with that jive-ass nigger. Now he had only a half-hour to get to the other side of town. He had the car up to fifty in a few seconds, weaving in and out of traffic, trying to quiet the anger buzzing in his head long enough to get his thoughts together.

Okay, now, the first thing to do is cool down. . . .

He flicked on the air conditioner, scrunched over by the driver's door, and pushed his stingy-brim hat farther down on his forehead. He drove like that for a while, the angry scowl on his face slowly replaced by intense determination.

As he thought back, he realized he'd had a feeling all along that something was not quite right. The Tones had acted funny all the time they were in town. They avoided him and seemed bored by the two recording sessions he'd arranged for them. When he went over to the Regal Theater to see them perform, let them know how things were going, they had a guilty, chickenshit look.

And then, there was the new Chrysler station wagon. There was no way they could have afforded that car after just a couple of months on the road, not with the kind of money they were splitting among four guys, not unless somebody had laid some extra bread on them.

Monroe glanced at his watch. A quarter to four. He might make it. And Goldman—he'd known that fucker was going to try to cheat him, but this was too much. That bastard had let him spend all that money, two or three grand, cutting dates on the group, mastering the tapes, making dubs, and all the time he didn't have the slightest intention of putting the record out. He had a contract with Goldman, an iron-clad written agreement to produce all the masters on the group. So why would he break the contract like that? There was only one answer: Goldman must have assumed that Monroe was broke, didn't have the money to fight back. He must have assumed that Monroe would get an Amos-and-Andy lawyer and try to sue him. But Monroe had been around long enough to know that the quickest way to go broke was to take somebody to court.

He flicked on the radio, just as Al Baxter was announcing the last record of the day. He tromped on the gas, ran a yellow light, and made a left turn.

He was still two blocks away when Baxter turned it over to the four-o'clock news. There was a Dixie Peach commercial. Just as the news started, Monroe slammed on the brakes in front of the little green cottage that housed the radio station.

He slid across the seat and ran for the gate of the Cyclone fence that surrounded the building. Locked. He ran another fifty feet, to the big sliding gate that blocked the driveway. He tugged it back and sprinted toward the side entrance of the house, reaching the bottom of the steps just as the tall, blue-suited figure of Al Baxter was emerging from the doorway.

Monroe, slightly out of breath, waited for Baxter to reach the bottom of the steps. He stuck out his hand. "Listen, man, my name is Monroe Wilcox. I own Monroe's Record Rack on the Southside, on Indiana Avenue. I met you a couple of times before."

Baxter shook his hand without enthusiasm. "Well, it's good to see you again, my man," he said, flashing the phony smile he reserved for his male fans. "I'm in kind of a hurry, what can I do for you?"

"You played a record about a half-hour, forty-five minutes ago, 'Going Down Slow,' by the Tru-tones?"

"Yeah?"

"Well, I, uh, wanna take a look at that record, okay?"

"I don't carry it around with me, baby," Baxter said a little sarcastically.

Monroe almost lost his temper. Why is Chicago so full of jive-assed, super-cool niggers? he wondered. He forced himself to remain cool. "Naw, man, I know that," he said. "But I just busted my ass to get across town in time to catch you. That's my group, the Tru-tones. I own them, and I think the Jews that own the company they're on are trying to pull some shit on me, you know? So I want to check it out."

"Oh, Monroe Wilcox!" Recognition came into Baxter's eyes. He put out his hand again, this time with sincerity. "Yeah, I heard a lot about you, man." The phoniness was gone, replaced by sympathy for a brother in trouble. He turned around and started back up the stairs. "C'mon in."

He held the screen door for Monroe and led the way through a dark corridor to a small makeshift office in the back. "Sit down, man." He waved Monroe toward a straight-backed chair. "I have to find it. The promotion man brought in two copies, if I remember right. One's in the studio, I know that. But I think I stuck the other one here in the desk somewhere. Have a seat."

"That's okay," Monroe said, still standing.

Baxter rummaged through the drawers for a few minutes. "Yeah, I found it . . . here it is." He passed a 78 record across the desk. Monroe snatched it out of his hand and pulled the record out of the sleeve. It was a Chartmaker Record. He read the label credits: " 'Going Down Slow.' The Tru-tones."

All the fight seemed to go out of Monroe. Until that moment he had been mad, incensed, but he didn't really think Goldman would pull something like this on him. His shoulders slumped, and he put one hand on the desk to steady himself. Baxter, still standing, looked down at him from the other side of the desk. "Them your kids?" he asked.

"Yeah, that's my little jive-assed, double-crossing group," Monroe said bitterly.

"What you think happened? The Jew laid a little bread on them? Blew a little smoke up their asses?"

"Yeah, I guess so, man. . . ." Monroe's eyes were stinging. He was afraid he might cry. He'd picked those kids up off the street, fed them, spent his own money recording, promoting them. Dave Washington had been pushing a goddamn ignorant stick at the Wrigley Building, sitting on the el platform until four or five in the morning, trying to get home. The other guys in the group hadn't even been working, just standing around on street corners drinking wine and trying to harmonize. Going nowhere.

Baxter reached in the top drawer and pulled out a pint of House of Lords and two paper cups. He poured a slug in each cup and offered one to Monroe.

"To the motherfucking Jew," he toasted.

Monroe shook his head. "Naw, man, I don't drink."

Baxter's laugh was dry. "You stay around this goddamn business long enough, you *will* drink. Smoke, too." He put his hand on

Monroe's shoulder. "Here, man, take it. Relax. Cool yourself down. I know how you feel."

Monroe took the cup, sniffed it once, tried a tentative sip. It was the first time he had ever tasted hard liquor, although he had drunk a little wine before he started boxing. He tossed the drink off. It burned all the way down, gagging him a little, but it settled his nerves almost immediately.

He sat down and put his face in his hands, running his fingers through his short kinky hair.

Baxter took a seat across from him and sipped from the cup in his hands. "Listen, man," he said sympathetically, "try not to be too hard on the kids. You might have done the same thing if you were in their shoes. Remember, until you got them that first hit, they probably never had a down payment on a pair of clean drawers, you know what I mean?"

As hurt as he was, Monroe had to nod in agreement.

They sat in silence for a few seconds, as Baxter tried to think of something to say to make Monroe feel a little better.

"You want me to lay off that record?" he finally asked. "I don't want to make no money for someone's trying to put it to a brother."

Monroe thought about that. It had been a shock. No warning, no nothing. But what Baxter said made him forget about the Tru-tones for a moment, refocused his thoughts on Saul Goldman. He began to feel a little better, as the anger inside him slowly edged the hurt aside. He didn't answer for so long that Baxter was beginning to think he hadn't heard the question. Baxter was just about to ask it again, when Monroe spoke.

"You're off tomorrow, ain't you?" he asked. Baxter nodded. "Okay, when you come back Monday, I want you to play it once, early, before the kids get out of school. Same thing Tuesday. Then, Wednesday, I want you to start playing the shit out of it. Lay on it! Push it as hard as you can!"

Baxter looked at Monroe like he thought Monroe had lost his mind. "Why? What the hell good is that going to do you?"

Monroe laughed, an angry little chuckle at first, that slowly worked itself up to a wide grimace. "It's gonna do me a *lot* of good, man. I'm working on a plan. I'm gonna fuck them over."

"Here, man," Baxter said quickly, pouring Monroe another shot of Scotch, "you'd better drink this." He thought Monroe was freaking out.

Monroe took it, tossed it straight down. The grin slowly faded as the anger returned. "Listen, man," he said, "I know you think I'm

• 113

crazy, but I ain't." He stood up, offered his hand. Baxter shook it, still looking perplexed. "Can I keep this record?" Monroe asked. Baxter nodded again. Monroe started for the door, put his hand on the knob, and turned around and spoke to Baxter again. "Listen, Al, do what I say, okay? Cool with the record until Wednesday, because by Wednesday I'm gonna have my dick so far up that Jew's ass he's gonna think he's Marilyn Monroe!"

When he got back to his car, the sweltering Chicago afternoon was just beginning to turn itself into a muggy Midwestern evening. He took off his stingy-brim hat and wiped the sweat from the band with his handkerchief. He got inside and turned on the motor. He sat there for a while, thinking, slowly rubbing the sweat from his neck with the handkerchief, feeling the car's air conditioner begin to dry the perspiration from his shirt. Al Baxter came out a few minutes later, got into his car, and drove away. Monroe sat there a little longer, then looked at his watch. It was four-thirty.

He pulled away from the curb, driving slowly, looking for a telephone. A block up the street some kids had turned on a fire hydrant and were wading around in the gutter, trying to stay cool in the sticky ghetto heat. As Monroe drove past them, a mulatto boy about nine or ten ran up to the car and slapped the fender and yelled something Monroe didn't catch.

Monroe smiled and continued on.

He pulled into a Sunoco station a few blocks farther on and parked by the phone booth.

It didn't take him long to find the number he was looking for, Windy City Distributors, on Rush Street. He dialed it, let it ring about ten times. He was just about to hang up, when he heard a young woman's voice on the other end.

"Good afternoon, this is Tom Milburn," Monroe said, making his voice as light and friendly and white-sounding as he could. "You handle the Chartmaker line, don't you?"

"Yes, sir, I believe we do. May I help you with something?"

"Yes, I'm glad I caught you before you left for the day. . . ."

"Well, as a matter of fact, I was just walking out the door when the phone rang."

"Okay, in that case I'll make it as brief as I can. I own several record stores in the north-central part of the state, and I just happened to be in town for the weekend, figured I'd give you a call. We seem to be getting quite a few requests for a new record by a group called the, uh, Tru-tones. I believe the record is called 'Going Down Slow,' although I'm not quite sure about the title. Do you happen to have it in stock?"

"Noooo . . . I don't think so." Monroe could almost see the woman's face screwed up in thought. "I'm pretty sure you're the first retail outlet that's called in for it."

Good, he thought. "Look, I need a favor. I know it's going to put you out a little, but could you go check for me? I'm pretty sure I'll be ordering very soon."

The friendliness in the woman's voice lessened a bit, but she said she'd go check. While she was gone, Monroe took the record out of the sleeve and held it up to the fading sunlight. It appeared to be a good pressing, unflawed. A thin coating of dust still covered the grooves, which meant it had never been played.

The woman was back. "I checked, Mr. Milburn, and all we seem to have in stock are maybe twenty-five copies. As I recall, the manufacturer sent, oh, fifty or so, for promotional purposes. I guess we must have used about half."

"Oh, is that so?" Monroe said. "Just as a matter of curiosity, when did they come in?"

"I really don't know, sir. One or two days ago, I imagine."

He could feel her becoming impatient. "Well, thank you. I appreciate you being so nice. I'll get back to you. Have a nice weekend."

"You're very welcome, sir."

He hung up.

All right, you cheap motherfucker, he thought. *That was your first mistake.*

He dialed another number. The phone rang for about two minutes. He was again thinking about hanging up, when the voice of a young black male came over the wire, "Concertone Recording. Willie speaking."

"Hey, Willie, this is Monroe Wilcox. How you doing?"

"Everything is pretty cool, Mr. Wilcox. How you doing?"

"Mellow as a cello, twice as nice as a mother's advice." He heard Willie chuckle. "Listen, Willie, is Mr. Gordon still there?"

"No, sir, he's gone for the day. I'm just around here cleaning up. Got about another hour's worth of work to do, then I'm gonna split myself."

"You don't have no more sessions scheduled for today, huh?"

"No, sir. Far as I know, we ain't got nothing coming in until Monday afternoon. I can go look in the book if you want."

"No, that's okay. Lemme ask you something, Willie. Did Gordon ever do what he promised, start teaching you how to do the sound engineering?"

"Naw, man," Willie snorted, "that jive-assed honky ain't teach-

• 115

ing me shit. When I first started working around here, he showed me a few things, but as time went on, he just played like he forgot. He's just got me cleaning up, going for sandwiches, rinky-dink shit like that." He hesitated a moment before continuing. " 'Course, I fool around with it some when ain't nobody here but me. I really want to learn, you know? It's a good trade, lotta money to be made if a cat knows his shit."

"You wanna make a hundred dollars?"

Willie immediately got suspicious. "A *hundred dollars*, man?" His voice sounded like he thought Monroe was queer. "What you mean, do I wanna make a hundred dollars? What you want me to do?"

"Just answer the question, man!" Monroe didn't have time to bullshit around. "You wanna make a hundred dollars tonight?"

"Yeah, well, of course I wanna make a hundred dollars, but I don't want to get in no trouble doing it. What do I have to do?"

"I want you to stay there until I get there. Just stay put, you dig?"

"Yeah, I dig, but I don't wanna get—"

"Don't worry, man, you ain't going to get in no trouble. I'll be there in a half-hour. Now, don't go nowhere. This is important!"

Monroe hung up, hurried back to his car, and headed for the Concertone Recording Studios on Michigan Avenue. He had done all of his recording there for the past two years, ever since he started his label. Tim Gordon, the big florid-faced white man who owned the studio, was one of those slap-you-on-the-back paddies who made a big thing about playing up to black people. As a result, he received the business of most of the small black rhythm-and-blues record producers in the city. The studio had a pretty fair little sound, and the rates were reasonable, twenty-five dollars an hour for two-track.

The late-afternoon traffic had thinned out considerably, and Monroe made good time. It was only a quarter after five when he eased the big green car to the curb. The front door was locked, as he had expected, so he went around the side and entered the building through the back door.

He was a few feet down the hall when he saw Willie come out of the doorway that led to the studio control booth.

Willie Jackson was a polite, bright young man in his early twenties. Monroe had already made up his mind, if he ever got in a position to build his own studio, he wanted to hire Willie and put him in charge of all recording.

They spoke, with Willie looking more than a little nervous.

"Like I told you on the phone, Mr. Wilcox, I don't want to get in no trouble, now . . ."

Monroe pushed past him. He went into the control booth and extracted the record from the sleeve and showed it to Willie. "Here's what I want you to do. I need a master tape, a *clean* master tape, from this record. Far as I can tell, it ain't got no flaws in it, but I ain't played it yet, so I don't know for sure."

Willie looked at the record kind of apprehensively.

"You think you can handle it?" Monroe asked.

Willie took the record from him and held it up to the light. "Yeah, I don't see where that should be no big problem," he said. " 'Course, you talking about a second-generation reproduction. There might be some tape hiss when I get through, but I should be able to equalize most of that out."

"Damn, nigger, you're smarter than I thought you were." Monroe laughed. "How'd you learn all that?"

"I ain't as dumb as I have to act, that's all." Willie grinned. "I watch that big fat honky like a hawk, man. Every time he sits down to that console to do a session, I learn something. I read all the books and magazines I can get my hands on about sound engineering, and . . ." He stopped, embarrassed at his sudden rush of words. " 'Course, I ain't never done nothing like this before." He looked at Monroe questioningly. "Is this what you gonna pay me a hundred dollars for?"

"No, I'm gonna pay you fifty dollars to make me a tape. And I'm gonna pay you fifty more dollars to keep your mouth shut. I don't want nobody to know I was here, you dig?"

Willie grinned, nodded, and took the record over to the turntable.

Most recording studios never turned off their equipment, except for maintenance, because it took more power to turn the machines on and off than it did to keep them running all the time, so the motor was already on. Willie touched the needle to the record. A few seconds later, the sounds of "Going Down Slow" came blasting out of the two twenty-four-inch speakers suspended from the ceiling.

Monroe sat down, put his head in his hands, and listened as hard as he could. It was the first time he had heard the record all the way through, really heard it.

After the first few bars, his experience and judgment told him that it was a good record. It was, in fact, better than any of the Trutone masters he had in the can.

He listened a little longer.

Halfway through it, he had to concede that it was a *damn* good record, a little more pop-white-sounding than anything he had ever cut them on, but a good record. His trained ear picked out one or two sour notes in the background harmony, but nothing a record buyer would notice.

The tune they were singing was instantly recognizable to him, since he owned a record store that had a fairly large religious section. It had been stolen from an old gospel song, "I'm Going Down Slow, Jesus, Take My Hand." Only instead of the word "Jesus," the "writer" had substituted "baby."

These were some cold thieves. Stole his group, stole the song. They would steal his money, too, if he was dumb enough to let them get away with it. It was going to be a righteous pleasure to put them in a trick bag!

The record ended. Willie had been fiddling with the knob on the eight-channel console while the record was playing. Now he slid his chair back to where he could reach the turntable, preparing to play the record again, when Monroe got a flash.

"Hey, man!" he called. "Before you play it again, look on the label and tell me who the writer is?"

Willie flipped the record up on its edge so he could see the label. "Paul Schultz," he said.

"Thanks, man," Monroe said, feeling a renewed surge of anger. *Okay, you cheap motherfucker,* he thought. *That's your second mistake!*

Willie played the record six or seven more times, all the time fooling with the dials on the console. Monroe was just about to tell him to stop, afraid he might scratch the record, when Willie called to him, "Okay, Mr. Wilcox, I think I'm ready for a take."

Monroe got up and went around the console and stood by Willie's side.

"Now, before I start," Willie said, making a few last-minute adjustments, "is there anything special you want to add on?"

"No, man, just give me what's on the record. Cut it flat, no reverb, no equalization, except whatever you need to keep the hiss down."

"You want it at fifteen?"

"Yeah, that'll give me more fidelity."

The take went perfectly, except for a little click at the very end, just as Dave Washington's high tenor voice was beginning to soul into the fade.

"Oh, oh . . ." Willie said, reaching for a dial.

118 ·

"No, man!" Monroe quickly grabbed his hand. "Let it go. We can't do nothing about that."

When the take was completed, Willie got up and went over to the big console Ampex machine and rewound the tape. He made a few more adjustments and played it over the system. It sounded like the record had been cut right there in the studio. The only perceptible difference between the master Monroe owned and the original was the small scratch at the end, and just a hint of tape noise. Nobody would ever notice.

"Okay," Monroe said, smiling, satisfied, "let's do the flip side."

The second take also went off smoothly. They listened to the whole tape again. When it was over, Willie smiled and rewound the two completed masters onto a smaller reel. He put the reel in a cardboard box, sealed it with a strip of Scotch tape, and handed it to Monroe.

"Here you are, Mr. Wilcox," he said, unable to hide the triumph he felt.

Monroe took the tape, flipped it once. caught it. Smiling, he took out his roll, peeled off two fifties, and stuck them into Willie's outstretched hand. "You got your shit together, my man," he said. "But remember, you ain't seen me."

Willie folded the bills once and jammed them into his pocket. He raised his right hand, waiting for Monroe to extend his palm. Monroe did, and Willie gave it a resounding whack.

"Seen who?" he asked.

It was almost dark, a little after seven-thirty, when Monroe pulled up in front of the grimy two-story red-brick building on the Northside, in the Polish neighborhood where Max Novikoff had his small pressing plant.

Novikoff did the majority of his business with small, ethnically oriented labels, mostly German, Czech, Lithuanian, and Polish. Surprisingly enough, those little companies released a fairly substantial amount of product to the "old-country" people who still loved and bought the native music of their respective homelands.

Monroe had done business with Novikoff several times before, whenever he needed a small number of records to test the market on a particular release. He was using Novikoff this time for two reasons: first, the product that the old man turned out of his little shop was first-class, very well done. And Novikoff could respect a confidence, since he probably didn't know anybody of importance in the mainstream record business anyhow.

As Monroe alighted from the car and crossed the sidewalk, he could see a few shopowners and their wives sitting around on wooden milk crates, brushing away mosquitoes, watching their kids run up and down the street. The women were fanning themselves briskly with clover-shaped cardboard fans, trying to survive the muggy Chicago night in as much comfort as possible.

There were a lot more blacks around the neighborhood lately, so they barely glanced at Monroe as he mounted the three stone steps next to Novikoff's shop and punched the bell that would ring in the upstairs two-bedroom flat that Novikoff shared with his wife and two teenage daughters.

There was no answer, although Monroe could hear lively music and laughter coming from the flat, and see the lights shining down from the windows above his head. He punched the bell several more times. He had his fist raised to knock, when he saw light flash on the other side of the glass door and heard someone descending the long flight of stairs.

Max Novikoff opened the door a few seconds later, stuck his head out, his bushy white eyebrows raised quizzically.

"Good evening, you remember me," Monroe said. "I own the record store over on the Southside."

Novikoff stared at Monroe for a few seconds longer before recognition slowly spread across his face, changing his frown into a wide grin. "Oh, yes! Mr. Wilcox! How are you?" He wiped his palms briskly on his pants, reached out and took Monroe's hand, and pumped it several times. "We are just having a little supper. Come in. Come in."

"No," Monroe said quickly. "Thanks anyhow, but I ain't got time." He liked Novikoff and knew the invitation was sincere. But he also knew if he went upstairs just to be polite, he would wind up wasting an hour he couldn't afford. "Listen, I got a very important job for you, okay?"

Novikoff nodded, wondering what kind of a job could bring this man out on a Saturday night.

Monroe handed him the box with the master tapes inside. He took out his roll and slowly counted out twelve one-hundred-dollar bills, seven fifties, and nine twenties, which was all the money he had on him, except for a few ones and some change. He counted the money into Novikoff's hands, the Pole's eyes growing wider and wider. "How many presses you got in your shop, Max?" Monroe asked.

Novikoff was so surprised he couldn't think for a minute. "I have six, ah . . . ah, *five*. No, six. I have six, but one of them is not working so hot."

Monroe nodded impatiently. "Max, you and your wife and kids do most of the work yourselves, right?"

Novikoff nodded, still staring at the money in his hand, still not quite believing what he saw.

"Okay, good." Monroe spoke slowly, making sure Novikoff understood every word correctly. "Now, listen, Max. I want you to start pressing right now. *Tonight*. Press around the clock. If you run out of blanks, wake somebody up and make them sell you some more. If you get tired, call somebody else in to help you."

Novikoff still looked to be in mild shock. Seventeen hundred and thirty dollars was a lot of money! God had certainly smiled on him and his family this hot Saturday night.

"You got somebody else you can call, don't you?" Monroe persisted.

"Oh, yes. Yes! I have people to come in and help me."

"Okay, fine." Monroe pulled a card from his wallet and handed it to the older man. "Call me tomorrow at twelve noon, sharp, and let me know how many pressings you got ready." He put his hand on Novikoff's shoulder. "Now, listen, pops, don't let me down. This is important, you dig? *Very* important!"

"Oh, yes. Yes, I dig . . . I mean, I understand! I will call you tomorrow at exactly noon. Don't worry, Mr. Wilcox, I will call you!"

"Okay, I gotta split now. I'll talk to you tomorrow, and don't let me down. You get any problems, you call me *immediately*."

He turned and started down the stairs. As he retraced his steps across the sidewalk to his car, he heard the door close behind him, and the muffled sound of Max Novikoff excitedly calling upstairs, saying something in a language Monroe did not understand.

It was almost eight-thirty when Monroe got back to his record store in the 5700 block on South Indiana Avenue. Southside Saturday-night action was just beginning, and he had to circle the block twice before he found a parking space.

Monroe's Record Rack was a small store, about forty by forty. Most of the time Monroe could handle it by himself, except on weekends. Friday and Saturday nights were his busiest times, because the neighborhood people stopped by to pick up the latest records for their house parties. Carleen usually helped him on weekends, and most of the time when Carleen was there Maudie would come by and keep her company. If things got really busy, Maudie would act as Carleen's gofer. Maudie never took any money for helping out, so Monroe always gave her a choice of whatever new releases he had in stock.

He had been so busy that afternoon, he had forgotten to call Carleen and tell her he would be late. Now, as he walked into the crowded store, she looked up from where she was standing behind the cash register and flashed him the kind of look that only a sister can give an older brother she idolizes—angry and thoroughly disgusted.

He made his way through the customers, stepped behind the counter, and pulled her off to one side. She lit into him before he had a chance to open his mouth. "What's the matter with you, Roe? Damn! I been here all day, and I'm hungry, and the least you could of done was call me and let—"

"Listen, baby, I ain't got time to jive around," Monroe interrupted. "Something important has come up and I got a lot of business to take care of. I gotta make some long-distance calls, and I'll probably be up half the night. Dig, take care of things for me. Don't bother me unless you really need something, okay? I'll be in the office."

Just as he turned, he heard Carleen's stomach give out a little growl. For some reason, the sound struck him as a perfect expression of the kind of day it had been. He turned back, laughing, and they stood looking at each other for a few seconds before Carleen came over and put her arms around his waist and laid her head on his shoulder. "What's the matter, Roe?" she asked. "Maudie said you were really upset when you left the cleaner's."

He held her for a moment, then gently kissed her smooth dark forehead. "Same old thing, Leen. Them Jews are trying to do their little dance on my head, you know? Nothing I can't handle, though." He gave her arms a squeeze. "What you want, ribs or hot links?"

"You heard my stomach talking." She laughed. "Both."

"How about Maudie? She coming in tonight?"

"She's already here, out back digging out some old records somebody wanted."

"Okay, I'll order something for you all."

He pushed his way through the customers until he got to his cluttered little office in the back. He closed the door and dropped down on the old swivel chair, flipped his hat at the lumpy couch, kicked off his shoes, and rested his stocking feet on the stack of bills and invoices that littered the desk.

God damn, he was tired and hungry, and the night was just beginning. . . .

He stayed like that for about five minutes, motionless, his hands folded behind his head, recharging his batteries. Then he picked up the phone and called Jack's Famous Barbecue in the next block and told them to send over two orders of hot links and three rib dinners, some soda pop, and some sweet-potato pies.

He hung up and rummaged around in the top drawer for a pad and pen. He stared at the Tru-tones' record on the desk in front of him for a full minute, fighting to control his rage. Finally, disgustedly, he picked it up and pulled it out of its sleeve, turned it back and forth in his hands, very carefully studying the label: CHARTMAKER RECORDS.

It was a simple two-color label, turquoise, with the name of the company in half-inch black caps. It would be easy to duplicate. He had gone to school with a boy named Rogers Thompson, who owned a small print shop a couple of streets over. He would call Rogers at home the first thing in the morning and start him printing the labels. He had to get them to Novikoff as soon as possible.

He was busy writing notes to himself on the pad, when the door opened and Maudie came in carrying a paper plate and several brown bags with grease spots on them.

"Here's your dinner, Roe," she said, her voice conveying the worry she'd been feeling ever since he had run out of the cleaner's that afternoon.

"Thanks, baby," he said, still writing, not looking up.

"Honey, are you sure you're okay?"

He glanced up, smiled, reached for a rib. "You remember what I told you this afternoon?"

"I don't remember anything but that look on your face."

"I said, 'I ain't okay yet, but you can bet your fine little ass I'm gonna *be* okay.' "

"You aren't in any kind of trouble, are you?"

"Baby, a colored man is *always* in some kind of trouble."

"Is there anything I can do to help?"

"Yeah, you can give me a kiss and get the hell out and let me do some work."

She picked up a napkin from the desk and gently wiped the grease off his lips, and gave him a long kiss. "I love you, Roe."

"You got good taste," he said, watching her leave the room.

He ate absentmindedly, pausing every few seconds to wipe his hands and scribble something on the pad. By the time he had cleaned the last rib, he had completed his plan.

He looked at his watch. It was almost nine-thirty now, which would make it ten-thirty in New York. He picked up the phone and placed a call, and sat there nervously tapping his pen against the edge of the desk while he waited for the long-distance operator to connect him with Yancey's Record Shop in Harlem.

Sam Yancey had been a friend of Monroe's for eight or nine years, ever since Monroe went to New York to fight in the Golden Gloves. Yancey, a boxing enthusiast, had handled a couple of kids on the New York squad. He had taken an immediate liking to Monroe, and they stayed in touch over the years. On the infrequent occasions when Monroe visited New York, or whenever Yancey came to Chicago, they usually got together to discuss boxing—and always ended up talking about the hassles of trying to run a record store. There wasn't a hell of a lot Yancey didn't know about running a record store. He had been in the business long before it really was a business. If Yancey hadn't urged him repeatedly to go into records, Monroe would probably be slaughtering cows at the stockyards.

"Yancey's," a young girl's voice came over the wire.

"Hello, lemme speak to Sam, please."

"Who's calling?"

"This is Monroe Wilcox calling from Chicago. Tell him it's important."

The girl must have been sufficiently impressed. A few seconds later Monroe heard the deep, rough growl of Sam Yancey on the other end of the phone.

The two men exchanged brief greetings before Monroe got to the point. Yancey already knew most of the story behind the Tru-tones, how Monroe had found them, produced the first record on them, leased the master to Saul Goldman.

Now Monroe explained to Yancey what had happened earlier that afternoon. Yancey listened attentively, punctuating the conversation with an occasional growl, but saying nothing.

"What you want me to do?" he asked when Monroe had finished bringing him up-to-date.

"A couple of things. First, lemme ask you a question. How many of the Tones' first record did you sell out of your place?"

"Don't know exactly, but we sold a bunch of them, I know that. Still selling them. At least a thousand, maybe twelve hundred."

Monroe smiled to himself. "Okay, now dig. I'm gonna bootleg this new release. I've already made a duplicate master, and I'm having pressings made up right now, tonight."

Yancey whistled softly.

"I'm gonna sell copies directly to record stores at a discount, ten cents under what you all pay your regular distributor. Plus, for every ten records you buy from me, I'll give you one free. Can we deal?"

124 ·

Yancey whistled again. "You really gonna try to put your foot up that Jew's ass, ain't you, Wilcox?"

"Up to the motherfucking knee."

"Well, now, man, you know we tight, but I ain't heard this new record yet. Is it any good?"

"Oh, yeah, it's a damn good record. It's gonna sell, I know it's gonna sell. I wouldn't try to put no con on you, Sam, I've known you too long for that."

"Wait a minute, I'll be right back."

Monroe heard the line grow quieter, while Yancey evidently put his hand over the mouthpiece and discussed the record with some of his help. Monroe could make out a few "uh-huhs" and "mmm-hmmms."

"Okay, Wilcox," Yancey came back on the wire, "I talked to a couple of my salesgirls, and they said the same thing you said, it's a damn good record. In fact, we got one or two calls for it already this evening. Send me five hundred copies, but you don't have to send no freebies. You my friend, you know? We don't have to do no business like that."

"No, no," Monroe said quickly, "I'm gonna be making the same deal to everybody I talk to, so you might as well get in on it too. Hell, it don't hurt me none, everything I make is gravy. I didn't pay for the session, and I don't have to pay for no promotion. Goldman is footing the bills for all of that."

"Okay," Yancey said, "in that case, send me six hundred, and sixty more freebies. I don't know how long it'll take, but I ought to be able to get rid of that many."

"Wait a minute, now," Monroe said. "I wanna make sure you got the *whole* picture. Dig. If I'm gonna con them, the only way I can get away clean is if he don't find out, at least until it's too late, you know what I mean?"

"So what you got in mind?"

"All right, I want you to take most of the records from me, but it's gonna look mighty suspicious if you don't order none at *all* from your regular Chartmaker distributor."

"I know that, but if I get six hundred-and-some-odd from you, that don't leave me very much to take from him, do it?"

"*Now*"—Monroe laughed—"you got the point. I just want you to order from him in dribs and drabs. Twenty-five, thirty-five, puny shit like that. He may get suspicious, but as long as you're getting a few from him, the only thing he can think is that the record ain't selling too good in that part of town. Let him sell the chickenshit records to the white folks."

Yancey chuckled. "You right, Wilcox, you right. You got a deal. When can you get them records here?"

"I'll get them out to you no later than Wednesday morning. That way you should have them by Friday at the latest. Now, lemme ask you another question. How much you paying your regular distributor?"

"Sixty-five."

"Okay, you got six hundred and sixty records coming in, Railway Express, at fifty-five cents apiece. Sixty-day open billing, two percent off on whatever you send me in forty-five days or less. Now, lemme see . . ."—he wrote a few figures on the pad—"that comes to . . . uh, uh, three hundred and thirty dollars. I pick up the freight. How does that sound?"

"It sounds like you taking care of some natural business, that's how it sounds," Yancey said. "I like that. I like to see a black man with some backbone. I admire you for that. We got a deal."

"I knew I could count on you, man."

"Oh, yeah, you can count on me, you know that. Listen, it's getting late, I gotta start closing up. I'll talk to you later, after the records get here—"

"No, you ain't," Monroe said firmly. "Sit down and pour yourself a taste, we got a lot of talking to do. I wanna know everything you know about every colored man in the country who owns a record store, is in charge of ordering records for one, or knows somebody who is."

"You asking a lot, Wilcox. I been selling records of some kind or another since nineteen hundred and twenty-six—"

"And I know that there ain't nothing you've liked to do better since nineteen hundred and twenty-six than talk."

"Well, you know I traveled on the old BB&O as a Pullman porter for twelve, thirteen years, traveled on the Illinois Central as a dining-car waiter for five or six more years after that." Monroe could hear Yancey settling back, getting comfortable. "Hell, I started bootlegging old Bessie Smith and Louie Armstrong records for two or three dollars apiece to people down home, when you could walk into any store in Harlem and pick them up for a quarter. I know a whole lot of niggers out there with big shops and little shops, trying to sell records. If I start telling you everything I know, this call is gonna cost you the whole three hundred and thirty dollars, and then some."

"Talk," Monroe said. "Don't leave nothing out."

Forty-five minutes later, when Monroe hung up, he had six pages of notes on the scratch pad in front of him. Names of stores all around the country. Names of the people who owned them, or ran them for somebody else, but who could still do the ordering. He had the names of disc jockeys that Yancey felt could be trusted to give him more information, without running off at the mouth to somebody about it later on. He even had the Black Muslim greeting down pat, along with a little Prince Hall Mason phrase Yancey had given him, to let certain people know that Monroe was a friend of a friend, traveling a lonely road, who could use a little help.

He went through his notes. It took him a few minutes to figure out that if he came on with the right approach, didn't get greedy, he could probably sell ten or fifteen thousand records on the phone before the night was over. Yancey had even given him the number of some black-owned record stores in Texas and California. He'd keep calling all night, or until he couldn't get anybody, and start again the first thing in the morning. And he had to check with Novikoff to see how the pressings were coming along.

Then, Monday and Tuesday, he'd drive up to Detroit, down to Cleveland, hit a few spots in between, and swing back through Saint Louis, taking orders. Later, when he got back, Novikoff should have more pressings for him, and he'd run up to Gary and Joliet. He could hit the Southside later. A lot of the people who owned record stores in his area were personal acquaintances. He knew he could do some business with them. Yes, he'd save Chicago for last. He could fill the stores here quickly, and the girl had already told him Windy City Distributors hadn't even ordered the records from New York yet.

By being cheap, Goldman had made a fatal mistake. A smart record company always sent out a few thousand copies of a follow-up to a hit, to be sure to pick up sales from the very first day the record went on the air. Goldman hadn't done that. If he hadn't done it in Chicago, the second-largest black market in the country, he probably hadn't done it anywhere else, either.

It was going to cost him. It was going to cost him plenty.

Monroe opened another bottle of ginger ale, swished some around in his mouth, and swallowed it. Yancey had told him about a record store in Philadelphia that stayed open on weekends until one or two in the morning. It was right on Fifty-second and Market, Philly's main stem for black people, and it sold a lot of records. The man who owned it was a friend of Yancey's. He was down on white people, even thinking about converting to the Black Muslim religion. Monroe looked at the number Yancey had given him and placed the call. He got his pitch together while he waited to be connected. A few minutes later, a gruff black male voice came on the line.

"Lemme talk to Amos Carter," Monroe said.

"This is Carter. What you want?"

Monroe cleared his throat. "*Ai Salaam a lincum*, brother," he said. "My name is Monroe Wilcox. I'm calling you long-distance from Chicago. I'm a friend of Sam Yancey's. You know, Yancey's Record Store in New York, on a Hundred and Thirty-eighth and Seventh Avenue?"

"Yeah, I know Sam. What you want?"

"I'm the guy that discovered the Tru-tones. I own the group, recorded them myself, and put the master with Chartmaker Records. Now the Jew who owns the company is trying to break it off in me, you know what I mean? I talked to Sam a few minutes ago. He said maybe we could do a little business."

There was silence on the other end of the line, while Carter thought it over. When he spoke again, his voice was warmer, friendlier. "You a friend of Sam's, huh?"

"A good friend, man."

"Well, if Sam told you to call me, you must be all right. What's on your mind, brother?"

Monroe smiled, leaned forward in his chair, and rested his elbows on the desk. His voice got quieter, more confident. "Okay, man," he said, "here's the deal. . . ."

HOLLYWOOD
AUGUST 1956

It was Sunday morning, a little after five o'clock.

While Monroe Wilcox was on the phone in Chicago, making arrangements to acquire the labels he needed for the record he was trying to bootleg, Carl Clinger was standing at the rear of a two-story building in the 5500 block of Sunset Boulevard, unlocking the heavy door that guarded the new Hollywood offices of Carousel Records.

He paused long enough to yawn at the first hint of daylight graying the black sky, then pulled the door firmly shut behind him, and with a clatter that echoed through the empty building, stepped, in his expensive shoes, onto the circular iron staircase.

He paused again at the top of the stairs, unlocked another door, and walked into a small entrance hall. There were two switches in the panel by his left shoulder; he flipped the one farther from him and watched a soft yellow-blue light appear in his private office ten feet away. He carefully hung his check sport coat in the closet by the door, and glancing appreciatively into the executive bathroom to his right, started along the short hallway.

His private office was furnished in gold and white. Gold rug, couch, and chairs, white-with-gold-trim tables, lamps, and accessories. He had hired an exclusive firm of Beverly Hills commercial interior decorators to do the job, which was: to make sure that nobody walked into Carl Clinger's office and doubted for one second that he was a big man in the record business.

But he didn't have time to stand there admiring their work, not this morning. He had some selling to do.

The thought drove all the drowsiness from his body as he strode briskly across the thick carpet, pushed aside the Remington reproduction that hung on the wall behind his oversize desk, and dialed the combination to a small safe.

The heavy brown envelope he removed contained eleven stacks

of typewritten paper, separately stapled together, each containing four or five pages. Included also was a personal handwritten note bearing the letterhead of J. P. MacNeil, Private Investigations, Nashville, Tennessee.

He settled his slight frame into the spacious swivel chair and sat for a few minutes quietly composing his thoughts, staring at the telephone like a puma about to pounce on an unsuspecting goat.

In the two months since his meeting with the investors, he had been a very busy man. The day after the meeting, he had flown out to the Coast with Bobbie Jean, and while she had looked for a new home for the family, he had found this property for Carousel.

After he signed the lease and made plans for the remodeling of the building, he had returned to Nashville for a few days to discuss production with Tommy Lee and complete some paperwork with Bob Blandings. Then he had flown to Boston, the first stop on a tour that would eventually take him around the country.

The purpose of the tour was to inform everyone of importance in the music business that Carl Clinger and Carousel Records were about to make themselves heard.

The journey from Boston to Los Angeles had taken him two days less than five weeks. It covered the eleven major markets that made up the foundation of pop-record sales. Without strong connections in each of those cities, no record company could ever hope to attain major independent status.

He had personally met, shaken hands with, bought lunches and dinners for—and gauged—more than two hundred people, from distributors and promotion men to radio-station managers, librarians, program directors, and disc jockeys.

Especially disc jockeys.

His years as a promotion man for I. V. Ware had helped him immeasurably with even the more sophisticated big-city dj's. Dj's were dj's, as far as he was concerned, and he still knew how to feed their egos and speak fluently in the non-language disc jockeys and record-company owners used to communicate with each other. Consequently, of the hundred-plus he eventually talked to at length about himself and Carousel Records, only a few were put off by his affected country-bumpkin manner and considered him to be a slick hillbilly. The others thought Carl Clinger was the greatest thing to come along since free pussy.

And now he was going to take advantage of it.

He was about to call eleven of the most influential radio personalities in the country. They had liked him—he was sure of that.

What he did not know was: could they be bought?

A record company never knew about dj's. There was no way to be sure how much they had going on the side, such as record-company ownership, publishing companies, stage shows, "consultant" fees from major labels. One of the big dj's in New York was grossing six hundred thousand a year, over and under the table. Guys like him couldn't be touched. There was nothing Carl Clinger or anybody else in the business could offer him that he didn't already have, certainly nothing valuable enough to make him want to jeopardize his prestige and position of influence.

Conversly, many other dj's did have their hands out, usually the number-two or -three men in their markets. They were playing catch-up, and whether it came down to a hundred dollars for a week or two of airplay or to a set of sterling-silver knives and forks for their wives, there was a very good chance that they would be receptive to any offer made.

These were the men vital to the success of a maverick company like Carousel. They could break records, but they were not strong enough to manipulate the company or demand control of the artist.

This morning, Carl was about to try to ensure a strong base of nationwide airplay by "fixing" one man in each of the major markets.

The way he intended to go about it was pure show-biz, corny and dramatic. But without hype, half the people in the record business, himself included, would be out looking for work.

He had already studied the dossiers in the envelope. Now he went through them one last time, to make sure he had them correct and in order as to the gifts and the times they would be delivered.

The first man was thirty-nine years old. He had been in radio for almost twenty years, thirteen of them spent as a staff announcer on various stations in the Philadelphia area. He had jumped on the rock-'n'-roll bandwagon less than a year ago, too late to pick up the first wave of active teenage record buyers, but early enough to garner a fairly substantial following. He put on a high-school record hop somewhere in the Philadelphia area every weekend, drawing anywhere from one hundred to three hundred kids, at a dollar a head. Occasionally he was able to coerce a moderately successful record artist, always local, into coming along to sign autographs. He had been married to the same woman for sixteen years, and his file indicated that he rarely played around. He had two children, a boy fourteen and a girl eleven. He had recently moved across the Delaware River from Philadelphia into the exclusive suburban community of Cherry Hill, New Jersey. From what MacNeil could uncover about his personal finances, he was living well above his income and had a "definite cash-flow problem."

During Carl's promotional trip, he had taken the man and his wife to dinner, analyzed them, and chosen the gift accordingly.

He looked at his watch. The gift should have been delivered ten minutes ago by the Carousel promotion man in the Philadelphia area. He had been given a ten-minute leeway. If any problems arose, he was to call Carl.

He had not called.

Carl picked up the phone. . . .

When the phone rang, Ted Blackman was just about to put it in.

The interruption irritated him, but he was also amazed that it had never happened before, not once in the last eleven years.

It had become a ritual with them. Every Sunday morning, Eloise would somehow manage to squirm around until her nightgown was hiked up to her belly button, and with her back to him, rub and press and push until she could feel he was ready. He always pretended to be asleep, and she always managed to work it so that her plump backside wound up completely outside the covers.

They had fallen into the game by accident when she was pregnant with Tricia, and except for the time she had been recuperating from the delivery, and on those infrequent occasions when he had to be out of town, they had never missed a Sunday. Some Sundays, of course, they had to go about things in a different manner, and those Sundays usually turned out to be the best of all.

He was pretty sure that this was one of those Sundays.

Eloise Blackman was irritated, too. Actually, she was furious.

Earlier in the week, Tuesday, she had been cleaning up Ted Junior's room and found a book hidden under some dirty clothes in the back of the closet. The title of the book was *Sex for the Modern Couple,* and it was absolutely filthy. With pictures. She had confiscated it, naturally, and when Ted Junior came home from school, she had given him the scolding of his life. Then, Wednesday, Thursday, Friday, and Saturday, when she had a little time to herself, she had studied it thoroughly. Some of the things in it were disgraceful. But promised to be absolutely delicious. Eloise knew that if Ted never strayed far from the farm it was due in no small part to their Sunday mornings together. This Sunday morning was to have been one of the best of all.

And now the phone kept ringing!

"I think you'd better answer it, dear," she said, trying to hide the irritation in her voice.

Ted Blackman felt himself start to wither. Who the hell could be calling at this hour? Probably some giggle-assed kid who had just gotten hold of his new unlisted number. He fumbled around and picked up the phone. Even in his anger, his trained announcer's voice came out warm and well-modulated. "Good morning, Blackman's residence."

"Ted? Good morning!" Carl Clinger's thick Southern accent came over the wire, bright and hearty. "Didn't wake you up, did I?"

"Who is this?" Blackman asked irritatedly. It sounded like a god-damned hillbilly.

"Who *is* this?" Clinger's voice was indignant. "Why, this is Carl Clinger! Carousel Records! I'm calling you from the Coast, all the way from Hollywood! How are you, boy?"

Blackman thought for a moment. Carl Clinger? Oh, *Carl Clinger*. The guy that took him and Eloise out to dinner a couple of weeks ago. "Hey, Carl, how are you?" he said, still not quite able to hide his anger at being disturbed. "Sorry I didn't recognize your voice."

"Ted . . ." Clinger's salesman voice dropped a full octave. "I couldn't be better. You know why? Starting tomorrow morning, Carousel Records officially moves to Hollywood. Open for business. And let me tell you something, we're getting ready to knock the record business flat on its behind."

"That's nice," Blackman said. "I wish you luck."

"I know you do, I know you do," Clinger agreed. "And that's what we're counting on, people like yourself who want to see some new ideas come into the business."

Blackman was sitting up now, leaning back against the quilted headboard. He was, in fact, happy that things had progressed well for Clinger, but at the present time his attention was more focused on the light brown hairs peeking out from between his wife's legs. "Hey, well, listen, Carl . . . you know I'm happy for you, and I do appreciate your calling—"

"Whoa, boy. Hold on a minute. You don't think I called you up from three thousand miles away just to say hello, do you?"

Hmmm, Ted Blackman thought.

"Nosirree," Clinger bubbled on, "you know better than that! Now, let me ask you a question, okay? You still in bed?"

"Yes," Blackman said, staring at his wife's behind, "I sure am."

"Okay, I want you to do me a favor."

"Well, Jesus, Carl . . . it depends on what you want—"

"Listen, do me a favor, okay?" Clinger's voice was insistent. "No questions asked, just do it. Okay?"

"C'mon, Carl . . ." Blackman's irritation was beginning to grow.

"Okay, okay. Now, I know this is gonna sound a little strange to you, but I want you to get up and go look out your front door."

The conversation had become so strange that Eloise Blackman now gave up all pretense of being half-asleep. She rolled over to face her husband. "What's the matter, dear? Who are you talking to?"

Blackman put his palm over the mouthpiece and told her.

"Ted, you still there? Listen, do you think I'd waste all this money calling you up from three thousand miles just to play games with you? Do what I tell you. Get up and go look out your front door. I've got something waiting for you. Now, go do it!"

Blackman folded the covers back, got up, and headed for the closed bedroom door.

Eloise sat up in bed. This Sunday was completely ruined! "What *are* you doing, Ted?" she asked angrily.

"I have no fucking idea," Ted Blackman said as he opened the door and started down the hall.

He padded through the house to the front door, the look on his face somewhere between anger and disgust, for allowing Clinger to make a complete ass of him.

He yanked the door open.

A package toppled over inside. As Ted bent to pick it up, a brown Plymouth convertible driven by a bald man pulled away from the curb across the street. Ted didn't notice, he was so engrossed in the package, a chocolate-colored box, about three feet long, a foot and a half wide, a foot deep, tied with a thick gold ribbon.

He didn't recognize the name on the box.

He absentmindedly pushed the door shut, walked back into the living room, and sat on the edge of the couch with the box in his lap, a puzzled expression on his face. He pulled the ribbon free and removed the top. Inside, wrapped in light blue tissue paper, was a mink jacket.

He let out a long, slow whistle and held the jacket up in front of him. Jesus! He didn't know a thing about furs, but this was beautiful!

He saw a nine-by-twelve envelope in the bottom of the box. He opened it. There was a note inside, along with two 45-rpm records. He read the note first: "You are a lucky man, Ted. She's one of the nicest gals I ever met. Carl."

He pulled out one of the records. Across the top, on a black background, the words "CAROUSEL RECORDS" were printed in jumbled merry-go-round type, each letter a different bright pastel color. He looked at the title: "Good Easy Loving," by the Caravans.

He checked the other record: "Something's Calling Me Home," by Bobby Joe Whitaker.

Eloise Blackman was still sitting up in bed when he came back with the jacket in his hand. She let out a squeal, climbed over the foot of the bed, and snatched it from his hands.

Still looking a bit puzzled, he sat on the edge of the bed and picked up the receiver from the nightstand. "Hey, Carl, uh listen—"

"Surprised, huh?" Clinger managed to hide the spark of relief he felt. He didn't know what he would have done if the coat hadn't been there. "She like it?"

"Oh, yes! But, Carl . . ." Blackman looked at his wife in front of the mirror with her chubby buttocks showing, adjusting the collar around her face, turning slowly, looking back over her shoulder, admiring herself. "Uh, you know, I don't know . . ." he finished lamely.

"I know what you mean, boy!" Clinger said heartily. "It's beautiful, ain't it? Picked it out myself, you know. And, Ted, I just want you to do two things for me, okay?"

Blackman frowned. "What's that, Carl?"

"I just want you to tell that pretty gal of yours to wear it for me the next time I get up that way and take y'all out to dinner again. Will you do that for me?"

"Hey, sure thing, Carl!" Blackman said quickly, half-relieved. "And, uh . . ."

"I'll tell you what else," Clinger said earnestly. "Every time you see a Carousel record, I want you to remember that we aim to be the classiest outfit in the business. And I want you to remember this morning, the Sunday morning that Carl Clinger called you up on the long-distance telephone and made that statement to you. Will you do that for me?"

"I don't think I'll ever forget this Sunday morning," Ted Blackman said honestly. "Nor Eloise. I just—"

"Good, then don't say a thing. Just tell your missus I said to wear it in good health."

"I'll do that, Carl. Absolutely."

"Okay, that's all I wanna hear. I gotta get off the phone now, but we'll be in touch, okay?"

"Oh, we certainly will, Carl, no doubt about that," Blackman said, anxious to hang up. "And good luck with—"

"Oh, by the way . . ." Clinger sounded like he'd just had a sudden thought. "Were there a couple of records in that package?"

"Uh, yes . . ."

"Good! I didn't know if he stuck them in or not. To be honest, I forgot to remind him. But, Ted, I want you to listen to them good. Those are our first releases from out here. The Whitaker record is brand-new, and the other thing was just starting to break when we picked the master up. You've probably already got the Caravans' record in the station library, but I just wanted to make sure. . . ."

He waited for a reaction.

Blackman was silent.

"Listen, I wanna tell you something." Carl's voice took on a little more enthusiasm. "You're gonna love that Whitaker record! It's great, the best thing we've ever done! It'll be number one in the country before it's over, take my word for it. Now, the official release date on it is this coming Wednesday, got that?"

"Yes, Carl, but . . . uh, Bobby Joe Whitaker may be a little too country for our format," Blackman said, making a stab at independence. "We're strictly rock and roll, you know?"

"Of course, I know that," Clinger said firmly, some of the salesman's heartiness leaving his voice. "But remember what I told you? About Carousel taking the country out of the country artist and going right across the board into the pop market? Remember me telling you that?"

Blackman looked at his wife, still turning in front of the mirror. "Yes, I guess I do remember you saying that. . . ."

"Good. Well, this is exactly what I was talking about. This is the record that's going to do that for us. And you, too. You'll be the first man to play that record in that town, and I'll guarantee you, you'll pick up a hundred listeners a day until the other stations get on it. You know what I'm talking about?"

"Umm-hmmm," Blackman said.

"Fine, fine. Now, listen, Ted, this is important. I want you to send me a copy of your playlist as soon as you get these records on. I'm gonna need it to force a few doors open in that part of the country, you know what I mean?"

"Yes, Carl, I do. I'll get it to you as soon as I can."

"Fine, fine! I'd appreciate that. Now, let me get off the phone, but I'll be talking to you in a week or so, okay? Take care of me, now, boy."

Blackman heard the line go dead. He replaced the receiver on its stand, a little harder than he had intended.

If Eloise Blackman had not already hung the jacket in the closet and had not already been climbing back over the foot of the bed with a familiar glint in her eyes, he might have felt a flicker of resentment at Clinger's last words: "Take care of me, now, boy."

It was not a request, it was an order.

But Bobby Joe Whitaker did sell a lot of country records, Blackman rationalized. And the Caravans' record had been on and off the charts for the past couple of months, and maybe all it needed was a little concentrated airplay.

He would have rationalized a little more, but Eloise was already cuddled next to him, teasing her tongue along the bottom of his ear.

"What's the matter, dear?" she asked when he didn't respond.

"Just thinking . . ." Blackman said.

"Wasn't that a nice thing for him to do?" she asked, trying to head off any second thoughts her husband might have about returning the jacket. "I mean, I know he wasn't just being nice. He wants you to play his records, of course. But to go to all that trouble I mean, to pick out a coat that fitted *perfectly* and go to all the trouble of surprising me, I mean us, with it and everything . . . I mean, he certainly is a thoughtful man, don't you think?"

"I don't know how thoughtful he is," Ted Blackman said wryly, "but he's a hell of a salesman, I know that."

The statement had a slight edge, as if self-anger were about to get the better of him.

Carl wasn't smiling when he hung up. He rarely smiled when there was no one to see it. Now he had his mind on the next call. If he was lucky, they would all go as easily as the last one.

They did not all go that easily. Two of the next three calls went unanswered. The dj's involved, however, were bachelors, and Carl's choice of gifts had allowed for their absences.

The next five men he called were home. They responded in essentially the same manner as had Ted Blackman: they were quite willing to be bought, but reluctant to admit they could be bought so easily.

The tenth call was to an important San Francisco dj. Carl reached him at his weekend apartment in Sausalito, in what sounded like the final stages of an all-night party.

The guy was stoned when he answered, and it took Carl the better part of five minutes to convince him it wasn't a prank call and that he must go outside and look in his mailbox. It took another ten minutes for him to get back to the phone. When he finally did, all he said was, "Clinger, you have got to be shitting me, right?"

"I ain't gonna call you up long distance this time of morning just to play games."

"Then it's true?" the guy asked.

"A little present from Carousel Records."

"All riiight!" the dj said.

And hung up.

The idea for the gift had come from Carousel's Bay Area promotion man, who was probably still at the party. He knew the dj's tastes ran to kinky sex, and the gift was a handwritten invitation from two classy hookers to come by their Post Street apartment for a prepaid private "party."

Carl figured he'd call the guy again later, when the dj was in a little better shape to talk business.

He had been on the phone for almost three hours now. He had one more call to make, perhaps the most important of all. The gift certainly was the most expensive.

The dj was local, young, in his middle twenties, and just beginning to acquire power. He broadcast daily from a pier in one of the beach cities. He was a pied piper to the kids in Southern California. He had them driving from as far away as Santa Barbara and San Diego, more than a hundred miles each way, just to dedicate their requests over the air.

Carousel's local distributor had told Carl about this guy, and Carl had traveled out to see his show firsthand. He could hardly believe the reception the kids gave the ugly little man with the terrible radio voice. His programming consisted primarily of black singing groups from the southeast Los Angeles area, and when one of them made a personal appearance on the show, traffic would tie up the streets a quarter-mile in every direction.

Los Angeles liked to think of itself as a city of pretty people, and common tastes ran toward the deep-voiced, smooth-talking dj's who played traditional pop records, so nobody in the industry took this young kid seriously yet. But he was hot. All he had to do was play a new record on his show once or twice, and the sales response immediately reverberated throughout Southern California. Carl had talked with him several times, and was surprised to learn that no company had tried to guarantee substantial airplay on his show.

The kid could break records. Carl wanted him.

When the phone rang in the bedroom of Ron Carson's little bachelor apartment on Queen's Road, two blocks above the Sunset Strip, he reached for it with immediate, unbounded gratitude.

It had been the weirdest night of his life.

He had mc'd a rhythm-and-blues "battle-of-the-bands" show at the arena in North Hollywood the night before, and met this little blond. She had approached him first and introduced herself as Judy, which was something he still had to get used to, a pretty girl like her coming up to him and introducing herself. Hell, until he'd gotten his show going, good-looking girls avoided him like he was the West Coast distributor for syphilis.

But this Judy was a cute little broad. She couldn't have weighed ninety pounds, and she must have been less than five feet tall, because she only came up to his chin. Just right.

After they had talked a bit, she asked him for a ride back into Hollywood. Sure, he'd said, and led her over to his fifty-five Chevy.

By the time they got halfway across the Cahuenga Pass, she had his pants open and her head in his lap.

That was once.

Then they'd stopped by the drive-in restaurant on Sunset and Highland for a late breakfast. Afterward, he'd asked her where she wanted to be dropped off. She said anywhere . . . nowhere. In fact, if he didn't have a steady old lady, she'd just as soon go home with him.

Okay, so he'd brought her up here to his place, turned on the record player, and fixed them both a drink. They had been sitting on the couch for about five minutes when she had his pants off and her head in his lap. Again.

Okay, so everybody had their thing, and that was hers. A little unusual, but hell, he was just about the most popular dj in Southern California now, and he probably could be considered some kind of a sex idol. And you did run across some strange shit when you dealt with the public.

He was completely satisfied after the second time, naturally, but he'd kept her there on the couch, trying to make conversation.

She didn't contribute much, mostly asking questions about the personal lives of the artists he played on his show. Was so-and-so married? Was so-and-so queer? Where did so-and-so live? Stuff like that.

Finally, tired, he'd suggested that they get some sleep. As soon as they got in bed, damned if she didn't go down on him again.

He'd pulled her head out from under the covers and asked her what was the matter with her. Was she having her period or something?

No, she said. She was still a virgin. And wanted to remain that way until she got married. But she loved his show, she thought he was about the cutest little guy she'd ever met, and she got off just as much doing this as if they were doing it the regular way.

Well, did she want him to. . . ?

Oh, no! Not unless he really wanted to.

He didn't really want to by now. But he did.

And so she did again.

And so did he.

Sleep came as a relief.

And now, a few minutes ago, she had awakened him with her head under the goddamned covers again.

Jesus fucking Christ!

So when the phone rang, his hand shot out from under the covers. So fast that it knocked the receiver off the stand and onto the floor. But as he reached down to pick it up, he did manage to give her head a sharp little punch with his knee.

"Hello!" he shouted into the mouthpiece.

"Ron? Is that you?" The Southern accent was bright, hearty, all salesman. "Carl Clinger, Carousel Records! How are you, boy?"

"Oh, Carl! Christ, I was just thinking about you! I'm glad you called!"

Carl couldn't figure out what the noise was that had just about busted his goddamn eardrum, or whether or not he was being kidded. Nobody should be *that* happy to be awakened before eight o'clock on a Sunday morning, especially by somebody he'd met only two or three times. But what the hell, you take what you can get.

"Listen, Ron, lemme tell you why I called. . . ."

"Hey, no problem! I'm glad you did! Why?"

"Listen," Carl said, dropping his voice an octave and a half, trying to settle Carson down, "we officially open tomorrow. Carousel Records, right here in Hollywood, with the big shots."

"Hey, I'm happy for you. You've got no idea how happy I am for you, Carl."

"I know, I know," Clinger said heartily. "And I'll tell you what I got in mind. We talked about it before, remember? A little something for you, something to keep Carousel on your mind, you know what I mean?"

"I know exactly what you mean, Carl."

Carson didn't have the slightest idea what Carl Clinger meant. The only thing he knew was, he wanted to keep Clinger on the phone long enough to figure out what to do with this goddamned broad. Jesus!

"Good, I knew you'd remember. Now, I want you to do me a favor, okay?"

"Anything you say, Carl."

"I want you to go look out your front door and tell me what you see."

"I beg your pardon?"

"I said, go look out your front door and tell me what you see out there."

Ron Carson didn't say another word, he was so grateful for an excuse to get up. He leaped from bed and fairly ran through the small apartment, naked, dragging the telephone cord behind him. He peered out the living-room window. The street was deserted. Nothing out there at all, except for a Cad convertible somebody had parked in the apartment-house driveway. He looked up and down the street, didn't see a thing. Nobody. Not a soul.

"I don't see anything, Carl," he said. "What are you talking about?"

Clinger felt a prickle of nervousness. He hoped the delivery hadn't been messed up; he wanted this boy in his pocket. "Don't you see *some*thing out there?"

"No, I don't see anything," Carson said, still peering out the window. "Just a Cad parked in the driveway. Don't know who it belongs to, though."

"You don't know who it belongs to, huh?" Carl said, keeping the relief out of his voice. "Tell you what you do. Run outside and take a look in the glove compartment of that Cad. I'll hold on."

The conversation wasn't making a lot of sense to Carson so far. But, Jesus, you don't suppose. . . ? Aw, hell . . .

He picked up his pants from where she had removed them by the couch the night before. The early-morning air was still a little nippy as he hurried down the stairs, and the concrete was cold on his bare feet.

Ron hurried across the damp lawn to the driveway, examining the car at close range. Jesus, what beautiful wheels. Two-tone beige and brown, with a dark brown top. The most beautiful car he'd ever seen! He stood there looking at it, almost afraid to touch it, afraid somebody might come out of the building and accuse him of trying to steal it.

He finally summoned enough nerve to try the passenger door. Unlocked. He half-knelt on the seat and tried the glove compartment. A nine-by-twelve manila envelope was inside. He opened it. A white piece of paper and two 45 records.

He read the registration.

The legal owner of the car was the United California Bank, Santa Monica Boulevard Branch. The registered owner was Ronald Vincent Carson, Queen's Road, West Hollywood.

He almost wet his pants!

He didn't bother to look at the records.

He took the steps three at a time, hurried back inside and grabbed the phone. "Carl? Jeez . . ."

"How do you like it?"

"Jeez, Carl . . ."

"Yeah, I know what you mean," Clinger said, pure joviality. "It's a beauty, ain't it? Picked it out myself, you know." He dropped his voice, again trying to use his own control to settle Carson down. "Listen to me, now. It's just what you need, boy. You're getting to be one of the strongest dj's in the country, you know. You deserve something like that to get around in."

"But, Carl . . . *Jeez* . . ."

"Whoa, son, hold on. You know what I told you about Carousel Records? That we aim to be the biggest and the classiest independent label in the business? Well, that car is just to let you know I wasn't pissing in your ear."

"But . . . Carl! I mean . . ." Carson was on the verge of tears.

"Now, settle down, son, listen to me. You got a seat there somewhere? Well, sit down and listen good."

"Anything you say, Carl."

Carson backpedaled a few steps and dropped on the couch, and immediately popped up again to stare out the window at the car.

"Okay, now, I just want you to do two things for me. First, I want you to drive that car in good health, got that?"

"Hey! Well, thank you, Carl. I really mean it."

"I know you do," Clinger said earnestly. "And the other thing is, just remember who your friends in the business are. Got that? Just remember who your friends are."

"Hey, well, I mean, that's no problem. I mean—"

"Now, lemme ask you something," Clinger interrupted. "Did you see those two records stuck in the glove compartment with the registration?"

"No, uh . . . yeah . . . oh, yeah!"

"Good. The official release date on the Whitaker record is this Wednesday. I want you to jump all over it, boy, you got that?"

"This coming Wednesday," Carson repeated. "Got it."

"Now, that other tune, that thing by the Caravans, is already a proven hit. This is the baby—you know what I mean? And I'll tell you something, those two tunes are gonna make us the number-one independent in the country. I'd stake my life on it. But we're still gonna need all the help you can give, got that?"

"You can count on it, Carl. I mean, no shit," Carson said sincerely.

"I know I can, son," Clinger said. "And as long as I can, you'll never have to worry about a single payment on that car, you know what I mean? Because the one thing you can always count on from Carousel is that we take good care of our friends."

"I can see that, Carl. I can absolutely see that."

"Fine. Now, I'm gonna let you get back to whatever it was you were doing . . ."

Carson remembered the blond in the bedroom, and grimaced.

". . . and I'll be talking to you in about a week or ten days. No, wait a minute, I got a better idea. Why don't you just swing by the office, say, a week from this coming Friday. I'll put you down for eleven o'clock in the morning, how's that?"

"Absolutely perfect, Carl," Carson said, nodding his head to the empty room. "I'll be there. You can count on it."

Clinger didn't answer immediately, allowing the inflection in Carson's voice to sink in, to make sure he had the young dj tucked away.

"I know I can," he said warmly.

Carl replaced the receiver, stroked his chin two or three times, leaned back in his chair, and rested his feet on a corner of the desk.

He had just spent three of the most profitable hours of his life. He was going to get airplay where no country-music label had ever thought of being played before, the same kind of airplay the majors and those slick boys up in New York were getting.

He did some calculating:

Among Jepstone, Leach, Jefferson, Blandings, and himself, Carousel had access to, or control of, thirteen radio stations, six of them in large or medium-size markets. They weren't necessarily the most powerful stations in those markets, but they were strong enough to put some juice under a new release. Now, today, on top of that, he had assured himself of airplay on nine more stations, in the biggest markets in the country. He could add to that the stations that regularly played his stuff, and a series of full-page ads on *both* his new releases in the two largest trade papers in the business.

There was no doubt about it, he was going to change a hell of a lot of things in the music business.

He thought about calling the two dj's who hadn't answered earlier, but decided not to. It could wait. He had already done enough for one day, and besides, Bobbie Jean wanted him to do some work around the new house. Louella would be coming out to visit them as soon as they got things in order, and Bobbie Jean really missed the old lady. Hell, he missed her, too. She was a good old gal.

He cleared the papers off his desk, replaced them in the safe, and stood there with his hands on his hips, revolving his torso, trying to clear the kink in his back from sitting in one position so long.

God damn! he thought, looking around the room one last time. This is about as far as a rednecked clay scratcher can get from Gaston County, Tennessee, and still live on God's earth!

He walked back down the hall and retrieved his coat from the closet, and not because he had to, but because he thought he should, stopped to take a pee in his private executive bathroom.

He was washing his hands when he heard the buzz.

There was nobody downstairs at the switchboard, and the only two people in the world who knew the number to his private phone were his secretary and Bobbie Jean. And Mavis didn't know he had come in this morning, so it had to be Bobbie Jean.

He hurried back to his desk and picked up the phone.

A male voice on the other end of the line asked "Is this . . . uh uh, . . . Carousel Records?" A southern accent even thicker than Carl's.

"Yes, this is Carousel. Who'm I talking to?"

"I'd like to speak to a Mr. Carl Clinger, please, sir. Is he around there right now?"

"Yes, this is Carl Clinger. Who'm I talking to?"

"Yessir. Er . . . uh, Mr. Clinger, this is Sergeant Jimmie Appleton of the Arkansas State Police. I called your home and your wife said I might be able to reach you at this number."

"Well, you did. What is it, Mr. Appleton?"

"You own a record company, is that right?"

"Yes, I do."

"Mr. Clinger, do you have a boy making records for you by the name of Bobby Joe Whitaker?"

"Yes, I do. . . ." Carl said apprehensively.

"Well, sir, it seems like him and his band was playing a dance down here last night, over in Fort Smith. And they had a pretty bad accident about ten or twelve mile north of there, 'fore day this morning."

Carl automatically reached for the pencil and scratchpad on the desk. "Was anybody hurt?"

"Well, yessir, it was a right bad one. One of the boys in the band told us we should get aholt of you right away."

"Yessir. Well, you did the right thing. How bad was it?"

"It was right bad, I'm sorry to say. Two of the boys got kilt."

Oh, my Lord! Carl thought, afraid to ask the next question. "Was . . . was one of the boys Bobby Joe Whitaker?"

"Yessir, I'm afraid so. He died right there in Fort Smith less than an hour ago."

Carl was silent.

"I'm truly sorry that I should be the one to give you that news," the voice said.

"I, uh, got a pencil and paper right here," Carl said, shaking his head, trying to clear it. "You better give me as much information as you can."

He listened a minute, and began to write.

CHICAGO
AUGUST 1956

The house was in a decaying black neighborhood on the Westside, buried between the noisy Lake Street elevated line and the old Illinois Central railroad yard.

It was little more than a shack, splintered remnants of rotten pinewood, beaten and warped into submission by sixty years of relentless Chicago heat and ice. The front had crumbled, and someone had jacked it up and stuffed fat, ill-fitting stones underneath it, to keep it from falling over completely. The yard was dirt, no grass at all, not even weeds. But neatly swept, the way black people used to do in the South to make their places look a little better for company. And the small picket fence that ran along the sidewalk and down one side had been mended again and again with scraps of wood, some of it no more than kindling salvaged from vegetable cartons. But each piece had been carefully broken off to fit, and neatly tacked on.

The house spoke of neglect, not by the people who lived inside it, but by careless friends and scattered relatives and overpaid city officials, all of whom had forgotten that it still existed.

But it spoke of virtue, too, of the inherent goodness of being neat and orderly, even if there was nothing to look after but an unpainted shack, a tiny yard of eroded shale, and a fence propped up with dignity.

Compassion, however, was not what Monroe Wilcox understood best. What he understood best was anger. And as he turned his eyes from the house and stepped from his car into the bright late-morning sunlight, his savage anger was directed toward Saul Goldman.

He was across the sidewalk and through the gate, almost to the steps, before he saw the shriveled old man in a rocking chair in a far corner of the porch, his slippered feet resting on a worn-out footstool, a blanket thrown across his legs.

Monroe skipped lightly over the two broken steps. As his feet touched the porch, the sudden noise from a loose board made the old man sit up quickly, and Monroe could see the white cane hooked over the back of the chair.

"Mr. Turner?"

"Yes, I'm Tom Turner," the old man said, leaning forward, offering his hand in the direction of Monroe's voice. His eyes were rheumy, clouded with a yellow film, but his voice sounded surprisingly young, and his handshake was firm. "You must be Mr. Wilcox."

"Yeah, I'm Monroe Wilcox. Glad to meet you."

"It's my pleasure, Mr. Wilcox."

Turner pulled a pyramidal bell from under his blanket and shook it several times. The screen door opened almost immediately, and a plump middle-aged woman bustled out, wiping her hands on her apron.

"Oh, you're here." She smiled at Monroe. "Wait a minute, honey, let me get you a chair." She looked past Monroe at the old man. "Can I get you something, Mr. Turner? A glass of lemonade?"

"No, dear, nothing for me, but maybe this young man would care for something."

"No, no," Monroe said quickly, "I don't care for nothing."

He waited while the woman hurried back into the house and returned with a straight-backed kitchen chair. "You all let me know if you need anything," she said, disappearing behind the screen door again. "I'll be right here in the kitchen."

Monroe took his seat next to the old man, trying to think of a way to begin the conversation. Blind people always made him nervous.

"Hardly get any visitors anymore," Turner said before Monroe had a chance to open his mouth, " 'specially those that sound like they want to talk a little business." He paused, waiting for Monroe to speak. When Monroe didn't, he added, "You want to tell me what's on your mind, or do you want to sit and rest a spell?"

"No, sir," Monroe said, ceasing his speculation of what it must be like to be blind. "I ain't got too much time, I better get right to the point. Like I told you on the phone, I own Monroe's Record Rack over on the Southside. We got a religious section with some of your songs in it, that's how I found you."

"Yes, I do remember you telling me that."

"Well, Mr. Turner, something's come up where you might be able to help me, and I might be able to throw a little money your way, too."

"If you've got a little money to throw around"—Turner chuckled—"you can bet you've come to the right place."

"Yeah, I think I have. Let me explain the situation to you."

It took Monroe several minutes to tell the story. He covered everything, except how he had been out of town bootlegging records for the past few days. The fewer people who knew about that, he figured, the better off everybody would be.

"So what you're saying," Turner said when Monroe had finished, "is that some record company in New York stole your group away from you and gave them one of my songs to sing, is that right?"

"That's it."

"Well, now, they can't do that," Turner said firmly. "That's against the law."

"They already done it," Monroe said just as firmly. "But we can do something about it. That is, if you're willing to trust me."

"Oh, I trust you, all right." Turner chuckled again. "The position I'm in, I've got to trust everybody."

Monroe laughed along with Turner. He was more comfortable knowing the old man could joke about his blindness.

"Okay, dig," Monroe said. getting back to business, "this is where it stands now. The man don't even know for sure that I've heard the record. I ain't even called him yet, but I'm gonna have to call him pretty soon, before he gets suspicious. And I'll probably have to run up there and talk to him. That's why I want you to sign the song over to me. If I can walk into his office with control of the song, the motherfu . . . uh, the dude's gonna wet his pants right there, you know what I mean?"

"I can see your point," Turner said.

Monroe looked at Turner to see if he was being funny, using the word "see" like that, but he wasn't.

"Umm-hmmm," Turner continued, nodding in agreement with himself, "the man in New York must have already assumed that the song was in the public domain or that it had never been copyrighted in the first place."

"I know he did," Monroe said. "But what I wanna know now is, is the copyright in good shape? I mean, it ain't expired or nothing like that, has it?"

"Oh, it's in good shape, all right," Turner said. "It's not that old you know."

"The book said 1941."

"That's right, I wrote it fifteen years ago. I should remember, it was the last song I ever wrote, or at least the last one I tried to do a little something with."

"It's a real good song," Monroe said. "I remember hearing it on the radio when I was a kid. The Wings Over Jordan used to sing it almost every Sunday morning."

"Yes, they did it for quite a while"—Turner couldn't help showing a bit of pride—"and the Hall-Johnson Choir did it quite often, too. In fact, several gospel groups recorded it around that same time. That was probably where that New York fellow got hold of it, from one of those old records."

"Ain't no telling," Monroe said. "The main thing is, he don't keep it."

"You know something?" Turner said. "You've got a lot of back-bone for a colored man."

"I don't know about all that. I just ain't gonna let nobody shit on me if I can help it," Monroe said, forgetting for the moment that he was trying not to swear in front of the old man.

"I like talking to you," Turner said. "Most of the people that come by here, what few there are, have got such sad stories, you know. All they can talk about is dying and going to heaven. Of course, I appreciate that, too, but it is nice to hear a little good news for a change." He was quiet for a minute. "Are you in a big hurry, Mr. Wilcox?"

Monroe looked at his watch. He was supposed to meet Maudie for lunch in an hour. Then he had to go see Ted Green about getting some money for his company. And after that he had to go by old man Novikoff's to pick up some more records.

"I got a couple of things I'm supposed to do," he said. "Why?"

"Well, it's just so funny that that old song should come up again. I was just sitting here the other day thinking about it, about how I happened to write it."

"I ain't in that big a hurry," Monroe said, interested. "I guess I got time to hear about it."

"Well . . ." Turner cleared his throat and began, "It must have been about eighteen or nineteen years ago that I found out my sight was beginning to fail me. I was still a young man, you know, still in my early fifties. Now, I know that doesn't sound young to you"—he laughed—"but when you get to be my age, you realize fifty is not too bad. And I still had my health at the time. I was working every day, waiting tables at the Union League Club downtown, bringing home good money for those days. But when the doctors first told me I was going blind, I'll tell you the truth, I couldn't even picture what it would be like." He shook his head sadly, trying to remember how he felt. "Lord, I guess I was scared to death."

"You must of been," Monroe said.

"Well, your sight is something you always take for granted," Turner went on, "and nobody ever heard of glaucoma or anything like that in those days, you know. But anyhow, I had been writing songs from the time I was a young man in Alabama. Used to write what they called 'honky-tonk' songs. There wasn't much good work for a colored man in those days, so I traveled all over the South, playing my songs in dancehalls and badhouses, places like that."

He adjusted his blanket and settled himself more comfortably.

"Of course, that was long before I met Mrs. Turner and decided to try to settle down and have a family. Mrs. Turner has always been a very religious woman, you know. And she finally got me to going to church regularly with her and the boy. It took some doing, but I guess you could say I finally got a little religion.

"Looking back, I'm kind of shamed of myself now," he admitted, "but when I first found my sight was failing me, I really turned on the Lord. I tried to accept it as his will, but I couldn't. I didn't know what else to do, so I finally decided to make a little deal with him. I said, 'Lord, to show you my appreciation for all you've given me over the years, I'm going to try to do as much of your work as I can before my sight leaves me.'"

"I don't know if I could of been that strong," Monroe said.

"Shoot, I wasn't being strong," Turner dismissed the compliment, "I was trying to con him. I figured if I went out of my way to do his bidding, he might spare me. But he knew: if I was such a good man, I should have been trying to do his bidding right along, isn't that right?"

"I got to agree with that." Monroe laughed self-consciously.

"So anyhow, I'll tell you what I did, Mr. Wilcox. I went back over all the old religious songs I had learned from the time I was a boy, all the old spiritual and gospel songs that, as far as I knew, had never been written down on paper. I made sheets on all the ones I could remember and mailed them off to the Library of Congress. It took me about three years, cost me a lot of money, too. Money I couldn't afford."

"Seems like that would of been the worst thing you could of done if you were going blind," Monroe said. "I mean, for your eyes."

"It was, it was. But I knew if somebody didn't do it, all those old songs would be forgotten someday. And not just the songs, but what they stood for, too. A lot of people think colored music is just about misery and bad times, but it's not, you know. It's history, too. And I knew that somebody had to take the time to put those songs down on paper for our children, if they were going to be preserved."

"I never thought about that before," Monroe said, "but I know it's true."

"Well," Turner sighed, "a lot of us don't have anything at all to leave our children, no money, no land. Most of us don't even have a decent education we can pass on to them. So those old songs are just about the only record we have to show that we've ever been on this earth."

Monroe listened, nodding in agreement, forgetting that the old man couldn't see him.

"And I might as well be honest, too," Turner continued. "I probably figured that if I put them all down on paper and tried to publish them myself, it would give me something to do, help me to take care of myself and Mrs. Turner when I couldn't see to get around."

"Did you ever make any money off them?" Monroe asked.

"Mr. Wilcox," Turner said disgustedly, "I'll bet you I haven't made five hundred dollars from all of them put together. And by the time I finished, I couldn't see much at all, you know, so I had to give the selling rights to a big publisher. He was supposed to collect the money for me and send it to me."

"Did he?"

"Oh, he did all right for a year or so. He never did send much, but he'd send a little every one in a while. Then, when the money started to get so tight around here, every now and then I'd get Mrs. Turner to sit down and write him for me, to see what he was intending to do. But six or seven years ago, the letters started coming back without even being opened. Maybe he went out of business, I don't know."

"I'll tell you something," Monroe said. "You'd be surprised at how many of your books I sell out of my little store alone."

"I know it, I know it," Turner agreed eagerly, "but I've never been able to catch up with the company that's printing them now. I went to see a lawyer a few years back, but he wanted too much money to take the case. More money than it was worth, I figured."

"Yeah, it ain't no sense getting a lawyer involved with nothing," Monroe said. "Not if you can help it. But what you're saying is, you own the song outright, publishing and all?"

"That's right. I always did. I never gave it to anybody."

Monroe slapped his palms together. "That's all I wanted to hear. I can hardly wait to walk in Goldman's office now. I'm sure glad I had enough sense to look for you. But you never did tell me how you happened to write it."

"Well, to tell you the truth, when I wrote that song I was just about at the end of my rope," Turner said sadly. "I had just about ruined what was left of my sight writing all those old songs down, and near the end I used to get these headaches, like my head was trying to split in two. The doctors had to keep me full of medicine all the time, you know, so I could sleep.

"Well, sir, I was asleep one night and the medicine wore off and woke me up, and I sat up in bed and saw this picture of myself. I could see myself just as plain as day, sitting right here on this porch, old and blind and useless. I knew I didn't want to live like that, so I got out of bed, quiet, you know, so I wouldn't wake Mrs. Turner, and went in the bathroom. I had two or three of those bottles of pills the doctors gave me, and I fumbled around and emptied them in my hand. I was meaning to do away with myself, but something stopped me. Now, I know that sounds foolish to some people, but I swear to this day it was the hand of the Lord on me. It just wouldn't let me do it. Finally I just put the pills back in the bottles and stood there leaning over the facebowl, crying, wondering what in this world I had done that was so bad that it made him want to put all these tribulations on me.

"Well, sir, when I came out of the bathroom, I knew my sight was just about gone. It had been coming and going right along, but this time I knew it wasn't coming back. I got down on my knees on the floor right there in the living room and put my elbows on the couch, and I started praying. The first words that came out of my mouth were, 'I'm going down slow, Jesus, please take my hand. . . .'

"I must have stayed down there praying half the night, and I must have started writing that song to keep from going back in the bathroom and doing away with myself. I can't even remember starting it. All I remember is sitting there at the piano before day came with a flashlight in my hand, trying to see good enough to put it down on paper." He shook his head abruptly, like he felt a sudden chill. "I never will forget that night."

Monroe cleared his throat two or three times, but he couldn't think of anything to say.

He watched a thin, dark-skinned girl of ten or eleven ride by on a rusted bicycle. Carleen had been little and skinny like that, after their mother died, and he'd had to go to work to take care of her. He watched the girl until she turned the corner in the bright sunlight.

"It looks like it might be a big record," he finally said to the old man. "You might have a nice little taste of money coming in before long."

Monroe didn't think the old man had heard him. Turner sat silently rocking back and forth in his chair, smoothing imaginary wrinkles out of the blanket on his lap. He opened his mouth two or three times, as if getting ready to say something, but remained silent, and went on smoothing the blanket.

"How much money do you think I might get out of it, Mr. Wilcox?" he asked at last.

"It really ain't no telling," Monroe said. "It's according to how big it gets. And you got to remember, too, that the white man don't want to see you with nothing. Before he'd see you and me with it, he'd rather give the money to a lawyer. But if Goldman will come right out and admit that the tune is stolen, and the radio people give us a fair count, you might come out with ten or twelve thousand. If we're really lucky, maybe two or three times that much."

Again the old man apparently hadn't heard Monroe. He sat rocking back and forth in his chair, slowly rubbing his palm across the blanket in his lap. Every now and then he would nod to himself, as if acknowledging different sides of a private conversation going on inside his head. When he finally spoke, Monroe could barely make out the words. It was as though Turner had forgotten for a moment that Monroe was still sitting there next to him.

"You know, that woman in there has waited on me hand and foot for fifteen years. There were plenty of times when I was as mean and ornery to her as I could be, trying to make her leave here and go find some good in her life. But she never left me. She took care of me like I was a child and never once tried to make me feel like I was a burden to her. Lord God, I've spent many a day sitting right here on this porch, wondering what will become of her when I'm gone." He turned his sightless eyes toward the screen door. "I think I could die in peace knowing she'll be taken care of."

And then Thomas P. Turner, the seventy-three-year-old blind black man who one night years before, in an hour of the most terrible anguish the human mind can endure, had sat down and knocked out what was currently the fastest-rising tune on the pop charts—the "down sound that was going around," the newest "red-hot," "can't-miss," "sure-fire" piece of wax—dropped his head on his chest and began to cry.

"Mr. Turner, I've got some papers here for you to sign," Monroe said, opening the briefcase by his feet, "and a nice little check already made out in your name. You don't have to worry none, I'll get your money for you."

He put the pen and the agreement of transfer in the old man's hand, and waited for Mrs. Turner to come out and witness their signatures. He told them he would be back in a day or so with a notary public. But in the meantime, this was all he needed.

They thanked him over and over, and thanked God for having led him to their house.

When he got up to leave, Mrs. Turner threw her arms around him and held him for several minutes, as though to let him go would be to let go of all the foolish, hopeful dreams he had brought with him.

When at last he gently pulled himself from her arms, the saltiness of her tears and the morning's heat had plastered his shirtfront to his body.

He left then, careful not to step on the loose board, remembering to avoid the two broken steps.

It was his tune now, he owned it, and they would collect every penny it earned.

NEW YORK SEPTEMBER 1956

It was the day after Labor Day. They were sitting at a back table in the Turf Café.

Saul Goldman was chewing at a corned beef on rye. A dab of mustard had attached itself to the side of his mouth, and Paulie was staring at it disgustedly, thinking what a dumb, sloppy old bastard his uncle was—not realizing that he himself had an even bigger chunk of mustard stuck to the frizzy little mustache he was trying to grow. Normally he would have said something like, "F'Chrissakes, Saul, wipe your goddamn chin, huh?" But he was still trying to patch things up with his uncle, so when he spoke his voice was pleasant to the point of solicitousness.

"Uh, Saul, you've got a little mustard on your chin."

Goldman looked at his nephew with the same expression he would have had if he'd just spotted a pile of horseshit in the seat across from him. He popped the last of his sandwich in his mouth and chewed it very slowly, never taking his eyes from Paulie's face. When the sandwich was thoroughly masticated, he swallowed it and reached across the table and plucked a napkin from the holder. He wiped his mouth very deliberately, catching part, but not all, of the mustard. He crumpled the napkin and dropped it in the paper plate in front of him.

"Fuck you," he said.

"C'mon, Saul—"

"Fuck you!"

It had been like this for almost a week now, ever since Monroe Wilcox had popped into the office unexpectedly and made them look like boobs.

Wilcox had held the upper hand from the beginning. He had called the day before, and Tracey, the secretary, had lied and said that Goldman was out of town for at least two weeks.

The reason Goldman didn't want to talk to Wilcox so soon was that he was afraid Wilcox might try to get an injunction to stop the sales of the Tru-tones' new release. He figured he'd bide a little time, get it moving good, then deal with Wilcox.

But he'd been sitting there talking on the phone to a distributor when the little black bastard had busted in on him.

Wilcox had walked out with the songwriter and publishing royalties. He'd torn up his production contract right in front of Goldman, saying he had some stuff in the can on the Tru-tones that he was going to put out on his own label, and if Goldman didn't like it he could kiss his ass. Then, for a closer, after Paulie had wised-off once too often, he'd chased the skinny little prick all the way out of the building.

That, Goldman decided, was the only good thing about the whole deal, that Wilcox had scared the piss out of his nephew.

Sitting across the table from his uncle, for once in his life Paulie had to admit that he was at a distinct disadvantage. He'd never known anybody to carry a grudge as long as his uncle. Christ, this morning, almost a week after the shit with Wilcox had ·gone down, he'd said something to his uncle and Goldman had thrown an ashtray at him.

Christ, he'd thought "Going Down Slow" was public domain. How the hell could he know that some blind old spade would have enough sense to copyright a goddamn three-chord gospel tune?

But one thing was for sure: he either had to make up with his uncle or get the hell out of the office. This situation was getting to him. He had a feeling his uncle was thinking about throwing him out anyhow, but he didn't want that to happen. He'd been in New York only a couple of months now. but he liked it. It was different from L.A. The people were different. They weren't so concerned about how you looked or how you talked. Hell, everybody in New York talked like him—tough, cocky, like they knew what they wanted. Even the women were different here. They didn't put him down because he didn't look like some faggot-assed beachboy. Hell, in the two months he'd been there, he'd already gotten two different pieces of ass, and didn't have to pay for either one. No, he definitely did not want Goldman to kick him out, so if he had to defer to his uncle for a while, it was worth it.

"Saul, did you see the new *Cashbox* yet?" he asked, making his voice as mild as he could.

Goldman looked at his nephew for a full ten seconds without answering. "Did you find a place to live yet?" he finally asked, ignoring the question.

"Yeah, I think I've got something in the Fifty-seventh Street Building. I gotta go check this afternoon."

"Well, go check. I want you the fuck outta my place."

"No problem, no problem." Paulie's voice was subdued. "I'll get out. I've been looking every day, but places are hard to find, you know what I mean?"

Goldman didn't answer. Paulie waited a few seconds longer before repeating his earlier question, "No shit, Saul, did you see the new *Cashbox* yet?"

"No, my nephew, the songwriter," Goldman said sarcastically, "I have not looked at the new *Cashbox* because I have had other things on my mind, like how to avoid a fucking lawsuit." He stared at Paulie in disgust, until curiosity got the better of him. "Why?"

"It's official. Carousel has picked up the master on 'Good Easy Loving.' "

"You already told me that two weeks ago. I thought it was official then. You also told me Jacob Weisenberg was going to send you six thousand dollars for your share of the front money. But on the other hand," he added caustically, "you have been known to lie."

"Oh, c'mon, Saul. Gimme a fucking break, huh?"

They were discussing the record Paulie had cut before he left California. The small company he'd leased it to couldn't get any major market exposure, and the record had floated in and out of the top hundred for more than two months, on a week, off two. It was a very unusual situation, because normally when a record hits the charts it either starts to rise, and keeps on going, or drops off and stays off. But Jacob Weisenberg, who owned the company, wouldn't give up. He kept making phone calls, bugging his distributors to continue working on it, begging radio stations for airplay. And somehow he'd managed to keep the record alive this time.

"Who the hell is Carousel Records anyhow?" Goldman asked disdainfully. "And what the hell difference does it make? The record can't do anything now, it's been out too long. If it was gonna take off, it would of took off by now. I told you before, you should of talked Weisenberg into letting me take over the master. I might of been able to do something with it."

Paulie felt better. At least he had been able to engage his uncle in conversation. Still, at the risk of making his uncle even madder, he had to comment on Goldman's last statement.

"But, Saul, he did offer to lease you the master," he said, careful to keep any recrimination out of his voice, "and you turned him down. I was sitting right there when you had him on the phone."

Goldman had been waiting for a chance to explode. This was it. "Goddammit, he was talking twelve, fifteen grand up front! For that piece of shit! Jesus Christ, you must of told him I was a half-partner in Chase Manhattan! I listened to the goddamn record, I know its potential, it ain't got none! It's a goddamn piece of shit and it ain't gonna sell!"

The last sentence came out like an uncontestable pronouncement from above.

Paulie wanted to tell his uncle to go jack off a mosquito, but he had to try to keep the conversation going. "I dunno, Saul, Carousel's supposed to be a pretty good company."

"Carousel's a goddamn piss-ant shit-kicking label! Take them out of the hillbilly market and they couldn't sell five copies of 'Stardust'!"

"I don't know, Saul, they're doing okay with that new Bobby Joe Whitaker record. It ain't been out but a couple of weeks, and every station in town's blasting it at least once an hour. You got to hand it to them, they must know something about promotion."

"They ain't doing the promoting, Bobby Joe Whitaker's the one doing the promoting. He got himself high on dope and promoted himself right into a head-on collision. Anyhow, I heard that record, and it ain't too bad, for a country record. It ain't like that shit you've been cutting. At least you can understand what the goddamn hillbilly was trying to sing about."

"They came up with twelve grand front money, Saul."

"Oh, yeah? I'll believe that when I see it, when you walk up to me and hand me some goddamn rent for the two months you've been staying at my place."

That shut Paulie up for a second. He didn't want to get into any discussion about rent money, at least not right now. The way his uncle was feeling about him, there was no telling how much Goldman might want to charge.

Paulie changed the subject. "Listen, now that we're finally talking to each other again, don't you think we'd better go over some company business? I mean, we gotta decide what our next move's gonna be, right?"

Goldman sighed and lit a cigar. He'd thought about it all week. At first, he was gonna kick the kid out, send him back to his goddamn mother. But the sales figures on the new Tru-tones record made him think that the little prick must have some talent. But it was a strange record. The initial sales response seemed to show that it wasn't doing too well in the black neighborhoods. Oh, in a few places, like Dallas and New Orleans, it was keeping pace with the first record. But in a lot of others—Philadelphia, Chicago, Detroit, and Cleveland, for example—they couldn't give the goddamn thing away to the black market. And the Saint Louis distributor had told him a week or so ago that three or four big stores had ordered the record, and then canceled, saying they had overanticipated the demand for it.

Still, total sales indicated that the record was going to do as well as or better than the first one had. Strange. . . .

So, he didn't know what to do with his nephew. But whatever he decided, he knew he was going to have to watch the little cocksucker like a hawk.

"We gotta decide what our next move's gonna be, huh?" He still had a couple of things to get out of his system. "Well, before we get into that, let me ask you a question. You written any new tunes lately?"

"Listen, Saul, like you told me when I first walked into your office," Paulie said, pandering to his uncle's ego, "I only been in the business a little while. So I made a mistake, right? So I'm new in the business. I won't make that mistake again. But I should of shown you by now that I do know colored music, right?"

Goldman offered a begrudging nod.

"Now"—Paulie put his elbows on the table, leaned forward, and lowered his voice—"I got two acts I wanna sign. I heard a group at the Apollo last Wednesday night, on the amateur show, that I think could be pretty big. I gave them my card and they've already called me two or three times. I don't know if they're lying or not, but they say they've got a couple of other companies trying to sign them. They say they wanna come with us because they admire the Trutones and they wanna be on the same label."

Goldman grunted noncommittally.

"And," Paulie continued, "I've got three colored girls I wanna sign. They're the ones who do most of the background work around town. They must of been on . . . oh, ten or twelve hits already, and nobody's thought to sign them up yet. They've already proved they can sell records. We can put them under a nonexclusive contract, give them a name, which we'll copyright, of course, and let them keep on singing background on other sessions, while we record them ourselves. That's a damn good idea, ain't it?"

Paulie neglected to mention that he was very close with one of the girls in the group, Juanita Harris. She was one of the two girls he'd taken to bed since arriving in New York. In fact, when he left his uncle this afternoon, instead of going to look for an apartment, he was going to meet Juanita.

Goldman made another noncommittal grunt.

"What," Paulie asked nervously, "does that mean?"

"That means I haven't decided if I'm even gonna keep you in the company," Goldman said. "You see, kid, you made the one unpardonable mistake."

"What's that, Saul?" Paulie tried to hide his panic. He knew that the only reason Juanita had made it with him was because he had all but come right out and promised her a recording contract for her group.

"The unpardonable mistake," Goldman said slowly, pointing his finger at Paulie's nose, "is: never lie to your business partner. Lie to the public. Lie to your friends. If you have to, lie to your wife. But *never* lie to your business partner. It even says that in the Talmud."

Never having read the Talmud, Paulie didn't know if his uncle was lying or not.

"Look at it this way, Saul," he said. "You, we, didn't lose nothing. We didn't have publishing on the Tru-tones anyway, right? It belonged to Wilcox. So you can't lose what you never had. Now, on the other hand, the Tru-tones' new record is hitting even bigger in the white market than their first, which is where most of the big sales are, right? And we've got another helluva record on them in the can. We couldn't even decide which one to put out first, remember?"

"Oh, yeah, I meant to ask you," Goldman said, "did you write that other tune, too?"

"So we really didn't lose that much," Paulie continued, ignoring his uncle's sarcasm. "The money's coming in just like before, and now we're really in a position to set up a first-class top-forty label."

Goldman nodded, puffing his cigar thoughtfully. "You're such a fucking *shvitser*," he said after a few seconds, "I should know better."

"And if it'll make you feel any better, I promise you I'll never lie to you again"—Paulie hesitated before adding—"about business."

"Okay, okay," Goldman said, forever struggling to remain in charge, "I told you we'll go on it. Just keep those session costs down."

"No problem," Paulie said mildly.

He looked at his watch. It was almost three o'clock. He had to run all the way up to Seventy-third Street, change, and get back downtown by five, in time to meet Juanita. He stood up. "I gotta go check on a place," he said. "You ready to leave yet?"

"No, I'm gonna have another cup of coffee. Then I gotta run over to my attorney's. I wanna check and see where we stand legally, see if Wilcox can violate his contract with me and start releasing tunes on the Tru-tones."

The incongruity of Goldman's anger at Wilcox's threat to ignore their already violated agreement somehow evaded both men.

"Fuck Wilcox," Paulie said, the old familiar, arrogant whine back in his voice. "We don't need him anymore. I'll bet you a million bucks he'll never get another hit. Settle up with him and forget him. He's dead, you know what I mean?"

Goldman grunted.

Paulie slapped his uncle on the back, pleased that they were back on speaking terms. He said good-bye again and pushed his way through the small crowd of people waiting for tables. He was feeling pretty good. He had given himself six months to bring New York to its knees, and he was ahead of schedule. "Going Down Slow" was going to be a biggie, and he had half of it. He had six thousand dollars coming in the mail any day for "Good Easy Loving," and when he and Juanita came out of the show tonight, he was gonna take her back up to his place and fuck her until her eyes popped out.

Just as he reached the door, he passed a black guy in a gray suit. A portable radio played on the counter near the cash register. Something caught Paulie's ear. Without excusing himself, he pushed passed the guy and lifted the radio up to his ear. Sure enough, they were playing his record, "Good Easy Loving."

Carousel Records had already moved the record into New York.

He had another hit.

He listened until the record was over, waiting to see if the dj had a comment to make, but the dj segued into a commercial.

Paulie set the radio back on the counter and started to walk away.

"Hey," the black guy said quickly, "ain't you Paul Schultz?"

It wasn't remarkable for the guy to recognize Paulie. Everybody in the Turf usually knew who everybody else was, sometimes before that person even knew himself.

"Yeah," Paulie said a little snottily.

The guy switched his hamburger from his right hand to his left. "Hey, my name is Billy Westerfield," he said, enthusiastically shaking Paulie's limp hand. "I've had a couple of things out. Ain't you the guy who produced the Tru-tones' new record?"

"Yeah," Paulie said, not bothering to sound modest, "and I also produced that record they were just playing, 'Good Easy Loving.' It's breaking bigger than the other one."

"No shit, man?" Westerfield was genuinely impressed. "You a soulful dude, man. Where's your office?"

Paulie told him.

"Groovy," Westerfield said. "I'm gonna have to bring you some material. I got a song the Tones could tear up, man!"

"Yeah? Well, I'm going to be taking them back in the studio in a couple of weeks," Paulie said, lying, but keeping his cool. "Bring it up and let me hear it. I may give them a shot on it."

"Groovy! Who else you got?"

"I'm just getting the label organized now. My uncle asked me to fly in from the Coast and help him get a couple of things on the charts, you know what I mean? In fact, I gotta run uptown and talk to an act right now."

He turned to leave.

"Hey, wait a minute, man," Westerfield said.

"Yeah?" Paulie turned back, irritated at being delayed.

Westerfield unwrapped the napkin from around what was left of his hamburger and offered it to Paulie. "Here, you got some mustard on your mouth."

Paulie took the greasy napkin and ran it around his lips. He looked at it, then smiled the first genuine smile he had enjoyed since he arrived in New York.

"That ain't mustard," he said. "That's gold."

BOOK TWO

Loud clamor is always more or less insane.

—*Carlyle*

§

If the first big break of Carl Clinger's business career came on that Tuesday afternoon in the spring of 1949, when I. V. Ware choked to death on a chicken bone, the second biggest break undoubtedly arrived on that Saturday night in the summer of 1956, when Bobby Joe Whitaker, stoned on barbiturates, tried to pass a green station wagon in the middle of a curve of Arkansas State Highway 71 and rammed head-on into a 1947 Ford pickup driven by an elderly farmer from Russellville.

There is no doubt that Carousel Records would have prospered anyhow. The first master Carl Clinger authorized for purchase by the company, "Good Easy Loving," proved that. It sold more than six hundred thousand copies, and rose to number three on the national pop charts.

But the Whitaker record, "Something's Calling Me Home," with its title of seemingly predestined disaster, rocked the music industry. The record sold more than two million copies within the first month of its release. And the next three Whitaker singles, rushed out to meet an overwhelming demand, each sold more than one million copies. An extended-play 45, made up of four tunes previously considered as not good enough for release, sold almost seven hundred thousand copies. The *Memories of a Country Boy* album, a memorial to Whitaker, comprising all his previous country hits plus the last four million-sellers, was certified by the Music Retailers of America as having legitimately earned a million dollars for its manufacturer.

Even Sarah Tindall's hokey, exploitative single, "Bobby, He Called Too Soon," was snapped up by what had turned into a cult of posthumous Bobby-worshipers, and attained million-seller status.

As a consequence, Bobby Joe Whitaker, the little-known country-music rockabilly singer, whose biggest single had sold no more than 340,000 copies while he was alive, and who had not been famous enough to appear at the lucrative state fairs and rodeos that symbolized the pinnacle of success in his profession, and whom, incidentally, Carl Clinger had seen and spoken with fewer than a dozen times, was responsible for grossing Carousel Records in excess of three million dollars during the company's first year of California operations.

Added to that were the seventeen masters of the company picked up from smaller companies, eight of which reached the top ten, two of them going all the way to number one.

And, for dessert, there were two other number-one records, performed by an aging female movie star with a slight drinking problem. They were cover records of previously recorded rhythm-and-blues hits, and the fact that they were snatched up so eagerly by the public served as dramatic illustration of just how rapidly the market for any kind of rock-'n'-roll music good, bad, or ridiculous was expanding.

So even if Carousel's first year in California did not quite see the company achieve Carl Clinger's aim of becoming the "classiest outfit in the business," it certainly surpassed all of his expectations for success. It was the most profitable independently distributed record company in America during the 1957 calendar year, grossing well in excess of eight million dollars. Carl Clinger was awarded a total of twenty-three plaques and citations from civic, business, and music-industry organizations. He was also named "Man of the Year" by the Music Retailers of America, not just for country music, but for the entire field of pop music.

Carousel's 45-rpm sales began to dwindle during the following year, 1958, as other companies, independents and major labels, began vying more competitively for the masters of small companies and independent producers. Carousel purchased thirty-three masters during the year. Only six of them reached the top ten nationally, and only one became the number-one record in the country. Nevertheless, because of increased album sales, the success of two newly contracted artists, more efficient methods of promoting, shipping, and billing, plus the rapidly increasing size of the rock-'n'-roll market itself, the company was able to return more than a hundred thousand additional dollars, in dividends, to its stockholders.

Sales figures for 1959 were proceeding along the same general lines as the previous year, when late in March a congressional committee was formed to investigate illegal payment by record manufacturers, to media employees for airplay of their products.

The popular name was "payola."

The payola investigations started on the East Coast, on a gigantic wave of media exploitation. But then they immediately bogged down because of tremendous pressure brought to bear by not only the companies currently successful in selling their products but also the major labels, the multimillion-dollar conglomerates that had been displaced by the new wave of music. The majors had, by far, the most influence. Their contacts and connections spanned a half-century and reached into the most hidden agencies and darkest cloakrooms of the federal government.

By the early part of 1960, heads began to roll. Dj's were fired, wholesale divestments were ordered, program directors were installed in large stations to control play lists, ostensibly to keep dj's from choosing their own records. "Format" radio was instituted in most major markets, so that, more and more, across the country, it would become increasingly difficult for small companies to "break" new records.

And, as is generally the case in such things, the public was misled. Nobody really wanted to clean up the record business. And nobody did, not for more than twenty or thirty minutes. The situation was: the major companies, publishing and recording, which had failed to anticipate or imaginatively respond to a change in public tastes, wanted to regain their original positions of power. To that end they had decided that there were a few people in key positions in the music industry they could better do without.

It wasn't until late spring 1960 that the Special Subcommittee on Legislative Oversight of the Committee on Interstate and Foreign Commerce reached Los Angeles and installed itself on one of the upper floors of the Federal Building on First and Spring streets.

It is significant that the very first subpoena issued upon the committee's convening in California was to Carl Aaron Clinger, president, major stockholder, and chairman of the board of Carousel Records.

Clinger was, he thought, quite prepared to ride it out. He had hired an expensive battery of attorneys who specialized in misreading small nuances into federal statutes. Clinger was sequestered in a small anteroom out of earshot of the proceedings. When he was finally called in to testify, he discovered that the information gathered about his activities during the preceding three and a half years was, indeed, thorough and totally incriminating. The investigators hired by the major companies had done their jobs well. He could not ride it out. He found himself sitting buck-naked on the crest of a tidal wave.

To pay a disc-jockey or program director to play a record was not against the law. The fact that it was not was an oversight, as the title of the subcommittee implied. But, like most things that allowed the little man to make a fast buck, it soon would be, just as soon as the subcommittee hustled back to Washington and got a few congressmen together and passed a few more laws.

In the meantime, fifty-six charges of bribery, attempted bribery, unfair business practices, and conspiracy to create a monopoly were returned against Carl Clinger and the other officers of Carousel Records. Clinger and the other stockholders were given sixty days to file a brief with the Justice Department, to preclude instigation of an official investigation of the company.

Alternatively, Carousel could hold a meeting and consider the idea of divestment.

The final meeting of the board of directors of Carousel Records was held in the rear banquet hall of an exclusive restaurant on Rodeo Drive in Beverly Hills. The meeting was called to order by Clinger. It consisted of two statements, both by Elmer M. "Red" Leach. They were: "Fuck it. Sell."

No other considerations, as the saying goes in the country-music business, amounted to a pile of week-old pigshit.

A final dividend was declared before drinks were brought in. Nobody was angry or even greatly disappointed. Carousel had been a profitable venture. For an initial subscription of one hundred and twenty-five thousand dollars, and financial participation of only one-half that amount in actual capital, each of the four minor stockholders—Leach, Tepstone, Blandings, and Jefferson—had realized more than three-quarters of a million dollars in declared dividends. Clinger, of course, had received considerably more than that, well in excess of two million dollars, including the salary paid him by the corporation during its four years of operations.

Carl was ordered to find a buyer.

Within a month he had seven firm offers. The most promising appeared to be that tendered by the International Transcription and Recording Corporation.

Negotiations were begun, and continued for several months. The accountants and officers of ITRC were perceptive enough to recognize that Carousel's catalog was almost totally lacking in musical substance. It was reflective of the company's past strict adherence to expediency and its flaming disregard for acquiring copyrights that might be strong enough to hold up through future musical trends. Still, ITRC could see that Carousel had several intangible assets.

First among these assets was the basic instability of the pop-music business itself. Buyers of pop records were becoming younger each day, and more fickle. As ITRC's preceding declining sales had dramatically illustrated it was virtually impossible to ascertain beforehand what a thirteen- or fourteen-year-old kid would buy. It was, at best, speculative, and Carousel did currently have records and songs on the charts.

On the other hand, purchasers of country-music records were much more stable, in some cases maintaining almost fanatical loyalties to the artists they accepted, and Carousel was an established country label.

Finally, there was Carl Clinger himself. Whatever else one might say about him, he certainly knew the country-music business. And more important, he was personally acquainted with most of the clannish, suspicious people who made it run. If he was put in a position to operate a country-music division of ITRC and strictly forbidden to continue the shady dealings that had put him in difficulties with the government, he alone might turn out to be worth the purchase price of the entire company.

The officers and accountants of ITRC finally concluded that the catalogs of Carousel's recording and publishing companies, the company's fixed assets, the market potential of its contracted artists, and its reputation within the industry for creating salable products were worth five million dollars. Carl Clinger, however, decided that, everything considered, the company was worth at least seven million dollars.

A compromise was reached, and as of midnight, January 1, 1961, Carousel Records became a wholly owned subsidiary of ITRC.

In addition to the $1,875,000 Clinger received as his share of the sale of common stock, he also was offered a five-year vice-presidency at ITRC and the position of general manager of a new country-music division that would open in Nashville immediately. His salary would be $200,000 a year, with various stock options and bonuses. To start.

He graciously accepted it.

§

As the fortunes of Carousel Records prospered, declined, and evaporated, Saul Goldman's company, Chartmaker Records, underwent a metamorphosis of its own.

First, Marge Bowlen married a heating-and-air-conditioning salesman from Paramus, New Jersey, whom she met while working at the Four Hundred Lounge in Atlantic City. She retired from the entertainment business shortly thereafter, never quite fulfilling her destiny of becoming the next Margaret Whiting. The Banjo Serenaders got their gig in Las Vegas and forgot all about Saul Goldman. They never received their royalty statements from him anyhow, so why record for him again? Sammy Patucci's sales declined in direct proportion to record buyers' increasing distaste for accordion music.

And when the Tru-tones played the Apollo Theater in New York City during the Christmas holidays of 1957, for their second and last time, Paulie again convinced his uncle to record them. It was again done surreptitiously, of course, because the contract between the group and Monroe Wilcox and Saul Goldman had now entered into litigation.

The Tru-tones' overexposed recording career only served to confuse the dj's. When Chartmaker released a new record by the group, Big City Records did the same. That happened twice. The second time it happened, the dj's decided to hell with it and stopped playing any Tru-tones recordings at all. The group broke up shortly thereafter. Dave Washington, the lead singer, signed with a major label, and immediately became musically incognito. The other guys, as far as anybody ever knew, went back to drinking wine and singing on the street corners of Chicago.

But even though Chartmaker Records was encountering a bit of difficulty, Paulie Schultz himself was not doing too badly.

He had produced two top-ten records, and now, with his successes, he could afford to put forth a slightly more attractive image. So after Saul Goldman finally succeeded in extricating him from the apartment in the West Seventies, Paulie moved into a penthouse over by the East River. New Yorkers have a curious habit of describing anything at the top of something as a penthouse, but Paulie's new place wasn't bad. He furnished it in early-bachelor, with large hi-fi speakers throughout. He even put one in the bathroom. He got a king-size bed, which took up almost all of his small bedroom, and put mirrors in the ceiling. He got the mirrors on the cheap. They were slightly warped, so whenever he looked up at himself, he saw either a skinny, mustached lollipop or a pale, mustached pear.

Then he made the mistake, or had the good fortune—depending upon the angle from which it was viewed—of producing the number-one record in the country using his trio of black female singers. Shortly thereafter, the girls were booked on a series of "package shows" and traveled around the country virtually nonstop for several years. Juanita Harris, the leader of the group, was supposed to have been Paulie's "main squeeze." But as she earned ever-higher amounts from personal appearances, she also gained somewhat more independence. She wouldn't put up with nearly as many of Paulie's obnoxious demands as she had when she was a mere background singer and needed the recording sessions he was throwing her way.

As a result, while she was on the road, or while she was home asserting her independence, Paulie acquired a fairly select catalog of low-to-medium-priced hookers. Two of them, Jennifer James and Candy O'Brien, he inherited from his Uncle Saul.

In fact, it was Candy O'Brien who called him late one night in August 1960 to inform him of his uncle's heart attack.

The way it occurred, according to Candy, was that Saul had taken her and Jenny to the Town and Country nightclub in Brooklyn. Later that night, they had returned to his place in the West Seventies. Saul had this thing about dirty movies, so he'd set up the screen in the bedroom and put on a film. When they'd started practicing some of the things they were watching on the screen, Goldman had clutched his chest, turned purple, and passed out.

The girls had panicked and run out of the apartment, leaving the projector still running and the vibrator still vibrating in Goldman's ass.

Candy made an anonymous call to the police from the pay phone in the restaurant on the corner. Then she and Jennifer came back and stood across the street and watched the ambulance arrive a few minutes later. Two white-coated attendants brought out what the girls thought was Goldman's dead body.

The two went to a nearby bar and had a couple of drinks and talked it over. If Goldman was dead, they decided, they would keep their mouths shut about what had happened. But if, by some chance, he was still alive, they would call Paulie. They waited an hour. Candy called Bellevue: Goldman was still alive. Candy found Paulie's number in her little red trick book and called him right away.

Paulie rushed over to the apartment in the West Seventies, cleaned things up, and called his Aunt Rachel. Rachel, of course, didn't know anything about the apartment, so Paulie told her Goldman's heart attack had happened at his place. He wasn't sure if his story fooled her, because she knew the man she was married to. Just to be on the safe side, when he got to the hospital, before his aunt arrived from Long Island, he slipped the policeman on duty in the emergency wing a hundred dollars for the police report, which hadn't yet been turned in.

Saul Goldman stayed in the hospital for three weeks.

When Paulie started trying to run the business, the first thing he discovered was that the books didn't make sense. All the expenses—sessions costs, pressing and shipping costs, travel, entertainment—had been jacked up, all the sales figures knocked down. They didn't balance with what he knew had been happening, and they didn't balance with what Saul had been telling him. Therefore, these books had to be strictly for the IRS.

Okay, fine, so where were the real books?

He tore the office apart, but couldn't find them. Then he went over to the apartment in the West Seventies. It took him two days to locate them. They were under a dresser, under a rug, under a loose board in the closet. If Goldman hadn't been too parsimonious to invest in a safety-deposit box, Paulie never would have found them.

But he did find them, and the first thing he discovered when he went through them was that his uncle had been robbing him along with everyone else.

During the four years between the summer of 1956, when Paulie arrived in New York, and the summer of 1960, when Goldman suffered his near-fatal heart attack, Paulie had produced eight national top-ten records for Chartmaker, including two number-one records. He had also produced two top-twenty albums. He had produced many other records for Chartmaker, most of which never became successful in the South, or on the West Coast, or even in the Midwest. But with the marketing base provided by his uncle's partially owned string of jukeboxes, almost everything Paulie produced became a small hit in some part of the Northeast.

Paulie Schultz may not have been very big in other parts of the country, but from Boston to Pittsburgh he was fairly heavy.

Operating expenses had gone up somewhat during the preceding four years, because they had moved the company offices to a larger suite in the same building, furnished it, and hired two more girls to handle the billing and increased paperwork. But with the salaries Goldman paid, the added help amounted to little, and session and promotion costs had remained nominal as well. Goldman had seen to that.

It took Paulie a week to figure it out. From what he could determine, his uncle- that sneaky, perverted, crooked, chickenshit cocksucker- had screwed him out of close to a quarter of a million dollars.

Just to be sure, Paulie hired a CPA to confirm his conclusion. After a few days of going over the books, the CPA said it was even more, about three hundred thousand. In fact, the CPA said, if Paulie wanted to get technical, it was exactly $312,417.33.

Goldman had been out of the hospital only a few days when Paulie confronted him with the evidence. Goldman denied everything. Paulie showed him the CPA's statements. Goldman still denied everything. Then Paulie showed his uncle the police report, which mentioned where Goldman was found, and the condition in which he was found, on the night of his heart attack. How would it be, Paulie asked his uncle, if Aunt Rachel heard the whole story? About the apartment. About Jenny and Candy. About the dirty movies. About the vibrator, f'Chrissakes, stuck up his goddamn ass!

Saul Goldman knew what a greedy, conniving bitch his wife was. If she learned the truth, she would pick him clean. With a little help from Paulie, he weighed his alternatives carefully. He didn't have any. He had to pay off his nephew to keep from losing everything to his wife.

That's when he decided to get out of the record business and move to Florida.

It took him only one phone call to find a buyer, one of his partners in the jukebox business. The asking price for the company would be one million dollars, plus another half-million under the table—in cash.

They could deal, his partner said.

Saul Goldman hung up and told Paulie it would take a few weeks to raise the cash to settle.

Fuck you, Paulie retorted.

Okay, Goldman said, how would it be if he gave Paulie a few thousand, just to, you know, show good faith? And after he had liquidated the business, they could settle up for good.

One hundred thousand dollars on account, Paulie said, or he would walk in the kitchen right now and lay the police report on the drainboard next to the potatoes Aunt Rachel was peeling for dinner.

Goldman capitulated and wrote his personal check for one hundred thousand dollars. Paulie waited right there while Goldman called the bank and had the money transferred to Paulie's account.

Goldman put his house up for sale the next morning, for one hundred and twenty-five thousand dollars. It was bought within two weeks. As soon as he was strong enough, he and Rachel left for Florida. He bought a luxury condominium on the water in Miami Beach. Since he was down there, he figured he might as well stay a month and soak up the sun.

While his uncle was away, Paulie tried to decide on his next move. He had built a reasonable reputation in the business, and most of the doors in New York were open to him.

He approached a few companies, but received no offers deserving of his self-proclaimed abilities. He was considering the idea of using the money he would get from Goldman to open his own company, when he heard some intriguing scuttlebutt: ITRC had something big in the works.

Paulie made an appointment to meet with Gino Turicotti. The rumor was true, Turicotti said, and they would be interested in discussing it with Paulie in a few weeks.

At that time, Saul Goldman came back to New York to sign the papers and collect the money for the sale of his company. He tried to duck Paulie, but Paulie finally caught up with him in a small hotel on the Upper East Side.

Goldman explained to Paulie that he had been looking for him to tell him he had changed his mind: he would no longer be *blackmailed* by a piss-ant, snot-nosed punk.

Paulie showed him the police report again.

Okay, Goldman said, he would go another fifty thousand, but that was it.

Then Paulie played a tape he had made while Goldman was in Florida. It was of Candy O'Brien, drunk, with plenty of urging from Paulie, going over the details of the night of Goldman's heart attack. Goldman listened impassively for a few minutes, trying to show his nephew that he didn't give a damn. But when Candy got to the part about sitting on Goldman's face while Jenny was going down on him and shoving a large vibrator up him at the same time, he almost suffered a second heart attack.

He would give his nephew another check for fifty thousand dollars, plus another silent fifty thousand in cash. That was it. Period. Take it or leave it.

Paulie took it.

§

During the years that Carl Clinger was climbing the golden ladder of corporate success and Paulie Schultz was learning the power of leverage in business, particularly as it applied to blackmail, Max Geary's prophecy of a few years before was beginning to fulfill itself.

As he had predicted, the 78 rpm, once the backbone of the record industry, had become obsolete. It was now 45's and albums exclusively, and the business of making music currently returned close to one-half billion dollars yearly to its manufacturers.

The water was warm, the booty was becoming more plentiful, and the crocodiles were beginning to slither in. The same syndicates and cartels and individuals who determined the cost of food, the price of oil, and the interest on borrowed capital were also beginning to determine what the public would hear when it turned on its radio. And what the public heard, particularly on those stations that catered to younger listeners, was a musically bland mishmash virtually devoid of roots or direction.

During the first nine years of the decade of the fifties, more than 15,000 black artists had recorded for the first time, almost all of them on small companies. And although their talents had been, for the most part, raw and undeveloped, their collective contribution to the whole of pop music had been overwhelming. But the pressures applied to radio stations by big-money interests, followed by the payola scandals, had effectively brought an end to their careers. Earl Bostic and Fats Domino and Bill Doggett and the church-rooted vocal groups, such as the Moonglows and the Dominoes, and the other influential black artists of the early and mid-fifties no longer received sustained airplay, and as a consequence could no longer dictate the direction the mainstream of rock-'n'-roll music would take.

They were replaced first by the horde of Presley imitators—among them Carl Perkins, Jerry Lee Lewis, Ricky Nelson, and Conway Twitty—and then by a "sound," a sound which, with an amazing show of contempt for the young people who purchased its products, the music industry called the "dumb" sound.

The artists who used this sound—groups such as the Capris, the Echoes, Dante and the Evergreens, the Dovells, and the Marcels—would neither achieve nor retain identity in any specific market. Yet they dominated the charts. The year 1959 saw sixteen of them achieve top-ten status. The year 1960 saw eighteen more, and before 1961 drew to a close, there would be no fewer than thirty-five groups of this type to reach the top ten—foisted upon the public by an industry consumed by greed and so prideless as to term its own produce the sound of stupidity.

But it was not the young record buyers who were stupid; they were merely gullible. It was the music industry itself that was exercising shortsightedness of immense proportion, because it was their disdain for the music of the black artists they had replaced with hastily concocted formula "hits" which would, in a few years, make them vulnerable to the onslaught of British artists and record producers.

And if the ascension of Gino Turicotti to the presidency of ITRC Records had signified for that company a realistic approach to coping with the way things had become in the music business, it also signaled the beginning of a certain ruthlessness within the company, as well.

By the summer of 1959, ITRC had pared its roster of contract artists from 345 to 116 More than four hundred key employees across the country had been fired, retired, demoted, or forced to resign. The International Recording and Transcription Corporation no longer operated like an old, worn-out conventional airplane, with thousands of creaking parts, each subject to breakdown without warning. It was now more like a sleek, modern jet—trim, capable of delivering to the market, within a few days' time, a payload of national airwave saturation and millions of singles, albums, and tapes.

Also, by summer 1959, company policy had been set. ITRC would not compete for the full-on, twangy rock-'n'-roll buyer. It would produce and promote a middle-of-the-road music. A softer, more musical rock and roll, designed to satisfy, simultaneously, some segment of the traditional ITRC market, and at the same time appeal, hopefully, to the least radical teenage purchasers of "hard" rock and roll.

It was as much of a compromise as the major stockholders and entrenched executives of ITRC would allow. They would not be convinced that rock-'n'-roll music, which they still basically, and accurately, perceived as black or imitation black music, was around to stay. They simply would not allow themselves to entertain the idea that rock-'n'-roll music would eventually become more profitable than dixieland, swing, jazz, and all of the preceding forms of

176 ·

American pop music put together. Soft rock and roll, they felt, would enable ITRC to retain a substantial amount of its prestige, and still return the company to its former sales power.

They were wrong.

Even though the 1959–60 fiscal year saw ITRC achieve the largest sales figures in the history of its record division, the company still found itself in control of less than twelve percent of the total market.

By mid-1960 it was obvious that ITRC still had a long way to go if it was to recover its position as one of the "majors."

Consequently, Max Geary and Gino Turicotti decided to consult with Robert Stermis and Associates once again.

Stermis had been intrigued by his first delvings into the pop-music market four years before. During the time his company was not engaged in researching the market for various political candidates, dog-food companies, and the like, he had returned again and again, fascinated, to his study of the music industry. What had begun as merely "educated guesses" and unsubstantiated "facts" had matured into comprehensive market analysis. Although most people in the music industry were unaware of his existence at that time, Bob Stermis probably knew more about the *business* of rock-'n'-roll music than anyone else in America. He could now portray with accuracy the "average" age, sex, education, and family background of every Caucasian teenager—from Klamath Falls, Oregon, to Milford, Delaware—who spent more than ten dollars a year on records.

Over a month-long period, Geary, Turicotti, and Stermis conducted a series of meetings at Geary's Connecticut mansion. Stermis was able to convince the other two men that his accumulated data proved conclusively that the market for rock-'n'-roll music had not even begun to peak. He was convinced it would double, perhaps triple, within the next decade. He suggested, indeed urged, that now was the time for ITRC to make as strong and total a commitment to rock-'n'-roll music as company finances permitted.

Geary and Turicotti digested Stermis' information thoroughly. Together they formulated a five-year plan, at the end of which time, barring unforeseen developments within the industry, ITRC would emerge as the uncontested front-runner in the race for the dollars of the contemporary music–buying public.

At the same time, the men knew that the climate and attitudes within the company would not allow for ITRC's hard-won prestige to be committed almost exclusively to the production of rock-'n'-roll music. They made plans, therefore, for yet another subsidiary label, this one to be called Arrow Records.

ITRC's previous subsidiary label, Champ Records, had long since expired—to be exact, eighteen months from the date it first became activated. But it had served its stated purpose. It had bought the company time. It had uncovered new and more effective ways of marketing and merchandising products. And while it had done no more than break even on the accountant's ledger, providing only one top-ten record during its period of operation, it had more than paid for itself in a dozen other ways.

This newly planned subsidiary would not be another cheap r&b label, as Champ had been, designed solely to explore the market. Arrow Records would be, they thought, the quintessential rock-'n'-roll label. It would represent a minimum investment of sixty-two and one-half million dollars, prorated over the first five years of its existence. It would advance its artists exorbitant sums of front money, to ensure their instant credibility, their instant respectability as performers. It would stage and promote their live concerts. It would exercise direct influence for television guest appearances for them. Whenever feasible, it would invest in motion-picture production for them. It would underwrite and control books and magazines featuring pictures and promotional—purportedly "factual"—material about them.

Geary and Turicotti forwarded their five-year plan to the ITRC division of corporate planning in the early fall of 1960, just as the payola investigations they had helped to manipulate were reshaping the inner workings of the music industry. It was returned for their approval shortly after the first of December of that year, in the form of a seventy-eight page booklet suggesting in part that the ITRC West Coast offices on Gower Street in Los Angeles be sold, furnishings and equipment intact, if possible, and that a new ITRC recording center be built on Sunset Strip on a parcel of land owned by ITRC since 1927.

A tentative logo had already been designed for the new label. Marketing and merchandising procedures were being formulated. Key distributors would be convened and given their sales programs and incentives during the early part of the fourth quarter of the 1960–61 fiscal year. Personnel would begin screening applications immediately.

The man recommended by Max Geary and Gino Turicotti to head the new subsidiary was presently national director of marketing for the ITRC Record Club of America. He had been heartily and unanimously endorsed.

His name was Mark Donovan.

§

Monroe Wilcox was right. They tried as hard as they could to put him out of business.

When he released a record and got it moving in a few places, they called him up and offered him a ridiculously low price for the master. When he wouldn't sell, they called him up a few days later and offered him a ridiculously *high* price for the same master. When he still wouldn't sell, they ganged up on him and blackballed his records from the big stations.

Anything to keep him from getting a firm foothold in the record business.

So he did exactly what he had told Ted Green he was going to do: he ignored them. He lost a lot of pop sales, but he sold a lot of records in the rhythm-and-blues market.

In one year, between the fall of 1956 and late 1957, his New York distributor alone owed him more than thirty thousand dollars. The distributor worked it very smoothly. He kept ordering records and sending back only a small payment on the balance due from each shipment. He made deliberate mistakes on the number and condition of records received. He promised to send back returns, which never arrived.

Monroe and Ted Green investigated the owner. He was "connected." There was nothing Monroe could do.

Many of his distributors pulled that on him.

When they didn't succeed in putting him out of business that way, they got more sophisticated. They allowed his records on the big stations, printed surveys that showed them beginning to break, and ordered larger numbers of records. As soon as Monroe shipped, they immediately took his records off the air, leaving him with huge pressing costs, which he had to absorb if he wanted to remain in business.

For almost two years, they forced him to sell the majority of his records through the mail, advertising in black magazines such as

Ebony and *Our World,* knowing that the mailing costs and extra paperwork would gnaw away at his profits.

But he stuck it out.

By the spring of 1955, his distributors owed him more than a hundred thousand dollars almost to the penny the amount he owed Ted Green.

But with all their tactics, all their private agreements, all their maneuverings, they had failed to cover one crucial angle: the music business was growing so fast, and so many records were now being made, the number of songs needed to keep the machinery operating was astronomical.

Consequently although Monroe couldn't get his records played on the big radio stations across the country, other companies did record his songs. The record producers of those companies didn't want to do it, but the white artists themselves—who were forever scrounging around in black record stores, listening to black radio stations for a tune, a piano lick, a guitar riff, anything to make them sound more authentic—insisted on it.

And by this time, by 1958, Big City Records was consistently putting out the highest-quality, most exciting music in the r&b market.

Still, the cash was not always there when Monroe needed it, so on occasion, when he was reluctant to ask Ted Green for more, he was not above jumping into his new station wagon with the Big City logo on the side, and driving through the Midwest and the East, selling records personally to the retail outlets in black neighborhoods, just as he had done with the record he had bootlegged on Saul Goldman.

In the summer of 1958, he put together the first convention of black dj's, NANRP, the National Association of Negro Radio Personalities. It was held in Chicago.

Most of the black dj's around the country were earning only staff announcer's wages, if that, plus whatever they could hustle. As a consequence, Monroe wound up paying transportation and lodging costs out of his own pocket for almost half of those who attended, some from as far away as Los Angeles.

But when the convention adjourned, he had sixty-eight dj's committed to playing his records on the black stations. He made no attempt to be secretive; he made certain they understood: if they gave him good, prime-time airplay, they could always count on Big City Records for a little extra cash.

He and Maudie had been married a year when the first baby came in November 1959. They named her Carleen, after his sister, and celebrated the occasion by moving into a four-bedroom split-level house in an all-white neighborhood on the far Westside. They had some trouble with their neighbors, until Monroe caught two men trying to burn a cross on his front lawn one night, and resumed his boxing career long enough to put one of them in the hospital.

He was overlooked when the payola scandals hit. After all, he had never wielded any influence with the big radio stations, even though his records were beginning to pop up fairly consistently in the trade papers on the r&b and regional charts.

It was about this time that the owner of Concertone Studios, where Monroe did all his recording, decided to sell and move to Nashville.

Monroe paid him a quarter down, forty thousand dollars and moved in. Now his recording costs were nominal. He could increase his amount of product considerably without raising his overhead. The first thing he did after he bought the place was hire Willie Jackson as his full-time engineer.

His dreams were beginning to materialize. Slowly, he was getting his nuts out of the dust.

By the middle of 1960 he was running as high as a quarter-million copies on some singles. They were records that still were not being heard by the majority of white buyers. But, more and more, white recording artists were seeking them out, recording them for their major labels.

For the first time, Monroe's publishing company—sheet music, mechanicals, and radio licensing royalties—earned him well in excess of six figures. You could walk into almost any black home in America and, among those people who consistently bought r&b records, find at least one Big City record in the stack by the stereo.

Old Tom Turner was dead now, and Maudie had invited Mrs. Turner to come live with them. Mrs. Turner was no trouble, still sprightly and full of life, and she helped Maudie take care of the baby and prepare the meals.

Christmas Day 1960 was a special moment in Monroe's life. All the time he had been trying to establish his company, Carleen had been running Monroe's Record Rack for him. Today Carleen came by with her new husband, and as a combination Christmas/wedding gift, Monroe made her a present of the store. She cried, Maudie cried, and Mrs. Turner cried.

It was a happy occasion.

Later in the day, after dinner, Al Baxter and a couple of other dj's dropped in with their wives and girlfriends for a drink. Max Novikoff, who still did some work for Monroe from time to time, came by with his little gray-haired wife, who spoke no English, and his youngest daughter, who was about eighteen and seemed determined to take Al Baxter to bed.

It was about nine-thirty when Ted Green arrived. Nobody, not even Maudie, really knew who Green was, except that he was a friend of Monroe's.

Green stayed only a few minutes, but long enough for Monroe to get him off to the side and tell him he would finally be able to start paying him back in the new year. Green told Monroe not to worry about it. Monroe said he wasn't worried about it, because he had already worked it out. He showed Green some corporation papers he had drawn up. There would be another publishing company within the Big City aegis. Green would own half. The way music publishing was now shaping up, it looked as though Green would get all his money back, plus a substantial income for as long as he lived.

Later, after Max Novikoff had taken his wife and daughter home, after Ted Green had left with his quiet Creole girlfriend, after Al Baxter and the others had drunk up most of Monroe's liquor and gone, after Carleen and Bill had descended the steps arm in arm, thanking Monroe again for his present, and after Mrs. Turner had tucked little Carleen in bed and herself gone to bed, Monroe sat on his overstuffed couch, sipped one last eggnog, looked at the huge Christmas tree by the picture window, and held Maudie in his arms.

He was about to become a father again, Maudie told him, and she was proud of him. He had worked hard and brought his dreams to life, she said—for himself, for her, for their children, and for all the people who loved and respected him. But most important, he had come through the fires with his body and his mind intact.

He had made it, she said.

He drank his eggnog and kissed her, and agreed with her.

But he knew better. He hadn't made it yet. All he had done was discover what it required to succeed. The answer was almost mystical, his eggnog told him: You busted your ass. You beat down doors. You held on as tight as you could and took care of as much business as you could. And one day, without even expecting it, you got a break and went all the way.

At least, at that moment, that's the way he and his eggnog had it figured out.

And they were right. It happened the first week of January. Just like that.

BOOK THREE

The world is full of hopeful analogies and
handsome dubious eggs called possibilities.

—Eliot

CHICAGO
JANUARY 1961

It was late afternoon. The building was quiet, the office staff already gone for the day.

Monroe and Willie were huddled over Monroe's desk, tightening up the year's album-production schedule, so engrossed in what they were doing that neither of them heard the man enter the room.

" 'Scuse me, y'all . . ."

They looked up, startled.

He was about thirty-five, wearing a baggy, one-button-roll suit and a shirt with a frayed Mr. B collar. He had a home haircut—chopped unevenly all over his scalp, the sides shaved—and the muscular, stocky look of a black man who has dragged a lot of sixteen-foot cotton sacks through a lot of furrows.

"How'd you get in here?" Monroe asked sharply, angry at the interruption.

"The front door was open. There wasn't nobody out front, so I just kept walking around till I found somebody." He smiled, showing a gap where his two front teeth should have been, and stuck out a callused hand. "My name's Rydell Mercer. I come to audition for y'all."

"You got to make an appointment," Monroe said, dismissing him.

"I can't make no appointment. . . ."

"What you mean, you can't make no appointment?"

"I don't live here, I lives in Indiana."

"Well, what you doing here, then?"

"I told you, I come up here to audition for y'all."

Monroe dropped his pen on the desk, sighed, and leaned back in his chair, resigned to spending a few minutes getting rid of him. "Okay, what do you do? Sing, write, what?"

"We sings and plays."

"We? What you mean, 'we'? What you got, a frog in your pocket?"

"I got my band outside. We all come up here together."

"From Indiana?"

"Yeah, Evansville."

"Damn! You brought your band all the way up here on the chance somebody might listen to you?" Monroe made a face. "You sure got a lot of nerve, man. How many cats in your band?"

"They's usually seven of us, but one couldn't come—one of his childrens is sick."

"Where you all parked?"

"Out front, down the street a little ways."

"Okay, as long as you came this far, I might as well hear what you niggers sound like. Pull your car around back and start unloading your stuff."

Monroe talked to Willie a few minutes longer, then walked down the hall and opened the back door to a burst of cold air just as a muddy brown DeSoto was pulling into the parking lot, dragging a dirty U-Haul trailer with an Indiana license plate hanging by one screw.

The six blacks who climbed out of the car ranged in age from eighteen or nineteen to a bald man who looked old enough to be Mercer's father.

Monroe shook his head. These were some of the most soulful blacks he had ever seen. He didn't know men like this were still around.

Mercer grabbed a ragged blue imitation-alligator saxophone case from the floor of the trailer and stood off to the side, giving orders. It took almost no time for the men to get their instruments inside. The last piece of equipment was an old Hammond B-3 organ with most of the shellac worn off. They set it on a splintered dolly with wobbly wheels and made a lot of noise pushing it over the hump in the doorway.

Monroe closed the door quickly, trying to keep some of the heat inside, and followed the musicians down the hall.

"What you niggers call yourselves, man?" he asked Mercer.

"Rydell Mercer and the Indiana Blues Boys," Mercer answered, making it obvious that Monroe should have heard of them before now.

Monroe shook his head disgustedly.

He went inside the control booth and watched through the window as Willie placed the microphones where the sound could be picked up and played inside.

Willie joined him a few minutes later, taking his customary seat behind the console. "You want me to tape them, Mr. Wilcox?"

"Hell, no! Man, if these niggers sound anything like they look, we about to hear some sad shit!"

He gave the band a few more minutes to finish tuning up, then pushed the button on the studio mike. "Lemme know when you guys are ready," he said to Mercer.

"We's ready now."

"You ready?" Monroe asked Willie.

"Umm-hmmm," Willie said, fooling with the knobs, already sounding bored.

"Okay," Monroe said into the mike, "lemme hear what you got."

He took his hand off the button and heard Mercer issuing some last-minute instructions, followed by four clicking noises as the drummer banged his sticks together to set the tempo.

Mercer had the introduction—a honking, preaching four-bar saxophone solo. It didn't take him long to set the groove. After the first couple of notes, he had his eyes rolled back in his head, the gap where his two front teeth should have been firmly clamped around the mouthpiece of his dented, silver-plated old saxophone.

Monroe was surprised: the nigger could play.

On the downbeat of the fifth bar, when the other instruments joined in, Monroe sat up straight in his seat.

God damn! Those raggedy-looking characters were cooking!

Monroe turned to Willie. Willlie was moving back and forth in his seat in time to the music, slapping the console with his palm, a wide grin on his face.

Monroe knew the sound blaring from the two speakers above his head was *exactly* what he had been waiting for. It was genuine, it was telling the true story:

> *Saturday night in the neighborhood . . . scraping up the rent money . . . hanging out on the corners . . . trying to jive some foxy little mama out of her phone number . . . or her drawers . . . chewing on a rib . . . drinking red soda pop . . . squeezing bedbugs . . . sitting on the back porch in your undershirt . . . sticky hot . . . swatting flies with a rolled-up* Pittsburgh Courier *. . . shooting rats with a .22 . . .*

He had their asses now!

There wasn't a white musician in the world who could "cover" the music that was coming out of that studio. Not yet. Not unless he had spent the last ten years of his life on the back of an Evansville, Indiana, dump truck, picking up trash in subzero weather, with the handles on the cans so cold that they stripped the flesh off his fingers when he set them back down.

The fix wasn't quite in. A year, maybe two, and it would be. But right now, today, there wasn't enough money or leverage in the music business to keep Rydell Mercer off the pop charts—not if he was promoted right.

The song ended. Mercer was getting ready to go right into another tune when Monroe pushed the mike button down. "C'mon on in, man. I don't need to hear no more," he said. He was already on his feet when Mercer came through the studio door. "Let's go in my office, we gotta talk."

Mercer followed him down the hall. When he had sat down across the desk from Monroe, he lit a cigarette, showing nervousness for the first time.

"That your tune?" Monroe asked.

"Yeah, how you like it?"

"What you call it?"

"We calls it 'The Up-and-Down Boogie.' "

"Umm-hmmm," Monroe said. "I might have to change that title. You write it?"

"Yeah, me and the organ player."

"Dig, you cats ain't signed with nobody, are you?"

"No, that's why we's here."

"Anybody ever publish any of your tunes before?"

"No, we ain't never played them for nobody before."

Monroe reached into the top drawer. "Here, read this," he said, thrusting a contract at Mercer.

Mercer took it, looked through it with a puzzled expression.

"It ain't nothing but a standard recording contract," Monroe said. "You can take it to a lawyer if you want."

"I don't need no lawyer, man," Mercer said defensively. "I can read it myself." He squinted at it for a few seconds, making it obvious that he couldn't. "I ain't got my glasses with me," he concluded. "What do it say?"

"All it says is, if you sign with me, you can't sign with nobody else. And that I'll pay you five percent of ninety percent of every record I sell on you."

Mercer thumbed through the contract. "It take eight pages just to say that?"

"No, it's got a lot of lawyer talk in it, too," Monroe explained. " 'The party of the first part,' 'henceforth and to wit,' that kind of bullshit, you know what I mean?"

Mercer looked a little dubious.

"Lemme tell you something," Monroe said firmly, looking Rydell Mercer straight in the eye. "I got one rule at this company: I don't fuck over nobody and I don't let nobody fuck me over. Can you dig that?"

Mercer nodded.

"So if you want to take it to a lawyer, that's cool. I ain't gonna try to con you into doing nothing you ain't sure about. But if you want to sign it now, I'll cut you as soon as I can, and get a record out on you cats immediately."

Mercer looked down at the contract in his hand, back up at Monroe, back down at the contract, back up at Monroe, trying to resolve his indecision.

"Okay," finally said. "This is what we come up here for. If you wants to mess over us, this piece of paper ain't gonna make a damn bit of difference. Where do I sign?"

"You don't have to sign right this minute," Monroe said. "It ain't filled in yet."

"That's okay, you done give me your word. If I'm gonna trust you, I might as well start trusting you now. Where do I sign?"

Monroe showed him.

Mercer signed three blank recording contracts and four blank publishing contracts, his scrawly "Rydell D. Mercer" so cramped and illegible that Monroe could hardly make it out.

"Okay," Monroe said, sticking the contracts back in his desk, "I got a girl coming in in the morning. I'll have her fill everything in. Then I'll sign them and make sure you get a copy, okay?"

Mercer nodded. "When we gonna make a record?" he asked.

"The sooner the better."

"The band's here, the stuff's already set up, the contracts is already signed. How come we can't go 'head and do it now?"

"The studio ain't set up yet for making a record. It'll take about a half-hour. You guys wanna go eat or something?"

Mercer's dark eyes shone with determination. "Man, we can eat anytime, but this might be the only chance we ever gets to make a record. Go on and get your studio ready while I rehearse my band. I got five babies to feed. I got to make some money!"

Monroe had the record pressed and shipped within ten days.

By the middle of February it was number one on the rhythm-and-blues charts.

That same week, it jumped on to the pop charts: number thirty-nine and with a bullet next to the number, which meant it was coming up fast.

The next week, it was number thirteen with a bullet.

The week after that, it was number three with a bullet.

The week after that, it was number one.

He had done it.

It had taken him the better part of five years to get another number-one record, but this one was all his. He owned the tune, the group, the company, the whole damned thing.

For the first time since he had formed his company, he had some leverage with his distributors.

It was what he had been waiting for.

He stopped shipment

Before he would send out more records, they had to pay him every penny they owed for delinquent accounts.

They paid.

The second week the record was number one, he had two pressing plants going around the clock. His publishing company already had five cover records on the song, including one country-and-western version in the top ten on the country-music charts. He had shipped out 1,750,000 singles. He had actually received payment for more than a million of them.

To date, including the squaring up of delinquent accounts, the song had earned him more than a half-million dollars.

It was the wildest, most exhilarating month of his life, like nothing he could have imagined. His whole catalog came alive. His label was suddenly the hottest line in the business. Young buyers, previously unaware of its existence, were now flocking to the stores to grab every Big City record they could get their hands on.

Friday morning, *Ebony* magazine phoned. They wanted to do a cover story on him.

He worked straight through the weekend, filling orders.

Monday afternoon, two white men came to see him.

They were gangsters.

NEW YORK
MARCH 1961

Almost five years had passed since Mark Donovan's first meeting with Sam Crockett, and the slow, sometimes agonizing process of learning and assimilating the intricate, high-stakes, no-limits rules that made up the music industry had changed him considerably. He was no longer the optimistic, personable young man he had been. He was wiser now, tougher, less trusting, sometimes impatient to the point of brusqueness. Somewhere along the way, in the vicious infighting for the dollars of young record buyers, his quest to become a man of form and substance had become conjoined with the pragmatism necessary for his survival in a business built almost without exception upon the frail egos of untalented people.

Three years before, following the Champ Records experiment, Max Geary and Gino Turicotti and the other ranking officers of ITRC had decided to find out once and for all if Mark Donovan was top-echelon executive material. To test him, they had given him an executive nightmare, the position of national director of marketing for the ITRC Record Club of America.

During the early and mid-fifties, the five major record companies had formed their own record clubs, with tens of thousands of dollars to invest in monthly advertising and huge catalogs of their own that could be repackaged and rereleased at will. Small manufacturers could not compete in prices or distribution. Eventually, if the situation remained the same, they would not be able to compete in quality of product, either.

At the time Mark assumed the directorship, the small manufacturers had just instigated a class-action, restraint-of-trade suit against the majors. They were determined to break open what they perceived as a tight-knit conspiracy to limit their respective markets. At the same time, ITRC and the other majors were equally determined to continue to exclude the products of smaller manufacturers, realizing that the exclusive operation of their record clubs was tantamount to a license to print money, for it gave them something they had never had before—a precommitted market.

As the record clubs thrived, their advertising programs began to reach upward of twenty-five million potential customers per month, in most cases more people than ever *heard* the hit records of smaller labels. But while it was clearly a fiscally rewarding program for the majors, for the smaller manufacturers it was, to understate the case, a severe limitation on their access to a lucrative market.

Upon assuming control of ITRC's record club, Mark's first official act was to meet with the heads of the major independent companies. He listened to their grievances and immediately acceded to their demands. Henceforth, ITRC would distribute the products of other companies through its record club. He even went a step further, limiting the selection of products of his own company to those which had proven their sales potential through prior release or through prerelease demands for the artist.

By striving to make the ITRC record club a vehicle for marketing the best music available, no matter who produced it, he automatically invalidated the free ticket that some of the old-line ITRC production people had been using to acquire sales for their otherwise unmarketable products. As a consequence, for the first time in his business career he found himself cast in the role of villain. And for the first time in his life he began to be overtaken by cynicism. He had to acknowledge openly that there were quite a few self-serving fools in the world, particularly in the music business, a great many of whom worked for ITRC.

But he was right in his decision:

In the three years that he served as head of the record club, he increased its billing from a half-million dollars per month to more than two million. He made ITRC's record club the cornerstone of the company's basic marketing procedures. The added competition within the industry for the products of smaller companies expanded the entire market, and primarily because of him, more companies were making more money than they had previously dreamed possible.

By accomplishing this, not only had he solidified his position as Max Geary's in-company protégé but also he had become the talk of the industry. Outwardly, things could not have been better.

Yet today, on this Monday morning, the beginning of his final week in New York, he stood before the window of his private office on the thirty-fifth floor of the ITRC Building staring out vacantly at the rain-drenched city with eyes clouded by indecision. In less than three months, as of June 1, he would officially assume the presidency of the newly created ITRC subsidiary, Arrow Records, the company's permanent entry into the burgeoning rock-'n'-roll market. He had been given the five-year plan several months before and had studied it thoroughly, trying to visualize its impact on the industry and the power it would wield over the musical tastes and minds of young record buyers. He was not happy with it. There were many aspects of the plan that he found difficult to accept, one in particular that he abhorred.

Basically, it relegated all the music that would be produced for the new label to the status of product, nothing more. It made no provisions for artistic growth of any kind. Artisans would be patently ignored. Fine musicians, accomplished singers, skilled writers, would become obsolete.

The five-year plan was a total abdication of the corporation's responsibilities to propagate the essence of music, aesthetically or emotionally. It was designed, purely and simply, to pick up the immediate buck, the dollar that was now in the pockets of the white American teenager.

That was what Mark disliked about the plan.

What he *abhorred* about it was its prescribed treatment of black artists.

It allowed him to sign as many black artists as he chose, but it put definite, unmistakable limitations upon the amount of money that could be spent for their promotion. (In fact, it was strongly hinted in the plan that it might prove good business to sign the most talented black artists merely to keep them out of the hands of competitors.) It was made quite obvious, however, that magazine promotions, newspaper ads, the pressures applied and gratuities extended to critics and music columnists, to radio people and producers of television programs, were to go directly for the benefit of the company's white artists.

Such a policy, on the surface, might appear to be no more than sound (if ethically questionable) corporate planning, simply seeking the most immediate return on what would be a huge financial commitment. But Mark had spent almost seven years in the executive suites of the music industry, and he knew better. He knew that the overriding motivation of almost all music business executives was an unspoken fear that bordered on the paranoid. It was the fear that the music industry might once again come to be dominated by small companies, as it had been in the recent past, and continue to be culturally dominated by black artists, as it was at present.

If ITRC were a small business, and if it were merely a question of the five-year plan aiding the company's survival, he would have had little difficulty arriving at a comfortable moral resolution. But ITRC was a huge corporation. Its history of artistic equality was the hallmark of the industry. Its present position, financially and within the industry, was not so precarious that it needed to compromise its reputation by attempting to purchase instant musical parity for a select group of generally ungifted artists.

And there was yet another, more important reason why he found it difficult to support the plan:

Less than a month before, in a private conversation with Max Geary, he had learned that one of recently elected President Kennedy's first acts upon assuming office was to write personal letters to the leaders of American industry, asking them to begin formulating a program whereby the various minority groups could be more easily assimilated into the mainstream of the American economy. It would be, the President felt, the most positive way to combat the invective and hatred that appeared destined to turn the country's urban areas into an internal battleground.

It was inexcusable for ITRC or any other major American music corporation to disregard the President's letter. Not one logical, rational executive in the industry could deny, with honesty, that a larger percentage of black artists could express the music of their heritage better, with more understanding and fidelity, than a similar number of white artists could attempt to express that same music. It was foolish and hypocritical to pretend otherwise, because it was an undeniable fact: *the music of black artists, both past and present, was the cornerstone upon which the huge rock-'n'-roll music industry was being built.*

But ITRC was not paying him eighty thousand dollars a year to moralize against company policies. He was a businessman, not a philosopher, and he was against the plan as it now stood from the standpoint of sound, practical business.

He could see, for ITRC to form a subsidiary label on such a calculatedly noncompetitive basis, and to finance it with such a substantial amount of capital, would almost assure that it would become a receptacle for every plagiarist and scam artist in the record business. Lawsuits against the company would increase because of their finaglings. Studio costs would skyrocket from the aimless creative meanderings of inexperienced so-called "young geniuses." It would only be a matter of time before distributor returns would double, treble, from the incessant hype of inferior products that even the gullible rock-'n'-roll buying public could not be forced into accepting.

In the end, instead of setting a standard for quality and leadership, Arrow Records would find itself nervously clinging to whatever temporary trends, fads, or momentary passions in which the music industry happened to find itself enmeshed. With three million dollars a year to spend on promotion alone, the label would undoubtedly achieve astronomical sales figures. But sales figures were not the bottom line. they were not even the middle line. The middle line was profit. The bottom line was stability and integrity. Stability for a music company could evolve only as a direct result of consistent quality in the product it turned out over an extended period. Integrity could come only from the dedication and corporate commitment of its administrative personnel.

As conceived, Arrow Records could offer neither stability nor integrity. Its concept was flawed. Its artists and administrative personnel would be dedicated primarily to the gratification of their own egos. Its music would be eminently forgettable.

And standing at the head of it all, in charge of serving up a sixty-two-and-a-half-million-dollar dish of tripe, would be himself. He would feel more like a procurer than a businessman.

He stood before the window, scowling at his reflection, his lower lip tucked between his teeth. It was raining harder. A fresh blanket of altostratus clouds had descended on the city, turning the mid-morning sky to dusk, giving it the eerie appearance of an immense cocoon dotted with patches of faded yellow light.

Mark was angered at the position in which he found himself. No one knew how tempted he was to walk away from it all.

The buzzer on his desk sounded. It was Turicotti's secretary, calling to remind him that the meeting would be as scheduled, in ten minutes.

He replaced the receiver and looked around the office, distaste locked into the corners of his eyes. He had never liked the room. It had always seemed dusty and oppressive to him, as though suspended on a barm of dirt and noise.

By Friday night, he would be home again, in his Malibu cottage, comforted by the roar of the surf beneath his bedroom window. He could visit his mother and father whenever he wanted, start seeing his old friends again. He could get in his car and drive for hours, without having his conscience prodded by rows and rows of squalid tenements inhabited by legions of human feculence that nobody cared about, not even his employer, that pillar of the American business community, ITRC.

He hated New York. Three years was long enough. He would be happy to get out.

It was only on those infrequent occasions when he was invited upstairs that Mark realized the great power and tradition of the company he worked for.

The presidential suite took up the entire northeast quarter of the fiftieth floor. It had been decorated thirty years before, with fine art and great attention to detail, by E. V. Calkins, as a testament to the position of preeminence held by ITRC in the artistic and financial communities of that time.

One room, more than any other in the building, expressed ITRC's rich musical tradition. It had witnessed some of the most significant announcements in American musical history. In earlier years, it was where the company's important contractual signings—duly photographed and publicized—had taken place. It had also been the meeting place for the "angels" of the musical theater, and the bankroll for many a Broadway show, featuring the company's artists, had been pledged there.

There was a time, until a few years before, when these rooms were kept open, though unpublicized, for the enjoyment of anyone who happened by. Their only guards were the procession of art students who worked there part-time, and a small white guestbook kept on a lighted pedestal by the front entrance.

But now, as the intrinsic value of art became translated into more absolute values of dollars and cents, and as the price of dope on the street of New York spiraled, the huge oak doors, and the doors to the drawing room and the gallery, were kept locked at all times, except for infrequent, special occasions. And although everything was dusted and cleaned daily, the overall impression was not unlike that of a dowager who has seen more exciting times.

There had been talk about remodeling the area, donating the collections to a local museum, but so far nothing had been done.

The suite remained intact, an elegant, anachronistic remnant of another era, casting its disapproving special glance across a corporation that had once been as proud of its aesthetics as of its quarterly financial statements.

The other entrance to Turicotti's office, the one Mark now found himself standing before, was approached by a circuitous route, through two slim corridors and behind the bank of elevators that rose through the center of the building.

The sign on the plain maple door read:

ITRC

RECORD DIVISION

OFFICE OF THE PRESIDENT

Mark paused a moment, then pushed the door open and stepped into a large reception area furnished in subdued shades of brown.

The woman behind the desk on the far side of the room, a stately brunette with carefully applied makeup, appeared to be in her mid-thirties. She had been watching the door, obviously anticipating his arrival. She made no effort to hide her anger.

"You were supposed to call me yesterday."

"I'm sorry, Ann." He smiled apologetically as he crossed to her desk. "It took me all day to pack. I didn't realize I had so much junk."

"Oh, is that so?" Her voice dripped ice water. "Well, first things first, I suppose. Did you find time to visit your sister?"

"Yes, I had dinner with her and Jules last night at their place in Westchester. Got home about eleven. Hit the sack immediately"

"You could have called. We could have had a late drink."

"I told you it wasn't definite, not to wait up."

"Well, I *did* wait up. I sat there until—"

"Hey, c'mon now. I told you I was sorry."

"Well"—she glanced at the door to Turicotti's office, then raised her lips to be kissed—"at least you can say hello properly."

He bent over the desk, preparing to brush her lips with his own. But before he had a chance to pull away, she took his face in her hands and gave him a lingering kiss, then sank her teeth into his lip.

"*Goddammit!*"

"That was for standing me up . . ."

He dabbed at his lip with a handkerchief, saw a speck of blood.

". . . and I'm not accustomed to being stood up."

He looked down at her, a tired expression on his face.

"Oh, him's mad!" She smiled, showing her perfectly capped teeth.

He ignored her words and nodded toward Turicotti's office. "Is he ready for me yet?"

"You *are* mad." She folded her hands under her chin and gave him her little-girl look. "That's too bad. I had a nice little going-away present for you . . ."

He shrugged.

". . . lunch."

He shrugged again and turned his palms toward the ceiling.

"You see, I have this friend who's got this nice little flat down in the Village, maybe fifteen minutes from here. She's a tall brunette with nice boobs and a terrific ass . . . gives great head, too. I thought maybe you and she could have a nice . . . long . . . lunch. Lie in bed, listen to the rain . . . maybe enjoy a little Irish coffee afterward."

He stared at her without expression, thinking how attractive she would be if she didn't try so hard.

"Maybe?" she persisted.

"Sure, why not?" The way he spoke made it obvious he wasn't serious. "In the meantime, maybe you'd like to tell Mr. Turicotti I'm here?"

"Dammit, Mark, I was disappointed! I sat there like an idiot until after midnight waiting for you to call, and your phone's disconnected, so I couldn't call you."

He dabbed at his mouth again with the handkerchief. "Maybe you should have eaten something while you were waiting."

"Maybe I should have eaten some*body* while I was waiting, for all you care!" She turned back to her typewriter. "Go keep your goddamned appointment!"

He started to speak, changed his mind, and headed for Turicotti's office. He knocked once briskly and entered. Turicotti was at his desk, immaculate in a dark green suit and matching paisley tie, the ever-present cigarette dangling from his lips.

Mark had seen very little of Turicotti during the past three years—the record club operated under a different section of the administration. But each time he did, the changes in the man's appearance were startling. Turicotti's hair was turning noticeably whiter, the lines around his eyes were deepening, and the impulsive gestures now appeared more deliberate. Three packs of cigarettes a day and the constant pressures of his job had put a slight tic over his eyes, made his voice hoarse, abrupt.

He motioned Mark to a seat and, as was his custom, started right in without amenities. "This is the last time I'll see you before you leave for the Coast, so I wanna go over a couple of things with you. Let's start with that Paul Schultz production thing."

"Did you talk to him again?" Mark asked, folding back the cover of the yellow legal pad in his lap, poising his pen to take notes.

"When are you supposed to see him?" Turicotti asked, consulting the memos on his desk.

"This afternoon, three o'clock."

"Yeah . . . that's what I thought." He shuffled through a few more pages. "Okay, here it is. I talked to him twice. The first time he came in was a couple of months ago, first of the year. He wanted a straight producer's job then. Asking fifty a year, plus two cents a record, plus half the publishing." He paused, lit a cigarette off the butt in his hand. "The last time I talked with him, he had changed his mind. Wanted a straight production setup."

"Wholly owned?"

"Well, that's what we're gonna decide now. He says he can go a hundred and a half easy, two if necesarry. If he uses his own money, he wants twenty percent."

"You think he's got that much money?"

"Naw . . ." Turicotti thought a moment. "Hell, I don't know. I know goddamned well he didn't have it the first time he came in. But he seemed pretty definite this last time. It's up to you to make sure he's got it, and can control it. We don't want to wind up doing business with some fucking buttonhole makers from downtown. We've got to be sure the money is clean."

"I can handle that, that's no problem. Anybody else?"

"Yeah, I'm giving you a couple of kids from here, Danny Weiss and Les Goodson. They're young, but they're on top of it. We've had them in the top forty a few times, but they're too goddamned far-out for us."

"I know Danny, nice kid. I don't know the other fellow."

"Take my word for it, he can do it."

"Are they coming out to the Coast with me?"

"Naw, I'm gonna keep them here. They can turn out a better product here, they know more people."

"That might make for communication problems. . . ."

"It might, in the beginning, until we get things organized. But you've still got product approval, you and Silverstein. And I don't want this thing to be 'California,' I wanna cover the whole country, you know what I mean?"

Mark nodded. "So who else have you got for me?"

"Are you ready? Tommy Lee Whitaker."

"Tommy Lee Whitaker?" A flash of anger darted across Mark's face. "He's a hundred-percent country."

"Country my ass! With *fifteen* top-ten records?"

"Yeah, all shit," Mark said disgustedly

"Listen to me, the King of the record business is a goddamned hillbilly, for crying out loud! And he still sells more records than any five artists you can name, put together. The hell with personal taste, Mark, we gotta get this Arrow thing off the ground."

Mark tapped his pen on the arm of his chair in irritation.

"I've already discussed it with him," Turicotti said. "I made it quite clear that we can't accept shit-kicking music from him, it's got to be pop all the way. He understands."

"I hear he's got a drug problem, too."

Turicotti slowed down for a moment, puffed his cigarette, and gave Mark an exasperated look. "Do you really give a shit?"

"No, but I do care about that Carousel thing. Anybody who was connected with it carries the kiss of death in the business, at least for the time being. If I put Tommy Lee Whitaker's name on one of my records as producer, it's going to make airplay just that much more difficult to come by."

"Bullshit," Turicotti said emphatically. "Sixty-two and a half million can buy a hell of a lot of airplay."

Mark flicked an imaginary particle of dust from his sleeve. "Okay, tell me straight, what choice do I have?"

"Now, listen to me." Turicotti folded his hands on the desk. "Whitaker has had *fifteen* legitimate hits. We've had him on salary for two and a half months, ever since we picked up Carousel. He's already recorded his first masters for us. He flew here a month ago and played them for Silverstein. Bob says they're fucking *monsters.* We need Whitaker, *you* need Whitaker. Okay, so he's a little weird, but he's no worse than any of the rest of those young assholes that are taking over production."

"What about Nashville? What's Carl Clinger doing down there?"

"Still setting up."

"For what?"

"Mostly country but some pop . . ."

"I get the feeling," Mark said, tapping his pen against the arm of the chair a little harder, 'I'm going to wind up releasing half of Carl Clinger's Nashville stuff, too."

Turicotti shrugged.

"Have I got a choice?" Mark said again.

"We got a contract with him."

"So he's got to come out on Arrow?"

"No," Turicotti said sarcastically, "I can always put him on the parent company, and go fifteen rounds with Max and the board."

"Okay"—Mark tried to smile—"who's producing for him?"

"A guy named Lonnie Pratt."

"I never heard of him," Mark said, frowning, "but I've been away from production so long it probably doesn't mean much. What's he had?"

"He's just moving into production," Turicotti hedged, purposely not mentioning that Pratt was Clinger's brother-in-law, "but he's got the experience."

"What kind of experience?"

"He picked up most of the masters for Carousel, as I understand it."

"As you understand it!" Mark blew up. "Give me a break, Gino! What's Arrow going to be, a goddamned garbage disposal?"

"For God's sake, Mark!" Turicotti stubbed his cigarette out in the ceramic ashtray on his desk and ran his fingers through his hair, trying to control his temper. "It's *all* garbage! I listen to as little of this shit as I have to. You know what I listen to when I get home? The goddamned opera. But if I tried to sell opera to some thirteen-year-old kid, you know where I'd be? I'd be somewhere in the Holland Tunnel right now, driving a goddamned truck!"

"I just don't like the way the label's shaping up."

"We've got no choice, Mark. We need these people. You think they're the dregs, right? Well, they may be, but they're the best we could find. It's a new thing, rock and roll. There's no labor pool, no fucking executive placement service we can go to to find the proper personnel. Take Whitaker. He's got a track record like Nashua. He can take his package anywhere, be snapped up in a goddamned minute, you know that."

"Okay." Mark sighed in resignation. "Has he signed yet?"

"We're finishing the contracts now. We'll put them in the mail the first of the week."

"How about a guarantee for Schultz, if we go with the production thing?"

"I didn't make a final offer—that's up to you. Try to keep it under a hundred if you can. If you gotta go up, go up. But keep it reasonable. Granted, we've got a lot of money to spend, but let's not spend it all in one place. We've got a lot of grease to spread around."

"How about additional staff producers for the Coast?"

"That's up to you, too. Just try not to get bogged down in a lot of unnecessary product. The secret to this whole Arrow thing is that every artist will be receiving maximum promotion, at least until we get a few off the ground."

Now was the time, Mark thought, to approach the subject. "Okay, let's go over this promotion thing again," he said, trying to hide some of the intensity he felt. "I mean, about policy toward Negro artists. . . ."

Turicotti's face clouded. He reached for another cigarette, tamped it on the corner of the desk a few times, lit it slowly. He appeared to be trying to cover up his embarrassment.

It made Mark think of a quote he had read, attributed to an Englishman who was visiting America for the first time. "The strange thing about you Yanks," the Englishman had said, "is that most of you are prejudiced, and all of you are ashamed to admit it."

Turicotti leaned back in his chair, gathering his thoughts. "It's all there in the plan," he said. "Fifteen percent of our total promotional dollar will be allocated for colored artists. It wasn't an arbitrary figure, Mark. Max and Bob Stermis and I deliberated a long time before we came up with it.

"The reason is simple, obvious. You get into the colored market, whether you like it or not, you're dealing almost entirely with a rhythm-and-blues concept. You got fucking animals all over the place. Your publishing goes to shit because the stations don't log their records most of the time, so you don't get decent performance money. Sales are unstable because every grifter and fast-buck artist in the business is down in the ghetto trying to bootleg records. You can't count on airplay because the colored dj's are promoting their friends. To ensure play you've got to fuck with the penny-ante stuff, a hundred bucks under the table here, a case of Scotch there. It's a pain in the ass, more trouble than it's worth. The goddamned r-and-b market is simply not big enough to warrant trying to service it full-time. Hell, you learned that with Champ. You worked your ass off for a year and a half and wound up with one goddamned hit. Eleven major markets, in a year and a half you only got three of them."

"Okay, I'll buy most of that," Mark said. "But look at Negro artists like Ray Charles and James Brown. You're going to tell me their sales don't justify maximum promotion?"

"They don't apply," Turicotti said firmly. "I'll tell you why. Both of them have been making records for years. They came up through a record business and a rhythm-and-blues market that was a lot less crowded and a lot more simple to do business with. They've both got strong, workable organizations, loyal followings, and they're stronger musically than most of the artists who are gonna walk in off the street. You *find* me a Ray Charles or a James Brown, we've got fifteen percent of a three-million-dollar promo budget to spend on them. That comes to . . . uh"—he figured in his head—"uh, four hundred and fifty thou. That'll buy all the promotion you want. The thing is, we can't afford to fuck around with marginal colored artists. The returns just don't warrant it. The hassles don't warrant it."

"Gino," Mark said quietly, staring at the older man, "you know what you're giving me? You're giving me the party line. You're shining up one side of the coin, trying to convince me that the other side doesn't matter. The fact is, right now, today, at this moment, colored kids make better records. You know that, I know that, and everybody else in the business knows that. If we hold promotion on our Negro artists to fifteen percent, we're going to flood the market with crap."

"I'm not going to insult you by calling you naive," Turicotti said, "but you're missing the whole goddamn point. We're not after the white kid who buys rock because he *likes* music, we're after the white kid who buys it because he thinks it's the best way to let his little buddies know how hip he is. We're forming Arrow to *visually* promote the young white artist. We want him to be attractive, easily accepted, easily identified with. In other words, we want the little pussies to wet their pants when they *see* him. Most of them couldn't care less what he sounds like anyhow. Now, face it, they might *want* to wet their pants over a James Brown, but their mommies and daddies are not about to let that happen, you know that as well as I do. Hell, seven or eight years ago, you couldn't even get r-and-b played on ninety-nine percent of the stations in the country. Then, here comes this hillbilly truck driver out of Tennessee, and the business doubles overnight. Fucking *doubles*. If it hadn't been for him, every major in the business would have gone broke trying to pretend that there was no such thing as rock-'n'-roll music."

"Okay." Mark sighed and shook his head in frustration. "Okay, you're right, but that's all history. Now we've got the capital, the marketing know-how to change that. Certainly not all of it, but enough to make a sizable impact. Hell, it's our *responsibility* to turn out the best music we can, no matter who it comes from. It's our tradition."

"You know something, kid?" Turicotti smiled. "I hear you talk like that and it gives *me* a little more dignity. It makes me personally feel proud to know that there are still a few decent human beings left in this goddamned business."

"Aw, bullshit!" Mark impatiently waved the compliment aside.

"Hey, goddammit!" Turicotti exploded. "You think I'm buttering your ass up? You think I'm sitting here in this goddamned chair making two hundred grand a year, pulling every string in the business, busting heads and rolling asses out the door, and I'm gonna take the time to butter you up?"

"I'm sorry," Mark said sincerely. "I was rude."

"I wasn't lying to you, kid," Turicotti said more calmly, "I *am* proud to know you. I've sat here and watched you walk down a lot of shit-filled highways in the last few years, and try to salvage a little of your self-respect. A lot of guys—hell, *most* guys in your position— good-looking, rich, successful, would have a head so fucking big I'd need a crowbar to pry them through the door. You don't. You're trying to find a way to do your job and still live with yourself. I know, I go through the same thing every day.

"But look around this office. Class, right? E. V. Calkins sat behind this desk for twenty-five years, as classy a guy as ever lived. And he loved this company as much as he loved his own wife. Every time he had to make a choice between what was morally correct and what was financially expedient, he went for conscience. And he wound up going down the tubes, and damn near taking the company with him.

"Listen . . . you think I'm prejudiced? You're so goddamned full of shit it's ridiculous! I was raised on a Hundred and Thirty-ninth and Amsterdam, for Christ's sake! I went to grammar school, to high school, to college, with colored kids. I slept at their houses and ate their ham hocks and greens, and they slept at mine and ate my old lady's cavatelli until it ran out of their goddamned belly buttons." He put a thick finger to his nose. "You see this? I broke this beak three times in three years, blocking for a colored tailback at Fordham. His name is Mike Eastman. My oldest boy, Mickey, is named after him. Mike Eastman's been my friend for thirty years! He's a big man in the insurance business, owns a split-level in Jamaica. You know why we're still friends? Because he's a winner, and I'm a winner.

"You wanna talk about responsibility? Okay, let's talk about responsibility. You and I have got one fucking responsibility here, to sell records. From nine to five, that's all we do, we sell records. We wanna change the world, we change it at night, on the goddamned weekends."

"I'm not talking about changing the world—" Mark began.

"That's *exactly* what you're talking about!" Turicotti exclaimed heatedly. "So, you wanna change it? Give to the NAACP, give to CORE, that's what I do. Give to the Jewish Anti-Defamation League, give to Toys for Tots. That's what I do. But if you start trying to change it from here, you know what's gonna happen to you? You're gonna wind up out of a job, standing on a soapbox in the Village, drinking wine and dissecting the universe with the goddamned potheads.

"Listen, Mark"—Turicotti's voice softened, the affection he felt for the younger man obvious in his eyes—"let me tell you something that might make you feel a little better, something it took me a long time to figure out. Those assholes out there"—he waved his arm at the window—"*deserve* what they get. They don't wanna listen to *music*. You try to get them to listen to some decent music, classical, jazz, they'll fucking go to sleep on you. They don't want to appreciate, they want to idolize. They *want* to look up to some cocky little bastard who knows three chords on a guitar, who rides around in a Rolls and pisses on all the nobodies. They *want* him to be common like them. The more common he is, the better they like it. That way, they can kid themselves into thinking: He made it, I can make it, too. They don't want reality, they've already *got* fucking reality, and it's kicking their asses every day of their lives. They want to pretend. *They* are the ones who insist on bullshit. So we sell them bullshit, and we stay in business. That's not absolving responsibility, that's just accepting things the way they are."

They sat across the desk from each other in silence, listening to the rain fall against the window in alternating sheets of volume, like rice being thrown by a giant hand. It was growing darker outside, more overcast, more ominous, and the darkness seemed to be seeping into the room, through the windows and the walls. It hovered about them for a moment before settling to encircle the confusion in Mark Donovan's eyes.

"Okay, let's tie this up," Turicotti said briskly. "I know you must have a few people to see, things to do before you go back to the Coast, so let's make sure we know where we are.

"The new building will be ready the first of June. As far as I know, it's on schedule. We're having some equipment problems, so the studios won't be ready until August, if then. But you can start moving your people in as planned.

"You'll see Schultz today—so that's covered. Whitaker will be in to see you out there week after next, sometime around the first of April. In the meantime, when you get there, take a couple of days off and get settled in.

"Oh, I almost forgot, Bob Silverstein will be moving out the early part of May. He's got a wife and two kids, right? Put somebody on finding him a couple of places to look at. He's well-fixed, making about fifty a year. It'll be a permanent move for him, he's already got his place here up for sale. You know the area, so you'll probably be able to choose a more suitable neighborhood than our regular agency.

"Your first releases, albums and singles, *must* be on the street by the fifteenth of June. Maximum promo. Planning will have a structural setup for you to go over in about two weeks. We'll send you some people from here, accountants, billing, et cetera. Those positions we can't fill, it's up to you to fill out there.

"We're moving into a different thing now, so we'll have a contract for you. Three-year tenure, one and a quarter per, plus options, three-quarters of the board before you can get dumped. Okay?"

"Fine."

"I'll be out there the second week in May. Anything I can do to help you get out of the gate, you got it."

He stood and offered his hand across the desk.

"Now, the last thing. . . . I know it's a fucking pain in the ass, but I'm gonna need memos every day. We've got sixty-two and a half million on this. Max is sweating it, I'm sweating it. He wanted to stop on the Coast on the way back from Japan, but he doesn't have the time—board meeting."

Turicotti came around the desk and gave Mark's face a tap with his palm, paisano style. ' Good luck, kid. I've got a gut feeling about this one. I know we've got the right man for the job. You do with Arrow what you did with the club, we'll be on top in two years, I guarantee it."

Mark stepped into the reception area and heard the door to Turicotti's office tick shut behind him. He started across the floor, head down, deep in thought. He was thoroughly disgusted with himself.

Sometimes he felt so fucking gutless! It was inexcusable for him not to have presented a stronger case for a more competitive label. He should have put himself on the line, refused the job unless basic policy changes were—

"Hey."

He was almost to the outer door. He turned. He had forgotten all about her. He started back across the floor.

"What were you going to do, just walk out of here without saying anything?"

"Well . . . yes, I guess I was."

"You don't give a damn about a girl's pride, do you?"

He could see, behind her flippant manner, she was hurt. "Yes, of course I do, Ann. I just have too much on my mind, that's all."

"Well, in that case, the offer still stands."

"No, thank you, I don't think I'm quite up to it today"—he kissed his finger and touched it to her lips—"but listen, if you're serious about coming out to the Coast later this year, call me. I'd really like to take you to dinner and introduce you to some nice people I know."

Ann Tilden prided herself in being a cold bitch. If she knew nothing else, she knew how to handle men. And it had been a long time since she had performed an act that was not calculated beforehand—to look cute, to look sweet, to look sexy. But now she heard the strain in Mark's voice and saw the lines of tension around his eyes, and in spite of herself, it touched something inside her.

"Here." She removed a key from her purse and dropped it in his pocket. "I won't be more than an hour behind you, just long enough to stop at the store and grab us something for lunch."

He opened his mouth to decline.

"No, *please*—I want to. I just . . . It's important to me, okay?"

An hour later, he was dozing on her couch in his stocking feet, a copy of *Newsweek* open on his chest, when he heard her key in the lock. He tried to rouse himself.

"That's okay, don't get up," she said quickly, balancing a small bag of groceries on her hip as she struggled to pull her key from the door. "I can manage."

She disappeared into the kitchen. He heard her plop the wet bag on the sink, heard the refrigerator door open and close. She was back a moment later, stripped down to her slip and bra.

"What happened to your clothes?"

"They're in the sink, covered with mud. Goddamned cabdrivers! Look at me, I'm drenched!"

"I'd better fix you a drink."

"Good. I could use one." She disappeared through the bedroom door, poked her head out again. "And put some music on, hon, something warm."

He got up from the couch, stuffing his shirttail inside his pants as he crossed to the kitchen. He entered, yawning, stepping carefully to avoid the puddles on the linoleum. He saw the cans of clam chowder on the sink, emptied them into a saucepan, and started them heating. She had already started the coffee, so he found two large ceramic mugs, filled them three-quarters, and poured a stiff shot of whiskey into each.

He padded back through the house and tapped on the bedroom door. There was no answer. He entered quietly and set her drink on the dressing table. Then, chuckling to himself, he went back to the kitchen and rinsed the mud from her splattered raincoat and dress and hung them on a hook in the small utility room. He went back to the living room and picked out a couple of Mantovani albums, a couple more by Percy Faith, dropped them on the turntable, and stood there sipping from his cup and listening to the music.

A few minutes later, the shower stopped and he tapped on the bedroom door again.

"Ummm. . . ?"

He pushed it open. She was sitting at her dressing table in a short white terry-cloth robe that barely reached past the curve of her hip, a white towel wrapped in a turban around her head. She glanced at his reflection in the mirror and put down her cup and reached for a tube of lipstick.

"Don't bother. You look fine."

She hesitated, the lipstick poised a few inches from her mouth. "I feel naked without it."

He crossed the room and leaned over her from behind, placed his cup on the table beside hers, and touched his lips to her neck. "Force yourself."

She shivered at his touch. "God, I thought I was long past the point of being nervous when a man entered my bedroom, but you make me feel like I'm about fourteen years old."

"You don't look it, take my word."

"You're telling *me* I don't look it!" She reluctantly dropped her lipstick on the table and reached for her cup. He continued to nuzzle her neck while she sipped. "Ummm . . . perfect."

"An old family recipe. I'll have my secretary type you a copy—"

"Now *she* looks fourteen."

"—and while I'm thinking of it, you're almost out of whiskey."

"I know, Harry was over here the other night and drank me out of . . . Oh, for God's sake, why did I bring that up?"

He smiled at her reflection in the mirror. "No problem. I can live with it."

"I know, but why can't I keep my goddamned mouth shut?"

"Doesn't bother me." He hoisted his glass to her reflection in the mirror. "To good old Harry."

She turned around on the seat to face him, a glint of anger in her eyes. "You really don't care, do you?"

"Hmmm . . ." he said, sipping his drink.

"*Do* you?"

"Well, you've already told me that you're seeing other men, so I don't have a hell of a lot to say about it, do I?"

"You could at least act a little perturbed."

"Why?"

"I mean, you could show *some* emotion."

He clenched his teeth and glared at the bathroom door. "*All right, Harry, you alcoholic bastard, come out of there before I come in and get you!*" He looked at her. "How's that? Better?"

"You're making me feel like a fool."

"Well, I'm not about to wring my hands and pace the floor over good old Harry, if that's what you mean."

She stared up at him for a moment without speaking, then slid her arms around his waist and rested her cheek against him. "Oh, I'm sorry, hon. I really wanted us to have a good afternoon."

"Let's not waste it, then." He tugged her to her feet and untied the towel from around her head. Her hair felt cool on his fingers. He bent to kiss her.

"Let me go." She tried to pull away. "I want to do something with my face. I feel like an old bat!"

"Yeah, sure"—he held her tighter—"thirty-four and fading fast."

"Oh, fuck you! What do you know? You look like a goddamned baby! When I was your age I had already been through two marriages and had a four-year-old kid to feed!"

Her outburst startled him. He pulled her over to the foot of the bed and sat her down. "Listen, if I'm going to have to go through all this to seduce you, I'd just as soon go out and get splattered by a cab."

His words made her smile. "By the way, how's your lip?"

"It hurts like hell."

"I shouldn't have done that. I'm sorry."

"Well, whether you believe it or not, I didn't stand you up on purpose. I had no idea you'd be waiting up for me to call." He reached for her again, and again she pulled away.

"Will you stop being so goddamned *nice.*"

He felt a flash of anger. "What the hell's the matter with you, Ann? Do you want me to leave, or what?"

"No!" She went to get her drink from the dressing table and came back and sat beside him again. As she sipped, her hazel eyes stared at him over the rim, framing a question. "Tell me," she finally asked, "what the hell are you trying to prove?"

"I don't understand what you mean."

"I mean, every guy I *know* is a prick, why should you be so different?"

"If that's true, maybe you should think about changing your friends. Take good old Harry, for instance . . ."

"Don't, please . . ."

"Okay, so what are you getting at?"

"What I said—what are you trying to prove?"

"Seriously?"

"Yes."

"Nothing."

"I don't believe you."

"I can't help that."

"Well, why are you just . . . just floating around, then?"

"What do you mean 'floating around'? I'm not floating around."

"You know what I mean—why aren't you married? Are you afraid of responsibility, or what?"

"You must be kidding. All I have are goddamned responsibilities. And, frankly, I don't see a hell of a lot to recommend marriage."

"That's not the reason."

"No, of course not, but you probably wouldn't understand my reasons if I told you."

"I'm curious. I want to know."

"Okay, I'm not ashamed to tell you. Because I'm Catholic and we're only supposed to marry once, for keeps. That's what I was taught and it's one of those foolish, outdated things that I still happen to believe. And I'm not about to worry about it. When it comes, it comes. My father was past thirty when he married my mother, and he was intelligent enough and secure enough in his profession to build a good marriage. I figure if I do half as well as he has, I'll be way ahead of the game. And don't try to convince me that what I believe is unrealistic, because I know damn well I'm not the *only* person in the world who believes that."

"I just want to know one thing."

"What's that?"

"Where in the name of God were you ten years ago when I needed you?"

He laughed to break the tension. "Probably hanging around Malibu beach on my surfboard."

"I was pretty then, I really was. . . ."

"Are you asking for a compliment?"

"Yes."

"All I can say is, I'll bet you were!"

"You lovable bastard!" She laughed. They kissed and held each other for a while, before she slipped from his arms and crossed the room to the light switch. The sound of the rain was suddenly louder in the darkness, and somewhere in the distance they could hear the crackle of thunder. They undressed and snuggled in each other's arms beneath the heavy quilt.

"I told you it would be nice."

"My first executive lunch, can you believe that?" He reached down to touch her.

"You don't have to . . . I've been ready since I walked in the door."

Her words were warm against his cheek, and he raised his body so she could slide under him. And then, in that quick, experienced way she had, she took him inside her. She spread her legs and made herself comfortable and began to move herself methodically, expertly. He held himself back as long as he could, and it was a while before she felt him begin to quicken. As she felt his juices flowing into her, she deliberately gouged her sharp nails into his back. Only when she heard him cry out in pain did she allow herself to finish.

Later, after she had washed and dressed, she came back and sat on the side of the bed and watched him as he slept. He was lying on his stomach with an arm across the pillow where her head had been, his face turned toward her. In the dim light of the bathroom, she could see his swollen mouth where she had bitten him earlier, and the four deep scratches in the middle of his back where she had dug her nails into him. She sat there for a while, looking down at him, remembering:

Three years before, when he had first come to New York, everyone at ITRC had been anxious to meet him. They had all known about him, of course—who his father was—and they had read occasional mentions of him in the Hollywood columns. Half the women in the building, married and unmarried, were already making plans to seduce him, herself included. Half the men were thinking of how to buddy-buddy up to him, to bask in his reflection.

And somehow, he had disappointed them all.

He was not what they expected him to be, the dashing swashbuckling son of a movie idol who went through the company's females adding notches to his gun. Instead, he was reserved and gentlemanly, courteous and dedicated. He was good at his job, which surprised them, and by demanding that they be the same, he made them uncomfortable. And he had such a terrible, penetrating honesty. And such a vicious . . . *fairness.* They could look in his eyes and see themselves reflected exactly as they were, no better, no worse. Unwittingly, he had divided the company into camps. On one side were the politicians, the climbers. On the other, the smaller, quieter, dedicated, hardworking group to which he belonged. And for those like herself, to whom being accepted by the "in" crowd was perhaps the most important thing in life, he remained an enigma. Being seen with him offered no particular status; he would just as soon have lunch in the employees' cafeteria as one of the expensive restaurants frequented by the successful people of the music industry. And no matter what they did, what kind of subtle pressures they applied, he simply refused to be drawn into their games. So she had avoided him—until she learned he was about to be transferred back to California. And then she had almost thrown herself at him. And in the short time they had known each other, the few dates they had enjoyed together had been memorable ones for her. She had found herself thinking of him, remembering things he had said for days afterward.

She got to her feet quietly, so as not to awaken him, and tiptoed to the bathroom. She returned with a small jar, touched her fingertips to the blue salve, and gently began to massage the ugly scratches on his back. She leaned down to brush his cheek with her lips and saw the traces of gray at his temple and realized, for the first time, that he was not the innocent, overprotected boy she had been trying to convince herself he was. He was a man, a very strong, decent, honest man. The realization filled her with a sudden rage at herself—for what, she didn't know—and she subconsciously drew her nails across the scratches and watched him pull away and sit up and blink his eyes.

NEW YORK
MARCH 1961

ITRC's production and sales personnel referred to the company's higher administrators as "the men in the tower"—which they were.

The higher an executive was in the company, the closer he was to the bottom line, and the more insulated he was from the day-to-day record business. And where production and sales people—especially production people—tended to think of themselves as indispensable/creative personalities, marketing and accounting executives thought of them as being merely effective or ineffective.

In "the tower," personality rarely entered into the decision-making process.

Saul Goldman's company, Chartmaker Records, had been a "singles" company. Its two fairly successful albums had been handled through the record club of an ITRC competitor and since ITRC had never dealt with Chartmaker on any level, there was only a slight chance that anyone in marketing would have known who produced the Chartmaker albums. For that reason, until a few weeks before, Mark Donovan had never heard of Paulie Schultz.

It is significant, therefore, that shortly after three P.M., when Paulie stepped into Mark Donovan's office to keep their appointment, Mark experienced a sudden and intense dislike for Paulie. He understood, without knowing why, that Paulie Schultz was exactly the kind of person who would be attracted to Arrow Records.

Nevertheless, his greeting was warm. "How are you, Paul?" he said, standing, offering his hand across the desk. "I've heard a lot about you recently, it's nice to meet you."

Paulie offered him a limp hand, took the seat opposite, and as was his custom, immediately tried to assume the upper hand in the conversation. "I didn't know if I had the right place or not," he said in his whiny voice. "Where the hell's your secretary?"

"I don't have one," Mark said, hiding his shock at the man's rudeness. "Officially"—he tried to smile—"I'm between jobs. She's still with the record club, and I'm setting things in order for Arrow."

"You're in charge of the whole Arrow thing, huh?" Paulie asked.

"Yes, I'll be president of that division of the company."

"Well, Jesus"—Paulie looked around Mark's office disdainfully—"to be in charge of one of the hottest labels in the business, they sure gave you a shitty little office!"

Mark almost took the bait.

He was tempted to explain that in less than three months he would be sitting in a spacious office at the top of Sunset Strip. It would be furnished in complementing shades of blue and gold, and there would be a large window behind his desk that would enable him to see all the way to the Los Angeles International Airport.

He started to explain, but he didn't. "Why?" he asked coolly. "Did you come in here to talk business, or buy furniture?"

Unlike Mark, Paulie couldn't keep the shock from registering on his face. Somebody had definitely given him the wrong information on this guy. He'd heard that Donovan had been handed the job on a silver platter because of his father's friendship with the president of the company.

He'd better step a little more carefully, until he had this one figured out.

"Listen, don't get pissed off," he said smoothly. "I just expected you to have one of those superimpressive offices with a good-looking broad out front. You know, the whole shot. You got to excuse me, though, I'm like that, I always say what's on my mind."

"In that case," Mark said, "we shouldn't have too much trouble communicating, right?"

"Right," Paulie said mildly, looking for a weakness in Mark Donovan, and temporarily finding none. "Okay, lemme tell you what I got in mind. I been thinking it over. I decided I wanna put up my own label, release through ITRC, you know what I mean?"

"No can do," Mark said. "What's your second choice?"

Jesus! What a cold son of a bitch, Paulie thought. "What the fuck kind of an answer is that?" he asked angrily. " 'No can do'? You wanna talk business, or you wanna sit there and play the role?"

Mark's fingers unconsciously began to tap the arm of his chair. He was becoming agitated. "We've got one label now," he explained, trying hard to control his temper. "ITRC Records. In two and a half months, we're going to be releasing products on another label, Arrow Records. We are working from a completely detailed five-year program, and we will not, in the foreseeable future, have the necessary machinery to distribute and collect for a third label. I'm not trying to impress you with my importance, Paul, I'm just trying to keep this conversation within the realm of possibilities."

Paulie clutched the attaché case in his lap. He was tempted to tell this turkey to go get fucked. He had a hundred and fifty grand to spend. He could put up his own label. He did not have to take any shit from anybody.

But on the other hand, he could also lose his hundred and fifty thousand dollars.

"Yeah, I know what you mean," he said placatingly.

"What's your second choice?" Mark repeated.

"Independent production. My own company, my own artists, no artistic interference, I keep the publishing."

"Yes, maybe we can do something along those lines," Mark said. "But before we get into that, I'd like to tell you what we're in a position to offer you as a staff producer:

"First of all, I want to say that we would like to have you join our label. We know your track record, we feel you can consistently produce a salable product for us. I'm prepared to offer you thirty-five thousand dollars a year for the first year of a three-year commitment. Forty thousand for the second, fifty for the third—at our option, of course. Also, royalties based on two percent of everything you produce that is bought and paid for by our distributors, plus a recording budget of three hundred thousand dollars a year, not including unlimited use of our recording facilities—"

"Not interested," Paulie said firmly.

"—plus, a full-time secretary and an expense account not to exceed four hundred dollars per month. Plus top-priority promotion on everything you produce that is accepted by our sales department, plus a minimum of two personal profiles a year, for the length of your contract, in our company-owned rock magazine, *Platter Talk*, which will begin operating with a guaranteed circulation of two hundred and fifty thousand copies per issue—"

"Not interested," Paulie said a little less firmly.

"Plus profit sharing and treasury stock, when and if it becomes available."

"Publishing?" Paulie asked tentatively.

"No can do."

Paulie had somehow manipulated himself into the big time, and the realization was shocking. He had prepared himself to wheedle and con, as he had been accustomed to doing when he did business with, and through, Saul Goldman.

But this guy, Donovan, was different. He came right out with it. This is the deal. No crap involved. We want you, do you want us? Make up your mind. You want security? This is it. You want recognition? Here it is. Take it or leave it. . . .

· 215

Jesus, he was tempted. "No," he said.

"You realize what you're turning down, don't you?" Mark asked. "The best job in the business. Nobody is spending the money we are. We're talking about a *minimum* hundred thousand a year, and everything that goes with it."

"I know. But I gotta pass."

"No problem, it's your decision," Mark said, dismissing the offer. "Let's talk about your production company, then. We can do business on that basis, but the requirements will be severe. If we contract with you for a certain amount of product, we must be sure that you can deliver all of it, without regard to any future royalties you might anticipate from us."

"I got the money," Paulie said.

"Have you incorporated yet?"

"No, but I got the money to do it right," Paulie said.

"Have you arrived at your capitalization figure yet?"

"Yeah, a hundred and fifty grand."

"No," Mark said patiently, "I don't mean your subscription figure. I mean, how much actual capital do you propose to have in your cash reserves when you open your doors for business?"

"I *know* what you mean!" Paulie said angrily. "I told you, I'm putting up a hundred and fifty grand."

"We'll have to know who your investors will be," Mark persisted. "We must be certain that you have complete control of the funds."

"That's easy," Paulie said smugly. "My sole investor will be me."

"When will you be able to show us some papers?"

It was the moment Paulie had been waiting for all his life. Maybe his father wasn't a big movie star. Maybe he didn't have a cushy job, sitting on his ass collecting a salary from a big company. But he had the money.

He had the goddamn money!

He opened the attaché case in his lap, flipped a brown envelope across the desk.

Mark opened it. Inside were escrow papers: one hundred and fifty thousand dollars in a trust account at the First National Bank of Manhattan, pending filing of the corporation papers for a record-production company to be called Dynamic Productions.

All of the money had been personally deposited by Paul Marvin Schultz.

"Very good," Mark said. "Do I owe you an apology?"

Paulie was tempted, checked the urge to gloat. This was one of the few offices in the music industry where a check of that size made no significant difference in the way business would be conducted. "Okay," he said, "now that we've got all that fucking bullshit out of the way, let's talk business."

And they talked.

CHICAGO
MARCH 1961

It was Monday afternoon, a few minutes past five P.M., and Monroe's office staff had just left for the day. He was on the phone to his Dallas–Fort Worth promotion man when they walked in on him.

The older man, clearly the boss, was in his early or mid-fifties. Moon-faced, heavyset, thick muscles dissolving to fat. Gray hair, cut short. Faded eyes that covered the room without expression. A small scar that dribbled from the corner of his mouth like dried spit.

The other man was twelve to fifteen years younger, a few inches shorter, perhaps seventy pounds lighter. Receding black hair combed into a ducktail behind oversize ears. Thin-faced and nervous. A dopehead, probably speed. He stood just inside the doorway, shifting his weight from side to side, exposing a brown leather strap across his chest and the edge of a small-frame automatic shoulder holster.

The gray-haired man approached the desk, motioning Monroe to get off the phone. When Monroe was unable to comply quickly enough, he dropped a thick forefinger on the telephone's chrome hookswitch, severing Monroe's connection.

Ted Green had given Monroe explicit instructions about what to do if this ever happened. Now, the one thing that Green had stressed the most clanged a warning in the back of Monroe's mind:

Whatever you do, little brother, don't try to show them how tough you are.

Fuck that! Monroe thought. I'll be goddamned if I'm gonna let this paddy motherfucker walk in my office and start ordering me around!

"Hey!" He glared up at the man. "What the hell do you—"

The hood slugged him.

It was a vicious blow—unexpected, the man's entire weight behind it. It whirled Monroe's chair around and sent him careening into the steel filing cabinet behind the desk.

He lost consciousness for an instant, regaining his senses as he was being carried across the room and dumped on the couch.

He shook his head several times, trying to clear it. When he could focus his eyes again, he saw the gray-haired man sitting behind the desk with his feet propped up in front of him, smoking a cigarette.

He was explaining to Monroe that he and his friend represented some "very important Chicago businessmen" who had been watching Monroe's progress for some time, and with great interest. They wanted in. Fifty-one percent.

Monroe tried to concentrate on what the man was saying, but at the same time, his mind was racing ahead. He was vulnerable. They could not have chosen a worse time to try to muscle in on him.

Rydell Mercer's record had hit so suddenly, and the money had started coming in so fast, Monroe had not had time to convert his company's assets to certificates, bonds, or any other nonnegotiables. At that moment, Big City Records had two separate accounts at two different Chicago banks. One held three hundred and seven thousand dollars. The other, two hundred and forty-one thousand dollars.

Monroe knew that if these hoods were smart and had as much backing as they claimed, they could own his company within a week.

So he let the man finish talking, then explained his own situation, just as he and Ted Green had concocted it beforehand:

He was not in a position to make such a decision on his own. He had two silent partners, a retired doctor and a real-estate woman, both of whom had backed him from time to time with operating capital. True, he was listed on the business license as the sole owner, but he was indebted to them, and still not able to sign away any of the company without repaying the money he had borrowed.

The gray-haired man wanted to see some papers.

They were at his lawyer's office, Monroe said. But he could have them there by tomorrow morning.

For the first time, the other gangster spoke from the doorway. "You're a lying piece of shit, nigger!" His voice was angry, brittle.

"I ain't lying, man!"

Monroe knew immediately that he had made a mistake. His words had come too quickly, too sharp-edged. He watched the big-eared hood pull a gun from beneath his cheap blue windbreaker, flick the safety off, and move toward him.

"Who do you think you're bullshitting, boy—some fucking clowns off the street?" The gangster's words fell on Monroe's head like pieces of broken glass. "Listen, we've already checked you out good. We know everything there is to know about you—about your old lady, your kid, your big house in Oak Park, your *three* fucking cars, f'Chrissakes. You're stupid, you know why? Because you're sitting on top of the world right now and you're going to fuck around and play games and get your lying head shot off!"

. . . don't try to show them how tough you are.

Monroe remembered Green's words again, made himself sound as cowed as he could. "I ain't lying, I swear to God I'm telling you-all the truth—"

"Lemme tell you something, you black son of a bitch!" the gangster interrupted angrily, touching the cold gun barrel to Monroe's nose. "You've got more than three hundred grand in the bank, that we know. It may make you pretty hot shit to some people, but it don't mean a goddamned thing to me. To me, you're just another nigger. And if I have to kill you, you won't be the first one I killed, and you damn sure won't be the last! What do you think I'm doing, standing here jacking off? I already told you—we know everything there is to know about you. There ain't no fucking retired doctor, and there ain't no goddamned real-estate woman, either! You tell one more lie, I promise you, I'll blow your brains all over this room!"

Monroe didn't want to die, but he had too much pride, too much self-respect, to beg this hophead for his life. He would rather die than crawl.

He raised his face to meet the gangster's gaze, to show that he was not afraid, but the look in the man's eyes sent a shiver through his body. He was looking up at two black sewers in a translucent skull—the look of death. Monroe had spent too much time on the streets not to recognize it when he saw it.

The man, he knew, was about to kill him.

He saw the hood's fingers tighten around the gun, and snatches of his life leaped into his brain: the good things—his wife, his child, his home, his business, the people who depended on him. Suddenly he didn't want to die. Not now, not when it had all come together for him. It wasn't the money, he didn't really care about the money. Fuck it, they could have it.

He just didn't want to die.

He opened his mouth to plead for his life, to beg if he had to—to tell them the truth—but the other man spoke from across the room.

"Back off! Jesus! You got the little nigger scared to death, can't you see that? What do you want him to do, keel over from a goddamned heart attack?"

"He's lying! He's trying to con us, I tell you—"

"Bullshit. Look at him. He ain't got enough guts to lie. Ease up, lemme talk to him. . . ."

Monroe waited. The gun wavered, pointed down at his belly for an instant, moved away.

"How long will it take you to get in touch with that doctor and that real-estate woman?" the gray-haired man asked.

Monroe gingerly touched his fingertips to the large welt that was beginning to rise on the side of his face, while he tried to remember what Ted Green had told him to say.

"Well, uh . . . Dr. Taylor had a heart attack a few months ago. He's out in California now, living with his daughter. I can call him tonight. The real-estate woman, Mrs. Griffith, lives here in town. I can get in touch with her anytime. But she didn't put up all that much money, Dr. Taylor put up most of it."

"Okay, I'll tell you what to do. You call your doctor friend tonight. You tell him to get his ass up here immediately, you got that?"

"Yes, sir."

"And you call your real-estate woman. Tell her the big boys came to see you. The big boys, you understand?"

"Yes, sir."

"Tell her we're moving in. No, fuck that—tell her we're already in!"

"Yes, sir."

The gangster removed his feet from the desk, stubbed his cigarette out in the ashtray, got up, and came around the desk.

Monroe kept his head down. He was watching the man's hands, ready to roll with the blow if the gangster tried to sucker-punch him again.

"Now, lemme tell you something very important, Mr. Wilcox . . ." The "Mr." came out mocking, disrespectful. "There had better be a doctor and a real-estate woman, because if there ain't, if you're trying to be cute, you're dead, understand?"

"Yes, sir."

"Remember this: you are still in business because me and my friends let you stay in business."

"Yes, sir."

"And you are still alive because we let you stay alive."

"Yes, sir."

"Okay, now that you understand that, remember what I'm telling you. This Friday night at six o'clock we sit down and sign papers—you and your doctor friend and your real-estate cunt. You try to pull any funny shit, Mr. Wilcox, and Friday night at exactly one minute after six, you will have been dead exactly one minute, understand?"

"Yes, sir."

"You sure you understand, boy?" the other gangster snarled from the doorway.

"Yes, sir."

"I can't hear you, nigger."

It was an old street trick, but Monroe fell for it. He turned his head to respond to the big-eared hood's baiting, and the other man hit him a shattering blow that sent him to the floor. He felt a sudden explosion of pain in his groin.

He heard them laughing as he lay there, his vomit mixing with the faint smell of blood.

An hour later, Monroe was sitting in Ted Green's little upstairs office, holding an ice pack to his swollen face while he recounted everything he could remember about the men, how they had looked and what they had said.

Green sat across the desk from him, chewing a cigar, sipping Scotch, listening in silence, his face impassive.

When Monroe had finished, Green made him go through the entire episode again. After Green had heard it a second time, he pulled a leather-bound scrapbook from the bottom drawer and slid it across to Monroe. "See if they're in there."

Monroe studied the book. It was similar to a police mug book, except, instead of posed front and profile photographs, it was full of snapshots. Some of them showed as many as five or six men. Most of the men were white, all of them looked like killers.

Monroe leafed through the book. Taking his time, studying each picture carefully. A dozen pages later, he found a photograph that resembled the gray-haired hood, but it was old and faded. He showed it to Green. "This might be him, but I ain't sure."

Green studied the picture briefly, grunted. "Keep on looking," he said. "See if you see him again."

Monroe resumed leafing through the book. A few pages later, he spotted another, later picture of the same man. He showed it to Green. "That's him."

"Umm-hmmm . . ." Green said, studying it carefully. "You sure that's him, now?"

"Yeah, I'm pretty sure. . . ." Monroe said, looking at the picture again, shifting the ice pack on his face.

"*Pretty* sure could get us all killed," Green said emphatically. "What we want is *damn* sure!"

Monroe stared at the picture for a full minute, squinting through a nearly closed left eye. The man in the picture was standing beside a pickup truck. Monroe studied the round face, the brush-cut hair, finally focusing on what looked like a small scar at the right-hand corner of the subject's mouth.

"That's him," he said, now positive. "That's the motherfucker."

Green chewed on his cigar, said nothing.

"You know him?" Monroe asked anxiously.

"Moe Fryman?" Green snorted derisively, nodded affirmatively.

"Is he heavy?"

Green's expression was knowledgeable. "Little brother, every son of a bitch in the world is bad when he's got the drop on you."

"Who is he? I mean, what's his thing?"

"Lemme see . . ." Green rubbed the bridge of his nose thoughtfully, trying to separate the faces in his mental file. "Well, he owns a little company over on the Northside, on Diversey Avenue, I believe. Runs five, maybe six dozen jukeboxes out of there. A half-a-hundred game machines. Makes a little book on the side. Does a little flunkying for the syndicate, Mickey Mouse shit. You know, 'gofering.' " He slid the book back across the desk to Monroe. "Here. We got one of them pegged—see if you can find the other one."

Again Monroe leafed through the book. He was almost at the end when he stopped over another photograph. This one couldn't have been more than a couple of years old. There were five men in it, evidently sitting at a restaurant table. The picture was slightly out of focus, as though taken by a concealed camera. But the man Green had identified as Moe Fryman was clearly identifiable. The other one, the one who had seemed so intent on killing Monroe, was on Fryman's immediate right.

"Here they are!" Monroe jabbed his stubby forefinger at the two faces excitedly. "There ain't no doubt about it this time, man, this is them!"

Hatred distorted Green's face. "Artie DeAngelo. I should have guessed."

"You know him?" Monroe asked.

"Yeah, I know him, all right, that punk motherfucker!"

"He's a killer, ain't he?"

"Got that right."

"Okay, so what do we do now?"

"We don't do nothing—yet," Green said, regaining most of his composure, puffing his cigar. "We gotta check them out first, see who they're working for these days. I'll handle that. All you've got to do is keep taking care of business, same as usual. But be cool, don't talk to nobody. They got a boy who works on Fryman's machines who's supposed to be pretty good at electronics. He might of bugged your phone already, maybe your whole office, ain't no telling."

"But I gotta tell Maudie. I can't walk in the house looking like this and not say nothing."

"Bullshit! You don't tell *nobody* what happened! Not your old lady, or nobody else! You tell her, the first thing she's gonna want you to do is call the fuzz. We don't want no cops in on this. Ain't no telling what might happen before this is over with."

"Yeah, but if I walk in the house looking like this . . ." Monroe removed the ice pack so Green could get another look at his face.

Green regarded Monroe's misshapen features with a trace of amusement. "Tell her a couple of paddies kicked your ass. If she don't believe that"—he chuckled softly—"tell her to call me. I'll vouch for it."

"Why don't you knock that shit off, man!" Monroe said angrily. Both of his eyes were swollen almost shut, there was a huge welt on the left side of his face, a steady, insistent bell was throbbing somewhere deep inside his skull, and his balls felt like they had been crushed with a hammer. The last thing in the world he needed right now was Ted Green's jokes. "I'm coming to you for help, I ain't coming here for you to get your nuts off on my bad luck!"

"Hey, little brother," Green chided gently, the singsong North Carolina *geechee* accent more pronounced in his voice, "I didn't mean no harm. Shit, you my main man, I thought you knew that. I wouldn't let nobody stomp all over you without trying to do something about it."

"Aw, I'm sorry, Ted." Monroe was immediately ashamed of his outburst. "I know you were just playing around, but I guess I just ain't ready for this shit. Them cats walking in on me like that . . . threatening to kill me, threatening my family. It ain't even getting beat up that really pisses me off. Shit, getting beat up ain't no big thing. I had that happen before. It's just that they didn't have no respect for me *at all*. I work my ass off all these years, get a little something going for me—and they think I'm just gonna let them walk in and take it away from me. Even if I didn't know you, I wouldn't let them get away with that. Man, you know, I wonder sometimes if most paddies ain't crazy?"

Green opened his mouth to speak, changed his mind, puffed his cigar.

"Dig . . . when am I gonna see you again?" Monroe asked.

"I'm gonna need a couple of days," Green said. "Call me Wednesday, day after tomorrow, noon sharp. I should know something by then. In the meantime, you'll be getting a long-distance call sometime tomorrow. Just act natural and go along with it. Let's see if we can't set these motherfuckers up."

"Got it," Monroe said.

The call came late the following afternoon.

The operator informed Monroe that Dr. Clarence Taylor was returning Monroe's call from Lancaster, California. A few seconds later, a distinguished-sounding black voice—it bore a faint resemblance to Ted Green's, but wasn't—came on the line.

Monroe's message had sounded urgent. Was there something wrong?

"Yes, Doctor," Monroe said. "I think you'd better come up here immediately."

"What's the trouble, Monroe?"

"I'd rather not say on the phone."

"How bad is it?"

"As bad as it can get."

"You can't handle it without me?"

"No, sir, I need you here. You'd better come as soon as you can."

"Okay, but I can't leave immediately. I have a couple of things I must attend to. I'll tell you what—I'll try to get there no later than Friday afternoon, how's that?"

"That's too late. The shit's gonna hit the fan Friday night."

"Very well . . ." The voice sighed resignedly. "I'll get there late Thursday afternoon. I'll call your office as soon as I arrive."

They said good-bye. Monroe kept the receiver to his ear for a few seconds. There was an almost inaudible click. Ted Green was right: the phone was bugged.

The next day, promptly at noon, Monroe made his call from the restaurant in the next block. The phone rang once.

"Wilcox?"

"Yeah."

"Take this number down." Green gave him an address. "Be there at ten o'clock tonight. Don't tell nobody where you're going, and make sure you're not followed, got that?"

"Got it," Monroe said.

He left the office shortly after nine o'clock. It was a dank, overcast night. The air was heavy, the streets almost deserted. The day had been warmer, a few flakes of snow had fallen intermittently with the late-winter rain. Now, as the night wore on, small mounds of muddy ice had packed against the curbstones, making driving slow and treacherous.

Monroe drove with the windows up, the heater on, the radio tuned softly to a jazz station. He had brought a gun from home—an old five-shot Colt .32—cleaned it, and loaded it with fresh ammunition. It was on the seat beside him, and he kept his hand on it most of the way, his eyes flickering back and forth between the windshield and the rearview mirror.

Twice he thought he detected suspicious headlights behind him.

Each time, he circled the block, parked, and waited.

Both times, the cars continued past without slowing down.

By the time he found the address, a small warehouse in an industrial district on South State Street, his skin and underclothing were soaked with nervous perspiration, but he was certain he had not been followed.

He circled the block to make sure. Returned, parked, and walked back to the corrugated-steel door at the side of the building. Before he had a chance to knock, a squat dark-skinned man holding a revolver beckoned him inside and quickly bolted the door behind him.

Leon Green led him along a darkened hallway into a small, dimly lit office at the back of the building, where Ted Green was seated behind a desk beside a far wall. Two burly blacks occupied a small couch across from Green; both held sawed-off shotguns, casually pointed at the concrete floor.

Monroe nodded at them. They half-nodded a return greeting.

"I checked things out when he got here." Leon Green's husky growl came from the doorway behind Monroe. "Everything looks cool, so far."

"Stay on it," Green said. Then, to Monroe: "Sit down, little brother, lemme run it down to you."

Green had done some checking. Fryman and DeAngelo were not presently connected. They were, in fact, badly *dis*connected, perhaps about to be murdered.

Fryman had flown out to Las Vegas over the Christmas holidays to do some gambling. He had gotten in over his head. Not bad, only for about eight grand. Since the Vegas people knew him, in lieu of payment they had requested that he do them a favor.

One of their bagmen was scheduled to bring a quarter-million in "cream" back to Chicago over the New Year's weekend. His bosses

226 ·

had been tipped that a girl he was seeing in Vegas had quietly, suspiciously, booked passage from Los Angeles to Mexico.

From there, to Buenos Aires.

For two.

The Vegas people were not absolutely certain the bagman planned to skip with the money. And since he had always played straight with them, they couldn't accuse him without arousing the anger of some of his highly placed Chicago friends. They decided the best thing to do would be to have him watched.

They had put him on a chartered junket to Los Angeles, and stayed with him until he boarded the plane for Chicago. Fryman, who had notified DeAngelo to be at the airport in Chicago, was already on the plane when he came aboard. Since the bagman had never met Fryman, he had no reason to suspect that he was being watched. If he remained straight, he would never find out. But if he tried to skip when he got to Chicago, Fryman and DeAngelo were supposed to grab him and deliver him and the money safely.

The plan was simple. The only problem was: Fryman and De-Angelo lost the bagman less than a mile from O'Hare airport.

The big boys were pissed. Not only did they put Fryman's eight grand back on the books, they gave him and DeAngelo three months to make up the quarter-million-dollar loss.

Time was now running out on them. They only had until the end of March to make good. They didn't have the money, and they were scared.

Fryman's youngest daughter had a boyfriend who worked in a downtown Chicago bank. From what Ted Green could learn, the boyfriend evidently told Fryman's daughter about the Big City Records account. She mentioned it to Fryman.

Who told DeAngelo.

But the most important thing was, it seemed pretty obvious that Fryman and DeAngelo were without real backup muscle. They were vulnerable, with nobody to jump salty if they were pushed around.

Green had a plan. The men would be conned, then taken up to the Canadian border, where their clothes would be removed, the fear of God laid on their heads, and they would be allowed to get back to Chicago the best way they could. With the trouble they were in, they would probably keep right on going. If they did, everybody would simply assume that they had skipped out on their syndicate debt.

Green's plan was a little involved. He had to be sure everybody was protected, just in case, so he and Monroe went over it for the next hour, until Monroe knew exactly what he was supposed to do.

At four o'clock Thursday afternoon, "Dr. Taylor" called Monroe again. This time, however, it wasn't the same voice, it was Ted Green's voice. Monroe recognized it because he knew who it was, but anyone eavesdropping would have been hard pressed to tell the difference.

"Mr. Wilcox, I just arrived from California. I've taken a room downtown at the Roosevelt Hotel. What time would be convenient for us to get together?"

"How about sometime this evening, Doctor—say, six-thirty, seven o'clock? Maybe the three of us, you, me, and Estelle, could have dinner there?"

"No, no, I really think it would be better to conduct our business in your office."

"Whatever you say."

"Have you spoken with Estelle yet?"

"No, I figured I'd wait for you to get here. You know how nervous Estelle is. It's gonna take both of us to keep her from falling apart."

"Yes, you're right. I'm the one who talked her into lending you money for your company, so I should call her. But I'd feel like a complete fool talking to her and not having the slightest idea what the problem is. For God's sake, will you please tell me what's going on?"

"Gangsters . . " Monroe said.

"Gangsters?"

". . . trying to move in on the company."

"I see." Monroe could understand why Green had been such a successful con man. His voice conveyed exactly the right mixture of anxiety and fear. "This is serious. I'll call her right away, Monroe, and get back to you within the hour."

"I ain't going nowhere," Monroe said.

Again, before Monroe replaced the receiver, he heard a slight click. Good, they were still listening.

He waited, hunched forward in his seat, his fingers nervously drumming the desktop.

The phone rang.

"Mr. Wilcox, this is Estelle Griffith!" an excited female voice came over the wire. "What's going on there? I just received the most frightening call from Dr. Taylor! He said something about . . . about *gangsters!*"

"That's right, Estelle. They're trying to move in on the company."

"My God! Why didn't you call me sooner?"

"I didn't want to scare you, and there was nothing we could do until we talked to Dr. Taylor."

"Have you called the police yet?"

"No, they said they'd kill me if I called the cops."

"Well, you should call the police. We have to have some protection, don't we?"

"Estelle . . . they said they'd hurt Maudie and the baby if I did."

"Oh, my God—no!" The woman sounded desperate. "I know you can't endanger your family, Mr. Wilcox, but we've got to do something. I've got almost everything I own tied up in your company. I had to use most of my savings and secure a second mortgage on my home to raise the money you needed to put out that Rydell Mercer record. I don't want to lose it all."

She began to weep, and Monroe could feel himself being caught up in her feigned anguish. She was one of Ted Green's people. Monroe didn't know her, had never even met her, but whoever she was, she was a hell of an actress.

"Now, listen, Estelle," he said firmly, "you coming apart ain't gonna do us no good at all. Pull yourself together, now. If we let them scare us, we don't have no chance at all. "Listen"—he lowered his voice to a confidential whisper, knowing the hoods were probably listening in on the conversation—"they don't know Dr. Taylor's in town yet. And we don't have to meet with them until tomorrow night, which gives us plenty of time to come up with a plan. And if we can't think of nothing by then, we still got plenty of time to call the cops."

"But, Mr. Wilcox—"

"Dr. Taylor is gonna call me back in a little while. The three of us can get together tonight, here—say, about seven o'clock. Don't worry, now, we'll come up with something."

"No, I can't wait!" She sounded determined. "I've already told Dr. Taylor to meet me at your office in an hour."

"Estelle—"

"Don't try to stop me, Mr. Wilcox. I've already told you, I'm on my way. I'll be leaving here as soon as I take a bath and get my clothes on."

She broke the connection. Monroe listened for the now-familiar click. It was louder this time. Whoever was listening was in a hurry.

Monroe had an hour to wait for the next phone call. This call would come from another of Ted Green's people, another woman, who was, at this moment, watching Monroe's house.

This morning, before leaving for work. Monroe had left the basement door unlocked. Two of Leon Green's boys were to sneak into the house sometime before four P.M., at the same time that the woman arrived to stand on the corner a half-block away. The men, heavily armed, would stand at the front basement window, watching the woman with the Jehovah's Witness magazines, who was watching to see if anyone approached Monroe's house. If the woman saw anything unusual, she would set her magazines on the curbstone and begin to apply face makeup—a warning signal to the men inside.

If nobody suspicious showed by five o'clock, she would leave the corner and walk the block and a half to Madison Street, where she would call Monroe from a drugstore and give him a prearranged all-clear signal.

Then she would sit at the lunch counter in the drugstore until she received a phone call telling her the plan had gone off without trouble. After the call, she would walk back to Monroe's house, get in her car, and drive away, which was the signal for Leon Green's boys to slip out of Monroe's basement.

That was plan A.

Plan B was what worried Monroe, because there was no Plan B.

He sat quietly, his head in his hands. Waiting. Wondering if he was doing the right things to protect his business and his family.

At five minutes to five, the buzzer sounded on his desk. It was Clarice, his secretary. She was leaving for the day. Did he need anything?

No.

A minute later, the buzzer sounded again. It was Charlie Crawford, the company's national sales manager. He was having dinner that evening with the new program director at WJJD. Did Monroe have anything in particular he wanted discussed?

No. Crawford could handle it any way he wanted.

It was a couple of minutes after five when Willie buzzed from the control booth. He had just finished the final mix-down on the final track of the Rydell Mercer album. He was excited about it. It might be good enough for a single. Did Monroe want to hear it now?

Not now, maybe tomorrow, when they were both fresh. Go on home and get some rest. Give it a night to cool.

He heard them leave. All of them—Clarice, Charlie, Willie, the two girls in accounting. The building was quiet except for the tick-

tick-tick of the faulty forced-air heating unit in a far corner of his office.

He waited. . . .

Ten minutes after five. The woman should be walking to the drugstore now.

He waited. . . .

His head was about to split open—whether from nerves or the aftereffects of the beating Moe Fryman had given him three days earlier, he didn't know.

Goddammit, he should have told Maudie! He should have made arrangements to get her and the baby out of the house. He didn't have any business fooling around with their lives, fucking around with this intrigue bullshit and maybe getting them all killed.

His throat was parched. He pushed his chair away from the desk and got to his feet, only vaguely aware of the dull ache that remained in his groin. He crossed his office quickly, continued through Clarice's reception area, and walked along the corridor to the small anteroom behind the main recording studio.

He took an RC from the little refrigerator beneath the coffee bar. As he reached for an opener, he thought he heard the phone ring.

He listened.

Silence.

He wiped the opener on his pants leg and slid it under the bottle cap, and noticed for the first time that his fingers were trembling.

He looked at his watch again. Five-twenty.

The phone rang.

He sprinted the length of the building and caught it on the third ring.

"Mr. Wilcox, this is Gladys Angston." The woman sounded young. "Did you have time to listen to those demonstration tapes yet?"

"No, I've been pretty busy lately. You in a hurry?"

"Oh, no, I'm in no hurry," the woman said. "Take your time."

That was the signal: *Take your time.* Nobody had shown up at his house. Green was right: Fryman and DeAngelo had been bluffing about harming Monroe's family. They didn't have the juice.

He hung up and made himself a bit more comfortable behind the desk, knowing that the woman would be dialing Ted Green's number now—wherever he was—telling him it was safe to proceed.

Fifteen minutes later, he was still sitting there, staring at the door, when "Estelle Griffith" walked in. An attractive dark-skinned woman in her thirties, with a fur stole draped around her shoulders.

She had a finger to her lips, telling Monroe to remain silent. "I got here just as soon as I could, Mr. Wilcox. I'm so frightened! I just don't know what we're going to do. . . ." She took a pen from the desk, hurriedly scribbled a note . . .

three men black Lincoln two doors down

. . . showed it to Monroe, tore it in half, and slipped it under the desk blotter, continuing to prattle on about how nervous she was and how they should probably call the police as soon as Dr. Taylor arrived.

When "Taylor" arrived, a few minutes later, Monroe barely recognized him.

Ted Green was wearing a pin-striped, vested suit, a black homburg, and professorial, rimless eyeglasses. The oversize suit and stooped walk he affected made him appear older, like the retired doctor he was pretending to be.

The woman greeted him excitedly, working herself up to the point that a few small tears began to trickle down her face. Green made consoling noises at her. He took a seat across the desk from Monroe, his back to the door.

Thirty seconds later, Fryman and DeAngelo walked in.

Fryman entered first. He had a proprietary smile on his face. His thick fist was closed around the handle of a black briefcase. He crossed the room, came around the desk, and motioned Monroe to get up. Monroe did, and Fryman sat down. He looked at Ted Green without recognition, stared at the woman smugly, and took his time lighting a cigarette.

DeAngelo stood guard at the door. He was wearing the same cheap blue windbreaker he had worn three days before. He made a point of letting them see his gun. Monroe avoided his eyes, afraid DeAngelo might see the hatred churning inside him.

Fryman got right to the point. He repeated what he had told Monroe, this time, however, embellishing it a bit, going into greater detail about how powerful he and his nonexistent "friends" were, and how lucky Monroe and the others were that the "big boys" had even bothered to take an interest in them and their little company. He explained that he and his friends owned dozens of radio stations scattered around the country, thousands of jukeboxes, and in the long run Monroe and the others would wind up making two or three times as much money owning only forty-nine percent of the company as they now did from the whole operation.

It was all make-believe, but Fryman did it very well. Very nicely, in a fatherly tone, as if trying to sell them a no-fault insurance policy.

When Fryman was through, Ted Green spoke. "What you're trying to do is against the law, you know. Suppose we call the police?"

Fryman laughed. He seemed to be enjoying himself. "Lemme tell you something, Doc . . ." He carelessly flicked ashes on Monroe's desk. "We *own* the cops in this town. You call them, they call us and ask *us* where we want the bodies dropped."

Ted Green seemed to be enjoying himself, too. "Let me put it another way," he said. "I happen to know that extortion of this kind is against federal law. Even if we sign whatever papers you have, what's to say we won't go to the FBI later and tell the whole story?"

"*I'm* to say," DeAngelo said from the doorway. "Lemme tell you people something—I don't laugh and joke around like my friend. When I tell you something, I tell you once. And if you don't get the message then, I take action. So I'm gonna tell you, *once.* You call the cops, you call the FBI, you call the fucking NAACP, you call anybody, and I'm gonna blow you fucking burrheads away!" He tapped the bulge under his windbreaker. "I mean, personally!" He looked at Fryman. "Quit fucking around, Moe. Get the goddamned papers signed and let's get the fuck out of here!"

So far, the meeting had progressed exactly as Monroe had anticipated. He and Ted Green had made their little token stand, and now he was ready to sign whatever Fryman put before him. Then, hopefully, the two hoods would leave, Leon Green's boys would pick them up outside. . . .

Everything would have gone perfectly if the woman who called herself Estelle Griffith had just kept her mouth shut. But she didn't. Maybe the same thing that made her one of the city's best con artists made her want to do somersaults along the edge of a precipice. More likely, it was the arrogance of the two thugs. But whatever her reasons, she spoke suddenly, without warning.

"You filthy pig!" She pointed at Moe Fryman. "How dare you come in here and try to steal this man's business, threaten his family, sit there behind his desk, like you belong there—"

What was she doing? Monroe stared at her in shock.

"Shut up, Estelle," Green said quietly.

"—when you should be emptying his trash and cleaning his toilets! You're nothing but a . . . an animal." She turned to face DeAngelo. "You and that . . . that—"

"Shut up, Estelle!" Green said sharply.

"—pathetic piece of filth standing there with his big brave gun!"

Green had been in tight situations before and knew that a quick way to get killed was to call an insane killer a "pathetic piece of filth." So while Monroe and the woman watched Moe Fryman sputter and fight to control his anger, Green kept his attention on DeAngelo. When the sharp animal cry came from the doorway, he turned just in time to see DeAngelo spring across the room toward the woman, his gun raised to smash her skull. Somehow, without losing his character of gentlemanly old "Dr. Taylor," Green managed to get to his feet a second before DeAngelo reached her. He stumbled into DeAngelo, taking the force of the blow on his own back. The two men tumbled heavily to the floor. DeAngelo's gun flew from his hand and skidded away.

They warily disentangled themselves and slowly got to their feet, DeAngelo first, then Green. DeAngelo's eyes were wild, darting back and forth between Green and the woman. Without turning his head, he held his hand out for the gun Fryman had retrieved from under the desk.

"Jesus, Artie! Knock it off, F'Chrissakes!" Fryman said in a tense whisper.

"Gimme the gun!" DeAngelo said, staring at Green and the woman.

"Not until you simmer down! Jesus, you're gonna fuck around and blow the whole goddamned deal!"

"No, I ain't—gimme the gun!"

Reluctantly Fryman slipped the gun, barrel-first, into DeAngelo's outstretched palm. DeAngelo's fingers caressed it gently, like a blind man holding a cane.

The room was quiet except for the woman's crying.

"Shut up, you black cunt!" DeAngelo shouted.

"I'm sure she doesn't mean any harm," Green placated, hoping to keep DeAngelo from going over the edge.

"Goddammit, who asked you? Keep your stupid nigger mouth shut!" DeAngelo's face twitched with rage. Without warning he slashed the gun butt across Green's face.

Green staggered back against the desk, but somehow managed to keep on his feet. He touched his hand to his face, it came away covered with blood. He pulled a handkerchief from his breast pocket and held it to the wound. Within seconds it had turned a dull, metallic pink.

"All right, that's enough!" Fryman screamed. "All of you, that's enough!"

DeAngelo stared at Green, challenging him, daring him to speak. Green resumed his seat in silence, still trying to stanch the blood seeping through the handkerchief in huge droplets.

Monroe was the only one in the room who could read the expression in Green's eyes. He had seen one exactly like it only three days before, in DeAngelo's eyes. Whatever previous plans Green had made for the two white gangsters had just been changed. They were now officially dead.

Fryman dropped his heavy body into the chair behind the desk. His colorless eyes flickered over the room. Satisfied the situation was back under his control, he opened the briefcase in front of him and pushed some papers across the desk at Monroe. "Here, sign these."

Monroe thumbed through them. Agreement of sale. Power of attorney. A cashier's check for twenty-five thousand dollars, payable to Big City Records and/or Monroe Wilcox.

"Don't hurry—just keep fucking around. . . ." DeAngelo spoke menacingly from the doorway.

"I think you'd better sign them," Green said.

Fryman kept careful watch. When Monroe had signed all the copies, he plucked them from beneath Monroe's pen, gave them a cursory look, and passed them on to Green and the woman.

When everybody had finished signing, Fryman leaned back in Monroe's chair and once again assumed his fatherly tone. "You did the smart thing, all of you. Hell, this business is too big for you folks now. I mean, face it, you're in over your heads. What are you doing, a million a year?" he asked Monroe.

"Something like that," Monroe answered.

"Penny-ante stuff, walking-around money," Fryman said offhandedly, but unable to hide the greed in his eyes. "Hell, with us handling things for you, you'll make two, three times that much. Easy."

"*If* you're smart enough to keep your goddamned mouths shut," DeAngelo added.

"Oh, we don't have to worry about that, do we *Mr.* Wilcox?"

"No," Monroe said, his voice devoid of feeling.

"Y'see, Artie, no problems." Contented with himself, Fryman tucked the papers back into his briefcase, stood, and offered his hand across the desk to Monroe. "Mr. Wilcox, it's a real pleasure to do business with you. You are a very smart man."

Monroe meekly took the proffered hand.

"See what I mean, Artie?" Fryman grinned. "We have gone into business with some very smart Negroes. Now, hear this." He directed his attention to Monroe. "I'll be here with my accountant tomorrow morning at eight sharp. I want the books right here on *my* desk. Understand?"

"I'll call my bookkeeper tonight," Monroe said.

"C'mon, Moe, let's get the fuck out of here!" DeAngelo was impatient.

"Coming," Fryman said, taking his time.

They left.

Green removed his blood-splattered glasses and laid them carefully on the desk, continuing to dab at the wound on his face. The woman kept her eyes averted. She fished in her purse, found a cigarette, lit it.

The sound they were listening for came from the rear of the building, four short beeps of an automobile horn.

The woman reached for the phone. Green sprang to his feet and hurried toward the door. He sprinted down the hall with Monroe right behind him.

A nine-passenger black limousine was parked just outside the back door. The name of a south Chicago funeral home was written on the front passenger door in gold script. The two burly black men Monroe had met at the warehouse the previous night were in the back on jumpseats, facing Fryman and DeAngelo and a third man Monroe had never seen before. They were the same shotguns pointing at the captured men. All three had been bound with heavy cord. Their mouths had been taped. Fryman's face was a sick gray. DeAngelo's left eye was puffed, beginning to close. A trickle of blood was oozing from his nostrils, running down onto the tape over his mouth. The third man sat on the far end of the seat. All Monroe could see plainly of him was his pants legs, muddy from the knee down, as if he had been knocked to the ground.

Ted Green reached inside the car and retrieved Fryman's briefcase for Monroe. "You want to say good-bye to these motherfuckers, little brother?"

Monroe couldn't think of anything to say. He looked at the two men and shook his head.

Green, still holding the soaked handkerchief to his face, slammed the door shut. "I got somebody tracking down that tap on your phone. He'll be over tomorrow to check out the whole building for you. Call me tomorrow afternoon about four o'clock, I should be back by then. Anybody ask you anything about this, just tell them you don't know nothing, which you don't."

He went around to the driver's side, tossed his homburg on the seat, and picked up a chauffeur's cap. Only then did Monroe notice Leon Green, who had been standing quietly at the corner of the building, coming toward him. He was hatless, his right hand still

236 ·

jammed into the pocket of his heavy overcoat. He opened the front passenger door and got in without looking at Monroe.

Ted Green put on the chauffeur's cap, tilting it at exactly the right angle of servility. He looked back at Monroe across the top of the car, without expression, then slid behind the wheel and eased the big car into the alley behind Michigan Avenue.

Monroe watched it disappear, then stepped back inside and pushed the door shut against the sharp March wind. He turned and slowly trudged down the hall to his office, his stomach a little queasy.

NEW YORK
MARCH 1961

At ITRC, as in most other large music corporations, the curtain of misunderstanding between the marketing and sales divisions was usually drawn; marketing dealt primarily with concepts, sales almost exclusively in precepts, and the common ground between the two remained, at best, tenuous.

Consider, the matter of jargon:

Marketing usually referred to a store as a "retail outlet," implying that it was operated by creatures without faces or names. Sales usually called a store, well, a store—often referring to it by name and location, and sometimes even including certain pertinent facts about its proprietor, as in: "The Acme Record Store on Twelfth and Maple—run by that idiot Pop Wilson."

Or a study that might take Marketing weeks to complete and which it would then grandly submit as a "visionary forecast," Sales might lightly dismiss as nothing more than "wishful thinking" or an "educated guess," depending on the conclusions offered. And a slow month—the period immediately before high-school graduation, for example, when record sales traditionally dipped—the sales division could explain away as a "slack season." Marketing could turn it into a major catastrophe by calling it "a period of sharp profit erosion," and therefore, by putting more pressure on Sales, draw the curtain of misunderstanding a little tighter.

Categorically, because of the fundamental differences through which they perceived their jobs, and therefore their lives, marketing and sales people rarely sought the company of each other away from work. Given those basics, plus a wide disparity in the ages and backgrounds and the fact that their temperaments were poles apart, it was remarkable that Mark Donovan and Bob Silverstein had become such good friends during Mark's three years in the city.

Silverstein was a rumpled, balding man in his middle years, settled and contented, who somehow managed to convey the impression that the same record industry that was presently being invaded by a worshipful army was of little more significance to the overall quality of life than a medium-priced comedy act on the Ed Sullivan show. He seemed antithetical to his job: married to the same homey woman for twenty-five years, the rock-music-hating father of two acne-stricken teenage daughters, one of whom, to his consternation, was actively seeking a third term as president of the New York chapter of the International Freddie Cannon Fan Club. His personality and life-style contrasted in every imaginable way to the younger, relentlessly introspective Mark Donovan, and the great differences between the two men would have seemingly precluded their ever finding a common ground on which to meet and exchange confidences.

But as comfortable and unassuming as he was, and as out-of-place as he appeared to be in the changing times, Bob Silverstein possessed one of the most astute minds in the record business. For that reason, he had been chosen by Gino Turicotti and approved by Mark for the key position of national director of sales for the Arrow label.

Silverstein was, like most good salesmen, a listener. From the beginning of their relationship, he had taken the time to listen to Mark's ideas, and because he had listened without prejudice, he had acquired great respect for Mark's integrity and business acumen, as well as an understanding of the depths of the struggle the younger man was waging within himself in an effort to combine business and ethical responsibilities.

During the time Mark had been trying to upgrade the quality of products offered by the ITRC record club, Silverstein, gently pushing aside the reserve Mark had covered himself with as protection against the incessant backbiting of company politics, had become his close and trusted personal friend. And he had tried to use that friendship constructively, to offer Mark occasional reminders that the music business did not comprise merely ideas, but also individuals, each separately engaged in a day-to-day fight for identity in what was fast becoming one of the most unenlightened industries in the world.

The two men generally had lunch together once a week at a kosher delicatessen-cafeteria on Second Avenue, far enough away from the music business to, as Silverstein liked to say, "get the bull-shit out of our ears." It was a noisy, hectic place, dishes clattering, shouts across the room, the kind of place Mark usually avoided. But Silverstein, born and raised in the city, was so comfortable in the bustling atmosphere that Mark had finally come to accept it himself and now found it a good place to relax and talk.

It was already early afternoon when he paid the cab and went in to find Silverstein in a back booth engrossed in a newspaper. He grabbed a tray and went through the line, choosing their lunches from the glass-enclosed counter They always went about it this way, the last man buying, and he already knew what Silverstein wanted—corned beef on rye, cheesecake, and a draft lager—since Silverstein always ate the same thing.

Waiting to pay, he enjoyed his usual mild flirtation with the owner's wife, an elderly woman with jangling earrings and a voice like a longshoreman's, before crossing the room to join his friend.

Silverstein glanced up as Mark set the tray on the table. "Aha, I see the goodies have arrived. I was just about to send up a flare. What kept you?"

"Last-minute packing. Been waiting long?"

"Oh, ten minutes or so . . . long enough to look through the paper and check on the Kid."

Mark cleared the tray and slid into the booth across from Silverstein, chuckling at Silverstein's customary reference to the new President. "What's he up to today?"

"Here, see for yourself. . . ." Silverstein handed over the paper.

Mark took a bite of his roast-beef sandwich, tucked a stray piece of meat into his mouth with a forefinger, and turned his attention to the news item.

PRESIDENT SIGNS ORDER

WASHINGTON, D.C. A.P.)—Earlier today, as leading civil-rights advocates looked on, President John F. Kennedy signed an executive order "to ensure that Americans of all colors and beliefs will have access to employment within the government and with those who do business with the government."

The expected order was met with general approval by government officials, including members of Congress, although some business leaders voiced the fear that . . .

Mark finished reading the article and pushed the paper aside. "Hmmm . . ." He chewed his sandwich thoughtfully. "What do you think?"

"I think he's had a busy week so far. First the Peace Corps thing, now this."

"It's too bad he has to pass an order to make people do what they should do anyhow. Do you think it will have any effect?"

"Well, if nothing else, it antagonizes the deadbeats. That in itself is worth something. And it lets them know that he intends to keep his word."

"Frankly, I admire him."

"Probably because he reminds you of yourself." Silverstein smiled.

"I'll tell you one thing, I wish I could issue a couple of executive orders around our place."

"Like what?"

"Like, Executive Order Number One: 'Duplicate copies of the ITRC five-year plan will immediately be distributed to all company employees, hereafter to be used as toilet paper.'"

"I guess that answers my next question—how you and Turicotti came out in that meeting Monday."

"Christ, we weren't even speaking the same language." Mark shook his head in disgust. "I don't know if it was impossible for him to understand what I was trying to say, or if he just refused to give it any consideration. But whatever the reason, I walked out of there feeling like an illiterate."

"What was it, what we've discussed? The promotional setup?"

"The whole thing. I'm just not comfortable with the way it sits. I think we're going backward instead of forward."

"Okay, suppose you had a chance to do it your way—say, you issue your executive order and dump the whole plan and start from scratch, what then?"

"I'd go slow. Give the label a definite direction and allow plenty of time and room for it to grow."

"How so?"

"Artist development. Go for the artists instead of the hit-record concept. Good artists, good songwriters, maybe even a nice little jazz division for creative input."

"In other words, another Atlantic Records?"

"Why not? You know how much I respect those guys over there, the Erteguns, Wexler and that bunch. They know their market and they know how to service it. And they're not going for the quick buck by turning their label over to the kids."

Silverstein covered the uneaten half of his sandwich with a napkin and reached for his cheesecake. "It seems to me what bothers you most is the fact that Arrow will be a 'young' label. Why should that bother you? Hell, you're little more than a kid yourself."

"No, I'm not saying we shouldn't have young artists on the label, of course we should. I'm saying, just because most of them are limited as to what they can accomplish musically doesn't mean that the whole label should be that limited. That's an asinine assumption. And it's even more asinine to spend millions to exclusively promote that kind of stuff. We can't pretend everything started with Elvis

Presley. If we want to have a decent label, we've got to have continuity—not just people who understand the market, but people who understand the music, as well. That's why I have so much respect for Atlantic. If it was up to me, I'd pay Wexler a half-million dollars a year to come over here and run Arrow."

"And where would that put you?"

"Exactly where I'd like to be, marketing decent products. But I'm not just talking about Atlantic. I mean labels that are being run by good solid record men. Kapp and Cadence are a couple of good examples."

"I wouldn't say that either of them is exactly setting the business on fire right now."

"Yes, but you know why—Dave's not well, he's still having heart problems, and Archie's just tired of going through the bullshit of getting a record played. I had a chance to talk with him at that BMI dinner at the Waldorf a couple of weeks ago, and he said it's costing him anywhere from twenty-five to thirty grand in promotion just to get enough airplay on a record to see if it has hit *potential*. He's so disgusted he's about ready to dump the whole thing."

"Oh, I doubt that. He probably just needs to change a couple of distributors."

"I'll tell you how serious he was—he said the Everlys' contract is coming up for renewal shortly and he'd try to steer them to us if we're interested."

Silverstein sat up. "What'd you say?"

"I told him maybe he ought to get in touch with Carl Clinger in Nashville."

"Beautiful." Silverstein reached for another bite of cheesecake.

"Well, he's supposed to be running a country label for us."

"Carl Clinger," Silverstein snorted. "Christ, what a politician! Every time I talk to him, I get the feeling he's running for office." He dabbed at his mouth with a napkin. "Okay, suppose you can't get Wexler, which you can't, what's your next move?"

"To get somebody, anybody, who really knows what they're doing. I mean, that's just common sense, right—if you don't know something, admit it and get somebody who does. That was the first thing I learned when I started trying to run Champ, and I'll tell you one thing, it made my job a hell of a lot easier."

"Probably didn't hurt the music, either." Silverstein chuckled.

"Well, you heard it. And you know we turned out some pretty good things on that little label. I learned a hell of a lot in that year and a half. That time I spent with Sam Crockett was an education. When he came to work for me I was as confused as everybody else in

242 ·

this business about what sells and why. And the most important thing he taught me was that hit records have absolutely nothing to do with age or form or any of the other misconceptions that we in the business use to outsmart ourselves."

"What do you mean by 'form'?"

"I mean, it doesn't matter what you call it, music is music, if it's good it'll sell. The lines between jazz and r-and-b and pop and rock and roll are arbitrary, they're where we set them, and we almost always set them euphemistically—r-and-b means colored, pop and rock and roll usually mean white, and jazz can mean anything from Henry Mancini to Louis Armstrong. It's pointless to pigeonhole an artist, because a good artist can cross those lines at will."

"Hmmm . . ." Silverstein weighed the statement. "I don't know if I can go along with that."

"Okay, look at Ray Charles. Two years ago he had the r-and-b record of the year with 'What'd I Say.' Last year he won the Grammy for the best male pop vocalist of the year with 'Georgia.' And it wouldn't surprise me a bit if he comes out next year with a country tune and hits just as big."

"Yeah, but you can't count him, he's a monster. Christ, what an artist! Can you imagine what we could do with him?"

"But that's what I'm talking about, heavyweights. That's what Arrow needs, and that's the weakness of the five-year plan. What would I do if a thirty-year-old colored man walked into my office to sign a contract? I couldn't even consider it. No matter how good he was, I'd have to turn him down."

"I'll give you a better example than him." Silverstein laughed. "Rydell Mercer. Have you seen his picture in this week's *Billboard*? That man's fifty if he's a day."

"And what did he sell, a million and a half copies of that thing?"

"Yeah, but who the hell would have picked that tune? It was a fluke, you know that."

"How about your kids? Do they like it?"

"Aw, Christ, they must play it a hundred times a day. I walked in the house the other night and they even had their mother jumping around to the damn thing."

"So . . . does that prove my point?"

"Not completely, but it's well taken."

"Okay, listen—since you brought up Mercer, I'm going to tell you something I've been kicking around for the past couple of weeks. No, that's bullshit, I haven't been just 'kicking it around,' I've been giving it serious thought. I was going to mention it to you sooner, but I hadn't completely made up my mind. And then last night, while I was going over that goddamned plan again, I thought about it some more, and it still seems like a logical solution to this whole thing."

"So how long are you going to keep me in suspense?"

"Well, I just want to be sure you hear me out completely before you give me your opinion. You may think I've gone off the deep end when I tell you."

"So tell me." Silverstein shrugged.

"Okay . . ." Mark leaned forward, elbows on the table. "Mercer's company is the hottest label in the business right now, right?"

"Right. So?"

"Bob, I swear, I would give my right arm to work out some kind of a deal with the guy that owns that label—what's his name?"

Silverstein thought a moment. "Wilcox—Monroe Wilcox."

"Right." Mark nodded. "I mean, absorb his whole operation, artists, catalog, everything, and bring him in as a vice-president in charge of production for Arrow. With his experience and our merchandising setup, we'd put a lock on the market immediately, and I mean a *consistent* market."

Silverstein was already shaking his head.

"Think about it a minute," Mark said. "The pop charts are a circus. 'Alley Oop,' 'Running Bear,' 'Itsy Bitsy Bikini,' 'Please, Mr. Custer'—and whatever dance Dick Clark's trying to push at the moment. And that's exactly the kind of nonsense we're going to have to compete with. On the other hand, the most consistent sellers are either coming off the country charts or the r-and-b charts. The Everlys, Brenda Lee, Roy Orbison, people like that. Or Jackie Wilson, Brook Benton, Jerry Butler and those guys. We can't go country, because we've got Carousel—"

"*If* they ever get anything going down there."

"—but we can come up with a strong r-and-b base with Wilcox, and we could probably pick up his whole operation for a million, a million and a half at the most. I know we could. He's got to be struggling, a colored man trying to take on the whole record business by himself."

"Hmmm . . ." Silverstein hedged.

"*Dammit*, Bob, if we can pay six or seven million for a label as unproductive as Carousel, mainly to get Carl Clinger, we can invest a lot less money with Wilcox and come out a hell of a lot further ahead in the long run. He's had tunes on the r-and-b sectional charts for years. And don't try to tell me we can't use him, I know damned well we can."

"The problem is," Silverstein said, "you're running into that

244 ·

same old bugaboo, the r-and-b thing. Nobody in the company wants to have to deal with that market on a consistent basis."

"No, you misunderstand me. I'm not suggesting we should bring him in to help us run an r-and-b label. I'm saying we could use him to help us run a label, period. If we do it to maintain control over the quality of our product, there's no reason it would have to be done with an r-and-b concept."

Silverstein nodded slowly, digesting the idea with the last of his cheesecake. "You're absolutely right, of course," he finally conceded. "I'm being guilty of the same limited pattern of thinking you've been talking about."

"All I'm saying is, without Wilcox or somebody like him, this whole Arrow thing is ludicrous. I mean, it's just simple logic that *somewhere* in the organization *somebody* should have enough knowledge of the music to say, 'No, you're not playing it right. *This* is the way it should go.' If we don't have somebody who can do that—and I mean somebody who's in a position to make it stick—we're going to have artistic chaos."

"Well, whether that's true or not"—Silverstein's expression was dour—"we both know you wouldn't have a prayer of getting that idea through Planning."

"Maybe not, but I can try. I can stay over tonight and draw up a memo and run it up to Connecticut to Max in the morning, and we'd know by this time tomorrow. I just want to know if you'll back me on it."

"No, I don't think so. . . ."

"Why not? I'm not asking you to put yourself on the line, I'm just saying I'd like to include your approval in a memo."

"No."

"Dammit, Bob—"

"Mark, you know I'd back you to the limit if it had any chance at all, but it doesn't. Even if Geary went along with you, you wouldn't have a chance of getting it past Turicotti, and even less chance of getting it through Planning. We've got people up there making thirty grand a year who have to get their secretaries to help them tie their shoelaces, and they're convinced they're underpaid. My God, you bring in a colored man and give him a million dollars and power like that, half the building would walk out."

Mark was silent.

"Am I right?"

Mark emitted a long sigh of resignation. The tension lines around his eyes became more pronounced. He stared at the newspaper on the table between them for a few seconds, then pushed it away. "Of course you're right. What the hell's the matter with me anyhow? Am I losing my mind, or what?"

"It's a good idea, a damned good idea. Twenty years ago I would have sat here and helped you craft that memo, but I seem to have run out of patience with lost causes."

"No, don't apologize. You've kept me from making a fool of myself more than once in the last couple of years, and I appreciate it. My problem is, I keep forgetting how ingrained self-delusion is in this business. I just need you to remind me from time to time."

"No . . . your problem is, you have a logical mind, and logic is the last thing this business will tolerate. Forget it. There's no sense in letting this thing get to you."

"If you really want to know what's getting to me, Bob, I'll tell you." Mark picked up his glass, studied it in silence before draining it. "I'm wondering who's going to take responsibility for this five years from now when we've got a couple of hundred thousand kids hanging around the fringes of the music industry, pounding on drums and beating on guitars and trying to sing like the Howling Wolf, grabbing for this carrot we're dangling in front of them. Is that what we want?"

Silverstein puffed his cigar thoughtfully, shook his head.

"Well, we should think about it," Mark continued. "We're a huge company with a good tradition. Over the years we've presented artists who have worked hard to develop their craft. Even if pop music is in the process of changing, we don't have to change that tradition, do we? I say, if kids like rock-'n'-roll music, fine. If they want to make it a part of their culture, great. But we do not have the right to merely sell crap to the kids, no matter how profitable it is."

"You know what I think? I think it's time for you to get the hell out of this business."

Mark waved the statement aside.

"I mean it. Face it, this business is not going to get any better, not with the caliber of people it attracts. And I'll tell you something, my boy, you keep on the way you're doing, and you'll end up with an ulcer or worse."

Mark kept his eyes on the table.

"How old are you now?"

"Twenty-eight, twenty-nine in June."

"So do it now, while you're still young enough to get your foot in the door somewhere. I'll tell you something, you're one of the brightest young men I've ever met, in this or any other business. You could write your own ticket out there—publishing, television, movies, anything you wanted. Hell, you've got a few bucks, and your whole life ahead of you. You know what I'd do if I was your age? I'd quit this goddamned rat race, find a good wife, and look around for something that would take advantage of what I had to offer."

"Well, I've thought about it a few times," Mark said. "You've probably guessed that. The first time was when we dissolved Champ and I approached the company about finding Sam Crockett a permanent job. I was shocked when they turned him down. I mean, here was a man who was exactly what we needed, qualified and experienced. Yet we couldn't find a place for him. I almost walked away from it right then, but I didn't. And I'll tell you why.

"You know, I didn't just *happen* to come to work for ITRC. Don't forget, I had known Max Geary all my life and I'd always respected him and the way he ran his company. For as long as I could remember, ITRC had put out nothing less than the very best music in the world. I wanted to be a part of that, and I always had the feeling that he expected me to. So maybe I think I *owe* him something for giving me a chance to do what I've always wanted to do. Jesus, I've been so fortunate that it scares me. There's nothing I've ever wanted that I couldn't have, so I have absolutely no right to ever become cynical about anything. That's why I don't say to hell with the music business and walk away from it. I know everybody can't live the way I have, but I believe everybody deserves some kind of chance, especially people who have earned it. I get impatient sometimes because I don't have that kind of power yet. But if I ever do, and a situation comes up where I can use it to influence decisions in a direction I feel is right, I think I would at least make an effort."

"You've given it a little thought, huh?"

"Yes."

"That's good." Silverstein smiled and drained his glass. "Got time for another beer?"

Mark glanced at his watch and nodded.

Silverstein was back in a few minutes with two fresh mugs. He plopped down in the seat across from Mark and saluted with his glass. "To less bullshit . . ."

They drank to that, and Mark smiled self-consciously. "Bob, I'm sorry, I didn't mean to get off on a tangent like that."

"So who's complaining?" Silverstein puffed his cigar and sipped his drink, trying to think of a way to put his own thoughts into words. "I have to admit, some of the things you say make sense, but some of them seem a little farfetched, too. I think you've overstated your case in a couple of spots. Like, rock-'n'-roll music being a part of kids' culture. I don't go along with that. Very little of our business has anything to do with culture. Popular music's a business, nothing more. It always has been and always will be. And it's a competitive business, like shoes or real estate or politics. If you're reasonably honest, it's based on the profit motive. If you're not, it's based on screwing your fellowman out of as much as you can. And it has the same inherent weaknesses as any other business in the free-enterprise system, which is: you don't have to be talented or dedicated to make it, merely ambitious or greedy.

"You know"—he paused to relight his cigar—"there's a phrase Galbraith coined a couple of years ago in his book *The Affluent Society* which fits in with what we're discussing. It has to do with accepted truths, what he calls 'conventional wisdoms.' He pointed out that there are a great many statements we've heard over the years that have been repeated so often that even though they have very little to do with the way things really are, or ever were, they've taken on the same values as truths in our society. And as time passes and people build additional premises on these 'conventional wisdoms,' before you know it, history has been rewritten. I think that's what's happened to you, why you tend to romanticize the music business. It's always been cold and opportunistic. I'll give you an example.

"You think that colored people should get a bigger piece of the pie? I go along with you on it a hundred percent. But the chances are they won't. I know 'conventional wisdom' has it that they've always done a little better in the music business than in other parts of society, but that's not true. The truth is, they've always had it a little *worse* in our business, in relation, of course, to their potential to accomplish. Hell, colored songwriters didn't even get performance money for airplay until 1940, '41, when ASCAP lost their licensing agreement with the radio stations and BMI took over."

"Why was that?" Mark asked, surprised.

"Well, I don't want to go into that now, because the point I'm making is this—as bad as things are for colored artists today, they've never had it as good."

"That's a terrible statement to have to make."

"But it's true, and you could apply it to a hundred other things. That's what I mean about 'conventional wisdom' being inaccurate. And I believe we're now in the process of seeing new 'conventional wisdoms' being created about rock-'n'-roll music. Magazine writers and sociologists and all kinds of people are starting to try to say it's the catalyst for some kind of upheaval. But that's completely inaccurate. Maybe it will become a part, an appendage, if you like, to some kind of cultural or social change someday, but I personally don't see why it should. When we talk about rock-'n'-roll music now, all we're talking about is a bunch of white kids trying to sing and play like colored people and usually doing a pretty bad job of it. And there's nothing unusual about that. Their parents and grandparents were doing the same thing in the twenties and thirties with dixieland and swing. And if you'd been around ten or twelve years ago and taken a walk down Fifty-second Street about three in the morning, you'd have seen half the white musicians in New York sitting around the clubs, trying to learn how to play like Parker and Gillespie and those guys.

"No, the upheaval we're seeing now has very little to do with either music or culture per se, except as how it applies to changes in business, the demographics we're always talking about, the fact that a few years from now half the population will be under thirty years old. The conventional wisdom might later want to hang everything on the music industry, but it's a coat that will never fit because the phenomenon is reaching far beyond *our* business and into the business community as a whole. A great many industries have now started to think of kids as nothing more than a market. They're not trying to teach them or give them anything of value, merely trying to sell them products."

"But that's all I'm really saying, that in order to make more profit, we're taking away their options."

"Yeah, but you're making *us* the goat. And it's not just the music industry who's taking away their options, it's all of business. We're *all* starting to pander to them, movies, television, clothing manufacturers, food companies. . . ."

"Does that bother you?"

"As a father, yes, because I find it hard to apply the 'buyer-beware' principle of business to kids—not just my kids, but anybody's kids. It think it's obscene to pander to them, opportunism of the worst kind. But as a salesman, I can understand it. The marketplace is simply becoming too crowded with too many people who don't have the intelligence or imagination to compete with integrity. In order to survive, they have to break the rules."

"How would you apply all of that to Arrow?"

"As a father, it's revolting. As a salesman"—Silverstein thumped the table with his palm—"I'd put my life savings on it. It absolutely cannot miss. It's as sure a thing as has ever existed in this business."

"What makes you so sure?"

"Because Arrow Records is coming along at exactly the right time. It will be what could be called the 'next logical conclusion—' "

"To what?"

"Well, let me put it this way . . ." Silverstein sipped his beer and puffed his cigar back to life. "I've been knocking around this business for nineteen, twenty years now, and it has always been a hit-or-miss proposition. I'd take a record out to get played or try to get it on the boxes with no idea whatsoever if it was going to sell or not. It was strictly catch-as-catch-can. That's not a comfortable state of affairs in business. In business, the manufacturer is supposed to dictate to the consumer, not the other way around. But the real power in the music business has always been inverted, until now. The consumer has always had the final say about what he would buy. He told *us* if the product was acceptable. Now, with Arrow, we will finally begin to tell *him* what he should buy. We've got everything we need, the money and the know-how, to put his mind where *we* want it. And from my standpoint as a salesman, that is the ideal state of affairs."

"How about the product itself? How much influence will the quality of what we're trying to sell have on the minds of buyers?"

"I think, in a couple of years, it will have very little. Our product will only need to be competitive, not necessarily outstanding, and we can still dominate the market. I'll tell you why—because we are the first major label to make a permanent commitment to crap. Not just crap in the quality of the music, but crap in the permanent structure of the music industry. It's already a corrupt business. As national sales manager of Arrow Records, I will be given a very large budget to ensure that it becomes even more corrupt, and therefore even more receptive to the crap I will be selling."

"Doesn't that upset you?"

"Not in the least. I was doing nicely, going about my job with a minimum of hassle, until rock and roll came along. All of a sudden I'm damn near out of business. Nobody wants to hear what I'm selling, nobody wants to play what I'm pushing. This is gonna sound strange to you, but my first ten years as a record salesman, I never paid off. Oh, I'd take the dj's or station managers to dinner every now and then, buy them Christmas gifts, stuff like that. But I didn't try to buy them. In those days they were really interested in what they put on the air, and all the payoffs in the world couldn't get sustained airplay on a tune if they didn't think it was a quality record.

"Today, it's a war between the record companies and the radio stations. We labor under mutual disrespect. They don't even hear the music anymore, they hear the dollars. If they don't hear the dollars in front, they make sure nobody ever hears the music. It's a fast track, and the only way to keep moving on it is with a lot of grease. I mean, a *lot* of grease.

"That's why I disagree with you about culture. Even if the public wanted to hear better music, which I doubt, there are a lot of people between us and them who could not care less about improving anybody's mind, including their own. You want to know how culture works? Okay, I'll tell you. Turicotti picks up the phone and tells some idiot TV producer: 'Hey, put my kid on your show and there's five grand in it for you.' And one of our young assholes gets on national TV and makes a goddamn fool of himself, and the next day the whole country is talking about what a great act he is, including the people in our business who should know better. There's your culture.

"That's why I say you can't take it seriously. This business is ninety-nine percent hype and one percent bullshit. On any given day, on any given chart, the number-ten record is outselling the number-one record, depending upon how much money is crossing palms. And even if you get a big record, it's only on the charts three or four weeks and it's gone. And then the whole cycle starts all over again. That's why I say I'll be damned if I, a forty-eight-year-old man, am going to get an ulcer worrying about what's going to turn on some pimply-faced kid whose only concern in life is how to get into my daughter's pants. I'm going to knock ten years off my life for that? Are you kidding me?"

"I wish I could look at it that way."

"I'm kind of glad you can't." Silverstein laughed his raspy laugh. "It makes me feel young again."

They sat there quietly for a few minutes, drinking their beer, mulling the conversation over in their minds.

"What does Lois think about moving to California?" Mark finally asked.

"Oh, she's excited about it. So are the girls. They think they're going to see a movie star on every corner." He drained the last of his beer. "Got time for one more?"

"No, I still have a couple of things to do—get my bags from the apartment, return the key to the real-estate office—and I promised Helen and Jules I would stop by and have a drink with them on the way to the airport."

"Need any help?"

"No, I can manage. No sense in you going through all that."

"Absolutely right," Silverstein said matter-of-factly. "It would be a pain in the ass."

He carefully wrapped the uneaten half of his corned-beef sandwich in a paper napkin, including the pickle, and stuck it in his attaché case. They walked outside into the bright early-spring afternoon.

"Going anywhere? We can share a cab," Mark said.

"On a beautiful day like this?" Silverstein spread his pudgy arms and did a quick dance step in the middle of Second Avenue. "This, my young friend, is the Big Apple at its very finest. You know what I'm going to do? Stroll over to Columbus Circle and buy a bag of roasted peanuts and spend the rest of the day molesting little old ladies in Central Park."

"Well, enjoy yourself. You don't have much time left here."

"Oh!" Silverstein snapped his fingers. "I don't know whether Turicotti mentioned it to you or not, but we're going to need a place out there. Something in the neighborhood of, say, a hundred grand. A nice place, but a *home*, you know what I mean?"

"Yes, he did mention it. I'll talk to my mother about it as soon as I get there. She's a genius about stuff like that." He hailed a cab.

"You're going to feel like a different man when you get back home," Silverstein said.

"I know, but I'm going to miss talking to you, Bob."

"For six weeks, you can stand it."

The airport lounge was nearly empty. Mark's sister, Helen, and her husband, Jules, had dropped him off a half-hour earlier. He had declined their offer to wait with him until time for his plane to leave, and now he sat alone at the end of the bar, already halfway through his second double Scotch.

He sat there with his chin in his hand, slowly making circles on the bar with his glass, and every few minutes he would punctuate a thought with a sip of his drink, look across at his reflection in the mirror, and shake his head at the quiet young man in the quiet blue suit and the quiet blue tie and the light blue button-down shirt, and then continue making circles on the bar with his glass.

He had no right to be dissatisfied with himself or his life. He had followed his plan, to work hard and move up in the company, and he had been successful. He had wanted to learn, and he had been given that chance. He had wanted responsibility, and he had been given it, sixty million dollars' worth. And now he was, in every sense, exactly what he had set out to become: the Rising Young Corporate Executive with the Bright Future. So what right did he have to complain? What did he really know anyhow? Maybe Turicotti and Silverstein were right in saying that he was trying to change the world. Maybe when he was older he would not believe any of the things he believed now.

Maybe he would look back at himself as a young man and laugh at his idealism, at his stupidity.

And so he did what millions of other young men before him had done at the moment of their first great accommodation to the wisdom of their elders: he angrily tapped the bar for another drink.

And a few minutes later, another.

He was still drunk when the young blond woman boarded the plane in Chicago.

He caught a whiff of her perfume as she took the seat across the aisle from him, and he thought she smiled at him, but he wasn't sure about that, so he turned his back to her, pulled the blanket up to his chin, and went back to sleep.

Sometime later he woke up again with a sour, hot taste in his mouth, and a feeling that he was about to reject the meal Helen had cooked for him earlier in the day. The plane rolled against a sudden turbulence as he pulled himself to his feet and bumped his way down the aisle to the toilet.

He stood in the tiny cubicle for a time, his stomach churning, wincing at the pallid face reflected in the mirror above the sink. Finally, when he thought it safe, he came out and gingerly made his way back to his seat.

The blond woman had turned on the reading light above her head, although she didn't appear to have any reading material nearby. She smiled at him again—unmistakably this time—as he resumed his seat, and even though his mind was not yet functioning as well as he would have liked, he was immediately struck by her beauty.

He returned her smile tentatively. "Do I know you?"

"I certainly hope so," she said, her voice seasoned with a spice of Southern accent. "I'm one of your artists."

Vaguely he remembered having seen a photograph of her a few weeks before in ITRC's biweekly house journal. He studied her, frowning, trying to place her.

She looked very young. Her short hair had been styled to give her a cute, boyish look. His wide eyes stared across the aisle at him in bright green innocence. Her nose turned up in a hint of a pout, and her smile was open and friendly. She was dressed for travel, in a chocolate-colored travelsuit and bright yellow blouse unbuttoned at the throat, exposing a gold chain with the initials ST scripted in small diamonds.

But as he continued to look at her, she seemed to change right before his eyes, as though she could enhance her beauty through the will of her own thoughts. Her eyes narrowed, became older, darker, more sensuous. A sudden intake of breath made her nostrils flare, and her small nose seemed to take on more character. Her tongue slowly caressed the edges of her mouth, and as her lips relaxed, they seemed to swell, become fuller, and curl into a tantalizing, inviting half-smile.

She had made herself desirable as he watched, and the impact was tangible. He felt himself begin to harden, and knew that he wanted to take her to bed. It was a feeling he almost never experienced upon meeting a woman for the first time. He felt his face flush, and he was grateful for the darkness inside the cabin. He remembered who she was. "Sarah Tindall, right?" he asked.

"I'm complimented. How are you, Mark?"

She had come to ITRC with the purchase of Carousel Records a few months earlier, but he had never met her personally, had probably never even listened to any of her recordings. He had no idea what her status was within the company's roster of artists, except he was fairly certain that sales and promotion had no plans afoot for extensive promotion of any of her records.

"Great, just great," he said. "Hell of a place to run into you, though, don't you think?"

"No, not really—sometimes it seems I meet half the people I know, or should know, on airplanes."

"You must do a lot of traveling."

"Too much. I'm just coming off tour now."

"How long were you out?"

"Seventy-five one-nighters in eighty-eight days. Just got back to Nashville the beginning of the week. I'm still so tired I don't know if I'm coming or going."

"I guess one-nighters can be pretty rough, huh?"

"Oh, my, yes—the nights just seem to melt together after the first few weeks. But"—she sighed—"that's where the money is."

"Well, whatever the circumstances, I'm glad I finally got to meet you."

"Me, too. It's funny, because I was just reading an article about you yesterday, in the new *Cashbox*."

"Oh?"

"Yes, they had some really nice things to say about you, about you taking over the new label and all."

"Well . . ." He laughed. "We buy a lot of ads."

"Hey, I hate talking across the aisle like this. Why don't you move over here?" She slid over a seat, patted the one she had just vacated.

Hesitantly he crossed the aisle and sat beside her. "So . . . uh, what's going on in Nashville these days?" he asked, trying to keep from breathing in her direction.

"It's growing. Lots of new studios coming up, and the city's really starting to promote itself."

"I know *we're* putting a lot of money there. We've got a new three-million-dollar studio that should be completed before long."

"It's already finished."

"No, I don't think so, not for another month at least."

"It's already finished," she insisted. "I should know, I just spent a week in it, doing voice-overs."

"You're kidding."

"No."

"What did you think of it? I mean, do you think it has a decent sound?"

"It's too early to tell, I think. Anyhow, we were having a lot of trouble with the board."

"What kind of trouble?"

"Mainly that it was new, and nobody knew how to work it right."

He shook his head in disgust. "Who was supervising?"

"Lonnie Pratt."

"I don't know him."

"Just picture the dumbest asshole you can imagine."

"You don't have to be tactful." He laughed.

"There's no way to be tactful when you're talking about Lonnie."

"What about Clinger? Isn't he supposed to be in charge of things down there?"

"Carl? He's worse than Lonnie."

"How so?"

She was quiet a moment. "Oh, I don't know," she said finally, irritatedly, "and I'm not sure I really care at this point. It's such a stupid goddamned business sometimes. . . ."

He thought about the past week, his conversations with Turicotti and Bob Silverstein, his meeting with Paul Schultz, and sighed in agreement.

"Well, maybe not for you so much . . ." She misunderstood his acquiescence, thinking he was merely trying to pacify her.

"For me, too."

He started to say more, but changed his mind. He was never comfortable talking with ITRC artists, because he invariably got the impression that they wanted him to intercede for them—to buck the production and sales departments—in order to acquire additional promotion for their products whether the quality of their records warranted it or not. He was tempted to divert the conversation to a more personal level, to avoid discussing company business, but there was something about her that made him want to help her, if he could. "Are you having trouble with the company?"

"Well, not exactly *trouble* . . ." She clicked her tongue and made a face. "Oh, look at me—I just met you and here I am already crying on your shoulder!"

"That's okay. Maybe I can help you."

"Well, it's just so confusing, Mark. I mean, Tommy Lee Whitaker was my producer on *Carousel*, right? And just before ITRC bought the company, he cut some tracks for me. He and Carl and everybody said they were good, with at least one top-ten record. That's why I okayed this last tour, I wanted to be on the road when the record was released. But after Carousel was sold, somebody decided—I don't know who—that the record had no potential, so it was junked. But when I got back to Nashville Monday, I got a call from Carl, saying to come back in the studio and redo the voice because they might want to use the masters after all. I mean, nobody seems to know what the hell they're doing."

"Well, you've got to remember, we're going through an involved reorganization program. *I'm* in charge of the new label and I'm not really sure I know what's going on, either."

"Yes, but I just wish they'd make up their minds!"

As she spoke, her slender fingers nervously intertwined themselves around the braided handles of the cloth handbag in her lap. Again he was touched by her vulnerable-little-girl quality.

"Maybe I can do a little checking for you," he said. "How long will you be in California?"

"Well, I *live* there, you know."

"No, I didn't know. I just assumed, you being a country artist and all, that you lived down South somewhere."

"Oh, no. I moved to California when Carl took Carousel out there, almost five years ago. But I'm not really a country artist anyhow, at least I don't think of myself as being just that. I happened to meet Tommy Lee Whitaker about the time I started singing professionally, and got stuck with that label. You know Tommy Lee, he's full-on country, right?"

"As a matter of fact"—Mark shrugged—"I've never met him, either."

"That's funny. I talked to him on the phone this morning, to let him know how the voice-overs went, and he told me he was just about to sign a production agreement with Arrow. In fact, he said he's supposed to meet with you sometime next week."

"Yes. I haven't seen the contracts yet, but as far as I know, the deal's already been worked out."

"He also mentioned that he might start releasing my records through Arrow."

It sounded like a question.

"My understanding is, he has complete artistic control. He can release anybody he wants through us."

Mark hoped he wasn't talking too much. Whitaker might not have said that to her at all. He might have other plans for Sarah Tindall. Or none.

"Well, at least you'll get to meet him. He's picking me up at the airport tonight."

Mark checked the trace of disappointment in his voice. "Good. It'll be nice to say hello to him before we have to sit down to talk business." He had a question to ask. He hesitated, then plunged ahead. "Are you and Tommy Lee, uh . . . ?"

"Lovers? Me and Tommy Lee? Oh, my goodness, no! We've been friends for so long we're just like brother and sister." She laughed. "We know too much about each other to be lovers."

"Why don't we have dinner together, then, and go over your contract?" He laughed embarrassedly. "No, I don't mean that at all. I mean, why don't we have dinner together very soon? I would like to see you socially."

"Sure, I'd love to. When?"

His pulse quickened. "Well, I'm just moving back to California after a couple of years in New York, so I've got a lot of unpacking and settling in to do. I know it'll take me at least a couple of days. How would Sunday night be?"

"Fine, I'll be looking forward to it."

The stewardess' voice came into the cabin over the sound of the engines, announcing twenty minutes until landing in Los Angeles.

Mark looked at his watch. "I had no idea I'd slept that long!"

"I thought you were going to sleep all the way to L.A., the way you were snoring."

"Really?"

"No." She smiled, and touched his face.

He excused himself and went back to the restroom again. He rinsed his mouth thoroughly with warm water and ran his forefinger across his teeth, trying to wipe away as much of the sour taste as he could.

The cabin lights were still off when he returned. He took the seat beside her again. They talked a few moments longer. Small talk, avoiding anything that might serve to make the following Sunday night less attractive. Just before the plane entered its landing pattern, she slipped a piece of paper into his hand.

"Here, I wrote this out for you while you were gone."

"Okay—seven o'clock Sunday night, at your place." He folded the paper, stuck it in his inside coat pocket. "And I'll call you Sunday, about noon, to remind you."

"You don't have to remind me, Mark. I won't forget."

It was past midnight, cool and raining slightly, when the plane landed at Los Angeles International. They walked together to the luggage-claim area.

They were standing there a few minutes later when a man of about twenty-five, in blue jeans and a worn pullover, came up behind them and put his arms around Sarah's waist—rather possessively, Mark thought—and kissed her neck.

"Oh! Tommy Lee"—she gave him a quick impersonal hug—"this is Mark Donovan."

"No shit? Mark Donovan, huh?" The hint of jealousy receded in Tommy Lee Whitaker's eyes.

Mark offered his hand. "Nice to meet you."

"We just met on the plane from Chicago," Sarah explained.

"Yeah? No shit?" Tommy Lee said, and Mark got the impression that maybe the young record producer was not quite as smart as Gino Turicotti had made him out to be. Then, as Mark looked closer, he saw that only a small circle of color showed outside of Whitaker's dilated pupils. He was high on drugs.

"I missed you, little lady," Tommy Lee said, turning his back to Mark, rudely placing himself between Mark and Sarah.

"It's good to be home, Tommy Lee," Sarah said noncommittally.

Her bags arrived first. She showed a porter her claim check, and the three of them waited in silence, watching him load the bags on a small cart.

"Hey, man, if you ain't doing nothing," Tommy Lee said to Mark, "why don't you come on up to my place? We can smoke a few, do a little rapping. . . ."

"Thanks, but I think I'd better pass on it tonight, Tommy Lee. All I want to do right now is take a shower and sleep for twenty-four hours. But we'll get together sometime next week. We've got a lot of business to discuss."

"Yeah, I know what you mean." Whitaker seemed relieved that Mark had declined the invitation. "I've got a couple of things to catch up on myself." He looked at Sarah meaningfully. "I'll call you Monday. You'll be at the old place on Gower, right?"

"Yes, but you'd better make it Thursday or Friday. I need some time to get organized, and that'll give me a chance to go over your contracts. They should be here before then."

"What's cool with you, sport, is cool with me." Whitaker shrugged.

Sarah extricated herself from Tommy Lee's hug and offered her cheek to Mark. "I'll talk to you in a couple of days, Mark."

As Mark brushed her face with his lips, he saw the glint of jealousy return to Tommy Lee's eyes.

They shook hands again, and Mark watched them follow the porter through the sliding glass doors. They made a strange pair, he thought, the well-dressed young woman and the unkempt, hostile young man. And it was clear that she had not been truthful about their relationship.

He experienced a twinge of disappointment at her dishonesty, felt a momentary urge to reach in his pocket and destroy the piece of paper with her address and phone number. But at that precise instant, the first of his bags appeared at the top of the ramp.

He smiled. He was home again.

HOLLYWOOD
MARCH 1961

The three houses, perched near the crest of a winding mountain road a few miles north of Sunset Strip, looked like expensive redwood Quonset huts.

The first was occupied by a nineteen-year-old rock "star" of recent emergence and limited phosphorescence, whose vocal range extended exactly two and three-quarter notes above middle C, and who, therefore, owed much of his recording success to his weekly appearances on his parents' network television show.

The second was occupied by a rather stylized couple, a delicate, moderately successful designer of women's fashions named Tony, and a leviathan former professional football player, sometimes referred to as "Sweetie," but more often, lately, as "you demented, inconsiderate brute."

The third house, the one at the far end of the road, was built the same as the other two. But having been erected upon a smaller lot, it hung out over the edge of the mountain a bit more precariously. This was Tommy Lee Whitaker's house.

It was a good neighborhood, small but first-class. Except when it rained. And since this particular Sunday morning marked the beginning of the twelfth straight day of direct precipitation, the whole neighborhood appeared to be quite literally on the verge of going down the drain. To hasten matters along, seemingly, sometime during the night the downpour had finally succeeded in washing away the last few bits of shrubbery from the steep incline across the road, turning the entire crest of the mountain into a thick, rufous slime— part of which now covered Tommy Lee's driveway, slopping against the wheels of the black Cadillac convertible that belonged there, and just beginning to envelop the driveshaft and rear axle of the yellow Austin-Healy roadster that had been parked beside it overnight for the first time in several months.

Inside the house, barefoot, wearing a pair of cutoff jeans, Tommy Lee sat cross-legged on his living-room rug, bent over his wrought-iron coffee table, engrossed in using a single-edged razor blade to chop and separate a small pile of leaves and twigs and seeds into what he hoped would turn out to be an acceptable mixture of first-class Mexican smoke.

Finally, satisfied, he allowed his slightly crooked front teeth to emerge from behind his thin lips, as he deftly rolled a joint to the thickness of a Lucky Strike, licked it lovingly, masturbated it twice, and lit up. He could tell right away that it was good—by the way he had to sputter and gag to hold the acrid smoke inside his lungs. He held it as long as he could, then, for Sarah's benefit as much as his own, leaned back against the couch and exhaled in a noisy sigh of appreciation.

"Hey"—he spoke across the room—"you'd better come get some of this. Maybe it'll turn you into some decent company."

She was lying on the floor on the other side of the room in front of the big picture window, on her stomach with her arms folded under her head. She was wearing one of his shirts—with nothing on underneath—which stopped about two inches short of covering her buttocks. She had been in that position for the better part of an hour now, motionless, morosely staring out at the dull morning, watching the cars inch through the flooded gutters of Ventura Boulevard three miles below. She made no sign that she had heard him.

"Fuck it," he said. "Suit yourself."

It took her perhaps thirty seconds to reconsider, before she half-crawled, half-rolled backward across the floor to where he was sitting. Wordlessly she plucked the joint from his hand, inhaled deeply, and handed it back to him.

"Sometimes I think the only reason you come up here is because you know I always keep some good dope around."

"No." She sulked. "I come here so you'll have somebody handy to put down."

"Christ, you still mad about what I said about your masters?"

She clamped her lips together, her eyes flashing, her expression telling him that she was.

"Jesus, Sarah, I just said that Carl and Lonnie did a shitty job of mixing it down. Why get so goddamned pissed off about that?"

"Because that's *not* all you said. You said my voice sounded 'tinny.' "

"Oh, bullshit!"

"Don't try to get out of it, Tommy Lee. That's what you said, dammit!"

"You just didn't understand me right. When I said 'tinny,' I didn't mean your *voice* necessarily, I meant the way the whole tape was equalized. I probably shouldn't have listened to the goddamn thing last night in the first place, I was too ripped."

"Well . . . you should have done it yourself, then."

"Stop talking like a fool. How the hell could I do it myself when I didn't even know about it? I didn't even know Carl had the goddamn tracks down there, let alone that they were planning to use them. And it's your own fault—I must have told you at least a dozen times, *never* let Carl or Lonnie fuck around with any of the stuff I do for you. You know as well as me that they've both got tin ears."

"Well, what else could I do? Carl called me as soon as I got back to Nashville. He just told me to come by the studio, that's all. I didn't even know until I got there that he was planning to do voice-overs."

Tommy Lee opened his mouth to say something, changed his mind, and busied himself with fastening the last of the joint onto a roach clip.

"What?" she asked.

"What-what?"

"What were you going to say?"

"Aw, c'mon, Sarah, I don't feel like arguing this morning."

"What were you going to say?"

"Okay, fuck it, you wanna know—I'll tell you. I was gonna say, instead of being so quick to do what Carl wanted you to do, maybe you should have shown some loyalty to me. Maybe you should have told him to call *me* and see what *I* thought about it, since I was the one who cut the goddamn tracks for you in the first place."

"I didn't even think of it."

"Bullshit! You knew what Carl was trying to pull. He knows Lonnie ain't never gonna cut a goddamn hit for him, not on his own he ain't, so he's trying to get Lonnie's name on anything decent he can. And instead of you trying to look out for me, you burn hairs running into the goddamn studio as soon as he crooks his finger at you."

"You make it sound like I planned it ahead of time, Tommy Lee, and it wasn't like that at all. The way Carl talked when I got in the studio made it sound like ITLC was really in a hurry for the masters. And I'm way overdue for a hit, you know that."

"Bullshit! You shouldn't have been so goddamn greedy! You're ready to fuck over me or anybody else, long as you get your fucking hit record!"

"Oh, kiss my ass, Tommy Lee!"

Sighing his impatience, he got up and went over to the stereo. The acetate she had brought over the night before was still on the turntable. He flicked on the power, set the arm on the record, and stood there listening. When it was over, he went back and sat on the floor beside her, his thumbs pressed to his lips in concentration.

"Well, don't just sit there like a bump on a log, say something."

"I'm thinking. . . ."

"Is it that bad?"

"Oh, it ain't that bad—it just ain't what I had in mind, that's all."

"Tell me the truth, now," she said, her eyes suddenly begging for reassurance. "You don't think it's got a chance, do you?"

"Well, it ain't no number-one hit, that's for damn sure. But I guess it really depends on how much promo ITRC wants to put behind the stuff that comes out of Nashville."

"Carl said they're really going to promote it."

"What else *would* he say? You know Carl."

"I know." She looked resigned. "I don't trust him, either. He always strikes me as being kind of, uh, sneaky."

"Carl don't give a fuck about nobody," Tommy Lee said, shredding the last of the roach into the ashtray. "He's a salesman, that's all. He'd sell you a goddamn rope to hang yourself. He don't care." Immediately he began to roll another joint.

"So what are you going to do about my record?"

"What am I going to do about it?" He looked up angrily, spilling a few particles of marijuana from the end of the cigarette. "I ain't gonna do nothing about it. It ain't up to me."

"Well, what are you going to do about me, then. I mean, are you going to take me over to Arrow with you when you sign your production contract?"

"I don't know, we'll just have to wait and see what happens," he hedged. "I haven't even signed the thing yet. I don't know if I *can* take you over there with me."

"You know something"—his evasiveness made her fume—"you're a damned liar, Tommy Lee!"

"God damn you! What right you got to call me a liar? You're the one that don't do nothing but lie!" Sometimes he wished he never had to set eyes on her again. She was a monkey on his back, a goddamn wound that would never heal as long as he had to be around her. "I told you, I don't know yet."

"That's not what Mark said," she baited, knowing she was about to make him even angrier. "He said your deal was just about set with them, and under the terms of your contract you'll be able to bring in whatever artists you want."

"He told you that?" Tommy Lee's anger was immediately redirected at Mark Donovan. "How the hell does he know that? You heard him say yourself, he won't even see the contract until the end of the week. He's just trying to snow you—trying to get in your pants, that's all."

"No, he's not," she said defensively. "He's not that kind of guy."

"The fuck he ain't!" Tommy Lee exclaimed jealously.

"Okay, I'm not going to beg you, Tommy Lee." She shrugged, deciding not to press matters. She was going to see Mark tonight anyhow. Maybe she could work the subject around to her contract then. "You just go on and do whatever you want, I don't care."

He drew deeply on the joint, held it, and began to relax. "Do me a favor, okay?" He sighed. "Just let me sign the goddamned contract first—before you start trying to tell me what I can and cannot do. If I promise you something now and I can't follow through on it later, you're still gonna think that I'm just fucking you around. So let's just forget about it for now, okay? Here"—he extended the joint—"you want some?"

"No." She waved it aside, glanced over his shoulder at the clock on the kitchen counter. "I'm already running late. I've got to be going."

"Why?" The remnants of his anger immediately turned to petulance. "It's not even eleven o'clock yet."

"I told you last night, I've got to take Millie to the airport. She's going back to Nashville today."

"No, you didn't. You didn't say that at all. You said you saw Millie *in* Nashville this week."

"I told you I saw her the first of the week, while I was down there. And I told you that she flew out here Tuesday night to sign a new contract to put her radio show on some more stations. And I told you I stayed in her house, like I always do when I'm down there. And now she's staying with me, like she always does when she comes out here. That's what I told you."

"That's funny"—he could hear the undertones of jealousy in his voice—"if she was at your place, how come I didn't see her when I dropped you off night before last?"

"God, Tommy Lee, will you stop hassling me! She was there. She was already in bed, that's why you didn't see her."

"Oh," he half-apologized, "maybe I didn't hear you right."

"That's because you never remember anything I say when you're stoned." She looked at the clock again. It was eleven. It would take at least a half-hour to drive home in this rain. And Mark was supposed to call her around noon. She stood up. "I've got to go."

"So go," he said, trying to sound like he didn't care.

He heard her moving about in the bathroom and the bedroom,

while he sat there on the floor finishing the joint. By the time she came back to get her record ten minutes later, he was very mellow.

"I looked out the bedroom window," she said, slipping into her raincoat. "The driveway's full of mud. You may have to give me a push to get out, okay?"

She was almost to the door, but she knew him well enough to know if she didn't kiss him good-bye he'd let her sit out there in the driveway until hell froze over before he'd help her. She hurried back, buttoning her coat as she crossed the room, and leaned over and quickly bussed his cheek. He grabbed her, pulled her down beside him.

"Dope always makes me horny. . . ." he whispered.

"Don't play around, Tommy Lee!" she said sharply, trying to free herself. "I'm in a hurry—besides, you got enough last night to do you for a while."

"What is this shit? Just because I don't have a contract ready for you to sign, you're gonna pull this shit?" His anger was half-feigned, but they could both feel an undercurrent of truth in it.

"That's not the reason . . . baby." She allowed him to taste the tip of her tongue. "I told you I'm in a hurry, that's all. And besides, I'm sore. I started getting sore last night while you were eating me. I think I'm getting ready for my period or something."

"There's more than one way to skin a cat," he whispered, making it sound like a recent discovery, "and the way I feel, it ain't gonna take but a couple of minutes. . . ."

His grip tightened on her, his left hand digging into her arm through the sleeve of her raincoat, his right hand fumbling clumsily at her breast. She kissed him again, perfunctorily, knowing she'd save more time by doing what he wanted than by tugging and wrestling with him. She thought about removing her coat, changed her mind, and hurriedly helped him slide out of his jeans. He closed his eyes as he felt her lips sliding down his bare stomach. A second later, her lips enclosed him. Softly, expertly, she drew him deep into her mouth. Then the familiar, exquisite sweetness that she gave better than any woman he had ever known. From a distance, he heard the delicate rain falling on the roof.

He was only half-conscious when he heard the front door close and felt the sudden stab of loneliness that always came when she left. He heard the grinding of the four-cylinder engine in the driveway as the Austin-Healy tried to extricate itself from the mud. And seconds later, another grinding of gears as the little car hurried through the first turn at the bottom of the hill.

He lay there on the floor awhile longer, feeling the dampness of the rug against the side of his face; then he sat up and slowly, dazedly rolled another joint, lit it, and reached for his guitar.

Hours later, he laid his guitar on the rug beside him.

Writing songs was hard work, hard work for anybody, but especially hard for him, because he was slightly tone deaf and couldn't hear the nuances of melody. He could, on occasion, write simple, fairly professional lyrics. But the more he worked on them, the more subjective they tended to become, until nobody knew what he was trying to say, including himself

He knew what was wrong. He was pressing too hard. Just let it come—that was the secret to good songwriting. But he was anxious, perturbed at himself. He should have been writing all along, instead of waiting until a few days before he was due to sign with ITRC to try to come up with some new material for his artists.

He already had six tunes in the can, recorded, mastered, and ready to go, the first half of a proposed album by a group of country-blues musicians he'd discovered at a club in San Diego. He had flown to New York and played the tapes for Bob Silverstein, head of sales at Arrow Records, a few weeks before, and Silverstein had been impressed. Unfortunately, he had led Silverstein to believe he had a lot more songs in the can than he really had.

And now, in the process of putting together a new production company, which enjoyed no reputation in the business yet, he was finding good, original material almost impossible to come by. At this juncture in the evolution of rock-'n'-roll music, a good song was a lot more recognizable than a good artist. Good melodies and interesting harmonies stood out from ordinary material like a diamond in a Cracker Jack box. And he knew that a good tune was the only thing record companies felt safe in putting their money behind, because of their limited knowledge of the artistic qualities of their products.

As he sat there stretching his legs and flexing his toes to get the blood circulating again, his stomach began to repeat the same growling noise it had started making an hour before, reminding him he hadn't eaten since morning. The day had been so dreary—it had been dusk outside ever since early afternoon. He had lost track of the time. He looked at the clock on the kitchen counter and saw that it was nearing eight-thirty. He still had time to run down the hill and grab a sandwich, and come back and get in a full night's work. He had to get this tune finished.

He showered quickly, changed into another pair of jeans, flung his green windbreaker on over a T-shirt, and stopped to roll another joint on the way out.

As he picked his way through the thick mud that covered his

driveway, he was glad to see that it had finally stopped raining. The night was a little chilly, but the crisp air felt good on his face after having been in the house all day, and the sky was clearer than it had been for several weeks. He was so stoned, a million stars seemed to be flickering just above his head, almost close enough to touch, going off like little precision-timed rockets. The bright mosaic that was the San Fernando Valley stretched below him like a blanket of Christmas-tree lights, and for a moment he felt like he had left his body and was floating in a vacuum, above and beyond everything and everybody he had ever known.

He slid behind the wheel and sat there smoking the last of the joint, while he lowered the top and revved the motor a few times, then took off in a splattering of mud, skidding the four and a half miles through the narrow canyon roads that led down to the Strip.

When he reached the intersection of Sunset and Doheny he drove a couple of blocks, trying to decide where to eat. Finally, dictated more by a break in the long line going the other way than by his own choice, he made a left across the double lines and pulled into Ben Frank's Restaurant, a gaudy coffee shop where street people, rock musicians, and aspiring actors congregated. It was now approaching nine o'clock, too late for the dinner crowd and too early for the rounders who would start spilling in after midnight. The lot was almost empty. He saw a familiar car, a blue Cad convertible the same year as his own, parked by the door.

Old Goose was in town. He was doing pretty well these days, having gotten in with a clique of country musicians who had settled in Bakersfield, about a hundred miles northeast of the city. They had built a good studio up there, already cut a number of national hit records, and seemed to be putting together a sort of mini-Nashville. Everybody in Bakersfield knew Halsey from his years on the road with the big-name country bands, but now he was in such demand for recording sessions that he rarely bothered to go out on the road anymore. Tommy Lee had seen him around town three or four times in the past month, and he looked prosperous.

Tommy Lee parked beside Goose's car and went inside. He spotted Halsey in the back booth between two girls, an attractive, petite blond in her early twenties and a taller, older-looking brunette with large breasts and too much makeup. He didn't feel much like socializing right then, and he thought about slipping unnoticed into a seat at the counter, but he knew Goose would invite him over as soon as he saw him, so he crossed the room and joined them.

"Hey, man, you still hanging around town?" Tommy Lee said. "I thought you'd be long gone by now."

Goose looked up, startled. A broad grin immediately covered his red face. "Well, shit—god damn, Tommy Lee!" he exclaimed, which was his usual greeting. "What the hell you doing here, boy?"

Tommy Lee edged into the booth next to the blond without bothering to introduce himself. "Just fucking around, that's all. What's the matter, they kick your hillbilly ass out of Bakersfield?"

"Hell, no, I'm moving down here. I got the job, man."

"What job?"

"The one I told you about . . ."

"Oh, yeah," Tommy Lee said, trying vainly to remember what job and when Goose had told him about it. "No shit? You got it, huh?"

"Yeah, I got the sum'bitch. You'd never guess how."

"How?"

"*Elvis,* man!"

"You're lying."

"No, I ain't. Swear to God. He got it for me."

"No shit? How?"

"Man, you ain't gonna believe this. . . ." Goose guffawed proudly.

"I probably ain't, so why don't you quit fucking around and tell me."

"I almost told you the other night, but I didn't know it was you till after you left."

"Huh?" That didn't make sense to Tommy Lee. He didn't know if that was because he was stoned or because Goose was talking double-talk. "You know something—I don't have no idea *at all* what you're talking about," he said.

"The other night," Goose said impatiently, "Friday, when you brought Sarah home from the airport. I was there in bed with Millie."

"Oh!" Tommy Lee tried to remember what Sarah had told him about Millie being there that night. "Yeah, I knew Millie was there," he lied, "that's why I didn't stay but a minute, I can't hack that fucking broad. But I didn't know you were there, too." It took a second to register. "What the hell were you doing there?"

"I told you, I was in bed with Millie. We had just got in a few minutes before you got there."

"From where?"

"*I told you,* from Elvis's."

"Well, what the hell's that got to do with you getting the god-damn job?" Tommy Lee asked in exasperation.

"Maybe I better tell you the whole story, huh?"

"Maybe you'd better, 'cause if you don't, I ain't gonna know what the fuck you're talking about."

"Okay, listen." Goose grinned, enjoying the attention of Tommy

Lee and the two girls. "You know me and Millie are pretty tight, right?" Tommy Lee nodded. "Okay, so I picked her up at the airport Tuesday night, and she told me Elvis was in town making a movie, and he was having a little party up at his place on Bellagio Road Friday night, and he had invited her because she was making his new record her 'pick of the week' on her new playlist." He regarded Tommy Lee quizzically. "You with me so far?"

"Hmm-hmm," Tommy Lee said dubiously.

"You didn't tell me you knew Elvis," the brunette said.

"Of course I know Elvis," Goose said, looking at the brunette as if he doubted her sanity. "I'm from Nashville, ain't I? Shit, me and him go back a looong time—"

"So how'd he get you the job?" Tommy Lee interrupted.

"I'm coming to that," Goose said, irritated at being interrupted before he could tell the brunette how well he knew Elvis. "Okay, so Millie invites me to go up there with her, knowing I know Elvis and all. And I guess sometime during the night she must have mentioned to him that I was up for this important job, knowing that Elvis would be interested and everything. So about ten o'clock he calls me off to one side and asks me how bad I want it. Well, I figured it wasn't no sense in trying to play it cool or nothing like that, so I told him the straight-out truth. I said, 'Bad, man!' And you know what he says? He says, 'Okay, I'll get it for you.' Just like that!" Goose snapped his fingers. " 'Okay, I'll get it for you.' "

"No kidding?" The brunette was impressed. "I heard he was like that."

"Oh, yeah, he's a cool sum'bitch," Goose said. "So anyhow, one of the gals around there gets the number for him and he picks up the phone right then and dials the head man's house. He talks to the maid, must of been, and tells her who's calling. Must of knocked her flat on her ass, 'cause, shit, a minute later the head man hisself is on the phone. . . ."

"No kidding!" the brunette said.

"What did Elvis tell him?" Tommy Lee asked.

"Well, 'course, ole Elvis ain't like he used to be when me and him was tight before, you know. He done put on quite a bit of cool since then, learnt how to act, and everything. When he talks now, 'course, everybody listens. So he says, 'I understand you're thinking about hiring my man Goose to head up your West Coast country-music office.' And the guy must of said he was, 'cause right away ole Elvis says to him, 'Well, if you're thinking about it, you better go on and take care of business, 'cause I'm just about to hire him to run one or two of my publishing companies myself!' "

"No kidding!" the brunette repeated.

"Umm-umm," Goose said, then explained, "Well, 'course, me and Elvis have been pretty tigh over the years, and I'd do the same for him."

"Boy, that's a bitch, ain't it?" Tommy Lee said. "What happened then?"

"Well, I guess the guy asks to speak to me. So I get on the phone and we talk a minute and he hires me right on the spot, so to speak."

"What kind of money he offer you?"

"Forty grand a year, starting off."

"Hmmm, that's pretty good money," the brunette said, snuggling a little closer to Halsey.

Tommy Lee didn't know whether to believe the story or not. It seemed every country musician in the world invoked the friendship of Elvis at the drop of a hat, especially when trying to impress a woman. Still, he knew that Goose was on good terms with just about all the country artists. And he deserved the job—that was certain.

"When are you supposed to start working?" Tommy Lee asked.

"Well, I'm *supposed* to start tomorrow morning, but I still got most of my stuff up in Bakersfield, so I'm gonna have to run up there tonight and start packing. I would have left sooner, but I wanted to stay around and see Millie off. And I probably should get me a lawyer, too, just to make sure everything's on the up-and-up."

"Hey, man, I'm really happy for you," Tommy Lee said sincerely. "I mean, no shit."

"Thanks, Tommy Lee. Oh, while I'm thinking about it, I'm gonna need a whole bunch of new tunes. You got any you can let me hear?"

"Yeah, I got some," Tommy Lee said, thinking about the songs still running around inside his head, "but I'm gonna need them myself. I'm signing with ITRC this week. Putting my production company with Arrow Records."

"Arrow Records!" Goose's eyes lit up. "Man, they're going to be the hottest label in the business! Shit, I didn't know you was going with them. I didn't even know they was getting into country music."

"They are, but I ain't. I'm gonna be cutting pop tunes."

"No shit? Pop tunes, huh? Boy, you gonna make some goddamn money! How much they gonna pay you?"

"We're talking about two hundred grand, for three years. Guaranteed."

"Hmmm . . ." the brunette said, unconsciously loosening her grip on Goose's arm, looking across the table at Tommy Lee with new respect. "That's pretty good money."

"But you got to pay for your session costs and everything out of that, ain't you?" Goose asked.

"Yeah, but I'm still gonna do all right. They're gonna pay me twenty-five thousand every quarter, and I have to guarantee them eight albums a year, so I can't go broke or nothing like that. I just got to be careful how I spend money, that's all."

"You know something—I'm proud of you, boy," Goose said, his eyes shining. "I mean it, I'm proud of you. All them hit records you cut for Carl Clinger, I knew they was gonna pay off sooner or later. I told you a long time ago you was gonna make it, didn't I?"

"Yeah, you sure did," Tommy Lee said, nodding, remembering.

"Yeah, this music-business thing came along at just the right time, all right," Goose said, nodding his head in unison with Tommy Lee's. "Everybody I know, seems like, is making a shit pot full of money. You, me, all them home boys up north—even Millie. You know how much she's gonna make off of that syndicated playlist this year? More'n fifty thousand dollars, she told me. Just for telling radio stations what records to play. Ain't that something?"

"Timing is everything," the brunette said knowledgeably, still staring at Tommy Lee, wishing he was a little better-looking so she could slip him her phone number.

"And I'll tell you something, Tommy Lee," Goose continued. "I'm glad to see everybody making it. Shit, I ain't greedy. There's more'n enough to go around. Me personally, I'm doing better than I ever thought I was gonna do. I'll be making forty grand a year, my own office, my own secretary. Shit, I'm wallowing in hog heaven!"

"Let me out," the brunette said. "I have to powder my nose."

"Me too." The blond spoke for the first time.

The two men stood, watched the girls slide out of the booth and disappear toward the back of the building..

"That ain't your old lady, is it?" Tommy Lee asked as they resumed their seats.

"Naw, I just met her at the airport a couple of hours ago. She's a promotion gal at Capitol, I think. She was coming in when Millie was going out, and Millie introduced me to her."

If Millie didn't go to the airport until a couple of hours ago, Tommy Lee wondered, why had Sarah been in such a hurry to leave his house that morning?

"Did Sarah go to the airport with you all?" he asked, knowing he shouldn't bring the subject up, but too curious not to.

"Hell, no, she was around there primping and going on when we left. She come rushing in this morning and got a phone call from some dude, and shit, she never did get her feet back on the ground after that." Immediately he saw Tommy Lee's face sag. "She'd just left your place, huh?"

Tommy Lee shrugged.

"Lemme ask you something"—Goose's face suddenly turned serious—"and you tell me the truth, hear?"

"What?"

"You know there's something wrong with that gal, don't you?"

"I know she's fucked," Tommy Lee said bitterly.

"She's in worse shape than you think. She's about to go over the side of the cliff."

"She needs to be *thrown* over the goddamn cliff, that's what she needs." Tommy Lee's clenched first jarred the table.

"No, that ain't it," Goose said quietly. "She can't help it none. I'll tell you something. Me and Millie talked about her all the way to the airport this evening, and Millie told me a lot of things about her, stuff that maybe don't nobody else in the world know but Millie." He shook his head compassionately. "That gal had a hard time coming up, Tommy Lee. Bounced around from pillar to post, you know?"

"Yeah, she told me about some of that," Tommy Lee said. He hesitated, gathering his thoughts. "But the thing is . . . seems like she could do a little better. I mean, she ain't no goddamn dummy. She's about the smartest woman I've ever known in my life, when she wants to be. Man, she could have everything she wanted, if she just didn't try to be so goddamn sick. I could help her myself—I'm in a position to. Ain't nothing else in the world I'd like to do more than sign her up on my production company and release her records on Arrow. I could make her a star, man. She sings good enough, and God knows she's pretty enough to be on TV and in the movies and all that stuff. And I know how to cut her. I should, I recorded every decent record she ever made. She wouldn't have nothing, not a goddamn thing in this world, if it wasn't for me, ain't that right?"

"I guess that's right," Goose said loyally.

"And the thing is," Tommy Lee continued, unable to stop the rush of words, "she don't have to be my woman. I guess there was a time when I did want that more than anything else in the world, but fuck it, them days are dead and buried. She's done fucked up too much. Every son of a bitch between here and Tallahassee's been wallowing around in that pussy by now. I mean, I *can't* sign her up on my company. I already been through too much shit on account of her. But if she would just quit lying all the time, quit fucking up so goddamn much . . ." He shook his head disconsolately.

"Yeah, but she probably don't even know what she's doing half the time," Goose said, reaching for a cigarette. "I guess if she hadn't lucked up and bumped into you and started making records when she did, she might be anyplace by now, whoring, locked up in a crazy house somewhere.

"I'm gonna tell you something, Tommy Lee." Goose sighed as he fanned the match out. "See, you ain't never been what you call dirt-poor, but I have. That's something you don't never get over, take my word for it. And lots of folks, me included, think being poor like that is harder on a gal than it is on a man, 'specially when she's growing up around people that don't care nothing about her. Dirt-poor, mean-assed kinfolks will ruin a gal quicker than anything in the world. I know what I'm talking about, boy." He slapped the table emphatically, then tilted his head to the side and looked at Tommy Lee. "You remember that time we was sitting in my car back home, and I told you what had happened when she was on the road with me and Bobby Joe?"

Tommy Lee nodded, recalling the painful episode.

"You was in love with her then, wasn't you?"

Tommy Lee shrugged noncommittally.

"*Wasn't you?*" Goose insisted.

"Yeah, I guess I was," Tommy Lee admitted.

"You should have told me, boy," Goose said angrily, " 'stead of letting me sit there half-drunk running off at the mouth like that."

"Too late now," Tommy Lee said.

"Yeah, I guess it is, all right. But I thought about that many a night—god damn, I wouldn't have told you about that for nothing in the world if I had known." He was quiet for a moment. "I hope you ain't *still* in love with her?"

Tommy Lee toyed with the matches on the table, grateful to have somebody to talk to about Sarah, somebody who wasn't going to put him down for being such a goddamn fool. "I truthfully don't know," he said. "Sometimes I am, sometimes I ain't. Sometimes we don't see each other for months at a time, and we don't keep no tabs on each other while we're apart. I do what I want to, and she does whatever comes in her head, I guess." Again he tried to put his thoughts into words. "But there's just something about her, man, that whenever I do see her, spend a little time around her, it don't take much for her to do a number on me." He tossed the matchbook at the ashtray, missed, and smiled wryly. "God damn, I must sound like a dumb son of a bitch, huh?"

"Hmmm." Goose nodded in understanding. "I been down that road, boy. That's the saddest goddamn road in the world. But you know what you got to do? You got to turn around and look back at yourself. You ain't the same little kid you was then. You prob'ly don't even know it, but you done come a long ways, farther'n me, farther'n most other folks, 'specially to still be so young. You just about to make it big, boy, with Arrow Records and all. And where you are now, that gal can't do you a bit of good. She's about the last thing in the world you need right now. You can't help her none, not a damn bit. All the hit records in the world couldn't help that gal. Can't nobody help her, 'cept herself. I'm telling you what I know: the best thing you can do right now is tell her to kiss your behind and go on about your business and make your million dollars and forget her. I know that sounds cold, Tommy Lee, but that's the way it is."

"I know you're telling me right. I just needed to hear somebody say it, I guess."

"And that's *all* I'm gonna say." Goose tried to smile. "I got a bad habit of talking too goddamn much." He stuck out his hand. "We still friends?"

Tommy Lee saw the sincerity in the musician's face, and remembered how Goose had praised him and encouraged him right along. "Yeah, sure—we're still friends. You might be the best friend I've got in this whole damn world," he said, taking Goose's hand.

"I'm ready to go," the brunette said.

They both glanced up quickly, wondering how long the two girls had been standing there.

"Okay," Goose said, bumping his leg on the table as he struggled to get out. Then, to Tommy Lee: "Do me a favor, huh? Call me one day next week, Tuesday or Wednesday if you got a little time. Maybe we can have lunch or something. And I wanna get the name of a good lawyer from you, to tighten up my contract. Shit, I don't know too many folks in this town, and the ones I do know, I don't trust worth a damn." He grinned and tapped Tommy Lee's shoulder. "Hell, we country boys got to stick together, ain't that right?"

"You can use my lawyer," Tommy Lee said. "His name is Blandings. Used to work for Carousel. He's pretty good about the music business. And if I run across any good country tunes or masters I can't use, I'll bring them by for you to listen to, okay?"

"I'll be 'specting to hear from you, then. Just call me at the office." Goose grinned broadly. "Did you hear that? 'Just call me at the office.' *Whooceee!*" He let out a rebel yell so loud that every head in the place turned around. "Ain't that a bitch!"

"For a goddamn hillbilly, that ain't too bad," Tommy Lee kidded.

"C'mon, let's go," the brunette said, embarrassed.

"Don't be ordering me around," Goose said, slipping his arm around her waist, tweaking one of her ample breasts, "unless you ready to come up off something."

He winked at Tommy Lee, and led her off toward the cash register with a noticeable strut in his step. Tommy Lee smiled and picked up the menu.

"Mind if I join you?" The blond was still standing there.

"No, I don't mind," Tommy Lee said. "But I thought you were going with them."

"No, I just came in for a cup of coffee and saw Gloria sitting here with your friend. Me and her used to room together, and I hadn't seen her for a while, so I just came over to say hello."

"You hungry—want a sandwich or something?"

"Yeah, sure, if you do. . . ."

The waitress came over to clear the table and pick up her tip. She took their orders and left.

"I, uh, happened to hear part of your conversation," the blond said. "I bet I know who you were talking about."

"No, you don't," Tommy Lee said.

"Sarah Tindall—right?"

Tommy Lee flashed a look of annoyance.

"I thought so," the blond said. "I saw her picture in a *Hit Parade* magazine a couple of months ago. I don't mean to sound conceited or anything, but don't you think I look a little like her?"

Tommy Lee hadn't paid the blond much attention before. He studied her now. She did bear a considerable resemblance to Sarah. Same face, same hairstyle, but she was a little smaller. The only thing wrong with her was her skin. It was pretty bad, like she had either been eating a lot of junk food or was using speed.

"Yeah," he said, "come to think of it, you do look a little like her."

"That's a compliment"—the blond smiled in appreciation—"because I happen to think she's very pretty."

They sat there for a while, making small talk, the blond trying unsuccessfully to provide interesting conversation. The waitress brought their sandwiches. The blond made several more attempts at small talk, again drawing only uninterested grunts from Tommy Lee.

He was lost in his own thoughts. When he finished eating, he wiped his mouth and picked up the check. "Well, it was nice meeting you," he said, leaving a tip under his plate. "What did you say your name was?"

"Judy. Maybe we'll meet again, huh?"

"Oh, for sure," he said without conviction.

He stood at the cash register and watched her go through the door, waving at a couple of people as she left. She was still standing outside by the paper racks when he started for his car.

"Listen . . . uh, I was thinking . . . ." She sounded unsure how to go on. "Look, if you don't have anything else to do, we can go down the street and check out some sounds. I know a few doormen, I can probably get us in for nothing."

"No, I can't. I gotta go home and do some work." He tried to smile. "Thanks anyhow."

"That's okay."

She waved good-bye and started walking east on Sunset. He stood there beside his car, watching her. From the back, she looked even more like Sarah. He called to her. She turned around.

"Listen, I was thinking . . . if you don't have anything to do, we can go up to my place for a while. You smoke?"

"Sure."

"Good. I got some right-on-shit. We can smoke a couple, drink a little wine, and kick back—you know what I mean?"

"Sure. Great."

She came over to the car. He found a rag and wiped the moisture off the seat for her, then went around to the other side and got in and started the engine. "I'm kind of ripped, you know," he said. "I'm sorry, I missed your name. Trudy, right?"

"No, Judy."

"Groovy."

The house was dark except for a small blue lamp by the stereo. They were lying on their stomachs in front of the window, looking down at the lights, sharing a joint, and drinking wine from separate glasses.

"This is a nice pad," she said. "I mean, *really* a nice pad."

"Thanks."

"You live here by yourself?"

"Most of the time."

She puffed the joint, held the smoke in while she talked. "How come you don't have a steady old lady?"

"I do, lots of them."

"That's too bad, you've got a lot going for you. You should have a steady old lady, you know. . . ."

"You wanna hear some music?" He was already getting bored with her.

"What've you got?"

"Whatever you wanna hear."

She called off a few names, mostly black singers.

"No, I ain't into that too much, but I've got some nice albums." He got up and went over to the stereo. A few moments later, Jack Scott's baritone voice floated into the room. Back beside her, he asked, "How's that?"

"It's okay. I'm not into hillbilly music too much, but it's okay."

He felt a flicker of irritation, but said nothing. Instead, he rolled her over onto her back and kissed her. He wasn't horny. He never got horny right after he had been with Sarah, but this one wasn't interesting enough just to talk with.

Her lips parted readily. But she had a slightly sour odor about her, which turned him off. He could tell that she used a lot of speed. Damn near everybody who did had that same smell. He wondered why she wasn't wired tonight. Probably didn't have enough money to score. He probably shouldn't have brought her up here to his place; she might come back later with some of her loser friends and rip him off.

"That was nice," she said when they had finished kissing. He picked up his glass, remained silent. "You know, it's funny that you should be in the record business," she continued. "I used to go with a guy that's in the record business. He owns his own company now."

"Oh, yeah . . . who?"

"You remember Ron Carson, the dj?"

"Yeah, I know Ron." He also knew that Carson had lost his radio show during the payola scandals.

"From what I hear, he's really going good, too. He's putting out a lot of old records, calls them Golden Oldies."

"Good for him."

Actually, she'd spent only one night with Ron Carson, four or five years ago. And what an unusual night that had been. Somebody had given him a brand-new Cadillac convertible that night. He'd said it was one of his fans, but she didn't believe that. It had been an odd night in a lot of other ways, too. But she was different now, more grown-up.

"Listen," Tommy Lee said, increasingly turned off by her smell, "I'm kind of sweaty. I been writing songs all day, and that always makes me sweat. You wanna take a shower with me?"

"Yeah, I haven't seen your bathroom yet."

"It's a bitch," he said.

They showered together, then went into the bedroom.

Later, after she had gone to sleep, he came back into the darkened living room. He lit another joint and lay by the window, smoking and drinking wine straight from the half-gallon jug, occasionally stopping long enough to strum a few chords on his guitar.

As he sat there, he thought about Sarah again, wondering who she was out with tonight. And that made him start thinking about Lonnie Pratt, and how he and Lonnie used to go out raising hell together back home. Then he thought about Carl Clinger and Bob Blandings, and Red Leach and old man Jefferson. And he had to chuckle to himself when he thought about how impressed he had been the first time he met Buddy Jepstone.

He thought about his grandmother for a long time, about how

much he loved her, and how tiny and wistful she'd looked in her black lace dress a few months ago, laid out in her casket in the Church of Eternal Understanding, in Goodlettsville, Tennessee.

He thought about his car parked outside, and how he had walked into Clarence Dixon Cadillac on Vine Street and paid cash for it. He thought about his house, right up here in the middle of all these rich, important movie stars. He thought about all the dope he could afford to buy when he started making a couple of hundred thousand dollars a year. And he thought about all the new women waiting for him out there in the world, that he hadn't gotten around to yet.

He was thoroughly stoned when he finished the second joint. He started strumming his guitar again, fooling around in the darkness with his tape recorder, until, somehow, he managed to erase most of what he had spent the whole day working on.

He couldn't tell how much later it was that he heard the blond— Trudy or Judy or whatever the hell her name was—calling to him from the bedroom. He ignored her. Sometime after that, he turned around and she was sitting on the floor beside him. He tried to concentrate on what she was saying. But couldn't, and gave up.

He had already passed out, so he didn't hear her when she called a cab. He was lying on the floor beside the window with the guitar in his arms when she took the ten-dollar bill from his pocket and went outside to wait.

REDONDO BEACH
MARCH 1961

Mark was anxious to see *The Misfits*, partially because he was an Arthur Miller fan, but mainly because Clark Gable had been such a close and longtime family friend, and he wanted to see him play his last role. Afterward, he'd have a late dinner with Sarah, take her home, and go straight home himself, so he could get up early and put the cottage back in shape after the mess left by the previous tenants.

That was the plan. Somehow, things didn't work out that way. By the time he picked Sarah up at her Beverly Hills apartment and drove out to the theater in Westwood where the film was playing, they were too late for the eight-o'clock showing. The box office had already closed. There would be a two-and-a-half-hour wait.

Okay, he decided, that posed no big problem. He had made their dinner reservations for after the movie, for ten-thirty, at a restaurant just a few blocks away on Wilshire Boulevard. And since it was still early and the rain had finally stopped, they might as well walk there and see if they could get a table right away. They still had plenty of time to enjoy a leisurely meal and get back to the theater before the last show.

They arrived at the restaurant to find it solidly booked for the night. The hostess suggested they wait in the bar, saying she would let them know if there was an unexpected cancellation. But the bar was so crowded that, twenty minutes later, when she came in to tell them that the possibilities of her getting them a table before ten o'clock seemed pretty unlikely, they hadn't even been able to buy a drink.

So they came up with another plan: they would walk back down to Westwood, grab a quick snack, and join the line already forming for the last show. But when they got back to Westwood, to the Hamburger Hamlet, it was overcrowded, as well. While they were waiting to be seated, a couple of UCLA students recognized Sarah and came over to get her autograph. Before long, her presence had evoked a minor furor. A half-dozen kids were milling around her and another dozen or so were looking at her, trying to figure out who she was and why the others were trying to get her autograph. In the meantime, two guys had guessed who Mark was and had him hemmed against the cigarette machine, trying to pressure him into arranging an audition with Arrow Records for their rock group.

Mark grabbed Sarah's arm and pulled her outside. While they were standing there on the sidewalk trying to plan their next move, it started to rain again. Not heavy, just enough to irritate them a little more. They decided it was probably time to go back to the car and think things over. Halfway there, Mark remembered a place. It was called Rugulo's near Redondo Beach on Pacific Coast Highway. They could have a nice, quiet dinner there—he hoped.

A half-hour later, the fog hit. It came without warning. It fell over them like a soggy blanket. Within minutes they couldn't see ten feet in either direction, and the inside of the car was like the interior of a refrigerator. That's when they discovered that the heater in Mark's rental car didn't work, except when the car passed over a bump in the road, and then for only a few seconds. The evening had become utterly ridiculous, and they began to laugh. The worse it got, the more they laughed.

And then, they were friends.

It took another hour to travel the few miles between Redondo Beach and Rugulo's. It was still so foggy when they arrived at the restaurant that Mark missed it on the first pass, then, realizing his mistake, turned around and inched his way back. As he was turning left into the parking lot, his car came within a foot of being broadsided by a Volkswagen going the other way.

Hungry, chilled to the marrow, and still half-scared by the near-accident, they parked and entered the building. Sarah excused herself to go to the rest room, while Mark waited in the small foyer.

Rugulo's was one of his favorite restaurants. He had been introduced to it as a high-school student, returning home with a group of friends from a Sunday-afternoon Stan Kenton concert at the old Rendezvous Ballroom on Balboa Island. In the ensuing years, except for his recent interval in New York, he had remained such a loyal customer that the Rugulo staff—mostly assorted nieces and nephews—had practically made him one of the family. Now, tonight, happy to see him, they showered him with hugs and kisses. Even dignified, white-haired Guglielmo Rugulo came out of his office when he heard that Mark was there, to give him a firm welcome-home handshake.

The way the night had developed, it was good to receive some extra attention. For the first time since Mark had stepped off the plane two nights before, he felt he was really home.

Sarah returned a few minutes later, and they were ushered through the candlelit dining room to a quiet table against the far wall. A waiter brought over a bottle of Pinot Grigio. Compliments of Mr. Rugulo

A half-bottle of wine later, they were ready to order the specialty of the house, *ciapino* made from fresh crabmeat, shrimp, chunks of lobster and gamefish, submerged in a spicy garlic-tomato broth and served in steaming ceramic casseroles. They ate ravenously. At the end of the meal the staff accorded them another complimentary bottle of wine. As the waiter uncorked it, they concluded that events beyond their comprehension had conspired to place them here.

The remainder of the evening rushed by in a warm glow of good conversation and easy laughter. It was late now, past midnight. They were well into the second bottle of wine, scarcely aware of the soft, invisible noises of the ocean splashing against the pilings a few feet below their window. It had turned into a good evening. They had discovered many things to talk about.

"Somehow," she was saying, "I just can't picture you as a football player."

"Why not?"

"Oh, you're too . . . dignified. I mean, I just can't see you crawling around in the mud, looking for a ball with a bunch of guys climbing all over you."

"That's because you're looking at an older and wiser man. But I was really pretty good. Not great, you understand, but pretty good."

"How good?"

"Pretty damned good. All-Coast, Honorable Mention, my senior year."

She looked impressed.

"Actually, I might've made All-Coast if I'd come along at a better time," he explained, trying to sound as modest as he could. "But there were a lot of good players that year. Southern Cal had this guy named Jon Arnett—"

"Oh, I think I've heard of him."

"He was a helluva ballplayer. Made All-Pro with the Rams later. And Oregon State had this colored kid who ran a 9.4 hundred. Probably the fastest back we played against all year. He would've been a cinch All-American if he'd had the right guys blocking for him, but they were too light. We cleaned them out on national TV. He got a hundred yards against us, though." He thought a moment. "What *was* that kid's name? I think he played a couple of seasons with the Colts after he graduated, until he got hurt. . . ."

"How about you? Did you ever get hurt?"

"Did I ever get hurt!" He made a face. "I got hurt so many times I had to wear a phone number on my helmet so they'd know who to notify in case of emergency."

She laughed appreciatively, puffed her gold-tipped cigarette. "You know, that's something I've always wanted to do, go to college. I know it would be fun. I had never even been on a college campus until I started playing them a year ago, but I enjoy it. The kids are always so nice and friendly to me."

"You could still go. You don't have to enroll full-time, just take a few classes."

"No, I'm too dumb. I didn't even finish high school."

"Really?" He was genuinely surprised. "Nobody would ever know it."

"You're just saying that to build up my ego, aren't you?"

"No, I'm not. You really do speak well. Matter of fact, the first time I heard you, I thought you might have taken speech lessons."

"Thank you, I did. After Carousel had been out here a couple of years, Carl got this wild bug up his ass about putting some of his artists in the movies. He paid for my acting and speech lessons for almost a year. No, I'd better change that—he talked me into taking lessons, and then wound up deducting the money from my royalties."

"That settles it, I have to meet Carl Clinger one day." Mark laughed.

"Don't bother," she said dryly, puffing her cigarette.

"What happened? Did you ever do any acting?"

"A couple of commercials, that's all."

"Anything important?"

"No, I never even saw them. Come to think of it, I don't know anybody else who ever saw them, either."

"I don't know why you should feel insecure," he said, refilling their glasses. "Sounds to me like you've done okay. Let's see . . . you've had a couple of hit records, you've been on TV a few times, traveled all over the country, made a few commercials. . . ."

"Oh, sure, I can't really complain. I've done pretty well, considering how I started. But I still feel a little unsure of myself sometimes, especially when I'm around someone like you. I mean, someone who is really well-educated."

"You shouldn't, you're doing fine. And I don't think college is all that important anyhow."

"Especially for girls, huh?" she teased.

"Very true." He smiled. Then, seriously: "No, I just think college is overrated, that's all. While you're there, you really think you're getting it together. You can't help but think so, the way they keep pumping your head full of all those so-called 'facts.' 'This is true,' and 'that is true,' and 'this is a common misconception'—you know what I mean?" She nodded. "So by the time you get your degree, especially from graduate school, you're really sold on yourself. But after you've been out awhile, you become suspicious of stuff they taught you. It just isn't that relevant."

"Why is that?"

"Well . . ." He paused, trying to frame his thoughts so she could understand. "All you really learn in school are the accepted theories of doing business, the main avenues. But when you get out and enter the business world, or, from what my friends tell me, just about any other field, you find that the main avenues are nearly deserted. The only people using them are people like yourself, the ones who just got out of school. Everybody else is taking the shortcuts—down the alleys, over the fences, through somebody else's backyard. . . ."

"But you've adjusted, haven't you?" She sipped from her glass, waiting for him to answer. "Of course you have," she said when he didn't. "You're probably the most successful man I've ever met."

"I doubt that."

She stared across the table at him in surprise. "You're kidding! You mean to tell me that you don't consider yourself successful?"

"Oh, sure I do. But I can't say I'm completely happy with my success. Sometimes it seems pretty trivial."

"Compared to what? You know something? That may be the dumbest statement I ever heard."

"No, it isn't. It's according to how you define success."

"Okay, in that case, define success for me."

He thought a moment, started to speak, changed his mind. "That would take the rest of the night."

"Okay, then, let me ask you something else. Who would you say is the most successful man you know—your father?"

"No, not really. I mean, I certainly consider him a success, but not what I would call an . . . uh"—he searched for the right word—"*emulative* success."

"You mean, the kind of person everybody else would like to trade places with?"

"Right."

"Why not?"

"Well, I guess knowing my father as I do, and knowing the kind of life he has to lead, I tend to think of him more as having a successful *image* than being an actual success himself."

"Don't you respect him? What he's made of himself?"

"Sure, of course I do. I'm not denigrating him. He laughs about it himself, how silly it is for people to treat him the way they do."

"But that's not your idea of success?"

"Hell no, I feel sorry for him sometimes, the things he has to put up with. I know I couldn't live like that, I'd go crazy."

"Personally, I think you're already a little fuzzy around the edges," she said in exasperation.

"I don't think we should have started this discussion."

"Why not? I like it." She sipped her drink. "So name somebody you think is more successful than your father."

"I would say my grandfather, for one."

"Is he anybody important? I mean, have I ever heard of him?"

"No, he's not famous. He's just a nice old man, past eighty now. Lives on a ranch in Idaho. My sister and I used to spend our summers there when we were kids. We had our own horses, stuff like that."

"It sounds like fun."

"Oh, it was. We really looked forward to going up there every year. In fact, when I was growing up I seriously thought about becoming a rancher myself."

"First a football player, and now a cowboy. You know something?" She tamped her cigarette out in the ashtray. "I'm beginning to feel like I'm out with somebody's little brother."

"We can fix that," he said with mock shyness.

"Well, I'm sure glad you changed your mind. I just can't picture myself sitting here with the Lone Ranger."

"Or his faithful Indian companion, Hiawatha?"

"Or his faithful Indian companion, Little Beaver, either."

"You have a very weird mind."

"*I* have a very weird mind? I never wanted to be a cowboy!"

"Well, I sure thought about it. I don't know, maybe it was because of my grandfather. You know, I flew up to see him a couple of years ago, before I moved to New York, and he looked better than ever."

"I don't understand how you can say he has it all together if he's not rich and nobody ever heard of him."

"Well, he's so completely at home with himself, inside and out. What I'm trying to say is, he belongs exactly where he is, in space *and* time. He knows the name of every tree and every wild animal and plant around there, and what they do. And every fish in every stream within a hundred miles of his ranch. He amazes me. He can sit on his porch at night and name every constellation in the sky. He can even sniff the air and tell you what the next day's weather is going to be."

"Oh, that's nothing. I know a million people back home who can do that—who can't even read and write. I wouldn't exactly call that being successful."

"Okay, then," he said, becoming a little vexed with her, "what would *you* call being successful?"

"Oh, that's easy—having a lot of money, being able to go where you want, whenever you want. Having people look up to you and respect you."

"How about love?"

"Sure," she said, reaching for another cigarette, "love, too."

"Well, at least we agree on one thing."

"Do you believe in astrology?"

"No."

"Then why are you wearing that ring?"

"Somebody gave it to me."

"But you don't believe in it?"

"No."

"Good. That's two things we agree on."

"You know something?" he said, his voice suddenly serious. "I like you."

"That's three," she said.

"No, I *really* like you."

The humor left her eyes for an instant, as her face assumed the same expression that had surprised him on the plane: her nostrils flared, and her eyes seemed to take on an intense, private passion. Once again he was struck by her startling sensuousness. She touched her tongue to her lips, making them glisten in the dim candleglow on the table between them. "That," she said, looking into his eyes very deliberately, "makes four. . . ."

"And I just got this uncontrollable urge to take you home and put you to bed."

"I would love you to. But we can't. Not tonight."

"What the hell"—he tried to sound nonchalant—"four out of five ain't too shabby."

HOLLYWOOD
APRIL 1961

Five years before, when Paulie Schultz first found himself walking the streets of Hollywood with a master to sell, he had been as rudely introduced to the rigid pecking order of the music industry as any budding record producer who ever dared proclaim his ass worthy of sharing a lavender throne among the Vine Street hierarchy.

The first thing he had discovered was that the Hollywood rock-music record business, contrary to common opinion, did not comprise only simple bullshit. It comprised one-third bullshit, the other two-thirds being, equally, horseshit and fear. But before he could ascend into the upper echelons of horseshit and fear he aspired to, he learned that it was absolutely vital for him to understand the spiritual and physical components of Basic Hollywood Bullshit. Moreover, it was not something that could be approached academically. True comprehension of the intricacies of BHB demanded that you endure it personally.

Spiritual BHB was the most urgent skill to master, because it was the essence of survival. It was the hustle, the scam, the con, the willingness to do whatever it took to make it. It was the ability to talk yourself into a favorable situation and to summon forth the requisite glibness and lack of character to take advantage of whatever, or whomever, you found when you got there.

From the beginning, Paulie had the spiritual thing pretty well covered.

Physical BHB, on the other hand, took a little more doing. It was tangible. It was the accoutrements—the fabulous pad, the expensive car, the foxy broad elected to the weekly communal top ten in reward for giving the best head. It was all the trinkets and accessories of success that might serve to bring envy to the hearts of those less fortunate but no less ambitious.

But the most important thing to remember about BHB, physical or spiritual, was that it was absolutely worthless until you acquired the ability to bullshit yourself.

286 ·

Hollywood Horseshit was much less complicated, merely a sort of latter-day Manifest Destiny, to wit, the God-given right of every entrenched, untalented asshole who had it made, or thought he did, to offer the middle finger of his right hand to anyone he deemed below his own level.

The final ingredient, the adhesive that held the business together, was usually described by the euphemism "ambition," although it really had very little to do with ambition. It had mostly to do with fear, the fear of being considered a loser. It was not even the fear of *being* a loser, merely the fear that others might see you with a few losers from time to time and remark how comfortable you looked among them.

To put it more succinctly, if you were a fairly normal, aspiring member of the Hollywood rock-music industry, bullshit was what you sought to acquire. Horseshit was what you handed out once you had acquired enough bullshit, and fear was what kept that great invisible thumb up your ass.

Paulie Schultz was attuned to most of this, and although he was not yet in a position to go around indiscriminately sprinkling horse-shit on his inferiors, nor quite perceptive enough to recognize that the ambition which kept him moving was nothing more than the fear of returning full circle to the Paulie Schultz of *"Oh, him!"* fame, he could now afford to indulge himself with top-quality, high-protein BHB.

And that is exactly what he did.

The morning after he had finalized his deal with Mark Donovan and Arrow Records—a three-year contract which guaranteed his company, Now Dynamic Productions, one hundred and fifty thousand dollars per year against twenty-two percent of the retail list price of all records, albums, and tapes bought and paid for by ITRC distributors—he caught a plane to the Coast. Within a week he had rented a very hip two-story A-frame house high in the Hollywood Hills. The following day, he had himself fitted for five thousand dollars' worth of elegant, casually tailored clothes at one of Beverly Hills' most exclusive haberdasheries. The same day, he bought a three-thousand-dollar diamond pinky ring, a fifteen-hundred-dollar diamond wristwatch, and placed an order for a twelve-thousand-dollar Italian sports car.

Whereupon, with the essentials taken care of, he went to work.

He leased a two-room office suite on Melrose Avenue, a few minutes down the hill from the nearly completed ITRC Recording Center, and furnished it with a tape recorder, a record player, a used spinet piano, a couch, a table, a coffee machine, three cans of Hills

Brothers coffee, four rolls of bennies—and locked himself in for a week.

Painstakingly he went over both sides of each of the four hundred and seventy-one 78-rpm records his mother's cleaning lady, Ruby Gadson, had given him seven years before, searching for any ideas he had not pilfered during the time he had been in New York producing records for his Uncle Saul. Anything of interest—a song lyric, a particular drumbeat, a vocal trick, a bass pattern, a guitar riff, a piano lick—anything that caught his ear, he immediately put on tape. By the end of the week he had accumulated several hundred "new" ideas.

He took a day off and went back up the hill to his new house, where he slept around the clock, showered, changed clothes, and went shopping again. He bought three more cans of coffee and four more rolls of bennies, and sequestered himself for another week.

By the end of the second week he had written four "records." Not songs, but complete records. That fact is important to note, because he was the first to do so, and in the years that followed, whenever rock-'n'-roll historians gathered, they would always refer to this phase of Paulie Schultz's creative life as his period of "blossoming genius."

Unfortunately, for the sake of accuracy, it is equally important to note that many of those same historians would be paid fairly large sums of money by ITRC, and later by Paulie himself, to perpetuate that myth.

But in the meantime, Paulie was confiscating everything he could lay his ears on, and now that he had assembled his musical vehicles, he had only to choose an artist worthy of recording them, which would not prove difficult, because he had only one artist to choose from, a singer named Terry Caulfield. And Paulie already had Caulfield under contract. This is how it had come about:

At the same time Paulie had been blackmailing his uncle out of two hundred thousand dollars, he had also talked Goldman into giving him the contracts of four artists from the small Chartmaker roster. After setting his deal with ITRC, Paulie had assigned those contracts to his own production company. Three of the artists were black, but Paulie knew from his conversations with Turicotti and Donovan that his black artists would be of no value to him at this time, certainly not as far as ITRC was concerned, because Arrow Records' complicated five-year plan did not include class-A promotion for black artists.

The very first record Paulie had ever produced, however, "Slow Easy Loving," had been performed by a group of kids from his old high school, white kids, who had called themselves the Caravans. Paulie had sold that original master to a man named Jacob Weisenberg, who had in turn sold it, along with the group's contract, to Carl Clinger at Carousel. Carousel had promoted the record to number three nationally, but Bobby Joe Whitaker had managed to get himself killed about that time, and in the excitement that followed, nobody at Carousel had taken the time to get out a decent follow-up.

The Caravans had managed to tour for a year on the strength of their one hit, before, one by one, the members of the group had been drafted. While they were in the service, Carousel allowed their contracts to lapse.

Terry Caulfield had been the lead singer with the Caravans. He had attended the same high school as Paulie, but graduated a year earlier. He was a handsome young man with Southern California beachboy good looks, a good-enough athlete in school to have been elected to the third-string All-City basketball team. His family was reasonably well-off, too. And to make it worse, he was still a pretty nice guy. In short, he was everything that Paulie was not. Of course Paulie disliked him.

But although Caulfield may have been the prototype of the artist Arrow Records was being formed to promote, he could not sing very well. His high tenor, pseudo-black voice had an embarrassing tendency to crack at inopportune moments. For that reason, he had been unable to secure a recording contract upon his discharge from the Army. So, as a last resort, he had called Paulie. Paulie had flown him to New York and signed him to a contract. Paulie never intended to do much with him, but it stroked Paulie's ego to show off his success, to put this big high-school hero under contract and be in a position to order him around.

Then, shortly after Paulie signed Caulfield, Saul Goldman had suffered his heart attack, and in the struggle over money and the problems connected with disposing of Chartmaker Records, Paulie had all but forgotten Caulfield. It had been, in fact, an afterthought for Paulie to negotiate with his uncle for Caulfield's contract in the first place. Nevertheless, the contract Paulie now held on Caulfield was still valid.

Yet, after Paulie had finished "writing" the material, he had absolutely no idea where to find Caulfield. It took two days of calling around to locate him. He finally learned that Caulfield had put together another group of Caravans and was working in the lounge of a bowling alley in Santa Barbara, about a hundred miles up the coast.

He left immediately.

Terry Caulfield was less than pleased when Paulie showed up unexpectedly at the motel where the Caravans were staying. He had been trying to reach Paulie for months, to try to convince him to record the new group. He figured, rightfully, that Paulie was jerking him around.

But when he saw Paulie's new Italian sports car, the diamonds, and the tailored clothes, his anger subsided considerably. Paulie took him to lunch and laid some first-class spiritual BHB on him, and by the time Paulie got around to paying for their meal with one of the hundred-dollar bills he had extorted from his uncle, he had Caulfield safely tucked away. Caulfield called work and told them he was suddenly taken ill. And would probably remain so for some time to come. Then he and Paulie drove back to Los Angeles together and started rehearsing Paulie's material that same night.

Unfortunately, it soon became obvious that Caulfield simply did not possess the vocal equipment to do justice to Paulie's material. So, after telling Caulfield to get lost for a few days, Paulie dropped a couple of bennies, poured himself a cup of coffee, and thought about what could be done.

The problem was technical, because nothing was likely to happen to change the scope of Caulfield's talent between that moment and the time when Arrow Records was obligated to release the first masters under the terms of Paulie's contract.

As Paulie sat there thinking, his eyes settled on a magazine he had bought at the newsstand on Hollywood and Las Palmas a few days earlier. The Sound Review was produced primarily for stereo buffs and people who made their living in some area of sound reproduction. With the Caulfield tapes playing in the background, Paulie idly began to leaf through the magazine, in his preoccupation almost overlooking the article that was to make him a name to be reckoned with among the young people who inhabited the dens and rumpus rooms of middle-class America.

It was a piece about a sound engineer who had left one of the major record-manufacturing firms to embark on a business venture of his own—redesigning the recording "heads" through which magnetic tape passed as sound was being reproduced. The man's name was Henderson. He owned a small electronics firm in the town of La Canada, a suburban community nestled in the foothills between Glendale and Pasadena. Impulsively Paulie dialed the number. Henderson answered the phone himself. An hour later, Paulie was standing in Henderson's workroom, listening to the slight, bespectacled young engineer demonstrate the capabilities of his new invention.

Paulie was impressed. And with reason. The invention was

290 ·

worth, roughly—give or take a few commas—five billion dollars. But to really understand the significance of Henderson's invention, it is necessary to have a perspective of how far the rock-music business had evolved by the spring of 1961.

In the immediately preceding years, impressive technical gains had been added to the recording process. Virtually no rock-'n'-roll records were now being made with a live band. Multitracking, sometimes referred to as "sound on sound," was the reason, the secret, and the necessity, because there was still only a handful of white rock-'n'-roll bands that had been together long enough to effectively imitate black music. Until multitracking came into widespread use, the general practice in the business had been to hire predominantly black studio bands, pay them union scale, less if possible, and, if record sales warranted, put together a band of white youngsters able to play passably well enough to pretend in live appearances that they had cut the record themselves. Most audiences were fooled, or allowed themselves to be fooled.

But as multitracking became more sophisticated—many established studios now had eight-track machines readily available, with twelve- and sixteen-track machines already on order—white bands were able to begin performing on their own records. Most of the time their attempts were labored and erratic. First, they would lay rhythm tracks; the more complicated the rhythms, the longer it would take them to complete the tracks. But multitracking allowed each musician to make as many mistakes as he needed in an effort to duplicate what he perceived to be a "Negro sound." And since the other tracks were not disturbed by a mistake, he could repeat a particular interlude again and again, until the illusion of a live performance was created. Finally, the most difficult task was undertaken, that of adding the lead voice, or usually voices, to the finished product.

In the years immediately following the advent of rhythm-and-blues music as an acceptable form of American pop culture, a widespread misconception arose among the people who ran the record industry, and later by much of the buying public, that gospel music was the one true foundation upon which black music rested. In reality, it was not. There were varied church-rooted expressions of black emotions, including hymns and spirituals, although gospel shouting undeniably carried the most impact. But the vocal turns, the tricks and syncopations necessary to creating a gospel feeling came from a different source. And they could not be easily faked. They were the end result of many generations of exposure to a particular cultural heritage. It was, therefore, virtually impossible for anyone who had not been exposed from birth to the driving, intricate rhythms and counterrhythms, the hypnotic, repetitive phrases of gospel music, to create an even passable vocal imitation. It is doubtful that most white artists, given their inexperience and cultural backgrounds, could have duplicated it at ten o'clock on a Sunday morning in a Pentecostal church on the wrong side of the tracks in Greenwood, Mississippi. Consequently, in the subdued atmosphere of a sound-proofed recording studio where the music was quietly fed to them through earphones, they often sounded ludicrous. But with multi-tracking, a vocal performance could be repeated endlessly until a "take" was completed.

The general hypocrisy of the rock-music industry in the early 1960's would not acknowledge the truth of the matter—that multi-tracking machines had been made more sophisticated primarily for the benefit of inept musicians and vocalists. Instead, those responsible for recording rock music claimed the chief benefit of multitracking to be that it allowed for the separation of instruments. Recording performers on different tracks, they said, enabled the listener to more easily identify any particular performer he chose, without being distracted by the other performers on the record.

True. But the problem was, separation usually made for a sterile record. Even though there was a minimum of mistakes on a recording made with sophisticated multitracking techniques, there was also a minimum of emotion captured. And as any experienced, competent musician knew, the purpose of a group playing *together* was not to create *separate* sounds, but to create a feeling of musical unity—for t was only when a band of musicians was playing in one musical piece that the dissonances and harmonics, the subtle changes in pulse and rhythm, could take place.

Most rock producers were not aware of all those things. They were aware only that—after they had laboriously pieced their products together, using "sound on sound," tape reverberation, numerous "patches" and equalizations, and finally, pressing the record itself at the highest decibel count possible short of distortion in the hopes that by sheer volume it would attract the attention of potential buyers—more often than not, something was still missing.

That something, of course, was usually talent, as witnessed by the fact that very few television producers allowed rock and roll artists to perform live. Even on those programs which maintained large budgets for musicians and arrangers, rock and roll artists were usually forced to lip-synch their deceptively produced recordings.

If the rock-music industry was to continue to grow, then, it was imperative for record producers to hide the lack of talent in the artists they featured. Only so much could be done technically. And so began the era of the black female background vocal groups.

One of the benefits of multitracking was that it allowed for the liberal use of these vocal groups to lend a feeling of authenticity to the recordings of white, usually male, singers. A few black female backup groups who could not get recorded or promoted on their own merits still found themselves earning upward of a hundred thousand dollars a year, merely by providing background for white recording artists. Sometimes, depending upon the particular singer or song involved, they were used simply to lend enchantment to the overall record. But, just as often, they were used to deliberately hide the flaws in the lead singer's vocal performance. By putting the girls and the lead voice on separate tracks, the producer could phase the lead in or out at will, creating the illusion that he was really performing the same vocal tricks as the black girls behind him.

Still, even with all the technical achievements, the basic problem of talent could not be submerged. Something was missing. That "something" was what Jim Henderson had come up with.

He called his invention "self-synch," a redesigning of the recording heads so that a sound engineer could push a button and cut into *any portion of any track at any point he desired,* without disturbing any other parts of the tape, including the track that was being reworked. If, for example, a guitarist was having trouble making a particular fill, the engineer could now play the guitarist's track back to him through earphones, and just before the flaw was reached, push a button that would enable the guitarist to try again. And continue to try until he got it right.

Naturally, this applied to singers, too. Which was what interested Paulie. He saw that now, theoretically, he could produce a record completely devoid of flaws, provided he had the money and the patience to remain in the studio the necessary amount of time.

Which he did.

Next Paulie borrowed Henderson's phone and called a small recording studio on Selma Avenue in Hollywood. He reserved it for *one month,* beginning the following Monday. He was determined, Terry Caulfield's musical limitations notwithstanding, to stay in the studio until he came up with a "perfect" record.

A perfect record!

"Once upon a time . . ." Thus fairy tales often begin, and with a benevolent wink from the gods, Paulie was about to make his personal contribution to the great events of mythical history: Ponce de

León, plunging headlong into the Fountain of Youth. Midas, consorting with Cronus in the Garden of Phrygia. Scrooge McDuck, gleefully stumbling upon the Lost Dutchman Mine.

Anything was possible, because Paulie had uncovered the perfect invention for his times—a machine that could turn noise into money.

HOLLYWOOD
JUNE 1961

On Monday, May 8, twenty-four days before Arrow Records was scheduled to open its doors for business, a rather dowdy young woman of thirty, wearing horn-rimmed glasses and a severe stipple-tweed suit, arrived at Los Angeles International Airport on the eleven-A.M. flight from New York, and immediately proceeded by taxi to the ITRC offices on Gower Street.

Belva Wiejocz, an honors graduate from the Wharton School of Business of the University of Pennsylvania, and a recent addition to ITRC's division of corporate planning, had come to Los Angeles to personally deliver to Mark Donovan a three-hundred-page volume that had been prepared by the firm of Robert Stermis and Associates at a cost of $200,000.

The disquisition was an econometric marketing forecast. It was a five-year projection of the anticipated sales and market impact of the new Arrow label, utilizing all the 1-0 data available before January 1, 1961, and covering: *consumer behavior, visionary forecasts, cross-impact analysis, time-series analysis and projection,* and *homogeneous aggregates.* Included in its appendix was extensive additional data based upon the Yankelovich Monitor—a method of measuring thirty-five separate and distinctive social trends that could directly affect consumer purchasing.

It was, by far, the most comprehensive study of the music industry, and of the buying patterns of white American youngsters between the ages of twelve and seventeen, ever attempted.

Mark greeted the woman cordially and saw to it that she was comfortably settled in a vacant fourth-floor suite of offices. Then, together, they spent more than a week assimilating the various concepts and implications of the study, combining their training and practical knowledge in an effort to circumvent the major problem of all environment analysis—the fact that the social sciences, as contrasted to the physical sciences, had yet to develop invariant laws of success.

They knew, generally, when a new company entered into a "fixed" market, as the record market presently was, the total units expected to be sold would not significantly change from previous levels. But for Arrow records to receive a satisfactory return on its immense investment, it would have to almost single-handedly change the existing market for prepackaged records and tapes into a "variable" market—which meant, it would have to expand the parameters of the market itself, and do so solely through the effectiveness of its marketing and sales programs.

Normally, with imagination, direction, and astute management of capital, a $12.5-million annual input into a fragmented $500-million annual market could accomplish that feat. But the record industry was different. It had created for itself a permanent bottleneck between the manufacturer and the consumer. That bottleneck was airplay. The fact was incontrovertible: consistent and strategic airplay was vital to the growth of every record company, but particularly a new company, because *all* other methods of selling records had proven subaltern to getting a record played on radio stations.

The appointed time was drawing near, and as they labored over the final plans for the operation of the new label, the matter of assuring sufficient airplay remained a gnawing, irresolvable problem. It loomed above the "success factor" of Arrow Records like a razor-sharp scimitar suspended by the thinnest of threads.

The day after Belva Wiejocz returned to New York, Mark received a terse memo from Gino Turicotti: "REGARDING AIRPLAY, SOMETHING IMPORTANT ABOUT TO HAPPEN WITH FM. CHECK IT OUT IMMEDIATELY."

FM radio had never entered Mark's mind. The idea was intriguing. The following morning, instead of returning to the office, he drove directly to the downtown Federal Building, where he discovered that, as of June 1, the same day Arrow was scheduled to open, a new FCC amendment would take effect which would allow FM stations to begin broadcasting stereophonic programming.

June 1. It appeared to be an omen.

Mark spent the rest of the day seeking to uncover more information. The only significant thing he learned was that the entire FM industry was in financial trouble. Although there were presently 1,092 stations in operation around the country, only one in four was making a profit. And the immediate future looked equally bleak. Government projections indicated that, collectively, FM stations were expected to lose at least $2.5 million for the calendar year 1961.

Clearly, all Mark had uncovered was a beginning. He recognized

296 ·

it as such, for he had now been in the upper echelons of the business community long enough to know that the federal government, especially a bureaucracy as manipulated by private interests as the FCC, did not arbitrarily begin to rewrite the books for a struggling industry unless somebody was about to pump in some new money. A *lot* of new money. Turicotti was right. Something big was about to happen.

That Monday, Mark flew to Washington.

Ensconced in a suite at the Shoreham Hotel, he quickly discovered that Washington, D.C., was a long way from Hollywood. There, he was a nonentity, merely another citizen seeking information. He would have received more preferential treatment had he been able to explain who he was. But he dared not mention ITRC, or his connection with the company, for fear of drawing undue attention to himself. So he devised a cover story, presenting himself as the representative of a group of California entrepreneurs who were considering FM as a possible long-term investment.

The story was worthless. He wound up wasting a full week, talking to elaborately made-up young women at public windows and keeping appointments with pompous G-3's and G-4's who could offer no pertinent information as to the future of FM radio, because they had none.

By Monday of the following week, he had decided to avoid as much of the bureaucratic rigmarole as possible, and began searching through the archives of the Library of Congress, poring over hundreds of ancient issues of the *Official Gazette,* the weekly magazine published by the United States Patent Office. He stumbled through dozens of dusty books and little-read digests. Slowly he began to piece the story together:

The stereo FM signal now about to be offered to the public for the first time had been available since 1934, with the invention of a process called "multiplexing," which allowed two or more signals to be sent and received simultaneously over a single frequency. In the intervening years, however, the leaders of the radio-manufacturing industry had been continuously guilty of producing equipment of less-than-adequate performance, to make sure that the listening public was not made aware of the considerable quality difference between AM and FM transmission. But now that the most costly FM patents were about to expire, radio manufacturers were preparing to produce modestly priced FM tuners. To deal with the anticipated upsurge of FM radio, the FCC was completely revising the rules governing the transmission of FM stations. There was about to be an FM "freeze," during which time the federal government did not intend to authorize any new broadcasting licenses for at least two years.

It was a marketing dream. The airplay bottleneck could now be broken. It would take time, and in all likelihood FM might never come close to supplanting AM. But it did offer leverage.

Mark decided to remain in Washington an extra day, preferring to think and work in the solitude of that strange city rather than resume the hectic schedule he would be forced to keep in his own familiar surroundings. While the information was still fresh in his mind, he began to outline a program he hoped would boost Arrow Records into its desired preeminence within the industry. He spent the night at his desk in the hotel, jotting ideas in a leather-bound notebook, pausing only to gaze pensively out at the quiet clusters of lights scattered about the grounds of the Naval Observatory a few blocks away.

The next afternoon he caught a shuttle to New York. Then, dinner at the airport with Helen and Jules before boarding the nine-thirty flight home.

Later that night, hurtling through the moonless skies six miles above the Arizona desert, bleary-eyed with fatigue, he sipped a Scotch and tried to ignore the sharp, insistent pounding at his temples. The cabin was dark. Quiet, except for the steady hum of the engines. Reading lamp on, papers spread out before and beside him, he began the final draft of a confidential report that would be typed and mailed to Gino Turicotti within the next few hours:

> The development of FM and stereo rests in large measure on hi-fi bugs. The connotation with the public seems to be that FM means high fidelity, implying that hi-fi is synonymous with quality. It would appear that we should begin immediately, on the marketing level, to align ourselves and the new label with FM management, and, from there, proceed to definite preproduct planning aimed toward taking advantage of this already existing consumer attitude. . . .

He paused, sipped his drink, and momentarily allowed his thoughts to wander.

He had been in constant touch with his office during the past eleven days. According to Barbara, everything needed had already been moved into the new building. The first products, she assured him, were already packaged and ready for shipment. Tomorrow, in his new role of president, his first appointment would be with Bob Silverstein and the other department heads. The entire afternoon would be devoted to a picture-taking session and an extended tour of the new building with photographers and writers from the leading music trade publications. . . .

Suddenly, irritatedly, he flicked the pen away. He turned to the window and stared at the reflected image in vague recognition. He searched the face for a sign of contentment, a glimmer of satisfaction, but found none. Only when a nearly forgotten ethos began to take shape in the haze of his memories, did he smile. And then, a smile of wonder. At how little, at that moment, it all really seemed to matter.

". . . *you know what I'd do if I was your age? I'd quit this goddamned rat race, find a good wife . . .*" Bob Silverstein's voice echoed in his mind.

"Would you care for another drink, Mr. Donovan?" The stewardess' soft contralto interrupted his thoughts.

Startled, he looked up, thought about it a second, and shook his head. "No, I don't think so."

"You look tired."

He tried to smile.

"Lots of work, huh?"

He nodded.

"We're going to be landing shortly, you know."

He automatically glanced at his watch, muttered an oath. "How long?"

"Half an hour at the most. But to tell you the truth"—she smiled sympathetically—"you don't look like you're going to stay awake that long."

He ran a hand over his face, blinked, squeezed the bridge of his nose with a thumb and forefinger. "Hmmm . . ." he said.

"Listen . . ." She hesitated, dropping her voice to a whisper. "If you need something to, uh, keep you going, I've got a couple of whites in my purse."

He looked at the papers scattered about his seat, thought about the long cab ride home, the hours of work still remaining before the night was over.

"Why not?" he said.

A few hours later, when the International Transcription and Recording Corporation officially opened its recording center on Sunset Strip in West Hollywood, California, every record company in the world, successful and struggling, was waiting to see what would happen.

For the first time in the short history of rock music, a major company was utilizing total market saturation to directly influence the tastes and buying habits of young people. Not for a particular artist, nor a particular record or song, but for a spectrum of rock-'n'-roll music. Within days, the complex machinery that had been set up to operate Arrow Records began to rumble beneath the foundations of the industry like the inchoateness of a giant earthquake.

Ostensibly, the product was music. In truth, it was image, a deceptive image of youth. The ploy, a penultimate con based upon the supposedly inherent virtues of being young. Not of being good, or wise, or caring, nor even honestly ambitious. Just young. That was enough. And beneath all the marketing jargon, the talk of profit erosion, input-output ratios, lay a verification overwhelming in its emptiness.

The image began with the new ITRC building, which rose up from the Strip to a height of twelve stories, sleek and majestic, pillars of sandstone conscripting an acre of tinted glass. The image of youth continued inside, where visitors to every occupied floor were greeted by a bright, bouncy "Susie," "Joanie," or "Debbie." Each girl scrubbed, smiling, and tanned. Each one secure in her own inefficiency, convinced of her own stardom. Simply for being there. The old guard, the last of the experienced and loyal workers from the outdated Gower Street building, had been displaced, restricted, hidden from sight like maiden aunts and eccentric uncles. They labored at the rear of the building in tight little offices overlooking the backside of the Strip, receiving their orders from budding executives who were still confronting the traumas of puberty.

Yet, even with all its newness, all its youth and bustling opulence, there seeped from the walls and floors of the building a pervading feeling of age, which caused discomfort among its occupants and tainted their movements with patches of hysteria. An unwanted inhabitant was about—a ghost who sat quietly in a corner of every office, who walked the building in the dead of night and came at daybreak each morning to sit in the still lobby and wait for intruders. It was his building. He owned it. He had owned it from the instant the first shovelful of dirt had been lifted. Impassively, fingers gnarled from overwork, black face lined with the sadness of ten thousand abuses, he watched—knowing that as long as the building stood, he could not be dispossessed. It would crumble without him.

He was the music.

Initial sales were massive. The first album, released on June 15, was produced by Tommy Lee Whitaker. Aided by national television exposure and magazine articles, it moved into the number-one sales position within a month.

Six weeks later, it was replaced in the number-one position by Terry Caulfield's first album. Rock-'n'-roll critics readily conceded that the musical quality of the Caulfield album was enhanced considerably by the genius of the "Paul Schultz sound."

Two weeks later, the first New York product, an album produced by Danny Weiss, skyrocketed onto the national charts.

Only a month passed before a single by Les Goodson found its way to number one. The artist was Sarah Tindall.

And while the quality of the products may have been debatable, the reasons for their successes were not. They had been guided onto the charts by the best-trained and most aggressive sales force in the history of the industry.

The bulwark of that force was the company's twelve regional sales managers, all college graduates with business degrees, who had been personally recruited by Bob Silverstein. Chosen for their appearance as much as for any sales ability they possessed, they maintained the company's image of youth, ranging in age from twenty-one to twenty-six. Before actually beginning work, they had attended an obligatory ten-day seminar in Rolling Hills, California, chaired by Silverstein. Following that, each man had been assigned to one of the eleven major markets. The twelfth man, based in Denver, was given the medium markets of the Mountain States and Southwest. Their basic pay schedules were minimal, small guarantees with an elaborate system of cash bonuses and incentives. Forced to operate under unrelenting pressures, they worked around the clock, traveled incessantly, did whatever was necessary to sell records.

The first quarter passed in a roar of success, yet it remained obvious to the more perceptive that rough waters loomed ahead. Executives at other record companies, long adept at earning their salaries from kneeling positions with their ears firmly to the ground, listening intently for the slightest changes in production and marketing procedures, now raised up as a body and rushed to copy every successful innovation of the new label. They studied the demographics, observed that each issue of *Plattertalk* increased Arrow's sales by 22.3 percent, and soon there was a proliferation of hurriedly produced teen-oriented record magazines on the market. They studied Arrow's sales-incentive programs, and before long they were pressuring their own salesmen.

Arrow's sales began to taper off. Slowly the company was being pulled back into the pack. Yet, inexplicably, Mark Donovan's carefully worked plans to begin concentrated marketing of products through FM radio remained unapproved by New York. He did not have time to press the issue, for each day found him more heavily engaged in a savage battle to maintain possession of his increasingly tenuous position.

Indications of mounting dissatisfaction in the company's executive suites began to be felt by regional sales managers, who began receiving daily phone calls from Bob Silverstein. As sales continued to decline, distributors began shipping records back. At the end of a particularly unsuccessful thirty-day period, each sales manager received an angry telegram from the main office:

ARROW RECORDS WAS FORMED TO BE THE NUMBER-ONE ROCK LABEL IN THE BUSINESS. WE HAVE THE MONEY AND THE TALENT TO ACHIEVE THAT GOAL. NUMBER ONE IS YOUR ONLY JOB SECURITY.

> GINO TURICOTTI
> PRESIDENT, RECORDS DIVISION
> ITRC, NEW YORK, N.Y.

The telegrams were abrupt and premature, but they dramatically pointed out that there was no longer any inherent prestige or job security in selling records for ITRC. By the end of the seventh month of operations, five regional sales managers were no longer with the company. Three had been fired. One was suffering hallucinations from abuse of amphetamines. One had been lured away by a rival label.

The young men who took their places were even more ambitious, if that was possible. They were more energetic, more innovative, more determined, and less secure. They seemed to be everywhere—radio stations, television stations, jukebox dealers, record stores, high-school hops, hot-dog stands, even paying to have their records played during intermissions at movie theaters.

Still, the one thing that Mark Donovan was afraid might happen was beginning to happen. The thread that held the sword over the company's "success factor" was beginning to fray. Product was being created too fast. Paulie Schultz and Tommy Lee Whitaker in Los Angeles, Danny Weiss and Les Goodson in New York, were each turning out an album every six weeks. So was Lonnie Pratt in Nashville, where Carl Clinger had recently signed another full-time producer. Turicotti had just contracted an independent production company in Philadelphia, guaranteeing them eight album releases a year. Added to that were the other independent producers around the country, who were trying to sell the company their masters.

It was time, Mark decided, to resubmit his FM marketing program. The program was rejected again. Reworked, and rejected still another time. Twice, within a month. Finally, seething with an anger born of fourteen-hour workdays and interminable pressures from above and below, he flew to New York and stormed unannounced into Turicotti's office. In the shouting match that ensued, he was able to learn why the plan had been discarded:

ITRC's division of corporate planning had seriously miscalculated the potential of FM radio, and in doing so had brought about a chaotic internal conflict.

Years before, when the company had first decided to diversify and enter into the stereo business through Japanese manufacturers, Planning had made a foolish and shortsighted recommendation. After a cursory study of the market, they had decided that FM radio was definitely not a growth industry. To save a few dollars in engineering design and production costs, they had recommended that FM tuners not be included. Turicotti had been a member of Planning then, but he had not sat in on the final meetings that led to the ultimate decision. From preliminary meetings he had known that FM was not to be included in any of the less expensive sets, but it had never occurred to him that Geary, the board of directors, and planning would all be so shortsighted as to continue to approve the spending of millions of dollars on sets offering only AM. Had he known that, he never would have alerted Mark to the changes about to occur in the FM industry.

Consequently, when Mark's confidential Washington report had arrived in June, Turicotti, unaware, had passed it on to Planning. The response had been icy. Later, when Mark's follow-up recommendations had come in, Planning perceived them as a deliberate effort on the part of the new subsidiary to embarrass that division of the company—for although all manufacturing of stereo sets had stopped more than a year before, ITRC still had more than 350,000 units of various sizes and costs gathering dust in assorted warehouses and retail outlets around the country. 350,000 units, at an average per unit cost of, including packaging and shipping, thirty-two dollars and eleven cents.

$11,238,500. Just sitting there.

There was no way ITRC could commit Arrow Records to expensive, concentrated marketing through FM stations, Turicotti explained. Not at this time. To do so would rub some very strong salt in some very raw wounds.

But what sense did it make to jeopardize the success of the new label, Mark wanted to know, by trying to stroke a few egos years after the mistakes had occurred?

Turicotti could not be moved. The matter had already been discussed at length. The answer was no.

Mark was furious. He would return to the Coast immediately. If the situation was not resolved to his satisfaction, he would submit his resignation as soon as he arrived back at his desk.

An hour later, Turicotti's call reached Mark in the airport bar. Turicotti had just spoken with Max Geary. Geary had acceded. Mark could proceed along the guidelines of his recommendations. It was a stilted, unremitting conversation, during which Turicotti made no personal acknowledgment of the situation, ending with a curt "Do whatever you want."

Given the go-ahead, Mark stopped in Chicago, where he put through a call to Bob Silverstein in California. He ordered Silverstein to contact the company's twelve regional sales managers and inform them of a meeting to be held the following Saturday morning. It would be a two-day affair, attendance mandatory.

That Saturday morning, in the sitting room of his suite at the Palmer House, Mark and Silverstein passed around a mimeographed twelve-page booklet containing all the informaton the two men had been able to obtain about the most potent FM stations in the largest markets in the country—management personnel, signal strength, potential audience, and current format. Ideas were discussed, changes made, suggestions entertained. The meeting continued into the night, resuming the following morning, and finally terminating in the O'Hare airport lounge.

Within the month, in key markets around the country, certain FM stations began extended, sometimes uninterrupted stereophonic airplay of Arrow records. Entire rock albums were played on the air and the dubious musical talents of the "artists" who recorded them extolled with the same flowery adjectives previously reserved for heavyweight boxing champions and World Series heroes.

FM radio and rock-'n'-roll music. It was a perfect marriage, because the majority of the stations were operated by young people, many of whom still lived with their parents, most of whom were not yet even aware of the vast amounts of money available and flowing into AM stations from record-company coffers. Equally important, Arrow's promotion men were the same age as the dj's they serviced. They dressed in the same casual manner, spoke the same pansophisms, were equally dedicated to being counted among the "in" crowd.

It was a nice little arrangement. But it could not go on forever. The Arrow promotion men knew they could not continue to ask for "favors." They eventually had to pay something, that being the nature of the business. And since almost everyone was smoking a little, dropping a few, sniffing a bit, it did not take long to fall into a comfortable medium of exchange. Dope. Not heavy. Not yet. Just enough to confirm the overall hipness of things.

The only irony was that it turned out to be Mark Donovan, who probably thought less of rock-'n'-roll music as a legitimate art form than any other top executive in the business, who took the first effective steps toward legitimizing that music.

But irony aside, he had once again proven his abilities, this time by creating a direct line to the young market. Now there was no longer any need to bow and scrape and beg at the doors of AM stations for airplay on every new release. An Arrow album that even by the questionable 1961 standards of FM radio could only be considered as mediocre, was still good for as many as fifty thousand units of national sales, without ever having been heard by half of its potential consumers. FM alone could generate enough sales to recoup the initial investment on a middle-range group and still return a sizable profit to the company.

As Arrow Records was claiming an increasingly larger share of the market, the familiar old ITRC landmark on Thirty-ninth and Seventh in New York was fast becoming an anachronism. Racked by poor management, lack of vision, politics, and petty bickering, it was beginning to smell of decay. The best creative minds in Production, Graphics, Marketing, Accounting, Sales, and Promotion were clamoring for a chance to move West and join the new subsidiary.

By the fall of 1963, after only twenty-eight months of operations, Arrow Records had already increased ITRC's total volume of record sales by 51.7 percent. Every single facet of the company was returning a profit. The reason, undeniably, was the business acumen of thirty-one-year-old Mark Donovan. Everyone, it seemed, who entered the ITRC Recording Center on the Strip—everyone who fit the image of youth and was smiled upon by the "Susies," "Joanies," and "Debbies" who inhabited the building—prospered.

But it could not continue.

On one particular Friday in October 1963, with the kind of peculiar coincidences that sometimes mark the natural order of things within the music industry, several events were taking place simultaneously in scattered parts of the world, all seemingly unrelated, but which would eventually come together and prove the undoing of a great many people:

At a few minutes after five P.M. in London, a young homosexual businessman from the north of England was emerging from the doorway of an imposing gray stone edifice to join the late-afternoon crowd hurrying along Manchester Square. He was experiencing gaiety in the very best sense of the word, having just concluded a meeting with three members of the board of governors of the world's third-largest body of money. He had convinced them that it would be possible for the four young musicians recently signed to his management to completely dominate the confused American record market, provided that adequate moneys for their extensive Stateside promotion were available. Now, after almost two months of meetings, those members of the board had finally concurred. A tentative budget of seven hundred and fifty thousand American dollars had been agreed upon, to be used for entry into the American communications system.

At the same time, more than four thousand miles away, in the forward section of a McDonnell Douglas DC-8, two men were sipping coffee from Styrofoam cups and nodding their heads in agreement. The younger man was trim, red-haired, nattily dressed. His companion, stocky and dark-featured, appeared sinister even in the bright glare of the morning sunlight streaming through the unshaded cabin window. They were on the 11:06 flight from Chicago to Las Vegas. They were discussing Monroe Wilcox.

At the instant the younger man set his cup on the pull-down shelf connected to the seat in front of him and reached for a cigarette, an elderly black musician was stepping into an elevator in the ITRC Recording Center in Hollywood. His face drawn with anxiety, he clutched a large sweat-stained manila envelope in his dark hands, as though his very life depended on the safety of its contents.

HOLLYWOOD OCTOBER 1963

Sam Crockett hadn't changed much. He might have lost a little weight, but the stern face was the same, punctuated by the same dark, sad eyes. He hesitated just inside the doorway, clutching the envelope, momentarily intimidated by the elegant surroundings.

"Sam!" Mark bolted to his feet and hurried around the desk. "Hey, it's good to see you again!"

They gripped hands in the center of the room. Mark put an arm around the old musician's shoulders and gently guided him away from the desk to an informal conversation area in a far corner, where he motioned Crockett to a seat on the couch. "You're really looking good, Sam. How've you been?"

"I been good, doin' real good!" Crockett said brightly. "Been catchin' a few dates here and there, you know, and scale's gone up a little, so I can't complain none."

"That's good."

"Ain't no sense askin' how you been." Crockett's eyes twinkled as they wandered the room. "I can see you been doin' just fine."

"Oh, I can't complain none," Mark playfully jibed.

"Yessir, I'm right proud of you."

"Well, I owe you a lot, Sam. The longer I'm in this business, the more I appreciate what you taught me."

"I know you do. But you would of learned anyhow—in time. And I appreciate what you did for me, too, or tried to. . . ."

"Sam, I did everything I could to keep that Champ thing going for you. I still believe you could have turned it into a good little label."

"I know, I know, but some things just ain't meant to be, ain't that right? The main thing is, you tried—when you didn't have to. Ain't no use cryin' over no spilt milk, I learned that a long time ago."

"But you deserved it, Sam. And I tried to tell them, if nothing else, it would have been a damn good source of new material."

"Well, you got to look at it from their point of view," Crockett said philosophically. "You were just learnin' the business yourself then, and you weren't in no position to be makin' no decisions of that kind. Anyhow"—he cleared his throat—"I didn't come up here to talk about that. I know you must be pretty busy and I don't want to waste—"

"No, no, we can talk. I told Barbara to bring us some coffee when you got here."

"Well, that's mighty nice of you," Crockett said, leaning back against the couch and reaching in his pocket for a Lucky Strike. "I was just sayin' to myself the other day . . ."

The door opened and Barbara entered with their coffee. She smiled at Crockett as she set the tray before them. "You still drink it the same way?"

"I'm too old to change now, girl." Crockett laughed.

"You know something?" She gave his face a quick pat. "I missed you, you old goat."

"Well, I missed y'all, too." He smiled, including Mark in the statement.

She pointed to the envelope on the couch beside him. "What's that, our latest hit?"

" 'One never knows, do one?' " Crockett quoted the old Fats Waller line.

"I sure hope so. Maybe then you'll have enough money to take me out on the town one night."

"Umm-hmmm . . . and what's your husband gonna say about that?"

"Clyde?" She wrinkled her nose disdainfully. "Oh, he's still got that little old gun, but we're not gonna let that stop us, are we?"

Mark smiled and sipped his coffee, remembering the constant byplay that used to go on between them in the old days. He missed it. Then he remembered the purpose for Sam Crockett's visit, and the smile slowly disappeared.

"You know, I sure miss bein' around that girl." Crockett chuckled as the door closed behind her. "I didn't even know she was still here till I called up the other day to get an appointment."

"To tell you the truth, Sam, I don't know what I'd do without her. Sometimes I think she knows more about what goes on in this building than I do."

"How long she been with you now?"

"Ever since I started here, except for the time I was in New York. Let's see, that'll be"—he thought for a moment—"ten years next March." The realization shocked him. "Ten years, Sam. Can you believe that?"

"Sure, I can believe it," Crockett said, enjoying his coffee and puffing on his cigarette. "Been five cr six since we had that little place down the street. Don't seem like it, but it was."

"The time sure slipped away. . . ."

"Speakin' of time, I don't want to waste no more of yours," Crockett said firmly, passing the envelope across the table to Mark, "and I'm on needles and pins to find out what you think of this thing."

"What's the story on it, Sam?"

"Well, a couple of months ago I was over at one of them little companies I do some arrangin' for from time to time, and they come in to audition for me. Little six-piece band from Watts, you know. 'Course, they didn't have no polish on them, but I thought they had a pretty good little sound I might be able to do a little something with."

"How good?"

"Too good for that little no-'count company, that's for damn sure. And they were nice kids—*are* nice kids, I should say—well-behaved, you know, and serious about tryin' to make a little somethin' out of themselves. Well, I like to see that in colored kids, you know, so I spent a little time rehearsin' with them, tryin' to teach them what I could."

"How'd they develop?"

"Mark"—Crockett nodded his head solemnly—"they came along damn good, if I must say so myself."

"How about the masters? Have they been mixed and eq'd and everything?"

"Oh, yeah, they're ready to go! I been in the studio for the past couple of weeks toppin' them off, tryin' to get them just so before I let you hear them."

"Well"—Mark got to his feet, knowing there was no sense in putting it off any longer—"let's hear what we've got."

He studied the label as he crossed the room to the stereo behind his desk. The group was called Windstone. The master had been recorded at Gold Star Studios over on Santa Monica, not too expensive, but good engineers and a bright, modern sound. He knew he was about to hear something special. Sam Crockett had too much pride to try to take advantage of a friendship by bringing in a weak master.

He was right.

As soon as he touched the needle to the acetate, the quality was evident. Sam had augmented the group with some of the best musicians in town. The voices came in strong, especially the lead. Untrained voices, so it had taken Sam a lot of work to bring them out. The violins caught him by surprise. Probably overdubbed, but still expensive—string players were notorious for almost always demanding union scale.

He turned it over. The second side was just as strong. Well-recorded, well-mixed, thoroughly professional. No flubs, no splices. Technically, it was as good as anything Arrow had ever released. As material, it might be better.

The masters, he knew, had probably cost Sam most of his savings.

He slid the record back into its sleeve and retraced his steps across the room, trying to think of the best way to handle the situation. He was limited as to what he could do, but maybe they could work something out.

"What you think?" Crockett asked anxiously.

"They're good masters, Sam."

"Well . . . what you think?" Crockett insisted.

"How much did they cost you?"

"I got about two thousand in them. I wouldn't tell nobody else this"—Crockett grinned sheepishly—"but I bootlegged the strings."

"Are they your tunes?" Mark asked, thinking if they were, maybe he could point out some imaginary flaws in the masters and let one of his staff producers rerecord them. That way, at least Sam would get the songwriting royalties.

"No," Crockett said, immediately killing that idea, "there's two or three kids in the group who does the writin' for them. I don't write too much no more, you know, music's changin', and I got to be honest with myself, most of the stuff I try to write nowadays even sounds a little old-timey to me."

"How about management? Are you handling them?"

Sam Crockett had been around so many jive-assed little companies, he had developed a sixth sense when it came to sniffing out bullshit. Now, slowly, the hope began to drain from his face. "No, they already had a manager when they come to see me—the mother of one of the boys. 'Course, she ain't worth a damn, but I wouldn't try to steal them from her."

"Listen, Sam"—Mark forced himself to look the old musician in the eye—"I'm going to tell you the truth, it's a good record, a damn good record, but it just might be a little too r-and-b for us. I just don't think we could do it justice."

"Hmmm . . ." Crockett said. "It ain't *that* rhythm-and-bluesy, is it?"

"Well, the thing is, we're simply not geared for that market,

Sam. We can take it, but I'm afraid we just might lose it for you, and it's too good a record for that."

"Umm-hmmm . . ." Sam Crockett said. He leaned over and carefully replaced his cup in the saucer on the table in front of him, then raised his mournful eyes to stare at Mark, not quite able to accept the words he was hearing, even though it seemed he had heard them a thousand times before. "Friendship is one thing, but business is business, ain't it?"

The look of disrespect in Crockett's eyes made Mark drop his head in embarrassment. He forced himself to look up. "Listen, Sam—hell, I may be wrong. Let me keep it and play it for Bob Silverstein, my national sales manager. Let me see what he thinks, maybe we can come up with something."

"That's okay," Crockett said, plucking the envelope from Mark's hand, getting up to leave. "I don't want you to put yourself out none."

"I'll tell you what you do, Sam. . . ." Mark followed him across the room. "Look around and see what kind of a deal you can come up with. If you can't get what you want, come back and see me. I'll do everything I can—"

Crockett spun around angrily. "You tryin' to make it look like I'm beggin' you for something! Well, I ain't! I didn't come up here lookin' for no favors! I just expected you to treat me like you would anybody else who walked in here with a decent master!"

"Dammit, Sam, my hands are tied. I told you, we're simply not geared to sell to the r-and-b market. We don't have the sales people, we don't have the dj connections to—"

"Your hands are tied!" Crockett waved the envelope under Mark's nose. "What about their hands? I wish you could see these kids, rehearsin' night after night in that dirty little garage. Arguin' and fightin' over their music, tryin' to get it right. Countin' up their little money so's they can pay down on uniforms. Tryin' to figure out how they can afford gas to get back and forth to their little gigs. I'll tell you the truth, I hate to go back and face them!"

"Sam, try to understand it from our—"

"Oh, I understand, all right! I understand that I acted like a damn fool and got to loud-mouthin' about how good I know you and what a decent fella you are, and now I got to go back and tell them kids the truth—that you ain't no different from nobody else in this business. You'll let a colored man work for you, all right. You'll pick his brains and kiss his behind to get what you want, but you ain't gonna let him try to do a little something for himself. Oh, I under-

stand, all right, but I bet you one thing, I bet you I won't be comin'
back up here to bother you no more, I bet you that!"

He gave the door a yank as he went out. It touched the jamb,
didn't catch, and fanned open a few inches. Mark could hear Sam
and Barbara talking in the outer office. He was tempted to go stand
by the door and listen. When he realized what he was thinking, he
felt his face flush. He stood there in the middle of the room clench-
ing and unclenching his fists, trying to turn his shame into anger.

Why should he care what Sam Crockett thought? Arrow Records
wasn't the only label in the business. Let Sam go peddle his masters
somewhere else. Hell, he'd been as nice to Sam as he could. He'd
bent over backward to be nice. And music was music. It belonged to
everybody. If colored people were so goddamned concerned about
their music, let them put up their own companies, their own radio
stations, their own everything. They didn't invent a goddamned
thing anyhow—the machines, the instruments, nothing. The business
was invented by white men. And Mark Donovan was one of the most
important men in that business!

Fuck Sam Crockett!

Unable to control his rage, he swept the serving tray from the
coffee table. It slammed into the wall with a noise like a gunshot.
Saucers, half-filled cups, the cream pitcher, and the sugar bowl flew
in every direction.

He stormed out. As he strode through the outer office, his voice
was hoarse, barely recognizable: "Cancel my appointments for the
day, and if New York calls, tell them to shove it up their ass!"

He drove aimlessly. On the freeway, off again. Down boulevards,
along side streets, unaware of his surroundings, the anger he had
misdirected toward Sam Crockett beginning to eat at his own
insides.

Finally, realizing he had to go somewhere and sit down to think
things out, he remembered the park. He hadn't been there since
college.

It was in Topanga Canyon, tucked away in the secant of Malibu,
Pacific Palisades, and Woodland Hills. It was just as he remembered
it, a few yards off a winding trail, down a half-dozen steps, cool and
secluded, like a rain forest, the overhanging branches of ancient oaks
so thick that the sun's rays fell on the ground like patterns of lace. A
slender waterfall came down from the mountains and formed a
stream. He took off his coat and tie and shoes and sat on the damp
bed of leaves beside the stream, staring at his reflection in the
water. . . .

Sam Crockett was one of the few decent human beings he'd met in the music business. Almost everything he had learned about the history and structure of pop music—what to listen for in a song or a record, how to determine if it was good or bad—he had learned from Sam.

"... it's a good record, a damn good record, but it just might be a little too r-and-b for us. ..."

How arrogant and insensitive to assume that Sam Crockett wouldn't see through that pathetic ruse. He had been listening to that kind of rationalization all his life.

And now he had heard it from Mark Donovan, too.

Well, one thing was for goddamned sure, Mark Donovan had endured just about as much of the music business as he could stomach. The time had come to make a change.

But to what? he asked himself, and emitted a dry, bitter, cynical laugh. Where could he go to exercise the personal integrity that Sam Crockett had just shown him was not nearly as deep as he would have liked to imagine?

He sat staring at the water, trying to see his true feelings in its reflection, trying to find some semblance of order in the chaos that seemed to surround him.

The old ways of responsibility and perseverance, those values of right and wrong which had him forever questioning his motives, had been instilled in him. To change now would be to lose his identity. And the only thing that had allowed him to put up with the hypocrisies of the music industry as long as he had was that sense of identity, a belief in the quality of his character—the belief that he would be fairer in a position of power than most other men in his profession. He had tried to convince himself of that innumerable times in moments of decision. No, he *had* convinced himself of that, which was why betraying Sam Crockett had disturbed him enough to make him consider quitting his job.

Yet, for all his conviction, he could feel the new ways of expediency and pragmatism and a callous disregard for the future tugging him forward. His job, the quality of his life, the way others viewed him, seemed dependent upon his acceptance of those new values. He could always rationalize, of course, that the true morality of business was to survive. To prosper exorbitantly was not moral, but to survive certainly was. But suppose, in the future, in a world of conglomerates, there could be no in-between. Suppose the stakes would be so high and the penalties for failure so heavy that there could, literally, be no room for personal integrity.

There were thousands of young men coming out of colleges and graduate schools every year with impressive credentials, but virtually devoid of imagination, wrapped only in blind ambition and a desire to cut the existing pie into smaller pieces and sell them for more profits. In another ten years, would there still be room in the business world for a man like himself? A man who sincerely believed that broadening services, improving the quality of products, and planning the future on natural market growth were not only the bulwarks against inflation but also the cornerstones upon which good business was built? Was there still a corporation that would even now hire such a man?

He had to find out.

Now, once again, he reaffirmed to himself his decision to resign from Arrow. But the anger that had racked him earlier in the day had cooled, and he decided to make his moves prudently. There was no hurry. By March of next year he would have been with the company ten years. He would leave then—take his ten-year pin and his treasury stock and go. And there was no sense in mentioning it to Geary or Turicotti yet. He would tender his resignation the first of January, allowing them three months to find somebody else. He would travel a bit, look around, decide if he was, in truth, an anachronism or a man who had the right to believe that business could be conducted with probity.

It was a pleasant thought. It made him smile.

He was still smiling when he turned into his driveway. He half-expected Sarah's car to be there, until he remembered her mentioning something that morning about a doctor's appointment.

As he climbed the stairs, he was beginning to itch from the bits of dirt and twigs that had worked their way next to his skin, so he went straight to the shower, then to the kitchen for a well-earned drink. Her note was taped to the refrigerator door:

Honey,

Had to stop by the house and pick up something to wear tonight. Also, Millie's having a cocktail party for some friends in town from Nashville. And guess what? She's finally decided to buy the place!

Don't forget, dinner at your folks' tonight. Your mother said seven-thirty *sharp*. Maybe you'd better pick me up, it's closer.

Love,
S

P.S. Something important to tell you!

314 ·

He plucked the note from the door and stared at it, a slight frown wrinkling his forehead. Her handwriting had changed noticeably in the last year. She wrote bigger now, steadier, the loops wider, the spaces between letters more even. Somebody had told him once that such things were significant in determining the improvement or decline of neurosis, or some such nonsense. In her case, he hoped it was true. He studied the note a bit longer before crumpling it and tossing it into the wastebasket under the sink.

He finished making his drink and took it outside to the sundeck at the rear of the house. The afternoon was still warm, the water a calm azure, lapping against the pilings below with a gentle sucking noise. To his left, a mile out, he could see a thirty-footer skimming the water, bright green spinnaker unfurled. It looked, at once, regal and snug, like a good place to be on a Friday afternoon. He'd spent some time around boats as a child, knew a little about them. Maybe he'd get one. It would be nice to sail along the coast, over to Catalina, maybe down to Mexico for a little fishing. Perhaps he'd even get something a bit larger, say, a fifty-footer. Put a little money into it. . . .

He watched the yawl clear the horizon, sipped his drink, completely at ease with his thoughts. He tilted the rocker back, stuck a bare foot up on the wooden railing, and closed his eyes.

He made an appealing portrait sitting there, a handsome, still-lean young man in cutoff surfer's jeans, the only concession to approaching middle age a distinguished touch of gray fluttering about his temples in the mild Southern California autumn breeze . . . plotting curves in a life that had been, until now, as straight and functional as an Indiana highway.

HOLLYWOOD
OCTOBER 1963

The doctor had called from the state university at Bloomington. Sarah had arrived earlier that day in a severe state of depression. As the time for her performance drew nearer, her condition had worsened. Someone had summoned him. He had just taken her to the infirmary and sedated her. Before falling asleep, she had asked him to call Mark.

Later, after she recovered, she told Mark that she remembered the night only as a series of surrealistic configurations. She seemed to be standing in the center of a group of forms that vaguely resembled people, but with no human faces or features. That was all she remembered. She didn't remember asking the doctor to call him, nor anything about the flight home.

Until that time, he had dated her only occasionally. They had been intimate, but nothing serious, at least not as far as he was concerned. She had told him once that she thought he would be "very easy to fall in love with," but he had attributed this pillow talk to the fact that after Tommy Lee Whitaker had failed to sign her to his production company, Mark had interceded to place her with Les Goodson in New York.

As far as Mark was concerned, Goodson was the most able producer on the label, an intelligent, hardworking young man who submerged his own ego into those of the artists he handled. Within a year he had produced two top-ten records for Sarah, good records, which made her playable on middle-of-the-road as well as rock stations. But the constant traveling, the interviews, the posing for pictures, the thousand and one details that went into maintaining the image of a successful pop recording star had simply been too much for her. And every time Mark saw her, he realized she was becoming more unraveled.

Nevertheless, the doctor's call had come as a shock.

He caught the first available flight to Chicago, from there to Indianapolis, then rented a car and made the hour's drive to the campus. He arrived that afternoon to find Sarah awake but obviously unfit for travel. A psychiatrist had been consulted and had already given her a perfunctory examination. According to him, she appeared to be suffering from "severe regressive schizophrenia, mild hallucinations, and definite symptoms of thanatomania," all apparently aggravated by continued abuse of barbiturates and amphetamines.

Mark spent the night on campus. The following morning, when the psychiatrist examined her again, she appeared to be more rational. Still, he was extremely reluctant to release her to Mark's care, acceding only after extracting a promise from Mark that he would seek professional help for her immediately upon their arrival in California.

She didn't speak on the drive from the campus to Indianapolis, nor did she say anything on the flight to Chicago, except once, to assure him that she was okay. She did talk a bit on the plane home, but in halting, tortured phrases. Mostly she'd put her head against the window and cry quiet tears. It was a kind of despair that Mark had never seen before.

After their arrival home, she wouldn't let him keep his promise to the psychiatrist. She was adamant, almost hysterical, in refusing professional help, saying that neither doctors nor medicines could help her—only she knew what was wrong with her and only she could reassemble the pieces.

He was afraid to let her be on her own, so he took her to his Malibu cottage. He hired his once-a-week cleaning lady, Mrs. Munoz, full-time, to keep an eye on Sarah while he was gone. Sarah would usually sleep all day, get up to have dinner with him when he came home from work, and immediately return to bed.

She behaved like that for several weeks, with no noticeable improvement. One morning she started walking on the beach, sometimes sitting on the sand for hours with her knees drawn up to her chin. He continued to watch her carefully, afraid she might decide to walk into the ocean, to try to drown whatever it was she found so hard to live with.

Gradually she seemed to improve. She started going shopping during the day, sometimes to a movie, sometimes for long drives along the coast. She appeared to be returning to normal.

When they went to bed, he would hold her in his arms until she fell asleep. After a while she began to trust him enough to talk. She told him about herself, sad things, almost as painful for him to hear as for her to recount. Until then, he had no idea of the terrible things people do to those they are committed to loving, nor the terrible

· 317

things people do to themselves when they are committed to forgetting.

She wanted to quit the business then, but he talked her out of it. Instead, he helped her to plan a career that would take her off the hit-record merry-go-round and allow her some control over her own life.

First he helped her obtain a Vegas-Tahoe contract, guaranteeing her eight weeks' work a year in each place at five thousand a week. Then he personally signed her to a new five-year Arrow contract which guaranteed her twenty thousand dollars for two albums a year. He'd purposely decided on that small guarantee so she would be under no pressure to keep coming up with hit records. That way, she could concentrate on good tunes and pleasant arrangements which fit comfortably into her act.

It had worked out well for her, because what she now had was essentially a part-time career that guaranteed her a hundred thousand dollars a year and left half of her time free to do whatever she wanted.

She was self-conscious about her lack of education, so he encouraged her to apply for her high-school diploma. She passed the test easily and began auditing classes at Santa Monica City College. Again, he tried to make sure she felt no pressure, encouraging her not to compete for grades, but, instead, to take only those subjects that interested her. She chose philosophy and drama.

More than six months had passed by now, and although she appeared to be completely recovered, she remained there at the beach house with him. Not formally, because she still had the duplex in Beverly Hills, but most of the time. After a while, most of her clothes were in his closets and most of the phone calls were for her. He didn't mind. They had grown into good friends.

As she became stronger, she began taking some of the pressures off him, as a bridge between the world of his few private friends and the world of parties and business functions he was obligated to attend in his capacity as president of Arrow Records. She could make even the dullest industry dinner fun, pointing out the pomposity and artificiality of music-industry executives. And when they went to the parties and after-parties of the label's artists, she had a talent for making him appear more relaxed and down-to-earth than he really was.

But there was so much dope around, he was never really comfortable at parties. Somehow he could not quite picture himself going to jail in the company of the musicians, the minor executives, and the assorted freaks who made up most of the guest lists at the so-called "hip" parties. He was always a little paranoid about that. There was a time, before Sarah, when he'd taken an occasional pill to stay awake, a habit he'd picked up in college. But now he didn't even do that. He knew if he did, she would, too, and the smallest amount of drugs would send her into a depression that could last for days.

They had built their relationship upon a tenuous rock of need, each one lending strength to the other, however temporary. They rarely spoke of love and there had been no talk of marriage. It was as though a permanent commitment might destroy the fragile thread of whatever it was that held them together.

Yet they would sit and talk for hours, thoroughly enjoying each other's company, laughing together, comfortable together. They made love often. She was the most sexually vibrant woman he had ever known, and the most unselfish. It disturbed him that she had been with so many men, but at the same time he appreciated her for not having tried to conceal her past from him, for giving him the chance to decide for himself whether or not he wanted to be with her. And after a while he rarely thought about it. As she became stronger and lovelier and more in control of her life, he began to feel a special kind of pride in himself, for he knew she had survived only because of him, only because of his faith in her.

He wasn't sure exactly when he began to love her.

It may have been the first time he touched her while she was sleeping and she came into his arms without hesitation. Or the first time she dressed up for him and cooked his dinner and sat across the table from him, smiling shyly, too nervous to eat until he had taken the first bite and given his approval. Or it may have been the first time he realized that she saw herself only through his eyes, and it was only from him that she could receive the self-respect that gave her the will to live.

But he was absolutely certain of *why* he loved her.

He loved her because of the way she made him feel, wise and complete and competent. She made him feel as though he had finally discovered a place for himself, a comfortable spot in a changing, manipulative world, a place where he really belonged. He saw in her a possibility no one else had ever seen. It was something he wanted to see and it was something that perhaps did not exist.

Those were the images bubbling beneath the surface of Mark's consciousness as they drove along the San Diego Freeway, north toward the Valley.

"Shame on you," she said.

"Shame on *me*!"

"Certainly. You have just insulted some of the cream of the record industry, including two of your finest producers, one of the industry's most successful female executives, one of country music's finest publishers—"

"Please forgive me," he said dryly.

She leaned over and studied herself in the rearview mirror, gave her hair a pat. "So, what do you think?"

"You'll pass."

"No, I mean about Millie buying the house."

"She acts like she already owns it."

"No, really."

"How much are you asking?"

"A hundred and a quarter."

"A fair price."

"And I know she's got the money."

"Great, sell it to her before she spends it all on dope."

"Umm-hmmm . . . I think I've already made up my mind." He felt her hand on his arm. "Honey, I'm sorry. I was embarrassed for you, I really was. God, I just hate those people sometimes! I can't believe they used to be my friends."

"They were never your friends. People like that don't have friends."

"I know, it seems like they only hang around together so they can stick knives in each other. They're so damned *destructive*." She pushed the cigarette lighter. "Did you see Carl?"

"No, I missed him by a couple of minutes. But he has an appointment with me for Monday."

"Have you seen him lately?"

"Not for almost a year. I talk to him on the phone every few weeks, though. Why?"

"What do you think of him?"

"Oh, he's a bastard, but not impossible to work with."

"I hadn't seen him for a couple of years, until tonight. You know, Mark, I really think he's the worst one of all. I mean, Millie's a bitch and Tommy Lee's got dope problems and ego problems, and Lonnie's got his brains in his ass, but Carl . . ." She waited for the pop of the lighter, touched it to her cigarette, and turned to stare out the window.

He drove in silence, waiting for her to finish the sentence. " 'But Carl,' what?" he finally asked.

"I don't know if I can put it in words. I mean, he's the one who got us all started, right? And everybody looks up to him so much that he seems bigger than life. It's like he's not just a man anymore, but a symbol—do I make any sense?"

"I think so."

"I mean, he used to act like exactly what he was, a creep. But now that he's got a lot of money, he acts so self-righteous he makes me sick."

" 'Whatever *is* is right,' " Mark quoted cynically.

"Who said that?"

"You're the one who's supposed to be studying Greek philosophy." He laughed. "Democritus, I think."

"Oh. We haven't gotten to him yet." She puffed her cigarette thoughtfully. "But that's not exactly what I meant. . . ."

"Want to try Plato?"

She pinched his leg playfully, thought a moment longer before the words came to her. " 'Had I succeeded well, I had been reckoned among the wise: our minds are so disposed to judge from the event'— that's what I wanted to say."

"Who said that?"

"Euripides."

"Very good." He kissed his finger and touched it to her nose.

"But you know what I mean, don't you?"

"Yes, I know," he answered, serious for a moment. "Carl Clinger is, in fact, a symbol—of the times. He's the American Dream, the poor, dumb redneck who took advantage of every opportunity to claw his way to the top. He's still a dumb redneck, only now he's a millionaire several times over, which makes him, to some people, a wise man, right?"

"To those who don't know any better."

"Right. 'A florist is not one who picks flowers and squeezes them to make poison. . . .' "

"Who said that?"

"Me."

"That's what I thought. It's not too heavy."

As they left the freeway, he suddenly remembered her note. "You said you had something important to tell me."

"Oh, it's not that important. I'll tell you later—on the way home maybe."

He heard the anxiety in her voice. "C'mon, now," he said gently.

"Not now, maybe later."

"It must be earth-shaking news."

"It could be."

"Okay, then, you'd better tell me or I'll be thinking about it the rest of the night."

"Are you sure?"

"Yes."

"I'm pregnant."

From the crest of the rise a half-mile away, he could see the amber lanterns atop the two pillars that stood on either side of the driveway.

He could remember when his folks had put the big iron fence up. He couldn't have been more than six or seven, but in the extended time zone of childhood it had seemed to go on forever. Even so, the fence had been erected only along the unpaved road that led to the entrance to the ranch, because the grounds were protected by a wide gully to the north and several miles of weeds and brambles to the rear. On the south, a hundred yards away, the property was divided from the land owned by Jim and Helen Hunt by a ten-foot hurricane fence with barbed wire on top and a sign that read "DANGER! HIGH VOLTAGE!" The fence was not electrically charged, but it had served to discourage Peter Donovan's fans from entering the property through the Hunt driveway. Jim Hunt was adamant in refusing to fence his property, even though in later years his wife became almost as well-known as their much-discussed neighbor.

It was only in recent years, after he was grown, that Mark learned how his mother and father had decided to move to the Valley:

His mother, May Price then, had been a bit player at the studio when Peter Donovan's star began to rise. At the time, she and Mark's Aunt Helen, who was a seamstress in the wardrobe department, shared a small apartment in Hollywood. Mark's mother and dad met on a picture. They began dating, and by the time they decided to marry, Peter Donovan was well on his way to becoming as big as Tracy or Taylor, or any of the others.

But May Donovan, realizing how difficult it was to keep a Hollywood marriage together, decided it would be best for her family to move as far out as convenient for Peter Donovan to commute to the studio every day.

She encountered little difficulty in convincing her husband, since he had been raised on a ranch in Idaho and was comfortable with the outdoors. Aside from that, he was a dedicated actor, and having spent a number of years on the Broadway stage before coming to Hollywood, was little impressed with the society of Beverly Hills and Brentwood.

They had managed the down payment on the property with an advance on his salary. The Valley was sparsely settled then, and the lot, the house, the furnishings, and all the landscaping together couldn't have cost more than fifty thousand dollars.

Then, with the verve that was to become legendary in the film colony over the years, May Donovan went back to the studio and quietly borrowed more on her husband's contract, for by this time her friend Helen had married a stuntman named Jim Hunt and May Donovan wanted them to be close to her. She lent the money to Helen and Jim so they could buy and build next door.

As a consequence, Mark's childhood had been happy and normal. And, for the most part, uneventful. Aside from visits by the famous and talented who were usually his parents personal friends, about the most exciting thing that ever happened in those days was fans either wading across the gully or finding their way through the brambles to the house. When that happened, likely as not, if Peter Donovan happened to be home, he would come out and chat with them and sign autographs.

Now, as Mark turned onto the private road, he saw that the front gate had been left open for them. Things were a lot less formal now. In the old days there had been a bell to ring and a telephone that had to be answered in the house before anyone could gain access to the property. But Peter Donovan had been around a long time, and there were younger faces to occupy the attentions of movie fans.

The house, beige with red trim, had been built in the days when California architecture was still under Spanish influence. It had never been plush, but as long as Mark could remember, it had always been comfortable. The Spanish decor extended to the interior. The floors were tile, with bright throw rugs scattered about. All four bedrooms were upstairs. In the rear, outside the kitchen, was a large brick courtyard which led to Emma and Will's apartment above the four car garage. To the left of the courtyard was a two-bedroom guest house which fronted onto the swimming pool. The guest house was, in fact, furnished more carefully than the main house, which said a lot about how Peter and May Donovan felt about their friends.

Mark parked his convertible behind May Donovan's blue station wagon and went around to help Sarah from the car. They crossed the patio, and Mark pushed the bell. A few seconds later, Emma swung the door open. She was the same as always, fat, dark, and bossy.

"My, my, will you look who's here!" she said before Mark had a chance to open his mouth. "You musta been in the neighborhood, 'cause I can't picture you comin' by for no other reason."

He stepped into her open arms and kissed the top of her frizzy head. "*Now* will you get out of the way?" he teased.

She stepped aside and gave him a loud whack on the backside as he slid past her. Then she spied Sarah standing behind him and touched her arm. "Come in, honey, come in! 'Scuse me for ignorin' you but I been tryin' to teach this boy some respect ever since he stopped dribblin' on hisself."

Sarah had never been around such open give-and-take between blacks and whites, and she was a trifle uneasy. Still, she had to laugh at Emma slapping Mark on his dignity, and was just about to peck Emma's upturned cheek when a distant reserve took hold and she stopped herself. Emma, not paying her hesitancy the slightest attention, reached out and gave her a quick hug. "Come on in, now, darlin'," she repeated in her no-nonsense staccato voice. "You gonna let the moths in!"

Sarah followed Mark inside. "Where is everybody?" he asked.

"Well, now, lemme see"—Emma undressed him of his sport coat without being asked—"your mama and daddy and your Aunt Helen is in the den, and your Uncle Jim is where he always is, out in the kitchen arguin' baseball with Will."

Their heels clattered on the hall's tile floor as they walked toward the den. Even from this distance they could both hear the familiar modulated voice of Peter Donovan coming toward them.

Sarah squeezed Mark's hand. "I'm nervous."

"Don't be silly," Mark said lightly. "You've been here before."

"I know, but I'm always a little self-conscious in front of your father. And I know your mother doesn't like me."

"Nonsense," Mark dismissed her fears again as they entered the den.

Although the Donovans had always called it the den, it was more like an open-air family room. At the far wall, sliding glass doors opened out onto the lighted swimming pool. There was a pool table in one corner of the room, and behind it a dart board that Mark had received as a present on his tenth birthday from his Uncle Jim. It still had numerous scratches and holes around it where Mark and his sister, Helen, had engaged in determined, winner-take-all games to see who would care for the horses or take out the trash, chores their mother had insisted they do. In another corner, couches had been arranged into a conversation area. Next to them was the spinet piano Mark and Helen had abused with their lessons when they were children.

Peter Donovan and Helen Hunt were seated on one of the couches, engaged in an animated discussion. May Donovan sat across from them, looking on with a slightly bemused expression. "You're late, dear," she said to her son without looking at the time.

"No, I'm not," Mark said, kissing the top of her head.

Without taking her eyes off Peter Donovan, his Aunt Helen stuck out her cheek to be kissed. He kissed it dutifully. Peter Donovan, who was leaning back on the couch with his slippered feet up on an ottoman, pulled Mark around to the side, and without breaking his conversation, encircled Mark's waist with an arm and drew Mark to him, as if he were still ten years old.

Mark's mother brought him up-to-date. "Your father just signed to do a television series and he's trying to convince your Aunt Helen to come along as the costume designer."

"Who's winning?" Mark asked.

"So far it's an impasse."

Helen turned to Mark. "Isn't that the most ridiculous thing you ever heard?" she asked, and turned back to his father without waiting for an answer.

"I don't know," Mark said; then: "Mother, you remember Sarah, don't you?"

May Donovan had been around Hollywood more than thirty years and she had rarely been mistaken when it came to people. She had taken an intense, instant dislike to Sarah. The girl was weak and vacuous, and from the way she carried herself, she probably had little self-respect. Lately, it seemed every time she called Mark's house, the girl answered, which meant they were living together. May had never interfered in either of her children's adult lives, nor would she this time, but her disappointment in Mark's judgment was acute. She had thought he had more insight.

All those thoughts flashed across her face in a fleck of time too quick for Mark to observe, but too long for Sarah not to notice.

"How are you, Sarah? It's pleasant to see you again," May said coolly.

"I'm fine, Mrs. Donovan," Sarah said.

"Dad, you met Sarah before?"

Peter Donovan had been an integral part of the American consciousness for two generations, loved, admired, and respected by those who knew him personally as well as by those who had merely been enthralled by his screen performances. He was a big, rawboned man, yet with the innate grace of the consummate actor. But if he had retained a personality of his own through all the years of pretending to be other men, it was one of kindness. He was, more than anything else, a gracious man. And now he turned his full attention on Sarah. "Why, yes, of course I have. How have you been, Sarah?"

"I've been very well, Mr. Donovan, thank you." Sarah could feel her knees shaking. His voice always sent chills through her.

"And it shows on your face, too, my dear. You look lovely. It's a pleasure to see you again."

Then, having immediately and completely charmed Sarah, he

returned his undivided attention to Helen Hunt, his friend, co-worker, and surrogate sister of the last thirty-five years, while May, with the unique grace that only a woman who has been loved by an extraordinary man can possess, watched them with affectionate detachment.

"Aunt Helen," Mark interrupted again, trying to finish the introductions, "did you ever meet Sarah?"

Helen Hunt was a tiny woman, under five feet tall, and her eyes, naturally weak, had been made even more myopic by years of straining over designing tables and sewing machines. She was the most lovable and unaffected human being Mark had ever known. Now, at his question, she darted to her feet and peered across the coffee table, her thick black-rimmed glasses two inches from Sarah's face. "No, dear," she said to Mark, "I don't think so."

Whereupon she immediately sat down again and resumed her dicussion with Peter Donovan.

It had been done so naturally, and so obviously without any slight intended, that Sarah had to laugh.

"I am quite lucky to have survived my Aunt Helen's love," Mark said to Sarah.

"You are quite lucky, period," Sarah answered.

"You see, dear," May explained to Mark, "the problem is, Helen doesn't feel that television, particularly a western, needs a costume designer of her reputation. And your father feels if it is to be a quality production, he should have the best people he can get, regardless of price."

Mark looked at his father, still slim and spry, but nevertheless beginning to bear the weight of time. He was past sixty now, too old for the rigors of a weekly television series. "Why did you sign?" he asked.

"Money, son," Donovan explained simply. "Your mother and I have been talking for some time about redoing the place in Palm Springs and maybe buying the adjoining property, and this will more than pay for it. The price for this thing is ridiculous—twenty thousand dollars per episode, complete syndication rights after three years. And"—he smiled—"various other considerations. . . ."

"Like what?"

"Like a three-day work week." He chuckled. "They have a young chap, Andy Nelson, who will carry the brunt of the workload, all the quick draws and fights, that sort of thing. All I'll do is stand by the old corral and introduce the show each week, and from time to time amble into the picture to offer sage advice and words of wisdom to my young charge."

"I met him," Helen said. "He's a very nice boy—don't you think so, May?"

"I haven't met him yet."

"You haven't? Oh, I thought you had! Well, he's a very nice young man. Rather delicate, you know. He reminds me of a young Myrna Loy."

The statement hadn't been made with malice, or even intended humor, but it struck Sarah as hilarious. Again she laughed.

"I think you need a drink," Mark said.

"I think so, too."

"Wine?"

"Yes."

But before he had time to move, Will appeared. Will Tillson was the only permanent concession to formality that the Donovans had ever had in their household. When Mark had been young, sometimes his parents had hosted "favor-returners," as his mother called them, for the movie moguls, and at those times a certain formality was required. But it had never mattered who was there, for even if it was just the four members of the immediate family, Will always made a formal announcement of dinner. Now he stood in the doorway in his stocking feet, wearing a pair of wrinkled corduroys and an unmatched, unbuttoned vest over a striped shirt open at the collar, and boomed:

"Dinnah is suhved!"

Nobody paid him any attention.

Behind Will, Jim Hunt stood in the hallway, holding a can of beer. Hunt was a huge, round-faced man who always reminded Mark of an overweight Joe Palooka. "Dammit, Will," he bellowed after the announcement had been made, apparently angered by something Will had said in their discussion in the kitchen, "don't tell me Vince Scully isn't the best announcer in baseball!"

"He may be the best announcer," Will said, backing out of the doorway, turning back down the hall toward the kitchen, "but he ain't the best *describer*. He don't tell you what's going on. And on top of that, he puts me to sleep."

"Don't tell Jim," Helen Hunt said to May Donovan as they walked down the hall together, "but he puts *me* to sleep, too."

Emma served their food family-style, then she and Will took seats at opposite ends of the table. Inga, the Hunts' Swedish maid, was still having trouble with some of Emma's recipes, so Emma was painstakingly going over them again with Aunt Helen. At the other end of the table, Will was relating to Jim Hunt his boyhood encounter with the legendary "shoeless" Joe Jackson.

And in the center of the table, the Donovans sat across from Mark and Sarah. It was a relaxed, enjoyable conversation. Nothing much of note was said, except that Peter Donovan made a special effort to draw out Sarah by asking questions about her career that evidenced genuine interest.

As the conversation flitted about, Mark was tempted to tell his parents about his episode with Sam Crockett that morning. He had mentioned Crockett to them before, and they had invited Mark to bring him out for dinner one night so Will and Emma could meet him. But Mark couldn't say anything to them about what had happened.

So he said nothing. But even as he held Sarah's hand under the table and basked in the warmth of his parents' love, he thought about Sam.

Finally, promptly at ten o'clock, the Donovans, the Hunts, and Will and Emma rose as one body, as though their minds had simultaneously heard the chimes of an invisible clock, and began saying their good-byes. They were working people, all of them, and the years of serving the studios—and serving those who served the studios—had formulated an unwavering discipline. Tomorrow morning at six o'clock, whether with a full day's work ahead of them or a day to simply enjoy their hard-earned leisure, they would be up and about.

Mark hugged everyone good night, feeling almost as though he should have put on his pajamas and said his prayers long ago. And everyone hugged Sarah. Even May Donovan, because the night had been warm and she had spent it with the people she loved most in the world.

The Hunts left through the kitchen, from force of habit and because that way they didn't have to go all the way around the long hurricane fence at the end of the property. Will and Emma followed them out, across the brick courtyard, and upstairs to bed. Mark and his dad stood in the doorway talking golf.

Did Mark believe that the old man, at sixty-four, was still playing to a nine?

No, Mark said, he did not believe it.

Good. A week from Saturday. Ten o'clock, Lakeside. Five-dollar Nassau. Loser buys.

A nine?

Absolutely!

"Who do I root for?" May Donovan asked Sarah.

"It doesn't matter," Sarah said. "They're both winners." And for an instant, May Donovan thought she might be wrong about the girl.

But only for an instant. She saw the weak tilt of the shoulders, the dull glow of capriciousness behind the bright green eyes, and she knew she was not mistaken. She was afraid for her son. She knew that he was troubled, as yet unfulfilled in his life and his profession, still searching for himself, and he needed a woman strong enough to help him shoulder the weight of his beliefs. She had raised him as best she could, and while she knew he had grown up to become a man of good character, she also knew he had no hidden resources to protect him from those who would hurt him. And this girl would hurt him. Sooner or later, perhaps not even intentionally, this girl would hurt him terribly.

Mark and Sarah walked arm in arm to the car. A clear October chill hung over the Valley. But with the warmth of the evening still with them, they lowered the top so they could see the stars, and rode along for a while in the comfort of each other's silence.

"What a strange night," Sarah said finally.

"Strange?" Mark looked surprised. "How so?"

"Well, we start off with a freak show at my house—"

"You mean Millie's house."

"—and we wind up spending a perfect evening with your parents. I didn't know they were really like that."

"Why not? You've been there before."

"I know, but always when there were other people around. You know, kind of formal. Never when it was just family."

"Oh, it's always like that around there. Jim and Will arguing about something, Aunt Helen and Dad talking back and forth at each other, Mom trying to keep things in order." He laughed.

"But they don't act like movie stars."

"Sometimes they do. It can get pretty star studded around there sometimes."

"But, I mean, you know . . . the cook and the butler sitting down at the table."

"They're friends," Mark explained. "They were friends long before I was even born. Uncle Jim and Will go to the ball games together, the three of them go hunting together. . . ."

"Together?" She was amazed.

"Look, Will used to help me with my golf game when I was a kid."

"I don't believe you."

"Yes, he did," Mark insisted. "My father was making a lot of pictures at the time, working six days a week, sometimes twelve hours a day, and he didn't have time, so he asked Will to teach me."

• 329

"They don't have golf clubs for colored people—I mean, places to play." She was staring at him. "Do they?"

"Sure, sometimes he'd take me to Brookside in Pasadena, sometimes to the course way out on Western Avenue. We'd go every Thursday morning, play a round, and sometimes, if he felt like it, we'd play another eighteen holes after lunch. I met a lot of colored stars then."

"Like who?"

"Oh, let me see . . ." He thought a minute. "Joe Louis, Sugar Ray Robinson . . ." He chuckled again. "I remember I played a round with Billy Eckstine once and won twelve dollars."

"I sure didn't know colored people played golf," she said, the amazement still in her voice

"Why not? They're people, too." The image of a disappointed Sam Crockett flitted across his mind. He quickly brushed it aside.

Two miles from the ranch, they reached the main intersection, but instead of making the customary right turn toward the beach, Mark turned left. Sarah was so caught up in what he was saying, she failed to notice.

"Did you ever see him again?"

"Who?"

"Billy Eckstine."

"Oh, sure, I've been to his house a couple of times. He lives right down the road from here, in Encino."

"From *here*?" She peered out the window, as though she could see the house in the darkness. "I guess I never learned about things like that," she said, turning back to him. "But now I can see why you are like you are."

"How's that?"

"About colored people. I mean, why you're always saying we shouldn't play their music."

"I never said that."

"Yes you did."

"No I didn't."

"Well, what did you say, then?"

"I just said we don't have the right to exploit it without giving them a chance to make an equal amount of money from it themselves, that's all. They catch enough hell as it is."

"I'm not sure I know what you mean. . . ."

"Okay, take Elvis, for example—all he was trying to do on 'Heartbreak Hotel' was imitate an old blues singer named Bill Broonzy. Most of the initial promotion on that record was simply to let dj's know Elvis was white. A lot of them still didn't believe it until they saw him on the Dorsey show, and the next day they jumped on his record. So he sells a couple of million copies doing a poor imitation of Broonzy, while the *real* Bill Broonzy dies penniless in some little town down South. That's the kind of stuff I'm talking about."

"Yes, but it's legal, isn't it?"

"Sure, it's legal—but that doesn't make it *right*, does it? And it happens all the time. I mean, Christ, I don't think I've ever gotten in a car with somebody from production whose radio wasn't tuned to KGFJ or some other colored station, trying to pick up the latest trends from Negro artists."

"Oh. I think I understand now—better, at least." They were quiet for a few minutes before she spoke again. "I heard your mother talking about your sister, Helen. Is she that way, too?"

"Which way?"

"I mean, like you all?"

"Like *y'all*?" He mimicked her every time her accent returned.

"Oh, *shit!*" She pinched his leg. "You know what I mean."

"Sure, she and I are a lot alike. The only difference is, she's more extraverted. But she's not prejudiced, if that's what you mean."

"Is she smart like you?"

"Smarter, especially when it comes to values."

"Just like you, huh?"

"Well"—he laughed again, pleased by her compliment—"our father loved us, but our mother raised us."

She suddenly sat up and looked around. "Hey, I think we're lost!"

"No we're not."

"We're not headed for the beach, are we?"

"No."

"Where are we going?"

"Vegas."

"Vegas! Why?"

"To get married."

"Mark, you . . ." The sentence caught in her throat.

"I know," he said gently, "but I thought about it all night."

"We could get rid of it, you know."

"Do you want to?"

"No!" she said quickly. Then, quietly: "Do you?"

"No."

"Why—because it's against your religion?"

"No."

"Are you sure?"

'I'm sure."

'Then why?"

'I made up my mind while we were sitting there talking to my folks: it would be nice to have a home and a son."

"How about a wife? They go together, you know."

"I know."

After a few minutes she said, "It's going to *kill* your mother."

"My mother has nothing to do with it. Besides, we can always marry again in the church."

"Mark . . ." She took his hand in both of hers and held it in her lap. "Honey, are you sure? We could just keep on living together, couldn't we?"

"No. I think it's time for us to grow up."

It was late when they entered the desert above Baker, the wind nipping their faces with the sharp bite of early winter. They left the top down and turned the car heater on, stealing glances at a sky speckled with stars that glittered down on them like millions of colored raindrops. Her head was on his shoulder. He thought she was asleep, until she spoke.

"Mark?"

"Umm-hmmm . . ."

"Stop a minute."

He slowed the car and pulled to the side of the road. The car radio was playing softly.

"Listen," she said.

He listened. It was one of her records. "Very pretty," he said.

"Did I ever thank you for saving my life?"

"Yes."

"Mark . . ." Her voice quavered. "You don't have to marry me."

"I love you."

"You hardly ever tell me that, you know, unless we're making love or something."

"It's not easy for me to say sometimes, but I do. Very much."

"I'll do everything I can to make you a good wife, I promise."

"I know." He kissed her and started to pull back onto the highway.

"Mark . . ." She tugged at his arm.

"Yes?"

"You're supposed to ask, you know."

He pulled her to him and kissed her again, longer this time. "Will you marry me?"

She stared at him in the light of the stars, trying to etch the memory of the moment in her consciousness, praying silently within herself that she would find the strength to be everything he thought she could be. She shook her head no, but she said yes.

A little while later, as they neared the Nevada state line, from the corner of his eye he could see her blond hair puffing out in the breeze, feel it tickling his neck and blowing softly against his face. And he thought about his decision to resign from Arrow and a different career and a wife and children, and loving friends and laughter.

It would be a happy, comfortable place in a changing world.

CHICAGO
NOVEMBER 1963

The blue-and-white sign atop the newly renovated Big City Records Building, the logo of two teenagers dancing, lit up Michigan Avenue like a musical beacon.

Monroe Wilcox now owned the busiest and best-equipped studios in the city. He had twenty-three acts under contract, seventeen of which had been on either the top-forty pop charts or the top-ten rhythm-and-blues charts within the last three years. He had thirteen full-time employees, plus six contracted songwriter-producers, all of whom were both prolific and creative. Since the day Rydell Mercer walked in unannounced with his ragtag group of Indiana Blues Boys, Big City Records had enjoyed a total of eight number-one hits, each one a million-seller, certified by the Music Retailers of America. Thus far, for the calendar year 1963, the company had already billed its distributors in excess of five million dollars, which did not include publishing. Publishing was not billed. It poured in like gravy—rich, tasty, and extremely fattening.

Today, on this chilly November afternoon, Monroe was sitting in his plush office upstairs at the rear of the building discussing the following year's production schedule with his vice-president in charge of engineering, Willie Jackson, and his musical director, Wilburn Minkler—formerly called "Redeye," but now, for reasons of dignity, shortened to "Red"—when his desk buzzer sounded.

"Mr. Wilcox, Mr. McDill is here to keep his appointment," Clarice announced.

"Gimme a few minutes," Monroe said. He turned to Willie. "Hey, man, who *is* Chester McDill?"

Willie shrugged.

"You know him?" Monroe asked Redeye.

"Naw, man." Redeye looked unimpressed. "I ain't never heard of the motherfucker. Why?"

"He's been calling me every day for the last week."

"What's he want?" Willie asked.

"I don't know. He won't say."

"I hate motherfuckers like that," Redeye said.

"Yeah, I'm hip. I tried to turn him on to somebody else, one of you cats or one of the producers, but he wouldn't talk to nobody but me."

"Did you finally talk to him?" Willie asked.

"Yeah, Friday. I figured I wasn't gonna get no peace till I did."

"Well, what'd he say?"

"He said he had something of 'pressing importance' to talk to me about, maybe we could get together and get some things down."

" 'Get some things down'?" Willie repeated.

"Naw man, he didn't say it like that," Monroe said impatiently. "But that's what he meant."

"What'd he sound like?"

"He sounds like a pretty nice dude—you know, for a paddy."

"Yeah, man you got to watch them paddies." Redeye's voice was suddenly knowledgeable. "Nice or not, them motherfuckers are generally out to burn your ass."

"Maybe we'd better go on and split so you can talk to him," Willie said.

"Yeah, I think so. . . ." Monroe's mind was already on his unknown visitor on the other side of the door. "Gimme a half-hour and come on back so we can finish this stuff. We got a lot of things to run over before we get out of here tonight."

Willie and Redeye picked up their notepads and left. Monroe sat there for a moment, staring at the door. He was sure he had never heard of the guy before, or seen his name in the trades, either. Probably just some ambitious manager trying to get an act promoted; he should be able to get rid of him quickly. He jabbed the buzzer on his desk, Clarice's signal to send the visitor in. A moment later, Monroe heard the door open.

He had learned a few tricks during his years in business, one of which was: whenever somebody pressured him into an appointment he didn't want to keep, to pretend like he hadn't heard the person come in, keep his eyes fastened to his desk and slowly count to thirty. Then, when he looked up, fix whoever it was with a cold stare and announce in a very unfriendly voice, "I'm Monroe Wilcox. What do you want to see me about?"

He did that, and found himself looking into the smiling face of a red-haired white man of about forty. The man crossed the room and extended his hand.

"Mr. Wilcox, I'm Chester McDill. How are you, sir?"

"I'm fine, couldn't be no better," Monroe said.

He took the card the man offered him. It was impressive, rice paper, the information engraved in gold:

GOLDENROD, LTD.
Box 12A
Las Vegas 12, Nevada
Cable: GORO

Monroe handed it back. "That don't tell me much."

"I know." The man was still smiling. "May I sit down, Mr. Wilcox? I promise to take no more of your time than necessary."

Monroe looked the man over. He was well-dressed, tailored dark blue suit, expensive suede loafers. Now that Monroe was able to afford the best, he knew clothes, and he knew that McDill's shirt alone had probably cost a hundred dollars. It might be interesting to hear what kind of scam this cat was trying to run.

"Sure, sit down, I got a minute. But try not to make it too long. I got some business to take care of."

McDill made himself comfortable across from Monroe. "I'll get right to the point, Mr. Wilcox. Goldenrod, Limited, an investment corporation which I represent, is very interested in becoming associated with your business."

"But, *I* ain't interested," Monroe said firmly.

"Well, perhaps the reason you're not is that you never gave it any thought before."

"Oh, I've given it some thought before," Monroe said, remembering Moe Fryman and Arie DeAngelo. "A *lot* of thought. But I ain't giving it no thought now. I told you, I ain't interested."

"Mr. Wilcox, just for the sake of discussion, let me throw a few figures at you, okay?"

"Help yourself, but you're wasting your time, I already told you that."

"Shall we start with, say, two million dollars?"

"Two million dollars, huh?" Monroe smiled. "Well, that ain't a bad figure."

"Tax-free."

"*Tax-free?*" Monroe was instantly suspicious. "What you mean, tax-free?"

"Cash," McDill said

Monroe's features tightened, a look of anger flashed across his face. "Who *are* you, man?"

McDill smiled disarmingly. "Oh, I'm just a workingman like yourself, Mr. Wilcox. But I do represent some very important people."

"Listen, man," Monroe said angrily, "I been through that 'very-important-people' bullshit before! I ain't interested in that shit *at all!*"

"Think about it—two million, tax-free. That's a great deal of money."

"You right, that's a lot of money. But it could be a lot of trouble, too. I ain't interested, so maybe you'd better split."

"Well, in that case"—the smile never left McDill's face—"I promised you I wouldn't take up much of your time, and I'm a man of my word. But I'd like for you to do me a favor, if you will."

"What's that?"

"I believe you have a partner in one of your publishing companies, a Mr. Ted Green?"

The alarm sounded in Monroe's head. The IRS was full of nice, mild-mannered paddies. He screwed up his face, as if he were thinking.

"Nooo," he said finally, "I think you're wrong there, I don't know no Ted Green. Now, if you'll excuse me, I gotta get back to work."

"Fine," McDill said, getting to his feet, "but if you should happen to remember Mr. Green's number, call him and ask him if he's familiar with this gentleman's reputation. . . ."

He wrote a name on the back of his card and showed it to Monroe. Monroe reached for it, but McDill held it out of his grasp. Monroe squinted across the desk at the name: Antonio Mauriello.

"If you will, check that name out with Mr. Green." McDill returned the card to his pocket and offered his hand. "I'll call you tomorrow morning at exactly ten o'clock."

"You can call if you want to," Monroe said, "but I don't expect to have nothin' to tell you."

"I'm not too sure of that, Mr. Wilcox," McDill said. "You know how it is in business, things can change very quickly."

He closed the door very politely as he left.

Monroe stood at the window and watched McDill leave the parking lot in a black Lincoln. He waited a few minutes, then told Clarice he had to step out of the office for a while, and left by the back entrance.

The Hawk was out, blowing off the lake like razor-sharp icicles. He pulled his overcoat around him tighter and walked the block and a half to the phone booth in the Sixty-six station, where he dialed Ted Green's private number. It rang once. Somebody lifted the receiver and held it without speaking.

"That you, man?" Monroe asked.

"Yeah—what's happening?"

"I gotta see you."

"What's the trouble?"

"I just had a visitor."

"Who?"

"Some cat named McDill."

"Never hear of him."

"He heard of *you*."

Green's voice suddenly became interested. "What did he want?"

"He told me to ask you about somebody named Mauriello—ever heard of him?"

"Yeah."

"Is he bad?"

"Is Sonny Liston ugly?"

Monroe automatically glanced around to see if anybody was watching him. "You gonna be there awhile?"

There was a noise on the other end of the line, a splashing sound, like Green was pouring himself a drink. "Little brother, a team of wild mules couldn't pull me out of here before I talk to you."

Twenty minutes later, Monroe turned his black Fleetwood sedan into the circular driveway of an exclusive apartment building on Lake Shore Drive, and watched the uniformed doorman come out to meet him. He hurried through the lobby to the elevator and pushed the letter P at the top of the row of buttons. When he stepped out, Green was waiting for him, dressed in his familiar silk bathrobe, a drink in his hand. He motioned Monroe inside.

Monroe had been there before. It was a spectacular apartment, furnished in shades of green with two of the living-room walls entirely floor-to-ceiling glass. The city of Chicago, blanketed by a misty haze, was spread out below as far as he could see. Green motioned him to a seat.

"Can I get you something?"

"Yeah," Monroe said, "gimme a light Chivas and water."

"Listen to him." Green chuckled as he went behind the bar. "I can remember when he didn't drink nothing but straight RC Cola."

"Oh yeah? Listen to *him*," Monroe said to the same imaginary person, "I can remember when *he* didn't live in no penthouse apartment with no white man parking his car, neither."

Green's laugh mixed with the rattle of ice cubes. He came back and handed Monroe a drink and took a seat across from him. "Okay, little brother, run it down to me."

Monroe told him the whole story—how McDill had been trying to get in to see him for a week. How nice the man seemed. How dramatically he had introduced Antonio Mauriello's name into the conversation, and concluded, "You say he's supposed to be pretty heavy, huh?"

"Last I heard, there were eleven Italians who sat on the board. He's one of them."

"Well, that answers that question, don't it?" Monroe said dourly.

"So tell me," Green said with a twinkle in his eye, "how did you get in bad with the motherfuckin' Mafia?"

"You ain't serious, man?"

"Naw, I'm just jivin' you, baby. The cat likes you. He wants to take you under his wing."

"He don't even know me, how can he like me?"

"Oh, he knows you, all right, you can bet your ass on that. He knows more about you than you know about yourself. He knows you legit. He knows you pay your help fair money. He knows you ain't trying to play no long string of bitches, wasting your time and money. . . ."

"If he knows me that well," Monroe said, "he probably knows that the last thing in the world I wanna do is get involved with him."

"You already involved with him," Green said matter-of-factly. "Everybody in the world is, in some way or another. You ain't no different."

"It ain't the same thing."

"What you think—he's tryin' to steal your business?"

"I don't know."

"No," Green answered his own question, "he ain't trying to muscle in on you. He ain't got no reason to steal your company. Shit, he already owns record companies worth millions of dollars."

"What's he want, then?"

"You."

"Fuck that!"

"Wait a minute," Green said. "Don't make up your mind too quick. Remember, now, you wanted to make it, didn't you?"

"Yeah, but—"

"Well, here's your chance."

"Damn, Ted," Monroe said angrily, "you make it sound like the motherfucker's trying to give me a promotion or something." He drank from his glass. "So tell me the truth, what you think'll happen to me if—I say *if*—I cut the motherfucker in?"

"That ain't the question. The question is, what will happen to you if you *don't* cut the motherfucker in?"

"What?"

"Well, lemme put it to you this way—anytime there's a game

going on, somebody wins and somebody loses. You been winning for a good little while, but now you playing against the house, so you'd better face it, you ain't going no farther."

"Ted," Monroe said soberly, "I ain't gonna bullshit around, I'm scared to be in business with them cats."

"That's good, you supposed to be scared. You wouldn't have good sense if you wasn't. But he wasn't trying to scare you, that's why he went to all the trouble of making an appointment and sending his man up to talk to you. Remember, now, just because a man's had to go outside the law to get his nuts out of the dust don't make him no animal. Look at me, I been a gangster damn near all my life. I had to dust a few motherfuckers here and there, but I ain't no animal. I always treated you good, didn't I?"

"Yeah, you been good to me," Monroe said.

"That's because you never tried to get slick with me. Same thing applies to him. You work hard and do what he tells you, make him a little bread, you'll probably get along with him okay, too."

Monroe sipped his drink and stared out the window, thinking back a few months. "I think there's something else going on, too," he said.

"Lemme hear it."

"Dig, I got this record in the mail from England a couple of months ago with a letter from some guy asking me if I would be interested in distributing it in this country. I didn't pay it no attention at the time, you know, just threw it in the drawer with the rest of my demos. Then one night while I was fucking around waiting for Willie to come back from dinner so we could mix some things down, I played it. I wasn't expecting much, but it sounded halfway decent, so I figured what the hell—it wasn't going to cost me but a few grand, I might as well take a chance on it."

"You got it out now?"

"Yeah, about two months."

"Is it doing any good?"

"Yeah, it's getting a lot of play on the pop stations. I shipped about a quarter of a million copies so far."

"On the *pop* stations?" Green gave him a penetrating look. "You mean, it's a white boy singing on it?"

"A white *group*. Their manager sent some pictures with the master. They don't look like much, just some long-haired, sissy-looking motherfuckers."

"I thought you said you weren't going to be fucking around with no white singers."

"I did, but I figured these cats were halfway around the world and—"

"—and you might be able to pick up a little gravy without stirring up too much shit, right?" Green completed the sentence for him.

"Yeah."

"Yeah . . . okay, go on."

"So a couple of weeks ago I got a letter from this lawyer in England making me an offer to buy the group's contract back for twenty-five grand. See, before I agreed to release them over here, I figured I'd better try to protect myself in case it hit, so I got a three-year exclusive contract."

"That was smart."

"Smarter than I thought. I was looking in *Cashbox* a couple of days ago and saw where they've got the number-one record in England right now. And not just that, they've got broads following them around, rioting, all that shit."

"Is that record the same one you got out on them?"

"No, it's another one, a new one. Mine's about a year old."

"But you got the rights to that new one for over here, though?"

"Oh, yeah, they've got to give it to me. That's our agreement."

"Hell, it ain't no wonder the lawyer's trying to buy the contract back from you. He's probably already been offered a whole bunch of money for it."

"Maybe so . . ." Monroe started to add something else, changed his mind.

"What were you going to say?"

"Ted, you're going to think I'm crazy. . . ."

"Shit, I already think that, so say what you got to say."

Monroe's brow furrowed in concentration. "You remember that first night I came up to your pad, when I was talking to you about the white man coming up with his 'King'?"

"Sure, I remember. You said he couldn't ever control the music business like he wanted to until he got his King. I dug that. That was one of the things that made me decide to go along with you."

"Yeah . . . well, I was right. Presley never amounted to much musically, him and the rest of that rockabilly bullshit he started. And they're trying to beat that folk-music thing to death. Ain't nothing really been happening musically since Ray Charles started to cool off. . . ."

"So what you getting at?"

Monroe leaned forward and unconsciously lowered his voice.

"Man, I know this is gonna sound silly, but I think this group I got may be his King."

Green raised an eyebrow. "How come you say that?"

"Well, for one thing, 'cause *I* like them. And I don't usually dig no white groups, you know that. They usually get on my nerves with that sewing-machine music they play. But this group is different. They got a little feeling. . . .'

"Well, I got to give you credit, baby, you know your shit. If you say they got it, they probably got it. But what I don't understand is, why did they send *you* the record in the first place? I mean, you doing pretty good, that's true, but you ain't all that big, as record companies go. I don't see how they even know about you."

"Oh, those cats over there are hip to American music, man, especially colored music. They've been writing me letters and asking for pictures of my artists ever since I been in business."

"You must be jiving!" Green exclaimed, surprised.

"No, I ain't. Some of those kids over there know more about r-and-b than a lot of American kids."

"Well, I'll be damned." Green shook his head in amazement. "When I think of English cats, all I think of is 'cheerio' and 'toodle-oo' and all that bullshit. I swear, I can't picture no Englishman sitting down digging on no colored music."

"I'm telling you, Ted, the cats are hip over there."

"That's a bitch, ain't it?' Green shook his head a few more times. "But they ain't never sent you nothing to put out before, have they?"

"Oh, yeah, a few times. They started sending me stuff a couple of years ago, back when they had what they called, uh, *skiffle* music, I think it was—cats playing harps and beating on washboards and trying to sing like Sonny Boy Williamson."

"English boys trying to sing like Sonny Boy Williamson? Ha, ha, ha . . . you a lying sack of shit, little brother!"

"It's true"—Monroe laughed—"and some of them didn't sound all that bad, either."

"So how come you never put nothing out on them before?"

"Well, for one thing, I could barely get pop airplay on my own stuff in those days. And couldn't you see me taking a record like that to Al Baxter or one of those other guys? They would have had me put away somewhere."

"Umm-hmmm . . ." Green was serious again. "So what you saying is, it ain't all that farfetched that this group of yours could come over here and take care of business, right?"

"If they got the right kind of promotion, I believe they would come over here and knock a whole lot of little jive groups off the charts right quick."

"But you can't give them that kind of push, can you?"

"No," Monroe was honest, "not like one of those big white companies. I ain't got that kind of juice yet."

"Umm-hmmm . . ." Green took their glasses back to the bar for refills. He came back and handed Monroe a fresh drink and resumed his seat. "Okay now, lemme see if I got this straight—you saying that group might have something to do with Mauriello wanting to come in on your company?"

"I don't know. They could have."

Green sipped his drink and stared out the window in silence, until a slight smile touched his lips. "Yeah, you could be right," he finally agreed. "They might have something to do with it."

"What you thinking?"

"Okay . . . suppose Mauriello got wind of the fact that somebody is about to put some money behind them. Suppose, say, he'd been checking your company out for a while, already thinking about buying in, and this just helped him make up his mind."

"No, I don't think so." Monroe shook his head. "Ain't no way he could have heard about something like that."

"Wait a minute, don't underestimate the cat, now," Green said quickly. "He's got gambling joints in England and all over Europe and the Bahamas. He must be pretty tight with some heavy people, otherwise he never would have been able to do all that. So if one of them big English companies was thinking about putting some grand-theft bread behind your group, it wouldn't take him no time at all to find out about it."

Monroe whistled softly. "God damn . . ."

"Okay, now, let's take it a little further. Let's suppose he's *already* made a deal with them—say, he buys into your company and they let him put out a few more records on the group, and then he tears up the contract and nobody has to take nobody else to court. Make sense?"

"Yeah, but what's the point of all that?"

"Simple. He makes a few million on the deal right off the top, depending on how the group does, and when it's all over, he's still got you and your company."

Monroe took a swallow of his drink. "That's how those mother-fuckers think, ain't it?"

"I ain't saying it's true. I'm just saying it *could* be true, give or take a few more scams."

Monroe nodded and forced a grin. "Shit, I can see how you made it as a con man."

"Got that right." Green nodded. "So what you gonna do?"

"I don't know yet."

"You gonna take Mauriello's offer, or what?"

"I told you, I don't know yet."

"Well, I can't make up your mind for you. It's your company. You the one who ate all the shit to keep it, not me. But I'll tell you one thing that's damn sure worth remembering: you buck the wrong motherfuckers, and they can put you out of business *anytime they want.*"

"Aw, they already tried that."

"Not *these* people. Mauriello ain't no Moe Fryman, remember that. Him and his people don't bother with nothing that don't have millions of dollars attached to it." Green took a slug of his drink. "Now, lemme ask you something, little brother—I ain't trying to get in your business or nothin', but how much you worth right now?"

"You mean me personally, or my business?"

"You, personally."

"I don't have no idea." Monroe saw Green's look. "No, I ain't trying to be slick, Ted, I really don't know. I guess, countin' my house and cars and insurance and money in the bank and all that, I'm probably worth a half-million now, maybe a little more."

"How about your business?"

"Lemme see . . . I should bill about six million by the time the year's out. Then maybe, altogether, another half-million from publishing."

"How much of it you owe?"

"Well, I owe about a half-million in pressing and album costs, stuff like that. And I got at least a million dollars' worth of stock sitting on distributors' shelves, not countin' the returns they're gonna be sending back on current releases. Plus, I gotta pay royalties and taxes and all that other stuff."

"That's what I mean, these motherfuckers can swoop down on you and hit the right spots and you're gone"—Green snapped his fingers—"just like that!"

"I think I'm open for suggestions." Monroe sighed.

"Okay, then, I'll suggest. Take it."

"But—"

"Goddammit, *take it!* This ain't no goddamned television show, man! You ain't Sidney Poitier riding over the motherfucking hill to clean up no turkeys! This is real life, and in real life, anytime a white man offers you two million dollars for anything, you fucking *take* it!"

"I don't have to take *nothin'!*" Monroe shouted defiantly. "I ain't no motherfucking slave!"

"Okay . . ." An amused look touched Green's eyes. "I'm gonna go along with you for a minute. Now, suppose these white boys from England really are the 'King,' like you say. They gonna wind up being worth, oh, maybe two, three hundred million dollars to somebody before it's all over, ain't they?"

"Maybe so. . . ."

"Well, that being the case, you ain't really dumb enough to think the white man's gonna let you keep them, are you?"

Monroe didn't answer.

"You livin' pretty good right now, ain't you?" Green persisted.

"I'm doing okay," Monroe agreed sullenly.

"And you aint' even a millionaire yet, right?"

"Yeah."

"Okay. You ever stop to think about how good you'd live if you had, say, three hundred million dollars?"

"Naw, I don't never think about no silly shit like that, man."

"Well, think about it a minute."

"Knowing me, I probably wouldn't be that much different."

"Oh, yeah, you'd be different, all right," Green said emphatically. "Hell, if you had three hundred million dollars, you could forget about them little white boys from England, 'cause *you* would be the King. Now, you know the white man ain't going for that. He may let you be the Prince for a while, but he ain't never gonna let you be the goddamn King!"

"What you talkin' about, man?" Monroe asked irritatedly. He already knew, he just didn't want to admit to himself that he did.

"Power, little brother, that's what I'm talking about. Princes ain't got no power, they just stand around looking cute. Kings has got all the power, and the man who controls the King got more power than that—dig where I'm coming from?"

Monroe thought about it a minute. "Naw, man," he said finally, "I ain't going for that. How about all them little countries like Cuba, where cats run off with hundreds of millions of dollars—"

"Yeah, but where do they run to?"

"What you mean?"

"I mean, they run put it in a white man's bank, don't they? And the white man who gave it to them goes and borrows it back, then he flips off a couple of bills and buys little niggers like you. Shit, you realize how many people you can buy with three hundred million dollars? How many radio stations and newspapers? How many ass-kissing motherfuckers you can pay to run around and tell your story for you? Three hundred million dollars would break a whole lot of grips on a whole lot of people's minds, little brother."

"I guess so. . . ."

"Umm-hmmm"—the twinkle was still in Green's eyes—"and the first thing you know, you'd be going around telling a different story from that bullshit you been hearing all your life, wouldn't you?"

"Yeah, probably so. . . ."

"And the second thing you know, people would stop buying all that 'sewing-machine music' you were talking about, right?"

"Probably so. . . ."

"And the third thing you know"—Green let out a cackle—"you done fucked up the white man's business! Now, what makes you think he's gonna let you do that?"

"That's some cold shit, ain't it?" Monroe said.

"Naw, that's just politics, little brother. But politics say you ain't going no further, so go on and take the man's money and try to make sure you in a position to get a little more when the time comes, and forget it."

Monroe sat there quietly, nodding his head, trying to absorb all that Green was telling him. Hating to acknowledge to himself how powerless he really was, but having to admit that, so far, Ted Green had never been wrong.

"You want another taste before you go?" Green asked.

"Naw." Monroe sighed. "I got to get back to the office and clean up some stuff before I go home. And I got a lot of thinking to do, so I better keep my head on tight." He stood up.

"Hey, ain't you forgot something?"

"What?"

"Sit down."

Monroe sat down again. "What?"

"The man said two million dollars, tax-free, didn't he?"

"Yeah. If I take it."

"Well, don't you think we ought to talk about my share?"

"How much you want?"

"I think a half-million would be cool."

Monroe didn't hesitate. He stuck out his hand. "You got it."

HOLLYWOOD DECEMBER 1963

It was a tiny speck of light, made up of soft golds and greens, of luminous whites and warm reds and browns. It shone on him and moved away, then returned with an even brighter glow and sent a quiver through him. He felt himself shiver and reach for it, but it moved away again. He searched the darkness with his fingers and found it and drew it to him. It seemed to melt beneath his touch, covering him with a buttery haze. He gasped and pulled away. It drew him back with an excruciating slowness. He felt himself begin to coil. A sigh escaped his throat. And for one clear moment there was nothing in his life but the relentless, agonizing sweetness of her mouth upon him. . . .

She was in his arms, a faint taste of him upon her lips. "Is that the correct way for a loving wife to wake her husband?" she asked.

He whistled softly.

"Good, that's one you owe me."

"You are very good at that."

"No, I am the *very best* at that," she corrected, "and if you're not convinced, I'll be happy to give you another demonstration."

"At the moment, you would be demonstrating on a very inactive model." He shifted his weight so he could see the clock without moving his arm. "Shit—it's almost eight-thirty!"

"So what? You're not going anywhere."

"Yes, I have to get up in a minute."

She snuggled closer. "What time does it start?"

"Not until noon, but I have a few things to clear off my desk."

"You have a few things you can clear up here, too," she murmured, sliding her lips along his neck.

"Don't worry, after today we'll have two weeks to catch up."

"I sure hope so. You've been scared to touch me lately."

"No, I haven't."

"Well, you act like it. I'm not made out of glass, you know."

"I know." He sat up, his back against the headboard, rubbing the sleep from his eyes. "You sure you don't want to come along?"

"I can't. I have to finish packing, and I'm supposed to meet the real-estate agent at noon to look at the new house. Oh, I meant to tell you, he says he has a firm offer of one-fifty-two, five for this place. He wants to know if he should accept it."

"What do you think?"

"Oh, honey, I don't know about things like that. Maybe you should ask your mother."

"I'm asking my wife. What do you think?"

"I don't know. Are you sure you want to sell it? I mean, I just can't picture you, us, living anywhere else."

"We have to have room for the baby, right?"

"Yes," she said wistfully, "our first and last child."

"What?"

"Well, I mean, now that you've given up screwing your wife . . ."

He kissed her. "Did I tell you Les is in town?"

"No, when did he get in?"

"He called yesterday, just before I left the office."

"Is he coming today?"

"Yes, I told him I wanted to talk with him before he goes back."

"Does he know you're leaving the company?"

"He probably has an idea."

"I don't think he'll take the job. He and Monique are too happy in New York."

"Maybe not, but I want to give him a shot at it before I put it up for grabs. It would be a big step up for him."

"Did Monique come with him?"

"Yes. They're going to stay out here for the whole holiday season, and he wanted to know if you've started choosing material for your new album."

"Did you explain to him that I've been busy getting married and looking at new houses and knitting booties and all that stuff?"

"He didn't want a whole newsletter, he just wanted to know if you've started yet."

"What time do you think you'll be home?"

"As soon as I can. I'll probably stay around until the presents are opened, but I'd say no later than—" He cocked an ear. "Is that the phone?"

She listened. "Yes, you want me to get it?"

"No, that's okay, they'll call back."

"I thought I heard it earlier. Why didn't you bring it in when you came to bed?"

"I figured you might have to get up and go to the bathroom or something, and I didn't want you to trip over the cord."

"Oh, shit, Mark!" she exploded. "I'm just pregnant, not spastic! I haven't had to get up and go to the bathroom in the middle of the night since I was four years old!"

"Oh . . . somebody told me pregnant women have to pee a lot."

"In that case," she said angrily, "maybe you should get me a bedpan!" He kissed her, laughing, and parted the covers to get up. She pulled him back. "I mean, let's not carry this concerned-husband bullshit too far."

"We probably should be careful, honey. . . ."

"You're being silly," she said, sliding a leg across him. "I was talking to Lois the other day, and she said Bob wouldn't touch her while she was pregnant, not for months. She said she used to lie beside him and cry because she felt like a toad or something."

"Lois said that? I can't imagine her saying that."

"Oh, yes, pregnant women are very insecure," she purred, reaching down to stroke him, "so I think you'd better start securing me as soon as possible. Besides, you owe me one. . . ."

She poured them another cup of coffee. "I told your mother we'd be there in time for dinner."

"When did you talk to her?"

"Yesterday, before they left. She was worried about you."

"I'm glad you two are getting along so well. I told you she likes you."

"No, she doesn't. She's just being nice to me because I'm your wife."

"C'mon, now, Sarah . . ."

"No, I can tell. She doesn't think I'm good enough for you."

"You're just being silly."

She shook her head once, sipped her coffee.

"I'll tell you one thing," he said, changing the subject, "I'm sure looking forward to getting down there. I feel like I could sleep for a week."

"That's what your mother said. She said you look sick, like you've aged twenty years since you took that job."

He grunted.

"Mark, I was wondering . . ."

"Hmmm?"

". . . if your folks would mind if Monique and Les came down and spent a couple of days with us over the holidays."

"We could ask. The place is plenty big enough."

"Oh, that would be great! Monique is pregnant too, you know. And I'll bet she's never been to Palm Springs. We could have a ball, go shopping for baby clothes together, swimming, all kinds of things."

"I'll mention it to him when I see him at the party."

"I mean, I like your mother, but two weeks alone with her would just destroy me."

"Why?"

"I told you, she doesn't like me."

"Oh, nonsense. I don't know how you came up with that."

"And I never know quite how to act, she makes me feel so damn self-conscious."

He set his cup down, determined to put the matter to rest once and for all. "Listen, do me a favor, okay? When we get there, just try to be friends with her. Give her a chance. She's a super lady and she has more love in her than anybody I've ever known. She'll do everything she can to make you feel at home, so stop worrying, okay?"

"Hmmm . . ."

"Okay?"

"Well, it just makes me mad that she thinks I don't take care of you."

"Dammit, Sarah—"

"Well, she doesn't! She kept saying how tired you look and how you've lost so much weight lately."

"Well, I am and I have."

"Well, it's not my fault. I don't make you live in that damned office."

"Honey, I'm sure she wasn't trying to give you a hard time. She's just accustomed to looking after my dad, that's all, and she wants you to do the same for me." He glanced at his watch. "I'd better get going."

"I'll walk you out."

She got his attaché case for him while he washed his hands. They walked down the front steps together.

"Don't forget to mention it to Les."

"I won't."

"What time will you be home?"

"Two-thirty or three, no later."

"Good. If we get out of here by four o'clock, we should have plenty of time without rushing, huh?"

"Yes, I want to take time and enjoy the drive down."

"I can't believe I'm going to have you all to myself for two weeks."

"You're not. You're going to have me all to yourself for one week, and the second week you're going to share me with about five different golf courses."

She hugged his waist and pressed her face to his chest. "I love you," she said.

"I love you, too. . . . Oh shit, there's the phone again."

Maybe I can catch it. Want to wait? It might be important."

"No, if it is, they'll call me at the office. I'm late, I'd better run."

He watched her hurry up the stairs. "Take it easy!" he called.

She paused long enough to throw him a saucy wave of her behind, then scampered inside.

He got off the elevator at the eleventh floor and peeked inside the conference room to see how things were going. The secretaries who made up the "Christmas Party Committee" were swarming about like bees festooning a hive. A few were standing on chairs, stringing lights and streamers. Another was busy choosing albums of carols. A couple more were trying to decide on the most strategic spots to hang mistletoe. They had commandeered several burly young men from the stockroom, who had already moved out most of the heavy conference chairs and pushed the tables against the wall beside the large brightly-decorated tree. They were now erecting and stocking the bar. One of the secretaries from Accounting, a bouncy little Chinese girl named Amy Chinn, left the mistletoe detail and hurried over to Mark.

"Merry Christmas, Mr. Donovan!"

"Merry Christmas, Amy. How're we coming?"

"Oh, it's going to be a blast! Betty—Mr. Silverstein's secretary— just took a couple of the fellows down to bring up the ice and Cokes and stuff, and Marcia Lowenthal and Debbie Anders—you know, from Billing—just went down to the catering truck to bring up the sandwiches, and—"

"Sounds like everything's under control."

"Oh, yes, it's going to be a blast! You're coming, aren't you?"

"I wouldn't miss it, Amy."

She heard someone calling her. "Oh! I think Stephanie needs me to hold the ladder."

She hurried away. He stood there in the doorway, smiling, watching them, thinking of the people he was going to miss when he left. But, he reminded himself, every day at Arrow Records was not Christmas, it was more like Halloween.

Instead of going down the hall to the elevator, he took the stairs up one flight and entered his office through the back door. He flopped down in the chair and swiveled around to look out the window for a few seconds. Then, frowning, he turned back to the papers on his desk.

He hadn't realized how much work was left to tie up until he started wading through it. As hard as he had tried to fight it, Arrow had become a paperwork company. Every time Planning held a meeting in New York, they seemed to come up with more intricate ways of keeping the lines of communication flowing. New procedures every month . . . forms, forms, forms . . . for cost projections, estimated quarterly distributor returns, revised studio maintenance costs . . . duplicates, triplicates, quadruplicates. . . .

He worked his way through one pile, pushed it aside, and looked at the other in disgust. "Fuck it!" He slapped the desk in frustration.

A few seconds later the door burst open and Barbara hurried inside. "I thought I heard you!" she said excitedly. "I've been trying to call you all morning!"

He looked up, startled. "Jesus, Barbara, you scared the hell out of me—what's going on?"

"Mr. Geary's been trying to reach you from Connecticut. He says it's urgent."

Mark's brow furrowed. "You'd better get him for me."

"I can't, he's driving into New York now. He said he'd call you again as soon as he arrives at his office, so stick close to the phone."

"When was the last time you talked to him?"

"About an hour ago. I called your house, but your wife said you'd just left."

"I wonder what the hell it is?" Mark worried aloud.

"I don't know, but it sounded pretty serious."

He calculated the time. It was normally an hour's drive into New York from Geary's house, but with Christmas traffic it could take twice as long. "Are you going to be at your desk, or do you have to go downstairs?"

"I don't know. Betty—you know, Mr. Silverstein's secretary"—he nodded impatiently—"will be here in a minute. We're supposed to start taking the presents downstairs."

"Can't she find someone else to help her?"

"I don't know. I'll ask."

"Okay, call her and check on it. And if you have to go, leave my line open so the switchboard can call through."

"I'll be back as soon as I can."

"I'd appreciate it."

She left, and he sat there wondering what Geary's problem could be. He hadn't talked to the old man in weeks. Well . . . He shrugged.

There was no sense in borrowing trouble, he'd just have to wait and see.

He turned back to his work. He had saved the most troublesome task for last, a cost-analysis projection for the first quarter of the following year.

Normally he merely estimated general market growth, tacked on the anticipated increase in the price of goods and services, and recommended that one percent be added to the previous quarter's budget. It was, admittedly, a lazy way of going about it, but the company was growing so fast that there was no point in trying to analyze and modify costs when the chances were that those particular services would have to be increased anyhow. The situation now was very different. The President's assassination had brought the company to a virtual standstill—indeed, as it had numbed the entire nation. It was such a stupid, senseless murder that the mere thought of it filled Mark with rage. And fear, to think that perhaps fate herself was determined to keep his life, all of their lives, trivial and without social conscience. And because of the assassination, much of Arrow's anticipated quarterly capital expenditures, except for salaries, of course, were still unspent.

This problem he faced today, that of increasing the budgetary allowance for the next quarter with a substantial amount of the present quarter's capital still unspent, was well outside the guidelines of any past memos he had received, but he was damned if he intended to spend half his Christmas vacation trying to come up with a solution that would pacify New York. That being the case, he had already decided on his customary one-percent figure and was busily trying to come up with a series of maneuvers to justify it, when Barbara returned.

"I'm sorry I took so long."

He looked at his watch. He had lost track of the time; it was already well past noon. Geary should have called by now. "How's it going down there?" he asked.

"Fine. They're already asking for you."

"Who?"

"Mr. Silverstein, for one. And Betty, who wants you there when she hands out the presents. And little Amy Chinn—I think she's got a crush on you. And Angela Dunn from the mailroom—"

"Miss Dunn, huh?" He grimaced.

"Mrs. Dunn," Barbara corrected. "Dirty old Mrs. Dunn."

"Great."

"Go on down. I'll wait here for Mr. Geary's call."

"You'll be okay? I don't want you to miss the party."

"Sure." She showed him her glass. "I brought some eggnog with me."

"Okay, I've one more thing to finish here, and I'll run down the back way." She turned to leave. "Barbara?"

"Yes?"

"Merry Christmas, and thank you for another good year."

She smiled, gleaming white teeth in a warm brown face, and left.

He worked a few minutes longer, then slipped into his jacket and headed downstairs. He paused in the doorway leading from the stairwell to the eleventh-floor corridor, and listened to the sounds of the party wafting toward him. Above it all was Sinatra's unmistakable baritone. . . .

> *. . . good tidings we bring you,*
> *For you and your kin;*
> *We wish you a Merry Christmas,*
> *And a Happy New Year. . . .*

He turned the corner to see that a dozen or so partyers had already spilled out into the hall, drinks in hand, clustered in small groups. Several waved to him as he approached. The grin on his face was abruptly erased by a groan as he saw Angela Dunn pushing her way through the crowd to get to him.

Angela Dunn was a forty-year-old redhead with slightly buck teeth, given to wearing black leotards with bright ponchos, who spent most of her evenings in the rock clubs that dotted the Strip around the building, and most of her salary trying to ward off advancing age.

She grabbed Mark's arm and fell into step beside him. "I've been waiting for you!"

"Well," Mark said dryly, "here I am."

"It's a lovely party. The girls have done a darling job, don't you think?"

"Yes, I looked in earlier. They've worked very hard getting it together, Mrs. Dunn."

"Angela. You can call me Angela today, don't you think?"

"How are things in the mailroom?"

"Perfectly awful, as usual, but we don't have to go into that, do we?"

"Probably not."

"And how is your dear little bride?"

"Fine, fine."

"Congratulations."

"Thank you."

"I haven't seen her yet—did she come to the party?"

"No—"

"Oh, that's too bad!" she exclaimed, taking a firmer grip on Mark's elbow. "I guess I'll just have to keep you entertained, then, won't I?"

"—she's coming to pick me up later."

"My, my, isn't that nice!" She immediately loosened her grip.

"Merry Christmas, Mark," Chuck Lichner, from Graphics, said.

"Good to see you, Chuck," Mark said, shaking his hand.

"Hey, you're falling behind, you'd better get a drink!"

"Oh, Chuck, I simply must talk to you for a moment!" Angela Dunn bolted off, yanking Lichner in the other direction.

Mark exhaled a sigh of relief, then felt a hand on his sleeve. "Here"—Bob Silverstein shoved a beer at him—"I was just about to come looking for you."

"Thanks. What did I miss?"

"The best part—Whitaker and Schultz just got into it."

"How bad?"

"Not bad, loud. They started scuffling and knocked the tree over."

"Oh, for God's sake!" Mark exclaimed in disgust. "Anybody hurt?"

"Whitaker got scratched up a little. He left a couple of minutes ago, so stoned he could hardly stand up."

"As usual, huh?"

"Worse than usual."

"How can anybody be so stupid, Bob?" Mark's face was contorted by frustration.

"That"—Silverstein shrugged—"is a four-beer question, and since I've only had two, I'll pass."

"It's a goddamned shame!"

"Fuck it," Silverstein said. "Drink up."

"You're right, to hell with it." Mark took a healthy slug of his beer. "Is Lois here?"

"No, she's home packing. We're going to New York for the holiday."

"You're going home for Christmas?"

"Not for Christmas, for Hanukkah."

Mark moved into the doorway to let a couple of people pass through the hall, and saw Les Goodson across the room, in a small group that included Paulie Schultz and one of the girls from Promotion.

"Listen, Bob"—he touched Silverstein's shoulder—"I want to talk tc Les about something, so don't go before I get back to you. I've got a call coming from New York. I think something's up. I'll know in a little while."

He slowly edged his way through the crowded room, smiling, nodding, offering greetings. He felt an arm around his waist.

"I told you it was going to be a blast, didn't I?"

"You girls did a good job, Amy."

"Yep," she said matter-of-factly. "Here."

"No, thanks, I've got a beer."

"I insist, Mr. Donovan."

He took a sip of her eggnog. It was generously laced with rum. "Wow!"

"I know, and the best is yet to come. Look up."

He did. He was standing beneath a sprig of mistletoe. "That's very nice," he said lamely.

"Sock it to me, please."

He kissed her.

She slipped the tip of her tongue between his lips, quickly withdrew it. "Ohmygawwd!" She pretended to swoon, before running off to tell the other girls in Accounting.

Laughing, he started across the room again, careful not to upset drinks, nodding and joking with the people who worked for him, some of whom he hadn't seen since the last Christmas party.

Goodson had his back to Mark. Mark tapped his shoulder. As Goodson turned, he looked like a younger version of Mark, a slender man with intelligent eyes and a slightly effacing manner that made him instantly likable. Aside from Silverstein, he was Mark's closest confidant in the company—a result, in part, of Goodson's patience in the handling of Sarah's career.

"Hey, I figured you'd show up sooner or later!" He pumped Mark's hand. "Merry Christmas! How's it going?"

"Great. How long've you been here?"

Goodson threw Paulie a weary look. "Long enough to see the Liston-Patterson rematch." He touched the girl beside him. "Honey, look who's here."

Monique Goodson was a willowy blond with sharp features and ice-blue eyes, easily the most attractive woman in the room. She had retired from a successful fashion-modeling career to marry Goodson, and they were now about to have their first child.

"Ahhh, zere's my baybee!" she squealed as soon as she saw Mark, and planted a juicy kiss on his mouth. It was a private joke between them. The first time he'd met her, he'd assumed, with the name Monique, she would be French. She was from Hamilton, Ohio. But

356 ·

from that time on, every time she saw him she did a broad burlesque of a French accent.

"I feel a lump against my stomach," he said, hugging her.

"I know, that dirty bastard's been screwing me again."

"When's it due?"

"April, which will be her name—April."

"Right," Goodson said. "April James Michael Goodson."

"See? Wrong again," Monique said; then, to Mark: "How's Sarah?"

"Good. She wants you to call her."

"I was going to. We can get together and talk baby talk."

"Where are you staying?" Mark asked Goodson.

"With her folks, in, uh . . . hell, I can never remember the names of these towns out here. What's it called, honey?"

"Buena Park."

"Buena Park, f'Chrissakes, no wonder I can't remember!"

"Hey, are you gonna speak or not?" Paulie erupted. He had been talking with the girl from Promotion, and Mark hadn't noticed him rejoin the group.

"I'm sorry, Paul. You were busy. How are you?"

"Great. Listen, while I got you here—"

"Merry Christmas, Mr. Donovan," the Promotion girl said, looking over the top of Paulie's head.

"Merry Christmas, Liz."

"Listen, while I've got you here," Paulie persisted, "did you get a chance to hear that new thing I did on Terry Caulfield?"

"No, I've been pretty busy. I got married, you know?"

"Yeah, I heard, congratulations—listen, you gotta hear it. It's a bitch!"

"Send it up to me. I'll check it out when I get back."

"I already sent it, two weeks ago. Ask your girl."

"I will. I'm anxious to hear it. We haven't been able to do much with Caulfield lately."

"I know, his fans are growing up. They're gonna be old enough to start having their periods pretty soon. That's why I'm getting him out of that goddamn bubble gum bullshit, you know what I mean?"

"Yes, I'm anxious to hear it." Mark pulled Goodson aside. "Les, may I talk to you a minute?"

"Sure."

They picked their way through the revelers, out the door and down the hall.

"What a prick," Goodson said.

"Shame on you. That's no way to talk about a genius."

"A genius at causing pains in the lower back." He lit a cigarette. "What's on your mind?"

"Les, I know this isn't the time to talk about it"—Mark's voice was unable to convey all the emotion he felt—"but I've made up my mind, I'm leaving here in March."

"I had a feeling," Goodson said quietly.

"I want to submit you for the presidency. It may not mean you'll get it, but I want to give you a shot."

Goodson shook his head. "I don't think so, Mark."

"It's probably the best job in the business right now."

"If it is, why are you leaving it?"

"Ten years is a long time."

"Not if you're happy."

"I'm just burned out, I guess."

"No, you're not. You're fed up." He shook his head again. "Would you be angry if I turned it down, Mark?"

"Not angry, disappointed."

"I'm sorry, but I have to. I talked it over with Monique, anticipating what might be on your mind, and neither of us wants to leave New York. We're both doing what we want, we've got a lot of good friends back there, and my folks and Monique get along great." He motioned with his eyes at the groups of people clustered around the doorway to the conference room. "I know what you're offering me, and I appreciate it, but I just can't see myself hassling budgets and lighting fires under those clowns. I don't have your patience. If I had to put up with asshcles like Schultz and Whitaker every day, I'd wind up punching somebody out in a week." He took a draw off his cigarette and regarded Mark with affection. "But I'll tell you one thing—when you go, a lot of us may be right behind you."

"I hope not," Mark said sincerely.

"Why not? Who wants to spend their whole life being seventeen years old?"

Mark saw Barbara pushing her way through the crowd toward him. "When are you going back?" he asked Goodson.

"We'll be here for the holidays, probably leave the second or third."

"How'd you and Monique like to come down to Palm Springs for a few days, say, sometime between Christmas and New Year's? Spend some time at my folks' place. I won't try to pressure you."

"Sounds good. I'll ask her."

"He's on the line," Barbara said.

"Okay," Mark told her, "I'll take it down here. Have a drink or something, but stick close, I may need you." He turned back to

Goodson. "It's Geary, from New York. I should be only a minute, but don't leave before I see you."

"I'll be here."

Mark pushed his way back into the conference room. It was completely packed now. The crowd was more boisterous, the shouting and rattle of glasses deafening. Everybody seemed to be getting pleasantly smashed. Sinatra had given way to Andy Williams, and Amy Chinn was busy trying to form a group of carolers to join in with the stereo, but nobody seemed interested.

A look of concern on his face, Mark threaded his way past the tree, to the door that led to the anteroom. It was dark inside. There was a shuffling of feet. He flicked the light switch by the door and saw Angela Dunn and Chuck Lichner in a corner, straightening their clothes.

"Excuse me," he said briskly, "I have to take a call."

They muttered apologies and scurried from the room. He found the phone, pushed a button, and Max Geary's voice came on the line. A few minutes later, Mark replaced the receiver and stood there staring vacantly at the wall, stunned, unable to move.

"What is it?"

He turned around in a daze. Barbara and Bob Silverstein were watching him from the doorway.

"Barbara, call my wife and tell her to pack a bag for me. I have to leave for New York immediately."

"My God, man!" Silverstein cried. "What is it?"

"Turicotti's dead. Heart attack."

LAS VEGAS
DECEMBER 1963

The steady drone of the engines shifted into an uncertain mutter as the plane began its descent through the clouds. Monroe hunched forward in his seat and peered out anxiously over the wing. He was disappointed at what he saw. What looked like downtown was no more that a few second-rate hotels cramped into an area of a few blocks. Farther away, he could see a cluster of tract houses, and beyond that a neighborhood of run-down shacks.

As the plane continued to dip in preparation for its final approach, he saw another group of buildings trailing out from town, spread out over several miles. Now, *they* looked like something. Newer buildings, ten or twelve stories high, interspersed with parking lots and golf courses and small patches of blue-green, which he took to be swimming pools. As he watched, a huge harp-shaped sign flickered once, before splitting the late-afternoon dusk with a pink-and-white glow that sprinkled light upon a thin ribbon of highway. He couldn't quite make out the letters on the sign. As the plane continued to bank, he unconsciously emitted a nervous sigh.

I must be crazy! he thought.

The stewardess came down the aisle toward him, wearing the same fixed smile she had worn since Chicago, pushing up trays, checking to see that seat belts were fastened, and passing out small packages. When she reached Monroe, she hesitated before dropping one into his outstretched palm. He looked at it. Suntan oil. Without turning his head, he handed it to the man in the seat beside him.

There was the sudden strain of the flaps being lowered, followed by the whine of the landing gear being locked into place, and, what seemed to Monroe an eternity later, the gentle shock of the wheels touching the runway. The last was greeted by a smattering of applause from the passengers around him. He was slightly embarrassed to find himself joining in with them.

He was at the front of the terminal, debating with himself whether or not to invest the two or three quarters in his pocket in one of the slot machines by the door, when he saw a young woman in a skin-tight pink pantsuit and white fur jacket walking toward him. She was about the same size as Maudie, built even better, if that was possible. Straight black hair and bold, dark eyes. He couldn't tell if she was black or not. But whatever she was, she was a stone fox.

"Mr. Wilcox?"

"Yeah?"

"My name is Tania. Mr. McDill sent me to meet you."

He thought he detected a trace of hostility in her voice. He showed her his bag. "I'm ready."

He followed her through the door. Her car, a bright red Plymouth convertible with the top up, was parked in front. He threw his bag on the backseat. She got in behind the wheel and steered the car into traffic.

"It's nice to meet you," she said. "I've heard a lot about you."

"Yeah."

"First trip to Vegas?"

"Yeah."

"You'll like it—lot of things happening."

"That's what I hear."

"Do you gamble?"

"Naw, not since I was in the Army. Used to shoot a little craps, stuff like that. Never won nothin', though."

"You could get lucky, you know?"

"Yeah"—he laughed—"I could dig that."

"Any idea how long you'll be here?"

"No more than a couple of days, I guess."

"Maybe I'll have a chance to show you around. . . ."

"Umm-hmmm . . ." he said, figuring he'd better check things out before he got himself committed to anything, ". . . if I have time."

It was almost dark now. She made a right turn. Immense glaring signs lit up the sky before him.

"Lot of money out here, ain't it?" he asked.

"Yes, and most of it stays here, too."

"How long you been here?"

"Not long—a couple of years."

"I don't mean to get in your business or nothing"—his curiosity finally got the better of him—"but you a 'sister,' ain't you?"

"No," she said shortly.

He was unconvinced. "Where you from?"

"Here and there. Name it."

"Yeah, okay . . . I dig." He got the message and turned to look out the window, dismissing the conversation.

They approached the group of hotels he had seen from the plane. Each one was like a small city within itself, spaced much farther apart than they had looked from the air.

"I didn't mean to get uptight"—there was no apology in her voice—"I just didn't want you to get on my case about, uh . . . anything."

"I ain't interested in your case, baby." He shrugged.

"Well, a lot of colored men—"

"Hey, listen, if you can jive these paddies into thinking you white, more power to you."

She looked at him out of the corner of her eye without responding, and continued on past several hotels before turning into the sweeping driveway with the huge pink-and-white sign beside it. A doorman approached, smiling, obviously recognizing the car.

She reached into her jacket pocket and handed Monroe a key. "You've already been checked in. You can go straight up to your suite if you like."

"Okay."

"I'm supposed to call you later. . . ."

"Save your dime," he said.

He got out and handed the doorman his key. As he entered the building, the casino was to his left, through an archway and down three steps. He paused and looked at the rows of slot machines, surprised to see that a few were being played by blacks. He'd heard that blacks weren't too welcome in Las Vegas, and seeing them made him relax. The people who strolled past were, for the most part, casually dressed. Nobody paid him any attention.

He felt a hand on his shoulder. "Mr. Wilcox?"

He turned, expecting to see the bellboy, but found himself looking at a massive chest. The face above it could have been carved out of rock, but at least it was smiling.

"That's right."

"I'm Jay Pastore." The man's hand swallowed Monroe's. "We've been expecting you. How was your flight?"

"Fine, no problems."

"Tania had no trouble finding you, I take it?"

"No, she came right to me."

"Good, let me show you to your suite, then."

Motioning for the bellhop to follow them, Pastore led Monroe through a shopping arcade, around the main desk, and to a bank of elevators. A few moments later, still chatting amicably, he led Monroe through a maze of ninth-floor corridors. The bellhop opened the door and brushed past them with Monroe's bag.

"I'm sure you'll find everything you need, Mr. Wilcox," Pastore said. "If not, just let me know, I'll be in my office. And you'll be having dinner in my suite tonight. Mr. McDill will call you shortly."

"Fine."

Monroe followed in the direction the bellhop had taken. As he entered the living room from the small foyer, he was unprepared for the plushness that greeted him. The room was furnished in varying shades of blue, except for the carpet, which was a thick, fluffy white. A large blue radio-television-stereo console occupied an entire corner, an antique-blue baby-grand piano another. Cut flowers, white roses in pale blue vases, were spaced about. One wall was entirely glass. The draperies were open, and spread out below was a breathtaking view of the fabled strip, more lights than Monroe had even seen before.

The bellhop returned with Monroe's other suit draped over his arm. "I'll have this pressed for you, sir."

"Thanks," Monroe said, offering him a bill.

"Nossir, everything's already taken care of."

He left, and Monroe went over to the piano and plinked a few chords, then crossed the room to the stereo and slid the accordion doors back and checked the record bin. Monk, Miles, Horace, Sonny Rollins, Ramsey Lewis, mixed with a few of his own company's albums. He grinned. They sure had him pegged, all right. He checked the bar stock. King's Ransom, Royal Salute, VSC, Ambassador 25, Crown Royal, Chivas . . .

There was a silver serving set atop the bar. An envelope with his name on it was propped against the ice bucket in its center. Inside was an engraved hotel gambling certificate for five thousand dollars. He replaced the envelope and left the liquor untouched. No sense in drinking their liquor and spending their money before he had made his deal.

The bellhop had left the light on in the bedroom. As Monroe stepped through the doorway, he sucked in his breath at the sumptuous furnishings. The room was dominated by a king-size bed covered by a dark blue crushed-velvet spread. A full-length mirror was attached to the ceiling above the bed. Mirrored doors hid a room-length closet, and a sliding glass wall opened onto a large balcony. He crossed to the bathroom, found a switch just inside the door, and flicked it on.

"God damn!"

He was looking at a sunken tub the size of a small swimming pool, made of light blue marble flecked with gold. There were three steps leading down into it.

A picture suddenly jumped into his mind—of a funky little nigger about ten years old, sitting on the broken stoop of a funky little house in a funky little neighborhood on Thirty-ninth and Wentworth, with a funky little haircut that didn't leave nothing but cockleburs, wearing a funky little stormcap with one flap torn off and funky little tennis shoes with the cardboard from a Kellogg's cornflakes box folded in the bottom to cover up the holes from riding a funky little scooter made out of two broken two-by-fours and one of Carleen's old skates.

"What am I doing here?" he asked himself.

It took him a few minutes of fiddling with the gold fixtures before he could get the water the right temperature. He found a bottle of bubblebath in the dressing alcove and poured some into the tub. A few minutes later, when he was reclining against the warm marble with soft blue bubbles up to his small black chin, another picture popped into his mind.

He was seventeen years old, standing on the Thirty-ninth Street el platform, pulling his cheap mackinaw around him tighter to try to ward off the chill of a bleak winter morning. Having lied about his age, he was working at the stockyards, bringing home $116.78 every two weeks—for hitting cows between the eyes with a sledgehammer.

And he used to be grateful for that!

It all seemed so silly—the pattern of his life—he couldn't help but laugh. And the more he thought about it, the sillier it seemed. Pretty soon he was rolling around at the bottom of the tub, delirious at the foolishness of it all. When he came up, he was sputtering and gagging and his hair and face were covered with blue bubbles and his stomach hurt from laughing so hard.

Just as quickly, the memory was gone, and he sat there quietly, finishing his bath, wondering how many other things there were in the world that he had yet to find out about.

The woman looked to be about fifty, a very well kept fifty. Her blond hair was expensively coiffured and the diamonds at her neck and ears were a perfectly matched set. She was wearing a floor-length flowered cocktail dress and her smile was as bright and friendly as Monroe had ever seen.

"Hello, there, Mr. Monroe Wilcox." Her voice held a teasing, informal elegance. "I don't know whether you realize it or not, but you are certainly the man of the hour."

He stepped through the doorway and found himself standing on a carpeted estrade as broad as the living room was long. A small group of people were staring up at him expectantly. Behind them, on another raised area, a maid in full uniform stood beside a candlelit dining table set for eight.

"I'm Jeanne Pastore," she said, taking his hand and leading him down the steps, "and these are my friends. . . ."

A tall brunette in a black cocktail dress came forward to meet him. "Hi! I'm Gertha Rubin." She smiled and extended her hand. "The way they've been talking about you, I fully expected you to arrive by way of the balcony—in long underwear and a cape."

"I never do that the first time," Monroe said.

They laughed appreciatively.

"And this is Gertha's husband, Ted," Jeanne Pastore said.

A tall bespectacled man gripped Monroe's hand. "I've been anxious to meet you, Monroe."

"My pleasure."

"And, of course, you know Chet. . . ."

"It's good to see you again, Monroe." Chester McDill clasped Monroe's hand warmly. "How was your flight?"

"Couldn't have been no better."

"Good." McDill placed an arm around another, younger brunette. "This is my wife, Hillary."

"So there really *is* a Monroe Wilcox!" Hillary McDill gushed. "I was beginning to think you were a creation of *Ebony* magazine."

"Not quite," Monroe said firmly.

"And last, Monroe," Jeanne Pastore continued, "this is a very dear friend of ours visiting from Los Angeles, Samantha Vogle."

Samantha Vogle was a slender redhead, perhaps forty, perhaps sixty, covered with diamonds. Glistening with diamonds. "Call me Sam," she said seductively, taking his hand, offering her cheek.

"Sam . . ." Monroe smiled, letting her hold his hand a fraction longer than the others.

Jeanne Pastore directed Monroe to a seat of honor in the center of the couch. "Jay just called a few minutes ago. He said to keep you entertained until he gets here. Would you care for a drink?"

"A little Scotch would be fine."

The maid standing by the dining-room table nodded and disappeared through a doorway.

"I'll bet you're hungry," Jeanne Pastore said. "I know plane rides always leave me starved!"

"Whenever you all are ready," Monroe said.

"Good. We'll eat just as soon as Jay gets here. Nothing fancy. Steak and salad, how's that?"

Monroe nodded and sighed an inward sigh of relief. He wasn't sure he could handle the fancy stuff with the foreign names.

"Now that we have all that out of the way"—Jeanne Pastore made herself comfortable in the seat beside him—"tell us about yourself and Big City Records. You seem to have accomplished an awful lot for one man."

"Well . . ." Monroe paused to remove his drink from the maid's tray. "There wasn't no secret to it. I just learned a long time ago, when I was a kid, the people who wind up with the money are, most and generally, the people who work the hardest, so I . . ."

A half-hour later, when Jay Pastore came through the door, Monroe was sipping his second Scotch, sitting there on the couch with his legs crossed, holding their attention like he'd spent most of his life in and out of drawing rooms. By the time Pastore had finished dressing for dinner and they were all seated at the table, they were old friends. Sam Vogle was on Monroe's left, flirting mildly. But he was being careful not to notice. Even if he was in the market, which he wasn't, she was a little too skinny for him.

Over the salad, they discussed the political theories of Malcolm X, and although nobody felt that violence was the correct remedy for past injustices, everybody agreed that it was certainly time for a change. Over the steaks, Ted Rubin told a few anecdotes about some of the men who were under his command in Korea. A few were black. . . .

They returned to the living room with their after-dinner drinks, and then, as if on cue, Jeanne Pastore gently directed the conversation to business—or to be more accurate, to the fringes of the reasons for Monroe's being there.

"I personally think the time is long past due," she said to Monroe, "to start bringing your kind of acts into our big room. I mean, let's face it, whether we like it or not, rock music is the music of the hour. And colored acts can draw—"

"That's right," Gertha Rubin interrupted, "Belafonte still holds every attendance record in this town."

Monroe's eyebrow raised. He didn't know that.

"The thing is," Ted Rubin added, "we've watched a few of your people on television and, as you know, we've had one or two of them in the lounges here, and we're really impressed with the way they handle themselves. We're convinced they can carry the big room."

"Hell, we might as well lay it on the table," Pastore said, giving Monroe a less innocuous look than the others. "This is not an open town. Everybody thinks it is because we promote like hell, but we're very careful who we let in here, especially in our big rooms, and especially our colored acts. That's true all over Vegas. The colored acts that work the big rooms in this town—Nat, Lena, Sammy,

Harry—are all first-class, onstage and off. We've had a little trouble with some of our colored lounge acts from time to time, and as soon as we do"—he made a slashing motion with his hand—"they're gone. We just opened this town up a few years ago, and the race thing is still a little touchy, so if we're going to start bringing in colored rock acts, we've got to be damn sure they're the right ones!"

"And we're very impressed with the way you've groomed your people," Ted Rubin interjected. "Beautiful costumes, fine arrangements, great choreography . . ."

"That's right," Gertha Rubin said, "we're very impressed with that."

"The reason for that," Monroe said, "is because we start getting them ready for personal appearances as soon as we sign them up. We select their clothes and choreograph their act. They got to pass my personal inspection."

"That says a lot for you," Hillary McDill said.

"Well, I ain't gonna have none of my artists walking on no stage in bare feet and T-shirts," Monroe said firmly.

"Hurray for you!" Gertha Rubin said.

"So when you want to start booking them in?" Monroe asked.

"We have a target date set for next fall," Rubin said. "Immediately after Labor Day. We have a few contracts due to expire and a few acts we want to get rid of, and we want to give your people plenty of time to correlate dates."

"Marvelous!" Samantha Vogle erupted. "This should have been done a long time ago!"

"I'll tell you what we want to do," Pastore said. "We want to kick things off with the whole Big City Cavalcade of Stars Revue. We'll give them so much promotion everybody in this town will be busting the doors down to see them!"

"In fact," Rubin said, "now that we've spoken with you personally, Monroe, I'm going to get on the phone this week with Tahoe and see if we can book the show up there for a few weeks this summer, just to make sure they're absolutely ready when they come in here. That way we'll . . ."

And so they talked, the eight of them, skirting the edges, keeping the conversation friendly and polite. They observed Monroe to see that he didn't drink too much, that he never pressed Sam Vogle on her implied offer, and that he showed no signs of being difficult to deal with in the future.

And Monroe observed them too—admiring, in spite of himself, their poise and tact.

And trying not to be taken in.

At eleven o'clock he got to his feet. "I can't tell you all what a pleasure it's been to meet you," he said, smiling at each of them individually.

"It's been our pleasure, Monroe," Samantha Vogle said.

"It certainly has been," Hillary McDill echoed.

"The next time you come to Las Vegas, Monroe, you simply must introduce us to your wife," Jeanne Pastore said.

"Absolutely," Ted Rubin said.

"Is she as cute as her picture?" Hillary McDill asked.

"Cuter," Monroe said.

Pastore stood, towering over Monroe. "You're welcome in my house anytime, Monroe . . ."

"Thanks. It's been a pleasure to meet you all."

". . . and remember, everything's on the house."

"I'll walk you out, Monroe," Chet McDill said.

At the door, Monroe turned to say good-bye again. The women smiled and waved, as did Rubin. Pastore made a circle with his thumb and forefinger.

McDill followed Monroe into the hall. "We'll be meeting with the stockholders tomorrow."

"What time?"

"Ten o'clock. I'll pick you up out front."

"I'll be there."

"And bring everything with you."

"No problem."

As McDill stepped back inside, Monroe heard Jeanne Pastore say, "He's quite a young man, isn't he?"

"He certainly is!" Gertha Rubin agreed enthusiastically.

Monroe shook his head cynically, knowing it had been said for his benefit. But he had to hand it to them, they were smooth.

He called Maudie as soon as he got back to his suite. She had been waiting up to hear from him. She had no idea of the true purpose for his trip, since all he had told her was that he was trying to make a deal to start booking some of his better artists into the big Las Vegas showrooms, and after that he had to stop in Los Angeles for a day or so for some additional company business before returning home.

She told him that little Carleen had made him something special for Christmas, a drawing of the three Wise Men—all black—to hang in his office. And the baby was toddling all over the house "looking for Daddy." And Mrs. Turner's rheumatism was still acting up from the cold weather, but not so bad that she couldn't keep her promise to bake some of Monroe's favorite sweet-potato pies before he got back.

They talked for an hour.

When Monroe hung up, he went back into the living room and put some records on the stereo and lowered the lights. He made himself a light Chivas and water and sat at the bar, thinking, trying to get himself ready for the meeting tomorrow. He wasn't kidding himself: he knew what he was getting into. All he had seen tonight was the civilized, manicured field upon which the game would be played. But that hadn't fooled him. He still knew it was a game in which loyalty would be considered a sign of weakness and honesty a sign of stupidity, a game in which nobody would be safe, not himself, nor his wife, nor his children.

But he knew, too, that he only had two choices—join them now and maybe continue to make a good living from his profession, or try to remain independent and have the life slowly squeezed out of his business over the next few years. Now he had to face it: Monroe Wilcox was no longer unique. Just as he'd predicted, the white boys had learned to copy the music. They had studied it to the point that now, even if they had to stay in the studio a month at a time, they could eventually come out with a product competitive to his own. They had effectively stacked the deck against him, by locking up prime-time radio, so he had to work doubly hard to break a new record. They had also kept the lid on TV, allowing his artists only a few isolated guest spots, certainly not enough exposure for them to acquire legitimacy in the minds of the buying public. There were only two things that kept Big City Records afloat: the songwriter-producers who turned out most of the hits, and the artists the company had continued to record over the years, who had built loyal followings among both black and white buyers. But the big companies had already started making overtures to his artists and producers, offering them sums he could not compete with. Eventually, he understood, the majors would break up his label and he would be right back where he started, promoting acts doomed to segregated, low-wattage airplay on all-black stations. . . .

He was deep in thought when he became aware of someone knocking at the door. Scowling, he got up from the bar stool and crossed the room to see who it was.

She had changed into a black miniskirt and white boots that came up above her knees. "I thought you might need some company," she said.

"I told you to forget it."

"Well"—she winked—"at least you can buy me a drink, can't you?"

He stood blocking the door for a few seconds, trying to make up his mind, then shrugged. "Come on in."

She sauntered by him to the couch, sat down, and crossed her legs. Her skirt slid up to the top of her thighs.

"Well?"

"Well, what?"

"Where's my drink?"

"I ain't the motherfuckin' butler, baby, I live here. You want a drink, get up and get it."

She got up and flounced behind the bar, and he heard the rattle of ice. She came back around and sat down next to him, eyeing him speculatively over the top of her glass. "Boy, you really think you're a hot little nigger, don't you?"

"I used to, about ten years ago when I was running around the streets trying to get my shit together."

"But it's together now. I suppose?"

He casually waved a hand around the room. "I ain't running up and down the streets no more, am I?"

A hint of respect crept into her eyes, and left immediately. She took a slug of her drink. "What's the matter, don't you like me?"

"You okay . . . I guess."

She gave him a sexy look. "Don't I turn you on, baby?"

"To tell you the truth, I never could get behind bubble-headed broads."

"You should never try to insult someone," she said coolly, "until you know what you're talking about."

"I don't? Okay, say something heavy, then."

"Like what?"

"Like, 'Good evening, Mr. Wilcox, how are you?'"

"Fuck you, nigger!" She slammed her glass down and got up to leave. Monroe sipped his drink and remained where he was. He waited for the door to slam. It didn't. A moment later she was back beside him. "I didn't want to come here in the first place."

"Didn't nobody invite you."

"I'm here because Mr. Pastore asked me to show you around, as a personal favor to him."

"That's cool, I can dig that. So why don't you get your heels clicking? . . . And you can call Mr. Pastore tomorrow and tell him that you met me but we couldn't find nothing to talk about."

She sat down again and reached for her glass. "The problem," she explained, "is that I don't usually date colored men."

"That's half the problem," he conceded. "The other half is, I ain't one of your goddamned tricks."

A flash of anger stripped her cool away. "You talk to me like that again, I swear to God I'll throw this drink in your face!"

"You throw that drink on me"—the smile left Monroe's face—"and the last thing you hear will be the sound of your ass hitting the floor."

Again respect darted into her eyes, lingered a bit longer this time. "You really think you're better than me, don't you—just because you've got a little money."

"Naw, baby, that ain't my bag, I ain't better than nobody. But on the other hand"—his smile returned—"ain't nobody better than me, neither."

She lit a cigarette and stared at him, trying to figure him out. "May I have another drink?" she asked finally.

"Help yourself."

"Will you fix it for me . . . please?"

"Sure, what you drinkin'?"

She told him. He went around the bar and fixed them both fresh drinks, came back and took his seat again. "I forgot your name," he said.

"Why don't you stop trying to be so goddamn cool, Monroe!"

"I know it's hard for you to believe, baby—fine as you think you are, and all that shit—but I really forgot your name."

"Tania," she mumbled.

"That's a pretty name, I never heard that before."

"Well, it's my real name, if that's what you're wondering."

"Good, that makes it that much prettier."

"You don't have to hit on me, nigger, I'm already paid for."

"I wasn't hitting on you, baby, I was just trying to be nice."

"That's why I don't date colored men, all they know how to do is shuck and jive!"

He swung around to face her full-on. "Hey, do me a favor, huh?"

"Anything you say," she said sarcastically.

"One day when you ain't doing nothing, dig up *Ebony* from a couple of months back. I want you to check my old lady out, see how fine she is."

"So what?"

"Maybe then you'll understand why I don't play around on her."

"You've never cheated on your wife?"

"No."

"I don't believe you."

"That don't surprise me none."

"You mean," she insisted, "you're gonna sit there and tell me you don't mess around on your wife? You're a liar!"

"Suit yourself," he said mildly.

"Damn, you piss me off."

"In that case, why don't you finish your drink and let the door-knob hit you? I'm tired and I got a busy day tomorrow."

In the short time she had been there, her expressions had changed from contemptuous to sexy, from anger to a kind of sullen pout, none of them quite real. But now, realizing that going to bed with her was really the last thing on Monroe Wilcox's mind, she showed genuine surprise. She wasn't accustomed to being turned down, especially for free, and she found it hard to deal with. In fact, at the moment, she found it impossible to deal with.

Abruptly she got up and carried her drink over to the window. "Why?"

"Why, what?"

"Why don't you want to go to bed with me?"

"I already told you, I don't fuck around on my old lady."

"Oh, I don't believe—"

"Listen, my old lady is a righteous fox! I don't mean no butt-shaking, street-walking, half-cute, motherfucking yard-dog, I mean a lady—and dead in my corner! If it wasn't for her, I probably wouldn't even be here, I would of killed somebody a long time ago. Now, the Lord is my Shepherd and I got what I want, so why would I throw it away on some jive-ass bullshit I outgrew ten years ago?"

She stood there at the window for a while, then came back and took her seat beside him again. "Mr. Pastore said I'm supposed to be nice to you."

"Well, you tried."

"He said I'm supposed to show you around."

"That ain't no problem. Just tell him you did, then get your money and forget it."

"You really don't like me, do you?"

"You okay."

"I mean, I wouldn't mind showing you around."

"Listen ain't but one place I want to go tonight, and you wouldn't want to take me there."

"Where's that?"

"Someplace called The Elks Club. You ever heard of it?"

The Elks Club! on the westside? She made a face. "There's nothing over there but niggers. What do you want to go there for?"

"One of my artists is playing there."

"Who?"

"Rydell Mercer."

"I've never heard of him."

Monroe looked at her, a trace of a smile on his lips. "You a goddamn lie," he said mildly.

"I don't listen to that kind of shit," she said.

"How you know it's shit, then?"

"That's all they have over there."

"Lemme tell you something, baby—two years ago he was riding around on the back of a garbage truck in Evansville, Indiana, making sixty dollars a week. Now he owns a hundred-thousand-dollar house in Chicago, four cars, and makes five or six thousand dollars a week."

"I don't care."

"So who's bullshitting who?"

She thought it over a minute. "Okay, I'll take you."

"You sure it won't mess up your image or nothing?" he laughed.

"I haven't been to the westside since the day I got here," she said haughtily, "they don't even know me over there."

"Better for me," Monroe said.

A few hours later she turned into the hotel driveway again, except this time, instead of following the sweeping curve around to the front entrance, she turned off into the parking lot. Monroe quickly covered her hand on the steering wheel with his own. "Naw, baby, you can let me out here."

"It's all part of the package."

"I know," he said, getting out and closing the door, "but I ain't."

"Monroe?"

"Yeah?"

"Will I see you before you go?"

"Naw, I doubt it. I'm gonna be tied up in a meeting all day tomorrow and I'll probably fly out of here sometime tomorrow night."

"Want me to call you, just in case? If you don't go, maybe we can have dinner or catch a show or something."

"Naw, baby, ain't nothin' happening with you and me." He smiled. "But thanks for running me over there, I dug it. You pretty good company when you get your ass off your shoulders."

She watched him walk around the front of the car and start up the driveway toward the hotel entrance, a concise little man bobbing up and down with the affected half-limp of the street black. It was a walk she detested. She had run as far as she could to get away from it.

But strong-minded men had always fascinated her, especially strong-minded black men, because there seemed to be so few of them, and she sat there drawing on her cigarette, watching him until the car behind her started blinking its lights for her to move.

A few hours later, he was standing in almost exactly the same spot when a black limousine pulled up to the curb. Chester McDill motioned him to get in. "You brought the papers with you?"

Monroe motioned toward his attaché case. "In there. You want to look at them now?"

"No, I'll wait until we get on the plane."

"What plane?"

"We're flying to Arizona."

"You should of told me. I didn't bring no clothes."

"We'll only be there a few hours."

"Oh." Monroe was about to say something else when he detected that McDill wasn't interested in holding a conversation this morning, so he turned to look out the window. They passed a construction site where men were working on the first floor of what would soon become another huge hotel complex. Beyond that lay a desolate beige-gray carpet that stretched all the way to the foot of the mountains. Monroe had never seen the desert before—nothing but a few cacti, and tumbleweeds that looked like balls of baling wire, rolling toward them, occasionally crossing the highway in front of the car.

They entered a private airport a few hundred yards north of McCarran Field. The limo crossed several runways and delivered them beside a sleek two-engine private jet, silver with blue letters on the tail. The chauffeur got out and opened the door for McDill. Monroe grabbed his case and hurried out the other side. By the time he reached the plane, McDill had already mounted the small ladder. A few minutes later they were airborne, making a wide sweep south over the mountains.

"I'll take a look at those papers now, Monroe."

Monroe handed him the case. "Who all's gonna be there?"

McDill opened the case and removed a handful of papers. "Everybody," he said.

Within the hour they had set down at a small private landing field on the outskirts of Scottsdale, where another limousine was waiting. Monroe recognized the chauffeur who held the door for McDill as a former featherweight contender who had been fighting pro when Monroe was fighting amateur. The man's face was heavily scarred, and one ear looked like a dinner bell. He sized Monroe up quickly, and accurately, as a man who had crawled through the ropes a few times. His nod was almost imperceptible, but the glimmer of respect in his eyes was unmistakable.

"Good to see you, Ernie," McDill acknowledged.

"You, too, Mr. McDill." The lumpy Italian face broke into a grin. "They didn't tell me it was you."

Monroe went around the car and got in the other side. The front passenger seat was occupied by a man who looked to be approaching thirty, also Italian, with curly black hair and challenging eyes. "What's happening?" he said to Monroe, offering his hand over the seat. "I'm Guy Pastore."

Monroe took his hand. "Nice to meet you," he said politely.

"Man, I've been wanting to meet you for years! You're supposed to be a heavy motherfucker . . ."

"Umm-hmmm."

". . . but nobody told me you were two feet tall and ugly as warmed-over shit!"

Monroe was glad he was wearing sunglasses so Pastore couldn't see his expression. He didn't go for that. He had been around white men like Pastore in the service, guys who would deliberately insult you and figure just because they were laughing you'd think they were playing.

"I wonder why they didn't tell you that?" he said quietly.

The car pulled out onto the highway, and Pastore turned around and put an elbow up on the seat. He regarded Monroe for a moment. "What's the matter, nigger, you don't like what I said?"

"Hey, man, lighten up."

"Shit, you 'bout ready to kick my ass, ain't you?" Pastore baited.

Monroe didn't say anything.

"Ain't you, *boy*?"

Monroe snatched off his glasses and flung them on the seat. His eyes were blazing. "All right motherfucker, what's your goddamned problem!"

Pastore threw his head back and guffawed. McDill started laughing along with him, and there was a raspy chuckle from the other side of the front seat.

"That's better," Pastore said. "I saw you getting off that plane carrying your little case and wearing your little hat and I thought you were one of those Uncle Tom insurance-selling niggers. I said to myself, 'No, this ain't the Monroe Wilcox I been waiting to meet.'"

"You come on too strong," Monroe said.

"Why—you think I ain't down, baby? Shit, I spent all my life around niggers."

"Umm-hmmm," Monroe said, "I can see that."

"You ever heard of Leroy Thatcher?"

"The football player?"

"Football player my ass! You mean All-Pro tight end for the Bears four years in a row!"

"Yeah, I know him."

"He was my roomie in college, man—that big ugly gorilla-looking motherfucker. If I hadn't been buying his pussy for him and keeping his nose happy and throwing him all those soft, easy-to-handle passes, he'd be somewhere hauling trash right now."

"I can dig it," Monroe said.

"Well, at least you can thank me, nigger."

"For what?"

"Didn't you get my presents?"

"What presents?"

Pastore looked at Monroe with feigned exasperation. "Boy, you is some kind of dumb!"

"What you talking about?" Monroe asked, trying as hard as he could to control his temper.

"I'm the one who set you up, nigger. I picked out your pad, stocked it with all kinds of his sides, made sure you had all the Scotch you wanted, and sent the best piece of ass in Vegas to meet you . . ."

Oh, Monroe thought, so *this* was the Mr. Pastore Tania had been talking about.

". . . and I bet you didn't have sense enough to take advantage of it, did you?" Pastore concluded.

"You took a lot for granted, man," Monroe said mildly.

"That's it!" Pastore threw up his hand in mock disgust and turned back around to look out the front window. "From now on, fuck race relations!"

Their destination was a two-story stucco mansion set back on a two-acre corner lot. The iron gates folded back automatically and the big car eased up the driveway, through an open carport, and halted in a concrete parking area. The got out and entered the house through a side door.

The three men who were watching the football game on television gave them a casual look. They were, Monroe noted, extremely hard-looking. One had his coat off. His gun looked like a .357 Magnum. Ernie, the chauffeur, went to join them, and Pastore led Monroe and McDill along a hallway, through a small shower room with swimsuits and towels neatly stacked on open cabinets, outside to the pool area.

Three metal poolside tables with umbrellas tilted against the sun had been placed in a semicircle. Six middle-aged men in various states of unanticipation were seated at them. One was talking on the phone. Two were playing cards. The man closest to the door was sitting alone, studying the financial pages of a Phoenix newspaper. Among the three men at the far table was Ted Rubin, one of the people Monroe had spent dinner with the night before. He glanced up and nodded a half-greeting to Monroe and went back to his papers.

Monroe immediately picked out the boss. He was seated across from Rubin, facing out from the table toward Monroe, leaning over with his arms resting on his knees, looking down at the ground. He didn't look up. The two men who were playing cards at the center table didn't bother to look at Monroe, either.

McDill motioned Monroe to a chair at the table with the man reading the newspaper. McDill took Monroe's attaché case and almost reverently approached the man bending over. He said a few words to the man and handed him the case. The man raised up and looked across the fifteen feet between himself and Monroe with unconcerned eyes, studying Monroe, but offering no greeting, then turned around and started going through the papers.

Pastore sat down next to Monroe, beside the man reading the paper. "Good morning, Mr. Venaro," he said respectfully.

" 'Morning, kid," the man answered in a voice that seemed to come from the bottom of a barrel, not turning from his paper. "How's your father?"

"He's fine."

"Tell him to call me, huh? I got some business for him."

"Yes, sir. As soon as I get back."

Monroe sat there quietly, observing. He didn't know who Venaro was, but he did recognize a few of the others. One of the men playing cards at the center table was a high union official, currently under indictment for federal-jury tampering. His playing partner was the president of a game-machine company which manufactured, reputedly, most of the slot machines in Nevada. He tried to place the man still talking on the phone, but couldn't. The man next to him, Rubin, he knew was an accountant for, among others, Goldenrod, Limited, Antonio Mauriello's company.

The boss, of course, was Manny Lebovitz. Ted Green had told Monroe all about him. He was the Big Jew, the man who had first taken gambling to Vegas, to the Caribbean, and who owned or operated several casinos in England. He was the liaison between European and American money, the connection between clean and dirty money. He was the one man who knew where every dime of skim money was supposed to go. He knew the number of every numbered bank account the organization held anywhere in the world, and how much was supposed to be in each one at any given time.

At the moment, he was flipping through Monroe's financial statements like he was reading photograph captions. It took him ten minutes to finish. When Lebovitz looked up, Ted Rubin put away his papers, the man next to him hung up the phone, and the two men at the center table neatly stacked their cards. Only Venaro paid him no attention and continued to study his newspaper. Lebovitz began the meeting without preliminaries. "Okay, I talked to Tony Mo in New York this morning. He wants thirty points."

"Down the line?" somebody asked.

"Down the line."

Ted Rubin nodded, satisfied.

"Gimme ten," the union man said.

"Down the line?"

"Down the line."

"Wump?"

"Fifteen," the president of the game-machine company said.

"Down the line?"

"Down the line."

Lebovitz turned around to face the man who had been on the phone. "Ikey?"

"I'll take ten."

"Down the line?"

"Down the line."

"Okay, we'll take fifteen," Lebovitz said. He looked over at the man reading the newspaper. "Mr. Venaro"—his tone was respectful—"would you like to pick up the rest?"

"What's left?"

"Eighteen points."

Venaro quickly looked up from his newspaper. "Huh?"

"Two points to the dealer," Lebovitz explained, nodding at McDill.

"Yeah, okay . . . I'm in."

Monroe sensed that nobody was going to ask Venaro if he was in for the whole ride, and nobody did.

"Okay, that's it," Lebovitz said. "One hundred of ninety-seven." He looked at Monroe. "Any questions?"

"Yeah," Monroe said.

Everybody turned to look at Monroe. Not angrily, not even questioningly. They just looked at him.

"What about my people?" Monroe asked.

Lebovitz' expression didn't change. "They stay—as long as *you* stay."

Monroe nodded. Lebovitz reached under the table and pulled out a black attaché case. He turned it end-up and gave it a casual push. It slid across the concrete noisily and came to rest an inch from Monroe's foot. The key was still in it. Monroe didn't know what protocol was, whether he was supposed to check its contents or not. But they had just auctioned him off, so he decided he was damn sure going to count it. He turned the key and flicked open the latches.

The bills were neatly stacked. Fifty packages of one-hundred-dollar bills, one hundred bills to a package. A half-million, but only one-quarter of the amount promised him.

"Satisfied?" Lebovitz asked coolly, measuring Monroe.

Monroe knew it was some kind of test. He closed the case and set it beside him. Then he removed his shades and looked around at the men, leveling his gaze on them equally and individually. He nodded his head a half-inch.

"So far," he said.

Lebovitz almost smiled. He liked what he saw.

"C'mon, let me show you the house," Guy Pastore said.

Monroe knew they wanted to discuss him. He reached for the money.

"I'll watch it for you, kid," Venaro said, still reading his paper.

They reentered the house through the same door, followed another hallway, went down three steps into a game room. There was a pool table in the center of the room, a cue rack behind it. Pastore stopped and extended his hand. Monroe gave it an unenthusiastic slap.

"They like you," Pastore said, "but I don't know why—you still ain't nothing but an ugly little two-foot-high monkey."

"You wanna shoot some pool, man?" Monroe asked.

"Shit yeah! You know you ain't gonna do nothing but get in trouble with all that money, boy!"

Monroe went to the rack and selected a stick. He rolled it around on the table a few times to make sure it was straight. Pastore did the same thing.

"Lemme see that," Monroe said. He looked at the end of Pastore's cue stock and broke out in a laugh. "I ain't never seen nothing but broads and cocksuckers shoot pool with a sixteen-ounce stick, man."

Pastore's face colored slightly, and Monroe knew he had pegged him right. He was one of those white boys who liked to talk a lot of insulting shit, but couldn't take it back.

"You get any bread on you, punk?" he asked.

"Shit yeah, you big-lipped baboon." Pastore pulled a roll from his pocket. "I got some money."

"I didn't know your daddy'd let you walk around with that kind of money, punk. Shit, first thing you know, some big-lipped baboon'll be taking it away from you. What you wanna play?"

"Up to you."

"Okay, I ain't got too much time, so I'm gonna have to take that little bread off you right quick. How about nine-ball? Hundred a game. Three games in a row, automatic push."

"Yeah, okay . . ." Pastore hedged.

"What happened to 'shit yeah'?" Monroe asked. "I mean, if that ain't enough, we can raise it right now."

"I said okay."

"That's better. I'm company so I break. Rack the balls, punk."

Pastore made the rack. Monroe broke. The two and seven went in. The one ball slid down the table. Monroe made a one-rail combination, two off the nine, and held out his hand. "Rack the balls, punk."

He was jammed up on the second break, so he ticked the one ball and slid the four ball across the table into the side pocket. The cue ball rolled down the table and shut him off, so he made a massé shot around the eight, came up and ticked the one ball into the corner pocket. Then he ran the table.

"Rack the balls, punk," he said, holding out his hand again, "and tell me some more about that pet nigger you used to keep."

This time the break was clean. Monroe systematically ran the table. When he got to the nine ball, he had a straight shot to the side pocket. He stopped and raised his eyes to the ceiling. "Oh, Lawdy! Doan lemme beat dis po' w'ite noah ag'in!" Then he called a cross-table bank and tapped the nine ball. It touched the rail and slowly recrossed the table. He was looking at Pastore's sullen features when it plunked into the pocket.

Monroe held out his hand. "That's three, baby." He pocketed the money. "Tell you what I'm gonna do for you—I'm gonna let you have the break for a hundred dollars."

"That's okay, you'll cool off."

"Don't forget, now, we pushing. . . ."

"Yeah, that's right." Pastore pretended to have forgotten. "Okay . . . here." He gave Monroe another hundred. Pastore leaned over the ball, concentrating as hard as he could, broke clean and ran eight straight, but scratched on the nine ball.

"This is a hard motherfucking shot here," Monroe said, spotting the ball.

"You ain't gonna make it, boy." Pastore tried to laugh.

"Tch! Tch! Tch!" Monroe clicked his tongue loudly. "This is a hundred-dollar shot, at least."

"No, it isn't."

"You ain't backing down to no big-lipped baboon, are you?" Monroe asked coyly.

"I'm not backing down. It's an easy shot, that's all."

"Yeah, you right, I was just jivin' you." Monroe laughed, reaching in his pocket. He pulled out a roll about the same size as the one Pastore had flashed, counted off ten one-hundred-dollar bills, and stacked them neatly on the table. "Yeah, you right," he said again. "It's an easy shot. You wanna cover that and go on and make it?"

"You're covered," Pastore said, trying to find a comfortable spot for the cue ball.

"No, no, no, no!" Monroe laughed, picking up the nine ball. "That ain't the way we do this shit. Put your money up, baby."

Pastore counted out ten one-hundred-dollar bills and slammed them on the table. Monroe picked them up and stacked them neatly on top of his own. Pastore made a bridge with his fingers and squatted down behind the ball. Then he straightened up and moved the ball a few inches and squatted down again.

"Listen, punk," Monroe said, "if you too chickenshit to shoot the motherfucker, I'll shoot it. Shit, I'd shoot *you* for a thousand dollars."

Pastore's jaw tightened. He stroked the cue ball. It was a good shot, except for being too hard. The nine ball flew into the pocket, bounced out, and came to rest an inch or so from the other corner pocket. Monroe had a duck. He casually leaned over the table and tapped it in, then picked up the stack of bills and stuck them in his pocket. Pastore's face was livid. He looked like he wanted to throw his stick at Monroe.

There was nothing in the world Monroe hated as much as a half-hip white man, but he knew he could not afford to have Pastore as an enemy. He was too close to the people Monroe had to answer to, so Monroe walked around the table and offered his hand.

"I know you pissed, man," he said, "but that's how we learn, ain't it—by picking on the wrong motherfucker? Now, like Ray Charles says, 'Understanding is a beautiful thing,' so let's you and me get an understanding: I'm gonna be seeing a lot of you from now on, I know that. So dig, I'll be your friend if you want me to, and I'll be your brother if you *let* me, but I ain't got no interest at all in hearing about how much you like niggers. If you all that cool, I'll find out for myself sooner or later, can you dig that?"

He could almost see the wheels turning in Pastore's head. Finally Pastore nodded.

"Good," Monroe said. "Now . . . what other games you got around here?"

They were still shooting pool, but for a dollar a game, when the chauffeur came for Monroe. "Catch you later," Monroe said, hanging up his cue stick.

"Yeah, I'll be in Chicago the first of the year," Pastore said. "Maybe you'd better start making room for me when you get back."

"That's what I thought," Monroe said.

McDill was waiting in the limo. The black attaché case was on the floor beside him. Monroe picked it up and moved it closer to make sure it was still full. The chauffeur turned the car back onto the street, toward the airport.

"They like you, Wilcox," McDill said.

"Yeah," Monroe said dryly, "I like them, too."

McDill flashed him a look of irritation. Neither of them spoke again until they were airborne, bouncing around in the midafternoon turbulence two thousand feet above the green-purple ridge of Squaw Peak.

"So when do I get the rest of the money?"

McDill handed him a folded sheet of paper. The address of a foreign bank was written on it, along with a number.

"Memorize that and give it back to me before we get off the plane."

"How much is in it?"

"There'll be a million and a half American dollars in it within ninety days."

"And after that I get three percent off the top, right?"

"That's right."

"That ain't much for doing all the work."

"Give yourself five years . . ."

"And then what?"

". . . and you'll be one of the richest Negroes in the country."

"What makes you think that?"

"Figure, oh, fifty million a year."

Monroe figured. Three percent of fifty million was a million and a half a year.

"And no worries."

"I'm already worried," Monroe said.

"Nothing will happen—as long as you're valuable to us."

"Suppose I stop being valuable?"

"If I were you, "McDill said, "I would try to remain valuable."

"How about papers? Do we sign any contracts?"

McDill pointed to the paper in Monroe's hand. "You're looking at it."

Monroe studied the number. As they made their final approach, he handed the paper back to McDill.

"You're sure?"

"For a million and a half dollars, man, I could memorize the Chicago phone book."

McDill struck a lighter to the paper. He waved it around a few times and dropped it in the ashtray. He pointed at the attaché case on the floor between them. "What are you going to do with this?"

Monroe had thought about that while he was shooting pool. "I don't know, I'll think of something. I don't want to be walking around with it, though."

"Put it in the hotel safe when we get back."

"I mean after that."

"Nobody knows you have it. And if they did, they wouldn't bother you. You belong to us now."

"No, I don't," Monroe said, watching the runway come up to meet the plane. "I don't *belong* to nobody. I just work for you, that's all."

A different chauffeur drove them back to the hotel. McDill stayed with Monroe until the money was secure in the hotel safe, then they shook hands and McDill said he would see Monroe in Chicago the first week of February. In the meantime, Ted Rubin would be in to go over the books with Monroe and start preliminary plans toward reorganizing the company.

Monroe went directly up to his suite. The phone was ringing as he stepped through the door. He crossed the room and hiked himself up on a bar stool and lifted the receiver,

"I saw you come in a little while ago," she said. "Have you called the airport yet?"

"Naw, I just got here."

"Want some company?"

He shook his head at the phone. "The last thing in the world I want right now, baby, is company."

"How about later?"

He was about to say no, when his eye caught the envelope still propped against the silver serving set. He picked it up.

"You still there?"

He opened it and took out the certificate with his name on it and tapped it against the bar a few times, trying to make up his mind.

"You still there, Monroe?"

"Yeah, I gotta get cleaned up. I'll meet you in the casino in an hour."

He was back on the Westside, in some fuzzy little joint, listening to some country niggers try to play three-chord jazz. He had never been drunk in his life before, but he was now, as drunk as those wineheads he used to see staggering down State Street when he was a kid. Somewhere, he knew, it was getting close to dawn. But inside his head, it was stone-cold midnight.

"You okay, Monroe?"

"Yeah, baby, I'm fine."

Well, at least he wasn't one of those evil drunks who wanted to go around jumping up and down in people's faces.

"You sure?"

"Yeah, I'm sure. Where's my drink?"

. . . A black case with a half-million dollars in it. And he'd opened it and felt nothing . . . not a goddamned thing! And he could never tell Maudie about it, not after all those principles he'd been talking all these years, about being your own man and not letting the white man get his thumb up your ass. All that bullshit! She'd lose all respect for him, selling out to some paddies who thought niggers were lower than snakeshit.

"I can't tell Maudie about this," he said aloud.

"There's nothing to tell."

. . . But he had to tell her. Suppose she walked in the office one day and saw a bunch of paddies sitting around with their feet up on the desk? Shit, she wouldn't know what to think, so he had to tell her. He'd have to sit down with her and show her the half-million dollars and tell her there was another million and a half in some bank in some little jive-assed part of the world that nobody ever went to, and he'd make her see that there wasn't nothing else he could of done. And he'd have to tell her about Ted Green, too . . . and about those two goons who beat him up and tried to steal his business . . . and how most of the big radio stations still wouldn't play his records and a lot of his distributors wouldn't pay him his money. . . .

"There wasn't nothing else I could of done."

"C'mon, baby, let's go," she said.

He felt her tugging him to his feet. The bar was almost empty, and nobody paid them any attention as they made their way to the door. He bumped into a slot machine and almost fell. She caught him.

"C'mon, baby, I'm going to take you home with me."

"No, you better take me back to the hotel."

"We'll see."

The parking lot was nearly deserted. Her red car was sitting in a corner by itself. He stumbled into the fender and almost fell again. She tightened her arm around his waist to hold him up.

"That's pretty."

"What?"

"Look up there. . . ."

He pointed to the mountains. The sun was just peeking over the ridge, and the sky was glowing with a soft pink haze. He stopped and turned in a circle, and he could see the mountains all around him.

"Damn, that's pretty!"

"Get in the car, baby."

"Oh, shit, I almost forgot. . . ."

"What?"

He was supposed to be in L.A. this morning to meet with some nigger named Crockett about buying a master. He'd talked to the cat on the phone. Old guy, sounded like. Sounded like he'd paid a lot of dues. But that was cool, everybody had. . . .

There was little traffic, it took her only a few minutes to get across town. He had the window down, watching dudes picking up garbage, watering lawns, unloading trucks. *If he wasn't where he was, that's probably where he'd be right now, somewhere breaking his skinny back!* She parked in the driveway of a new two-story apartment building and turned off the motor.

"This is it."

"Umm-hmmm . . ." He sat there looking out the window, letting the wind sober him up a little.

She came around the car and reached to help him out.

He pushed her hand away. "God damn, I ain't no motherfuckin' invalid, baby!"

"Shhhh . . ." she said, helping him out of the car.

He wobbled toward the building. "You know what's gonna happen when your nice white neighbors see you walking in with me, don't you?"

"Nothing."

"Pull the covers off your ass, that's what. Blow your whole bullshit scene sky hiiigh!"

"Shhhh!"

He made it through a courtyard without bumping into the flowerpots, through a sliding glass door, into a ground-floor apartment.

"This ain't too bad. . . ."

She pushed the door shut. "Thanks."

He started for the couch, but she grabbed his arm. "C'mon, I'll put you to bed."

He stiffened. "Naw, baby, I better cool with that."

"C'mon, you're in no shape to do anything anyhow."

She led him into the bedroom and pulled the green spread back from the bed, then left the room while he got undressed and slipped under the covers. She came back carrying a glass of water.

"Here, take these before you go to sleep."

"What's that?"

"Just . . . something."

He swallowed the two capsules and washed them down with the water. She stood there, a slight smile tugging at her lips, looking down at him, then got undressed herself and crawled in beside him. They lay quietly, not touching, while she smoked a cigarette.

"I probably should of gone on back to the hotel. . . ." he mumbled under his breath.

"Shhhh . . . go to sleep."

"How come you being so nice all of a sudden?" he wanted to know.

"I don't know—maybe because you think you're so hip and you're such a dumb little nigger."

"I'm starting to think there ain't no such thing as hip."

"Oh, yeah, there's hip." She laughed. "And then there's *hip*."

The way she said it pissed him off. "If there is, you don't know nothing about it, that's for goddamned sure!"

"Okay, you want me to tell you something hip?"

"I told you, you don't know nothing hip."

"You know that mirror over your big pretty king-size bed back at the hotel?"

"What about it?"

"There's a camera up there."

He tried to sit up, but it was too much for him, and he plopped back on the pillow. "How you know that?"

"I know. Take my word for it, I know."

He rolled over on his side with his back to her and folded his arm under his head. He was motionless for so long, she thought he had fallen asleep. She tapped her cigarette out in the ashtray on the nightstand and drank the last of the water she had brought in for him.

"Is that why you were trying so hard to get me to take you to bed last night?"

"Umm-hmmm . . . that's what they paid me for."

"Then what? I start getting out of line and they threaten to show it to Maudie?"

"Umm-hmmm . . . that's how it works."

"Who put you up to that, Pastore?"

"Umm-hmmm . . ."

"Which one?"

"Guy."

"Some cold motherfuckers in this world, ain't it?" he said bitterly.

"Umm-hmmm . . . now you're getting hip."

He was quiet for a little while. "So how come you didn't do it tonight? I mean, take me up there instead of bringing me over here?"

She touched his back. "Roll over a minute. . . ."

He turned to her. She put her head on his shoulder. Her feet were cold and she ran them up and down his leg a few times to warm them.

"How come?" he persisted.

She kissed his chest and made herself comfortable in the crease of his arm. "Don't make me sorry I didn't," she said.

CONNECTICUT DECEMBER 1963

There had been a time when the windowsill came all the way up to his chin and he had to strain on tiptoes to see outside.

That was the year his father was suspended from the studio in a salary dispute and decided to return to New York and appear in a play on Broadway. And to keep from having to make the long drive up to Connecticut from the theater every night, his folks had taken an apartment in the city, while he and his sister had stayed with the Gearys—Uncle Max, Aunt Glemmie, and their son, Maxie, who must have been about ten or eleven then.

It all seemed so long ago, he could barely remember it now. But one thing he could remember vividly was that the word "estate" had been a little too mellifluous for his four-year-old tongue in those days, and so he had dubbed the Gearys' imposing English Tudor mansion, with its surrounding acres of meticulously tendered grounds, Uncle Max's "park." It really had seemed like a park, too. It was so big and the grass was so smooth and everything was so clean and well-kept. And trees. He had never seen such trees before. Huge, friendly, rough-barked trees that seemed to reach into the sky!

He and Helen must have arrived in late summer or early fall, because he could still remember Maxie teaching him to roller-skate down the long driveway, and later, when the weather grew cooler, he could remember playing touch football on the lawn with the bigger boys. And he could remember getting a sled that Christmas, a "Li'l Flier," and Maxie teaching him to bellyflop on the hill outside the front gate. How he loved that sled. So much so that, when the Donovans returned home to California, he had insisted on taking it with him. It still stood in a corner of the closet in his old room at the ranch, completely out-of-place, but a pleasant reminder of an exciting time in his young life.

And there was a later time, another Christmas Eve, like today, when he was older and the windowsill had only come up to his chest.

He and his mother and sister had come East by train to be with his father, who had been given a seven-day Christmas furlough. The four of them were having breakfast at their hotel in New York when his folks decided that Uncle Max and Aunt Emmie might need some true and sympathetic friends to help them through the holidays. It was the first Christmas after Maxie had been reported missing in action.

The Donovans arrived to find the house shrouded in tragedy. Mark and Helen muddied about all afternoon, until Mrs. Grebbins, the housekeeper, collared them off to the village to get them from underfoot. They wandered about the winding brick streets and lingered in the pet store and ice-cream parlor until dusk, before returning home. After dinner, he went upstairs to Maxie's room and listened to the radio and read the dog-eared comic books until time to go to bed, never imagining that the death of young Maxwell Geary III would eventually work such an influence upon his own life.

And then there was today, yet another Christmas Eve, with the smell of snow in the crisp New England air, and the premonition that everything he had ever been or done in his entire life had somehow served to bring him to this inevitable moment.

They had not talked until today, he and his Uncle Max, although they had attended Gino Turicotti's funeral together, visited the cemetery and paid their condolences at the family home. Nor had Geary invited him to attend the board meetings that had been taking place during the past few days. Geary had attended them alone, returning each time seemingly more shaken and uncommunicative than before.

The fact that something was seriously amiss within the inner chambers of ITRC was obvious, but how serious, he could not have guessed, not until Geary's words of a few moments before. Now, trying to regain his composure and feeling that peculiar lack of confidence all men experience when discussing painful subjects with someone who has known them from childhood, he turned from the window to look across the paneled study at the white-haired man sitting before the fireplace. It was a disheartening sight. Max Geary, for most of his life, had been a man of vitality and accomplishment. But today, as he sat there staring vacantly into the flames, he looked beaten.

"Would you care for a glass of wine, Uncle Max?" Mark asked, rousing the old man from his thoughts.

"Yes, thank you, Mark. I believe I would."

Mark crossed the study to pour them each a glass of sherry from the decanter on the ancient cellaret beside the bookcase, then returned to his chair next to Geary's before the fireplace. They sat silently, sipping from their glasses, each momentarily lost in the subtleties of his own resolutions.

Mark finally broke the silence, but he took care with his words. The last thing in the world he wanted to do at this moment was castigate this dignified man he admired so much. "Uncle Max, I'm sorry I'm finding it so hard to accept, but the whole thing just seems so . . . so utterly preposterous. Are you sure nothing can be done?"

"If anything could have been done, my boy"—Geary sighed—"the time has long since passed. I think I've finally accepted the situation as it is. Now I'm just trying as hard as I can to continue to live with it."

"But how in the name of God did it ever happen?"

"Oh, hell, Mark, I'm not a businessman, nor have I ever claimed to be." Geary appeared to be more impatient with himself than with Mark's question. "I'm an engineer. Everything I've ever accomplished in my life has come from my ability to understand and solve difficult technical problems."

"That's not true. You're one of the most astute businessmen in this country.

"A businessman by necessity, perhaps, but not by choice. Account ledgers have never held my attention for very long. My concerns have always been the product we produced, never particular financial choices or options. And for years I was lucky enough to have some of the most brilliant men in the world of business by my side."

"Men like Mr. Calkins, you mean?"

"Oh, yes, Everett—such a brilliant man! I never realized how much I, we, depended on him until he was forced out."

"But that's what I don't understand—with men like you and Mr. Calkins and Whitley Rogers and the others running the company, how could they have gained such a foothold?"

Geary stared into the fire, the successes and disappointments of a half-century etched upon his craggy countenance. Where could he begin? In a lifetime of decision-making, how could he isolate the first fatal mistake? Or was there even such a thing as a *first* mistake? Perhaps business mistakes gathered as indolently as cobwebs, only to entrap the unsuspecting blunderer when he least expected it. He gave Mark's knee a fatherly pat. "We've never talked, have we, son?"

"Oh sure, we've talked, plenty of times."

"But not like we should have. We should have sat down together a long time ago. I owed it to you. I had no right to spring this on you the way I did."

"No, no, you don't owe me anything. You've already given me more than I deserve."

"Nonsense, I could have given you something a hundred times more valubale than a job and a few promotions."

"What's that?"

"Perspective, my boy—the one true gift of time, and the most valuable thing the old can offer the young." His eyes clouded. "I think that's the one thing I could never handle about losing Maxie, not being able to pass on to him some of the things I've had to learn to survive this life."

"I understand."

"I should have done it with you, I know that now. You're such a smart, decent person. You always have been. I like to think Maxie would have turned out just like you if he had lived."

"Thank you, Uncle Max, that's a compliment."

"I meant it to be. I see a lot of myself in you, especially in the way you analyze business. I've kept a file on every report you've written, every suggestion you've made since you came with the company, and I swear"—he chuckled—"it's almost like reliving my own dreams of fifty years ago. Just like you, I never placed money ahead of integrity or the other intrinsics. I never set out to become wealthy at the expense of what I felt was my true purpose for being put on this earth. All I ever wanted to do was build a company strong enough to survive the years, and maybe leave something worthwhile to my heirs when the time came."

Mark watched a shower of sparks flutter against the fireplace screen. "Perspective would indicate that that kind of rational thinking is somewhat outdated, wouldn't you say?" he asked cynically.

"No. If I've leared anything at all in my life, it's that nothing of true value is ever completely outdated."

"I'm afraid I've reached a point where I find that concept, as appealing as it is, difficult to accept."

"You really have been overtaken by cynicism, haven't you, son?"

"Yes, sir, I'm afraid so."

"That's sad, because to me that indicates a belief in predestination, that no matter what we do, evil must eventually triumph. And that simply isn't so. Nothing is inevitable, good or bad. There are merely forks in the road, and the ultimate destiny of men or corporations or cultures is determined by the choices we make."

"I'm amazed you can still believe that after all that's happened to you."

"If I didn't believe that, my boy, I'm sure I would have done away with myself by now."

"I wish you'd tell me the whole story, Uncle Max. Please. I want to know."

"The whole story, huh?" Geary forced a laugh. "I'm afraid the *whole* story would take quite some time, and probably bore you in the process."

"I'd like to hear it."

"Well, you certainly have a right to hear it." Geary was quiet for a moment, as he sought a way to begin. "How much do you know about the company, Mark? Where it came from. How it got to be as large as it is."

"Quite a bit, I think. I know that your father started it in New Jersey in 1912 and you moved it to New York in the twenties, and somehow you became involved in the radio business about that time. Am I right so far?"

Geary nodded and extended his glass. "Here, pour us some more wine. We can talk about it if you like. It may help us both to better understand why things have evolved as they have."

A moment later, Geary took the refilled glass from Mark's hand and held it up in front of him, gazing thoughtfully through the amber liquid at the logs burning in the fireplace. From the slight smile that tugged at the corners of his mouth, it was easy to see that his early memories of the small family busines that eventually grew into the conglomerate ITRC were good ones.

"You know," he began, "it's so common nowadays for successful men to cry about what a hard time they had coming along, but I can't do that. To tell you the truth, I honestly can't remember a time, as a kid, when I wasn't happy and full of dreams. I think it was because my folks put in my head from the very beginning that a man's happiness is built on hard work and accomplishment. I must have been about twelve years old when I discovered my first real hero, Charles Steinmetz. I read *Radiation, Light, and Illumination,* and it seemed to me that the whole future of mankind depended on our imaginative uses of electricity. So I decided right then to get my BS from Rutgers and go up to Union College in Schenectady and do my postgrad work under Steinmetz. But just about the time I entered college, he left there and went to work full-time for General Electric, so it never panned out."

"What did you do?"

"Well, I got my BS, all right, and applied at MIT instead. As I remember, I got to Cambridge just about the time we were getting into the war. And that was where I met Everett Calkins and Whitley Rogers, who would later form the nucleus of ITRC."

"I didn't know Mr. Calkins went to MIT."

"No, no, they were Harvard men, both of them. In those days we used to take the train down to New York weekends, to gad around, you know, and that's how I met them. After a while the three of us became pretty good friends."

"How about the company? Was it doing much in those days?"

"No, hardly anything, just staying in business. My father was really interested in only the technical aspects of recording, and he had only one other full-time employee, Cameron Dibley, who had just finished Rutgers on a student visa and had taken the first job he could find so he could stay in the country."

"It doesn't sound too promising at this point." Mark laughed.

"Well, yes it was, because by the time I left MIT I wasn't too concerned about recordings anyhow. I could see that radio was the coming thing. I went back home and convinced my father that we should get into it. He started building a plant, and while that was going on, I designed our first models. We came on the market early in '23 with what was generally conceded to be the best product in the business."

"Did the recording end improve during that time?"

"No, it was still having problems. And the main problem was Dibley. He's the most loyal, hardworking man I've ever known, but he just has no feel for music. We just couldn't trust him to make decisions. He'd put out *anything*, he didn't know the difference. So as soon as I found distribution for our radios, I went back up to Boston and hired Everett. And I had already made up my mind by then that we could never do much in the entertainment business stuck way out in Jersey like we were, so I established an office in New York, at Thirty-first and Broadway, and put in a nice little studio and got Everett to run things for me. Then I hired Whitley as my controller and shuttled him back and forth between Everett and the plant in Jersey."

"So that's really how you got started?"

"That," Geary said firmly, "is how I got started."

"I've never heard that part of the story before. It's fascinating. Please go on."

"Well, a couple of years later we decided to go public. Everett and Whitley and I drew up a prospectus, and between the fall of '25 and the end of '26 we sold over five million dollars' worth of shares. We tore down the plant in Jersey and built a four-story building a block long. Then, in '27, the real boom came. The public bought more than three hundred and fifty million dollars' worth of radios that year. And after the crash it seemed like people bought more radios than ever. By 1930 we had the biggest cash reserves in the history of the company, and that's when we started putting up the building on Thirty-ninth and Seventh."

"Had the record end improved yet?"

"Improved? My God, it was dying! I'll tell you how bad it was—American Columbia was about to go into receivership, that's how bad it was. You couldn't *give* records away in the early thirties. But I've got to give Everett credit, he had faith and he insisted that we put in the best studios we could afford. We brought in the best engineers, and by the time it was finished, nobody could touch us. Then, of course, a couple of years later Decca came out with their cut-rate line and forced the prices down, and the business started to move again. And thanks to Everett, we were ready. We immediately became one of the majors."

"Where are we now—I mean, chronologically?"

"Well . . . now the thirties are over"—Geary's voice took on an edge—"and we've got trouble staring us in the face. In December 1940, I get a call from Secretary of War Stimson asking me to come down to Washington for a conference. I meet with him and he tells me it's just a matter of time before we're in it. He wants to know when I can start getting things ready for government contracts—radios, radar, electronic surveillance equipment. Within three months we've started converting our plant. A few months after that, the Japs hit Pearl Harbor."

"How did the war affect ITRC?"

"Christ, we made a bundle! Just like everybody else. I guess I must have been pretty naive up until then, because I had no idea how much profit there was in war. In two years we doubled our employees and quadrupled our net. In '44, we had our first hundred-million-plus year."

"But wasn't that only temporary?"

"It would have been *if* I'd had any goddamned sense!" Geary exclaimed bitterly. "But when the war ended, I wasn't smart enough to go back to regular business. By this time I'm pretty involved in government, you know. I'm hanging around with the Washington big shots, having lunch at the White House once a month and swallowing crap as fast as they can feed it to me. They're convincing me that a conflict with the Russians is inevitable, and I don't have enough sense to question it. Hell, I was sick of war. Everybody was. The Russians didn't want a war and the Chinese couldn't have licked a Harlem street gang at that time. But I listened to the Washington big shots and I fell for it. I've been cursing myself ever since."

"But what was it you did?"

"Well"—Geary took a second to gather his thoughts—"I sank the majority of our profits from the preceding years into research and development. We purchased property here in Connecticut, out in Kansas, and way out in California, and started building. In addition, we started hiring engineers right out of MIT and Cal Tech, putting them on the payroll at premium salaries. Then the government started sending me all these cloak-and-dagger types. They're sneaking into my office at all hours of the night, bringing me mock-ups and blueprints with about as much chance of working as a sparrow has of making the Knicks."

"What was the point?"

"Well, that's why we were there—research and development."

"But you're an intelligent man, Uncle Max, how could you get sucked into that?"

"Perspective, son, that's what we're talking about. Remember, now, at that time there was a Communist under every rock, Truman was spending billions of American dollars to feed the same people who had been trying to blow us to kingdom come a few years before, and J. Edgar Hoover was running a PR office out of the Justice Department. In the meantime, I'm losing my shirt. I've got engineers all over the country staring up at the ceiling and catching up on their Dostoevsky, and maybe tossing an occasional glance at these blueprints for a perpetual-motion machine that we're supposed to be building to win the next war."

"It sounds ridiculous."

"Oh, no, my boy," Geary said quickly, "it was a lot of things, but ridiculous wasn't one of them. It was probably the most inglorious moment in our history, because that's when most of the shenanigans started. You see, there were a lot of businessmen in this country who had never made a decent living until the war. Now they were fat, and the opportunity to continue to receive billions of dollars in government contracts was too much for them to turn down, even though it was obvious that the country would suffer from it in the long run. But that wasn't the worst of it, not for us."

"How's that?"

"Well, after I had spent all that time and well into eight figures of the stockholders' money getting R-and-D set up, Truman's got to win another election so I can see who's going to be handing out contracts for the next few years."

"And the record end?"

"It was pulling its weight. Of course, there was that strike that Petrillo pulled on us right after the war. It went on for a year and damn near broke all of us. But except for that, for the most part, the record division did pretty good. Still, there was no way it was going to carry us until we started receiving all the government money we were building for. And we're talking about a different kind of money now, don't forget that. Before the war, it had been millions, now it was hundreds of millions.

"So about that time I met with the board and we decided to float the largest bond issue in he history of the company—dependent, of course, upon whether or not Truman gets reelected—fifty million dollars in five-year conve-tibles, redeemable at any time after three years. Follow me?"

"Yes, sir."

"Well, he does and we do. We get our SEC clearance in May 1949 and make our first ssue of twenty-five million in June of that year. It was all gone within ninety days, most of it over the counter. We checked. It looked good. No hanky-panky. Six months later, we've got some of our government money and a half dozen additional contracts pending. And a war in Korea, to boot, so we're back in the black. But we've got big plans, right? So we issue the rest. Do it the same way. Time passes and we do great. R-and-D is paying off, record sales hit an all-time high. But the problem is, you start depending on government contracts for the majority of your income, and you're juggling a ho turnip. On top of that, now, after twenty years, the Democrats are on their way out."

"Great," Mark said dryly.

"And ITRC has never played politics, you know that. We've never given a dime to any political party, except through individual contributions from our employees. But the Republicans get in and see where we've been doing business with the other fellows for a decade and a half, and they don't want anything to do with us. They don't take into consideration that we've been doing honest business all those years, which is nore than a lot of companies could say. All they see is, we've made a few friends in government, who are mostly their political enemies. And what's worse, we never contracted directly through the Pentagon or any of the intelligence agencies. We always went through the Secretary of War, the Secretary of the Army or Navy, the Justice Department, follow me?"

"Yes, political appointees."

"Right. So I start finding out that if I want to keep on doing busines with the government, I'm going to have to begin playing footsie. About that time, thank God, I begin thinking clearly. I'm sick of all the political games, so I start disposing of my remaining contracts."

"Where are we now?"

"Let's see . . ." Gear thought for a moment. "We're coming into

1954, just about the time you were joining us. Anyhow, by the time we get through regrouping, clearing the books, and getting ready to start functioning again as a normal civilian corporation, we've got . . . oh, maybe thirty million to do something with. Now, as you know, at this point we're entering a crucial time in the record business. We've been going along great for seven or eight years. But nobody knows that rock-'n'-roll music is about to turn the whole thing upside down. All we know is there is about to be a push on 'hi-fi,' and RCA and Columbia and some of the others are going to promote it to try to get their LP and EP's off the ground."

"But hadn't LP's been around long before then?"

"Oh, sure, for twenty, twenty-five years. But the industry never had a peg to hang them on until the hi-fi thing, that's when people first started becoming conscious of sound quality."

"I'm sorry, I didn't mean to interrupt. Go on."

"Well, as I was about to say, I'd already made some pretty solid contracts with Japanese manufacturers through R-and-D, so I decided we should jump on the hi-fi thing. My idea was, we'd put out a nice little inexpensive line in the thirty- to forty-dollar bracket, a good little machine, but nothing spectacular. For the kids, you know, mainly to help sell albums. Our research had indicated that the war babies were starting to grow up and there would be a steadily increasing market for that sort of product over the next few years. Oh, and while I'm thinking about it, I want to take full responsibility for that FM fiasco. I should have been aware of the FM growth potential from my radio-manufacturing days. Hell, we used to make sets to catch every conceivable piece of racket that came over the air—AM, FM, shortwave, marine-band, and anything else you could mention. I know you blamed Turicotti, but it was really my fault. I take full responsibility for the whole mess."

Mark acknowledged the statement with a nod. "So now I guess we're at the point where Mr. Calkins comes in to see you, right?"

"Yes, my boy, I guess we are. . . ." Geary rubbed his hand along his upper arm as if to fend off a sudden chill. "Why don't you pour us another glass of wine while I put a couple of logs on the fire?"

Mark got fresh drinks, returning in time to catch the look of anguish on Max Geary's face. There were, obviously, very few pleasant memories in ITRC's recent past.

"Uncle Max . . . you don't have to say any more if you prefer not to."

"No, no, I'm fine!" Geary said quickly. He took a sip of wine, forced a smile, and settled farther back in the cushions. "Anyhow, one morning in March 1954, I believe it was, Everett came in to see me. I knew from the look on his face that our worst fears had been confirmed—less than fifteen percent of our bondholders had responded favorably to our notice of intent to redeem. Generally, bondholders are more conservative than stockholders. Only a small percentage even consider conversion to stock. They want to take their profits and get out. Not always, but usually. And, frankly, our stock was not that attractive at the time. We were in a state of flux, solid certainly, but not good enough for eighty-five percent of the bondholders to be considering conversion."

"What had alerted you?"

"Well . . . in the immediate preceding year, we had gotten an inkling that something might be wrong. We ran a check to try to determine what was happening, and the first thing we learned was that a union pension fund out of Detroit had picked up about twenty percent of the bonds immediately after the first issue—"

"But that's fairly common, isn't it?"

"Yes, that didn't bother us too much, except that they had done it on the qt and we didn't like the idea of so many convertibles being in the hands of one party. We checked further and learned that Artists Management Corporation had also invested in a block, not a great deal, less than ten percent, but still a little unusual. But what *really* disturbed us was that a company called Telemetrix had very quietly come into control of about thirty percent. The reason it bothered us so much was that after a while you automatically distrust holding companies.

"So we investigated. It was, essentially, a John Doe company, the principal shareholder in a Florida bank and a Bahamian gambling resort, with extensive real-estate holdings in Arizona. We didn't like the resort thing, but the bank allayed our fears. We assumed it might have purchased the bonds and placed them with Telemetrix for later trust investments, or something of that nature."

"I think I would have been pretty concerned about that."

"No, no, we felt we had a right to make that assumption. After all, we had been on the market for thirty years at that point, and we had never failed to return a dividend to our shareholders, so we considered ourselves a blue-chip company. And as far as we could determine, Telemetrix had nothing to do with the casino end of the resort. That part of it was owned by a Nevada corporation called Goldenrod, Limited. We looked into Goldenrod and discovered that they were also tied to some union pension fund, but with the majority of the stock held by a Chicago gaming-machine company. Nevertheless, even though we could uncover no corporate connection between the two, it made us uncomfortable. So Everett and Whitley and I, along with a few of the old guard, immediately held a private meeting—right here in this room, in fact—and decided to make every effort to cover our tracks."

"What about the second issue of bonds?"

"I'll get to that in a minute—but in the meantime, I guess it was April or May of '54, I got a call from Palm Springs, from Rich Bentley of AMC, asking me to fly out there to talk to him as soon as possible. Hell, I'd known Rich for years, ever since he was a kid trying to book dance bands into Atlantic City. I trusted him. If he said it was important, it was important. So I jump on a plane. I get out there and rent a car and drive down to Palm Springs. He greets me with some very disturbing information he learned during his own disastrous proxy fight with an outfit called the Rhondo Corporation."

"I never heard of them, either."

"They're a limited corporation whose principal stock is held by American Indemnity and Life."

"Insurance?"

"Yes."

"What did he tell you?"

"He said he had pretty good information that the same people might later try to pull a takeover on us."

"How did it all tie in?"

"As soon as I got back here, I hired one of the best firms in the business to investigate the whole thing. Two months later, they turned in their report. The principal stockholder in American Indemnity was Telemetrix."

"Which meant that they had close to forty percent of the first-issue bonds and a substantial amount of common stock, plus some kind of a connection with the pension fund, right?"

"Unfortunately, yes."

"Who the hell was Telemetrix?" Mark asked angrily.

"We never could determine who the John Does were. It was set up by a genius, whoever he was. We traced it from Delaware to the Bahamas to Europe and back to Delaware, through a half-dozen dummy corporations."

"How about the bank?"

"The bank, huh?" Geary made a sour face. "Oh, the bank has a *very* select clientele, all right, including several high elected government officials, a television network, two of the largest shipping lines in the world, a half-dozen big insurance companies. . . ."

Sometime during the past few minutes the color had drained from Mark's face. The enormity of Max Geary's revelations was almost too hideous to comprehend. Mark's hand was unsteady as he set his glass on the hearth beside his chair. "When did they begin to apply pressure?" He could barely get the words out.

"Well, to answer your other question now—despite what Rich Bentley told me, I don't think they seriously considered a takeover until after this rock-'n'-roll thing hit. The reason I say that is, they hadn't picked up as much of the second issue of bonds as we'd expected. We checked that thoroughly, immediately after the meeting here with Everett and the others. So we worked hard at redeeming those bonds. In the meantime, throughout 1955, we painted as dismal a corporate picture as we could to discourage conversion to voting stock. But when the bottom began to drop out of the record business . . ."

"I think I know what happened then. Some of the old stockholders got scared and started to jump ship, and as fast as stock became available, Telemetrix snapped it up, right?"

"Exactly. And remember, our stock had been floating around for thirty years by that time. People had died and passed it on to their heirs. It had been used for collateral all over the world. Some of it was squirreled away in safe-deposit boxes. Frankly, we didn't have much of a chance to keep up with Telemetrix in tracking it down, because we still had a company to run—a company that was in serious trouble, I might add—and most of our efforts were spent on trying to keep those second-issue bonds from falling into the wrong hands. I was desperate, so I did the only thing I could. I sent a letter to Buzz McCandler at SEC, notifying him that we might have to go into a Chapter Eleven."

"That must have hurt Uncle Max."

"God, it absolutely killed me to do that! I was smearing a reputation it had taken us forty years to build. But I had to do whatever I felt was necessary to keep our stock from being traded. I had gone to Rutgers with Buzz, known him practically all my life, so as soon as he got my note, he drove up here to see me personally. I told him the whole story exactly as I'm telling it to you now. He tried to discourage me. The changes in the administration had shot the market to hell. We were already in a recession while the money shifted, and ITRC was 'one of the cornerstones of optimism,' as he put it. He promised a quiet investigation, but I didn't have much hope. I knew he had to table it."

"Why?"

"Well, actually, he had no choice. All he could do was raise a stink and solve nothing. It wasn't within his province to question the character of those who bought stock, just those who sold it. And the entire operation was legal."

"Jesus! So who eventually came after you?"

"American Indemnity, in the first stockholders' meeting of the year, January 1956."

"What were they like? I mean, normal people don't just walk in and steal your life!"

"They were kids—the same age as you, polite, neat . . . but icicles. They had their information, their proxies, and their orders. I had twenty-seven percent of the outstanding common stock, they had nineteen. I had proxies for twenty-two, they had proxies for thirty-two."

"But . . . where did they come from?"

It was such a naive question that Geary, in spite of himself, emitted a small chuckle. "Where do *you* think they came from?"

"I don't know." Mark reflected a moment. "I honestly don't know."

"Well, as I recall, one came from the University of Southern California, the other from Harvard Law. They had no ax to grind with me personally, they were just doing a job. And doing it very well, I might add. I'm sure they could not conceive of the years of work and love I'd put into the company. And even if they could, I'm sure it was beyond their capacity to care."

"But they certainly must have known whom they were working for?"

"I'm not sure I understand you, son."

"Well, if Telemetrix is involved with gambling resorts and Arizona land deals . . ."

"You mean, you think they're gangsters?"

"Yes, of course."

Geary sighed and sipped from his glass. When he spoke, his voice rang through the quiet study. "I'm going to explain something to you, my boy, and I want you to remember it, because it will help you to understand a great many of the things that are happening in business today: the parameters and intentions of the law have been manipulated to the point that there's practically no such thing as a real gangster anymore, certainly not at this level of finance. I mention gambling casinos and pension funds to you, and you automatically picture characters like you see on *The Untouchables*, guys riding around on running boards, shooting at each other with machine guns. Well, there were only a few of those to begin with, and most of them are long since dead now. No, in those days, just as today, most crooks were small-time, petty. They booked horses out of the backs of stores, ran illegal gin mills, pandered, extorted money from small business, things like that. And some of them made pretty good money, too. They got married and raised families and eventually became respectable.

"On the other hand, there were the people they did business with—the crooked politicians, cops on the take, greedy lawyers, corruptible zoning boards, and so on. And standing right in the middle of them were the average citizens. And after a time, a great many of those average citizens became disillusioned. They saw the others breaking and bending the law, promoting and manipulating and growing wealthy, and they decided that hard work was for fools. They decided to cut themselves in for a piece of the pie.

"So now we have their kids, all of their children, writing our news and setting our fashions. We have them making our laws and controlling our economy. So what we're dealing with in business today is not a gangster as much as a 'gangster mentality,' the conviction that there really is something for nothing. And, you see, it doesn't matter whether a man owns an insurance company or a music company—if he has been taught to think like a con man and a hustler, whatever he does will reflect it, and eventually he will destroy everything decent he comes in contact with."

"You're the one who sounds cynical now," Mark chided.

"No, angry perhaps, but not cynical. And I still hold to the belief that there is honest money and tainted money, and it serves no good purpose for the line between them to become nonexistent."

"What demands did they make?"

"They wanted a trade-off. They offered to let me keep the chairmanship if I would allow one of their people to assume the presidency without a fight. But I convinced them that the way the economy was at that time, if I stepped down from the presidency, our stock would go through the floor. And it was true. After all, for better or worse, I had become a fairly large patch in a kind of living security blanket to the American economy. I was finally able to convince them of that, so then they zeroed in on the record division. They became adamant in their demands for Everett's resignation."

"What was it? Did they think he was incompetent, or outdated, or what?"

"How could they think that when he practically built the record division? No, it was something altogether different. It seemed to me they were not so set on taking Everett's job as they were on destroying the image he gave the company. To most Americans of my generation, E. V. Calkins symbolizes the very epitome of culture. He was one of a handful of men whose foresight had created the industry in the first place. He had done as much for recorded music—classical, pop, all kinds of music—as, say, D. W. Griffith did for films.

"But these kids wanted him out. They were inflexible about receiving his resignation immediately. They wanted dynamics. Energy! I fought them to a standstill. I simply refused to ask him for it." Geary's thoughts turned inward, and for an instant he seemed to be talking to himself. "I simply don't understand why an image of culture should be so offensive to them. . . ."

"Is that where Turicotti came in—force, energy?"

"Yes, they had already chosen Gino to head the record division, even before they walked into the meeting. But I wouldn't hear of it. I told them Everett had a year remaining before he would be eligible for a full pension and it was unthinkable after all he had meant to the company to ask him to step down before that time. There was simply no way I could make a graceful public announcement of it."

"If I remember correctly, it wasn't until later in the year that he did offer his resignation. About the time I was chosen to head that Champ Records thing, right?"

"That's right. We were approaching our second stockholders' meeting of that year, and they warned me if Everett did not step down before then, they would force him to resign publicly. I couldn't allow that to happen, so I acceded—but only after making certain he could withdraw his treasury stock and go on full pension immediately."

"Uncle Max, I . . ." Mark began, and not being able to find the words to express his feelings, shrugged helplessly.

"I know, son. It's a terrible shock to you, and a situation I'm sure I'll never be able to fully reconcile, either. But if I'm going to be completely honest, I must take a certain responsibility for it—and again, we must think in terms of perspective. I sincerely believe in my heart that if I and the other business leaders of my generation had not been so timid, if we had fought a little harder and stood up a little taller for the things we knew to be . . ."—he searched for the right word—"*substantive,* especially in the years immediately after the war, there is a chance that the young people coming along now would feel a little more respect toward our traditions."

"I disagree. Absolutely, totally!"

"I can understand how you might," Geary spoke with kindness, "but at any rate, after all the ponderings and retrospectives, we must come forward to the present. And as you know, I've been meeting with the board all week—"

"I'm quitting, Uncle Max."

"—and they, we, have arrived at several important decisions."

"My mind's already made up, I'm quitting."

Geary's eyebrows creased in a frown. "You're not serious?"

"Yes sir, I am."

"It's out of the question. As of the first of the year, they want you to step into Turicotti's job."

"No."

"You have to take it."

"*No*, I don't have to take it." The strength of Mark's refusal surprised even himself. "I had already made up my mind that, as of the first of the year, I would offer my resignation."

"And what you've heard today merely strengthened your resolution, eh?" It was the only expression of cynicism Mark had ever heard in Max Geary's voice.

"You know me better than that, Uncle Max!" he said sharply.

Geary dropped his eyes in embarrassment. "Forgive me, son. I certainly do know you better than that. When did you decide?"

"Two months ago."

"Why didn't you tell me sooner?"

"I wanted to stay with the company a full ten years. It will be ten years in March."

"I see." Geary nodded. "What brought it on?"

"Nothing, everything. . . ."

"Did your getting married have anything to do with your decision?"

"No. If anything, it made me deliberate longer."

"Then, what? Why? You must know how much we need you?"

"I just don't fit in the music industry, that's all. I'm totally out of step with the people in it. I can't seem to find any level to communicate with them. Most of the time I feel like a self-righteous fool."

"You're hedging, son," Geary chided gently.

"Okay—I pay my artists hundreds of thousands of dollars a year and they urinate in my hallways and vomit in my studios. If I walk into a recording session unexpectedly, I find my engineers reading comic books and my producers smoking dope. I can't accept that. I *refuse* to accept it any longer!"

"Well, I can't fault you for that." Geary nodded solemnly. "Was there any specific incident that hurried your decision along?"

"Yes, there was. But it had nothing to do with that type of thing, it was something . . ." Painfully he recounted his confrontation with Sam Crockett.

"The way we have treated our colored talent over the years has been disgraceful," Max Geary admitted when Mark had finished. "The shame of it is, they have always been the main source of creativity in the industry, although most people in our profession would rather be strung up by their fingers than admit it. For years, you know, we had our 'race' label, the same as every other major company. It was a cut-rate line which retailed for as low as twenty-nine cents per unit in some depression years. In our case it was no attempt to denigrate the quality of the music, but rather a simple acknowledgment that the colored market did not have the money to spend on recordings at regular prices. We tried to cross our colored artists over from time to time, to integrate our music, as it were, but the majority of radio stations refused to play them.

"And the level of resistance inside our own company as well as throughout the business was tremendous. I don't think you have any idea how deeply ingrained opportunistic racism is in this business—"

"Oh, yes I do!" Mark exclaimed heatedly. "I've confronted it since the day I joined the company, ever since I realized that racism was part of most of the foolishness, the incessant bickering and ego problems."

"You're a sensitive man to realize that," Geary said. "Very few others in our business do—or even devote much thought to it. At any rate, the absolute best we could have hoped for at that time was that the most qualified of our colored people would not continue to be denied an opportunity for major-market success. Everett was trying very hard to do something positive and long-range along those lines when the rock-'n'-roll thing hit. Then, of course, we suddenly found ourselves excluded from the mainstream of sales, and there was not very much we could do at that point even with our established white talent.

"But I'll tell you—frankly, I had more hopes for that Champ venture. Actually, what I was really hoping was that the colored dj's and retailers would be more receptive to us, especially since they only had one or two labels of their own of any substance. But we simply could not deal with the colored market on any kind of a consistent basis. We encountered the same rampant opportunism in trying to reach them directly as had begun to destroy the traditional pop-music sales structure, except at a much less profitable level. As I said before"—Geary shrugged helplessly—"it's a situation which has never been reconciled and probably never will be. . . ."

"I know that now." Mark's face was resigned. "I couldn't accept it a few years ago, but I can now—I mean, as a fact of life. I just can't accept it any longer as an irrevocable fact of *my* life."

"And *I* can't accept the board's second choice for Turicotti's job."

"Who's that?"

"Carl Clinger."

"Carl Clinger, for Christ's sake!" The shock of Geary's words made Mark sit upright in his seat. "That's the most ridiculous thing I've ever heard! Why him?"

"Because he is, above everything else, a salesman. And a damned good one, at that. He's spent the last two years of his vice-presidency selling himself to the board. He's a clever man, you know. It's virtually impossible not to be taken in by him, if your mentality operates on the same level as his, and I'm sure by now he must have told them everything they want to hear."

"Oh, they can't seriously be considering Clinger," Mark dismissed the idea. "He doesn't have the background or intelligence to run the entire record division on his own."

"Perhaps not—not with any degree of judiciousness, that is. But he's smart enough to do exactly what they tell him to do."

"He couldn't hold that job fifteen minutes." Mark shook his head contemptuously. "The very idea is preposterous!"

"No, it is not preposterous!" Max Geary's eyes blazed with fury. "What is preposterous is that those people should be operating ITRC in the first place, that is what's preposterous! But let me tell you something—Carl Clinger can hold that job long enough for them to reorganize and consolidate all their other record holdings, long enough for them to bring in whoever they want on a permanent basis. Then they can hustle Clinger back to Nashville and give him his own label, which they'll distribute for him—and further along, they can back a nationally syndicated television program for his artists and provide financing for him to enter motion-picture production, which is what he really wants."

"Okay, suppose you're right. They'd do the same with me, wouldn't they? They'd put me in just long enough to reorganize the company and then bring in their own man, right?"

"Maybe so, maybe not. You're certainly a different-caliber executive than Carl Clinger"—Geary spat the name out—"and they're insightful enough to realize it, otherwise they wouldn't have made you their first choice. But that's not the important thing. The important thing is, *I* need you there."

"Why? It's their company now, you said so yourself. What could I do, except sit there and follow orders like Turicotti did, or Clinger will?"

Mark's words tore at Geary. The old man flinched as though he'd been slapped. He dropped his head for a moment. When he looked up again, he tried to smile to show that the outburst had not angered him, but all he could muster was a wistful sigh.

"You know something, my boy? A few weeks ago I realized that soon, ITRC, which has been my whole life, will not have one single employee whom I personally approved to come to work for us, except you. My company has been cleaned out from under me. I hardly know a soul there now. I seldom even bother to go into New York anymore. I walk through that building and I feel like an apparition, like a ghost haunting the past.

"I still have the key to Everett's old office. One night a year or so ago, after I had just come from visiting Glemmie at the hospital, I went up there and let myself in. It made me sick! All those beautiful paintings, those lovely antiques and first editions, just sitting there, rotting. I think of all the love and dedication that went into those rooms, into putting up that building, and . . ."

Mark touched the old man's hand in a gesture of understanding— for Geary, for his parents, for all those who had passed before him, who had labored so painstakingly to try to build a world that he could enter and find a comfortable, satisfying role for himself. He tried to speak, but his voice was unable to bear the weight of his emotions. He drank the last of his wine, now warmed by the heat of the fireplace, and tried again.

"Uncle Max . . . please try to understand what a difficult decision this is for me to make. I've reached a crossroads in my life, maybe the same kind you were facing at the end of the war, maybe even worse. I'm not well, I haven't mentioned it to anybody, not my parents, not even Sarah, but I have an ulcer that could begin hemorrhaging at any time. And I'm taking medicine three times a day for my blood pressure. But even worse than that, I can feel myself losing touch with what I want to believe are the realities of my life. I look around and I can't see anything of value anymore. All I can see are people like myself, running in no particular direction and with no particular purpose. I'm lost and I know if I don't make some kind of drastic change to try to find myself, I'm never going to be able to make any sense at all out of my life."

Geary peered at him with compassion, silently acknowledging Mark's words with his eyes, debating with himself whether this was the time to declare his own mortality. Then, wordlessly, he got to his feet and crossed the room to the wall safe behind the desk. He returned with an envelope.

"Here, read this, son. . . ."

Mark's hands were trembling as he broke the seal. Inside was a copy of a will:

I, Maxwell P. Geary, residing in the township of Morganville in the county of Fairfield and state of Connecticut, being of sound mind and disposing memory, do make, ordain, pub-

*lish, and declare this to be my last will and testament, hereby
revoking all former wills and codicils by me made . . .*

Mark read it through. It was dated March 20, 1955, a year after
he had joined the company.

"I don't deserve this, Uncle Max " He spoke sharply to try to
hide the tears welling in the corners of his eyes. "Why did you do
it?"

"Why?" Geary smiled. "I knew I was going to do that from the
moment Cameron Dibley phoned me to tell me you had submitted
your application with us. I guess I knew even before then, when you
were still a kid, the first time you mentioned that maybe someday
you'd like to come to work for me. Then, after you'd been with us a
year and I saw that spark of intuition that makes a good and decent
businessman . . . well, it just seemed like the logical thing to do."

"I'm grateful, Uncle Max, you know that, but I—"

"I'm not trying to bribe you, son. If you don't change your mind
about leaving, it still stands. Who knows, with the vultures we've got
in there now, by the time I pass on, ITRC stock may not even be fit
to paper a wall. And the money's not important to me, not at this
stage of my life. Glemmie's had two operations now, so there's no
telling how long she's going to be with us. And if I go first, she's well
taken care of, I saw to that years ago."

"But . . ."

"Mark, I'm well fixed My personal assets, excluding my shares in
the company, run eighteen to twenty million. We have this place
and the house in the city and the place in Palm Beach, all paid for.
And Glemmie and I only have a few distant relatives between us.
Don't worry, we'll leave plenty for them to fight over."

"I know. That's not . . ."

"The business has been my life, son. I poured all my energy and
dreams into it after Maxie was killed. I have to leave it to someone
who can see it for all it is, as a means to improve the intrinsic quality
of life, not just as a vehicle to make money. Who else but you is
there?"

Geary could see the confusion in Mark's face, and he knew that
nothing else he could say would register at this moment. He tried to
make his voice reassuring. "You're still young, my boy. And I don't
intend to start paddling my canoe down the River Styx for a while
yet, so you make whatever decisions you must at your leisure. The
main thing is, you must get your health in order. Promise me you
will."

"Yes, sir."

"And you tell your wife. Take my word for it, nothing makes a woman happier than to find out her husband is fallible. Promise me you'll tell her as soon as you get home."

"Yes, sir, I will. I promise."

"Now, then . . . I know you have to catch your plane. How much time do you have?"

Mark looked at his watch. "I should be leaving now. I didn't realize it was so late."

"Okay, why don't you run upstairs and get your bags and say good-bye to your Aunt Glemmie, and I'll tell Henry to bring the car around for you."

They got to their feet, the flames from the fireplace lending a warm glow to their faces. They looked at each other for an instant, seeing the years of affection they'd shared reflected in the other's eyes, then gripped hands and walked to the study door together.

"I'm sorry I can't stay for the party."

"Oh, it won't be much, believe me—just a few old friends in for some eggnog."

"How is Mr. Calkins doing these days?"

"Great, strong as a bull. He's involved in putting together a big-band anthology for the Reader's Digest people at the moment."

"Give him my regards and wish everyone a Merry Christmas for me."

"I will, I will . . . and the same from us to your parents and your new bride."

They shook hands again and Mark started toward the staircase, then stopped and turned back, tears glistening in the corners of his eyes. "Uncle Max, how can I ever thank you—for everything?"

"You already have, my boy, by giving me years of honest labor and more loyalty than I could ever ask for. Merry Christmas, and good luck to you. . . ."

CONNECTICUT DECEMBER 1963

Mark rode along the quiet countryside in the late-afternoon dusk, lulled by the drone of the car's engine, his leg draped across the backseat. Christmas lights blinked at him from fenceposts and driveways. Stately old elms, undressed and asleep in the brittle arms of winter, rested their trunks against the landscape. Occasionally he caught a glimpse of an inviting living room, drapes parted, decorated with stockings and piled high with bright, unopened presents.

A few miles south of Darien, it began to snow. Huge flakes the size of cotton balls, covering the earth with a gentle, luminous quilt and reminding him of past lives he had known through the calligraphy on Christmas cards.

Sometime later, Henry, usually stiff and competent behind the wheel, was nervously scrubbing at the windshield with a towel and nursing the limousine through the inert traffic of the Van Wyck Expressway with all the confidence of a calvaryman riding a cow into the Battle of the Bulge. It was the beginning of the worst December snowstorm in the recent history of New York City.

Mark missed his plane by an hour.

He shoved his way into a line of frantic travelers, and another hour passed before the harried young woman at the reservations counter was able to put him on standby for an eleven-P.M. flight. It was the best she could do. She couldn't even promise that the airport would still be open then.

He found an overnight locker and left his bags, then joined another line of people waiting for a public phone. When he finally got through to Sarah, the bustle around him and the crackle of static on the line made it difficult to hold a conversation.

". . . doesn't matter what time, honey, I'll come pick you up."

"No, I don't know when I'll get out of here. It's a madhouse. You'd better go on to bed."

"How did it go?"

"Okay."

"You don't sound like it."

"I'm just tired, that's all. I miss you. I'll be happy to get home."

"Honey?"

"Yes?"

"Millie called a little while ago. She wants me to come over there for a Christmas Eve party."

"I thought she was going home for Christmas?"

"No, she changed her mind at the last minute."

"What did you tell her?"

"I told her no—but I thought you'd be home in a little while."

"Do you still want to go?"

"Oh, I don't really *want* to go, I just don't want to stay here by myself. I'm lonesome, that's all."

"I told you, you should have gone down to Palm Springs like we planned. I could have met you there."

"No, not without you. . . ." Silence. "You don't want me to go, huh?"

"Well, I guess it's not fair for me to ask you to stay home by yourself, if you don't want to. . . ."

"I have to take Millie her present anyhow."

"Well, be careful. You know how I feel about those people."

"I'll be careful, I promise. . . .Uh, how was the funeral?"

"Just a funeral."

"You sound tired."

"Yes, I guess I am."

"Honey, if you really want me to say home . . ."

"No, that's okay. Have a drink for me. Just don't stay out too late. We'll be leaving early tomorrow. I promised the folks we'd get there in time for Christmas dinner."

"Oh, I will. It's still early here, not even five o'clock yet."

"Okay, I'd better hang up now. There're some people waiting to use the phone."

"Mark?"

"Yes?"

"Are you sure it's okay for me to go?"

"Yes, *go.* Have a good time."

"Throw me a kiss."

"Honey, there are people watching me. . . ."

"I don't care, throw me a kiss!"

He did, and glanced around. The man behind him was scowling back. "I'd better go, honey."

"I'll probably see you in the morning, then, huh?"

"Yes, if not before."

"I love you."

"Me too . . . good-bye." Before he had time to replace the receiver, the scowling man snatched it from his hand.

"Merry Christmas," Mark said sarcastically.

"Fuck you, buddy—get out of the way!"

He walked around the waiting area, looking for a vacant seat. He heard the dispatcher announce a flight and saw an elderly woman stand up and begin to gather her shopping bags. He took a few steps toward her before he changed his mind and headed for the bar.

He had a feeling the day was just beginning.

HOLLYWOOD
DECEMBER 1963

Cantor's Delicatessen on Fairfax Avenue was turning into a West Coast counterpart to the Turf Cafe in New York. At almost any time of the afternoon or evening an interested party could drop in and do a little table-hopping and pick up the latest gossip about the Hollywood music industry.

Tonight, however, the place was quiet. There were only two customers in the large dining area, an elderly, bearded gentleman comfortably ensconced at a rear table behind a potted palm, and a skinny, dour-faced younger man in a front booth, staring morosely into an empty coffee cup.

Paulie Schultz was lonesome.

He did not recognize the symptoms, of course, having arrived at the conclusion a few minutes before that he was merely bored. But the truth was, he was lonesome. He was also more than a trifle confused. His life was not progressing quite along the lines he had anticipated, especially with women, and he was now turning over in his mind the painful possibility that a sportscar, a bachelor pad in the Hollywood Hills and two records in the top-hundred did not necessarily make one a swinger.

Earlier in the evening, after having been stood up for the second time in a week, he had decided to visit his mother. But after spending an hour or so listening to her describe in some detail the rapidly declining condition of her health, he had left in the middle of a sentence and driven around the corner to Cantor's to see what was happening.

Nothing was and now he was in the process of narrowing the remainder of his evening's activities down to one of three possible choices. He could return to his apartment and watch a group he had just missed signing make their first appearance on the Tonight Show. Or he could cruise the Strip and check out the available pickups. Or he could drive down to Santa Monica Boulevard and look for a dirty movie. Or he could get another cup of coffee before the place closed and continue to mull over the first three choices.

He was so intent upon arriving at a decision that he failed to notice the door open and the tall, well-muscled young man with sun-bleached hair enter, take a quick look around, and approach his booth. The first time he realized that he was not alone was when he heard the familiar voice extend a somewhat personalized yuletide greeting.

"Merry Christmas, prick."

"Aw shit, just what I need . . ." Paulie groaned without looking up. But he was nevertheless grateful for the company, as Terry Caulfield plopped down across from him, stretched his long legs under the table and gave Paulie a nudge with his foot to make more room for himself. "If I'm in your way," Paulie said, "I'll get up and move."

"While you're up, bring me a beer."

"What the hell are you doing here, Caulfield? I thought you were supposed to be in Denver at a dj convention or something?"

"A dj Christmas party—I was, until this morning."

"How was it?"

"Lotta dope. That's why they call it the 'mile high' city."

"Did you hear about Turicotti?"

"Yeah, a couple of days ago."

"A bitch, huh?"

"Way it goes," Caulfield shrugged.

"Well, just in the way of polite conversation, I can't help but wonder what you're doing here?"

"Looking for my car," Caulfield explained.

Paulie made a big production of looking under the table. "It ain't there," he said.

"Yeah, I was afraid of that." Caulfield leaned back against the booth, folded his hands behind his head and burped loudly.

"What do you mean you're looking for your car?" Paulie persisted.

"It's a long story."

"That's okay, I got time."

"Well—I left it with this broad I know while I was out of town. She was supposed to meet me here tonight so we could go to a party."

"Look at it this way, it's only a Rolls."

"Yeah, I guess you're right. I shouldn't get worked up about it, should I?"

"Right, especially since it ain't even paid for yet."

"So why don't you help me relax and take my mind off it?"

"How can I help you take your mind off it? I ain't your goddamn psychiatrist."

414 ·

"—By sliding over here and nibbling on my knob while I'm waiting. That always helps me relax."

A pair of headlights slowed outside and Caulfield sat up and peered anxiously through the window. The car pulled away in the darkness and he slapped the back of the booth in irritation. "Goddamn bitch, where the fuck's my car?" He stared out the window a moment longer, then began fumbling through his pockets.

"It ain't there. If she'd parked it here you would have noticed."

"Wait a minute . . ." Caulfield pulled a scrap of paper from his pocket and studied it in the dim light, ". . . called and left the address a couple of days ago."

"Who?"

"How should I know. I was out of town. Here," he handed it to Paulie, "I can't make out the writing."

Paulie squinted at it. "Yeah, this ain't too far from my house. . . ."

"You want to go?"

"I don't know. Who's gonna be there?"

"What do you care, a party's a party, and you're not exactly swamped with invitations."

Paulie briefly considered his options. "Okay, but don't change your mind later and expect me to bring you all the way back down here. I already told you, I only live a couple of miles from there."

"Don't sweat it, I'll score a broad at the party and go crash with her someplace."

"Yeah—well, if you don't you can flop on my couch."

"What do you mean 'if I don't'?" Caulfield sneered. "You're talking to a star, asshole, and a star always scores, remember that."

"—And another thing, if I meet a broad there and wanna leave before you're ready, you're on your own, I just wanna tell you that in front."

"Let me tell you something, Schultz. If you meet a broad and leave before I do," Caulfield shook his head in amazement at Paulie's speculation, "it will be the true fucking Miracle of Christmas."

A few miles away, high in the Hollywood Hills, Sarah Donovan guided her yellow convertible into the small driveway and turned to the woman in the passenger's seat beside her. "Millie, why don't I just drop you off and go back home? I shouldn't even be here. I told Mark—"

"You're right, you shouldn't be here. You should be down in Palm Springs with his folks, doing whatever it is movie stars do on Christmas Eve. But instead of that you were getting ready to mope around the house all night feeling sorry for yourself."

"No, I wasn't. I really thought he was coming home earlier, and I didn't want to go down there by myself. I told you, his folks make me nervous, especially his mother."

"Oh, shit, everything makes you nervous! I don't know what's wrong with you, Sarah, you've got everything a woman could ask for, including the sexiest-looking man I've ever laid eyes on. And all you do is complain. Sometimes I don't think you realize how lucky you are."

"Yes, I do. That's what I was telling you on the way up here, I don't know what he sees in me. He's so patient and everything. I mean, he could have just about any woman he wanted. I can't understand why he married me. I'm dumb and half-crazy and I just make his life more complicated."

"Oh, Sarah, he loves you because you're pretty and talented and you know it, and I'm not going to sit here all night boosting your ego. You can go back home and sit in that house by yourself all night if you want to, but I'm going to go in there and have some fun."

"Well, maybe just a drink . . ."

"That's better, a couple of drinks won't hurt you, and they may do you some good, you've turned into such a wet blanket lately."

"Okay, I'll come in for a little while. But I want to be home in case he calls."

"You can leave anytime you want, that's why we came in your car."

"And, Millie, kind of watch out for me, okay? I mean, I don't want to drink too much or anything . . ."

"No, dammit, I am *not* going to watch out for you. That's what's wrong with you, Sarah everybody babies you so much. You're a grown woman and all you have to do is go in there and say hello and have a couple of drinks and go home. No big deal—now come on!"

"God, you don't have to act like such a bitch!"

"But I am a bitch," Millie Michaelson smiled in the darkness, "that's why everybody loves me."

They were speeding north on Highland Avenue, Paulie behind the wheel, Caulfield sprawled in the passenger's seat beside him smoking a joint. Paulie was in the middle of one of his monologues.

". . . So when Peter, Paul and Mary covered a couple of his tunes I went back and listened to that first album again and checked out 'Man of Constant Sorrow' and I said to myself, shit, all I gotta do is put a little punch in it. Lay down a good beat, move the guitars around a little, and change a couple of words, you know what I mean . . ."

"Umm . . ." Caulfield said, not wanting to waste good weed on an answer.

". . . so you know how long it took me to come up with the record? Two fucking days, can you believe that? See, it's like I told you a hundred times already, Caulfield, the tune don't mean a goddamn thing, it's production that counts. Nobody listens to the words anyhow, they want some fucking excitement. I don't give a shit if it's folk music or what, you lay out what you want before you go in the studio and you stay there until you get the *big* sound, you know what I mean? And the main thing is, you don't listen to nobody, that's the secret. Remember how you kept telling me 'this ain't gonna work,' 'that ain't gonna work'? But I didn't listen, did I? You wanna know why, because I don't listen to nobody, that's why. And that's why you're so lucky to have me handling you, Caulfield, you know what I mean. . . ."

"Ummm . . ."

". . . So I see Donovan at the Christmas party, right? And he ain't even listened to the goddamn thing yet, can you believe that? I mean, here I am running around busting my guts to cut hits for him and he's sitting there on the phone with his thumb up his ass saying Hail Mary's to New York, him and his buddy Silverstein, and in the meantime the fucking business is passing him by. I ain't one of their fucking contract producers, you know, I got a company to run. And I'll tell you something else, Caulfield, something a very wise man in this business once told me, 'when you got it in the grooves, you gotta move.' And he was right, because that's how you stay alive in this business, Caulfield. You stay a little ahead of the trends and come up with good production and you can't get hurt, you know what I mean . . ."

"Ummm . . ."

"Right. So you know what's gonna happen six months, a year from now? That folk music bullshit's gonna be dead and they're gonna be asking whatever happened to Dylan. Like I say, they're mishandling him. If it was up to me I'd of never let the sonofabitch record. I'd of stuck him in an office somewhere and just let him write tunes. He ain't a bad songwriter, his problem is he has a tendency to get a little far out. . . ."

Tommy Lee Whitaker's living room was overflowing with the buzz of conversation, the sound of Johnny Cash—and the rattle of bad vibes.

It had been Barbara Jean Clinger's idea to have the party there. She had intended it to be small, with just a few Nashville friends present, music people who, like herself and Carl, happened to be in California for the holidays. She had chosen Tommy Lee's house because of the view it offered, which was breathtaking when Tommy

Lee saw fit to wash the windows, and because her brother Lonnie was worried about Tommy Lee and felt it might do him some good to spend Christmas Eve with a few folks from back home.

But the night before, Tommy Lee had made the mistake of mentioning it to a couple of people he knew who happened to be in Ben Frank's restaurant at the time, and tonight shortly after the party began the half dozen or so friends from Nashville were suddenly augmented by a dozen of Hollywood's hippest street people, none of whom had any particular place to be on Christmas Eve.

Millie Michaelson, drink in hand, sat on the floor in front of the couch, her eyes restlessly probing the room for the young guitar player she had been introduced to a few moments earlier. Beside her, already passed out drunk, wedged in between the couch and the wall, lay Goose Halsey. Above them, slouched into a corner of the couch, wearing his customary T-shirt and jeans, sat Tommy Lee, stoned from the marijuana he had been smoking since morning, along with the pills he had been dropping since early afternoon and the wine he had been drinking ever since the party began.

At the other end of the couch sat a dumpy brunette wearing large earrings, looking nervous and out of place. On the floor in front of her, overweight and perspiring profusely, sat Lonnie Pratt. Another couple occupied the dining room table. The man's face was pock-marked and his hair vintage Presley. He was Tommy Lee's principle dope supplier. The girl beside him, underweight, pinch-faced and considerably younger, looked like one of the girls who were now starting to hang out on the Strip near the ITRC offices. They sat drumming their fingers on the table, impatient for Carl Clinger and his friends to leave so they could light up.

Behind them in the kitchen doorway, talking with two young men who looked like musicians, stood a big-chested brunette named Gloria. On the far side of the room, half hidden by the stereo and oblivious to their surroundings, a young man and woman stood kissing. Another half dozen or so people were scattered in various places about the rooms, most of them sitting on the floor, including a fairly attractive young woman in red who sat alone with her back to the wall and her legs stretched out in front of her.

The party was being quietly dominated by a group of five people, all but one of them approaching middle-age, who were positioned in front of the big picture window that looked out on the Valley and the winding trail of lights that was Ventura Boulevard. At the center of this group, dressed in a black mohair suit and expensive, brightly-polished shoes, stood Carl Clinger. To his left, his chubby wife Barbara Jean, with her blond hair teased into a beehive that rose a full six inches above her head. To Clinger's right, punctuating his sentences with occasional nods, stood Buddy Pruitt, a Nashville music publisher whose facial features bore a startling resemblance to those of Roy Rogers. Beside Pruitt, but not taking part in the conversation, stood his wife Mary Ellen. She was occupied in surveying the guests whose appearances did not meet with her approval. Clinger was holding a drink in one hand, gesturing broadly with the other. His conversation was directed to Sarah Donovan.

"Honey, I'm tellin' you what I know—you'll never be a genuine star until you come back to Nashville and country music. And I just wanna do one album on you, that's all, me and Lonnie and Tommy Lee, if we can get him straightened out and talk him into coming back home where he belongs. And this is the time for it, country music is gettin' ready to explode."

"He's right, honey," Barbara Jean Clinger said. "You ought to see Nashville now. You wouldn't believe how much it's growing."

Sarah Donovan did not respond well to pressure of any kind, and she could already feel herself beginning to overreact to the attempted coercion of Clinger and the others. She tried to keep her voice steady. "I keep telling you all that I don't want to come back to Nashville. I don't want to be a country star even if I could, which I don't believe for a minute. I like what I'm doing. I like the kind of music I'm singing and I like playing Vegas and Tahoe with big orchestras and good arrangements. I'm going to do another middle-of-the-road album as soon as the baby's born and next year I'm going to sign with an agency and start doing commercials."

"Commercials?" Barbara Jean snorted. "You're going to waste your time and talent doing commercials? You ought to be ashamed of yourself, Sarah."

"Barbara Jean, I can make more money doing one commercial for a big company like Clairol than I can in six months of singing country songs, and I don't have to do all that traveling."

"That ain't the point," Clinger injected himself back into the conversation. "Commercials are fine, we all know that, but as a sideline. What we're talkin' about here is your overall career. You're a country girl, pure and simple, and you ain't got much of a future at all singin' middle-of-the-road tunes. I mean, face it, there ain't no sense in you tryin' to imitate Vikki Carr and Jackie DeShannon and them gals."

"That's right," Barbara Jean said, "look at Skeeter Davis. She's been singing country music for years, and this is the biggest year she's ever had. Of course she sells to the pop market, too, but she's a good Christian girl who doesn't try to get above herself."

"I'm not trying to get above myself," Sarah said defensively.

"Listen, I'm gonna tell you somethin', honey"— Clinger lowered his voice and moved in a little closer—"I was talkin' to Buddy here about you a couple of days ago—"

"That's right, honey, he sure was," Pruitt said.

"—and I was sayin' to him that there's a big hole in country music right at this moment that's got to be filled, and you are just the gal who can do it."

"Oh, Carl, are you still talking about Patsy Cline? I don't know why you keep bringing her up. You know I don't sound anything like her."

"Yes, you do, honey," Barbara Jean said. "You've got that same little sad sweetness in your voice."

"That's right," Pruitt said, nodding his head vigorously, "and I got just the tune for you. Carl knows—right, Carl? I was just gettin' ready to play it for Patsy when she and Hawkshaw and Randy and them got killed goin' up to do that benefit for that boy in Kansas."

"What's it called?" Sarah asked.

"Well, now—"

"You know he can't tell you that, honey," Clinger interrupted quickly. "Good titles are just like money in the bank, you know that as well as I do."

"I wasn't trying to be tricky, Carl. I was just thinking that maybe he could send a demo to Les Goodson in New York, and if Les thinks it's right for me—"

"Well, if that ain't something," Barbara Jean said angrily. "Here we are straining ourselves as hard as we can to get you back where you belong, and you're ready to sell us down the well to some Jew in New York who—"

"Now wait a minute, honeybunch," Carl soothed, "I know Les. He's a good boy and he's done a lot for Sarah, but the thing is"—he returned his attention to Sarah—"you got to decide where you belong, and we both know where that is."

"I don't need you to tell me where I belong, Carl."

"Well, I declare!" Barabara Jean huffed. "If you're not the most ungrateful—"

"Listen, honey," Clinger said to Sarah, "you're makin' too big a fuss over this thing. Remember now, we ain't talkin' about but one album."

Sarah drank the last of her wine and set the empty glass on the floor by the window. She fished in her purse for a cigarette and waited for one of them to light it for her. Buddy Pruitt flicked his zippo lighter and she inhaled deeply and sighed. "Carl, let me talk it over with Mark when he gets home, okay?"

"You don't have to talk it over with him," Barbara Jean said, still angry, "Carl's the one who—"

"No, I want to talk to Mark about it."

"Now, honey, you don't have to worry him about it," Carl said. "It's just a small thing and he's already got enough on his mind tryin' to run Arrow. So why don't I just set it up myself? All it'll take is one phone call to New York and—"

"And that song ain't just gonna sit there," Pruitt said. "I got an option coming up on it the first of the year. I got to give it to somebody or give it back."

"Well, just let me talk to Mark about it."

Sarah's hesitancy finally became too much for Barbara Jean to put up with. "You know what's wrong with you, Sarah—you're ungrateful! I mean, after all Carl's done for you, you should jump at the chance to come back home and make a record with him. But you've got the big head, sitting out here with your rich movie star in-laws, thinking just because they let you play Las Vegas—"

"Oh, Barbara Jean, will you stop it?"

"That's right, you think you're too good for all the people who stuck by you when you didn't have a pot nor a window. You think you're too damn good to sing country music, that's what's wrong with you! Well, I'll tell you one thing—"

"Barbara Jean, just leave me alone—*please!*"

"No, I'm not going to leave you alone, Miss-high-and-mighty, not after all Carl's done for you. If it wasn't for him you'd still be running around Nashville in Tommy Lee's pick-up truck, sleeping with every man you could get your hands on!"

Sarah felt herself fighting to hold back the tears. It seemed like the harder she tried to pull herself up, the more they wanted to hold her down. "Dammit, what did Carl do for me," she heard the hysteria in her voice, "except work me to death and cheat me out of half my royalties? And spend half his time trying to take me to bed! And when I got sick he didn't even send me so much as a card, not even a damn card! So you get off that subject right now!"

"When you got sick? *Sick?* You weren't sick, the only thing wrong with you was you were full of dope and—"

"*Bobbie Jean!*" Millie Michaelson's voice covered the room like a peal of thunder. "If you say one more word to her I'm going to come over there and smack the shit out of you!"

"Alriiight," a woman's voice came from the dining room table, "let's get down!"

"The hell with you all," Sarah said, "I'm going home!"

"I wish you would come over here," Barbara Jean shouted at Millie.

"Now wait a minute," Pruitt tried to calm things down, "you gals know better than that. You been friends for . . ."

Millie grabbed Sarah's arm as she passed. "Wait a minute."

"No, I'm leaving."

"Fuck her, let her go," Tommy Lee said thickly as he moved toward them. "She don't belong here anyhow."

"He's right, let me go."

"Dammit, Sarah, are you going to spend the rest of your life letting people walk over you?" Millie threw Barbara Jean Clinger an angry look. "She's jealous, that's all. You know it as well as I do. What are you going to do, let her chase you away like you've done something wrong?"

"Millie, it's getting late. I really should go."

"Okay," Millie released her arm, "go. Keep on being a damn doormat if you want to, I don't care!"

Sarah stood there for a moment feeling unsure of herself, exposed, then she forced herself to take a quick look around the room. Nobody appeared to be watching her, they had already returned to their conversations. The dumpy little brunette at the other end of the couch gave her a tentative smile of encouragement, and Lonnie Pratt, still sitting there on the floor, pointed toward his sister, who was now engaged in an animated conversation with Carl and the others, and made a funny face. Sarah thought about the long drive back to Malibu and sitting in the house all by herself waiting for Mark to come home, and she knew she would be miserable. She couldn't make up her mind what to do. It was Tommy Lee who decided for her.

"Aw f'Chrissakes, Sarah, one more goddamn drink ain't gonna kill you."

It wasn't what he said, it was the look in his eyes that touched her. The sullen jealousy had been replaced by a sadness she had never seen there before. It was a pleading look, almost like he was trying to tell her something.

Millie reached under the couch for her purse. She removed a small vial of capsules and stuck them in Sarah's hand. "Here, go fix your face and take a couple of these, you'll feel better."

"I'm not supposed to—"

"They're just tranquilizers, they're not going to hurt you. Hurry up, don't be a party pooper."

Outside Paulie had been standing with his ear to the door. "Jesus, will you listen to that shit? Yelling and arguing, Johnny Cash on the record player—what is this, a fucking hillbilly party?"

"Do me a favor, Schultz, quit bitching, okay?" Caulfield said. He gave the door a couple more loud thumps with his fist. There was still no answer.

"They can't hear you with all that noise going on. It sounds like the fucking OK Corral in there."

"Schultz, I've got an idea. . . ."

"What?"

"Why don't you go hop in your little green car and split?"

"What the hell, I'm here now, I might as well check it out."

"Then shut up." Caulfield raised his fist to bang on the door again, just as an overweight young man of thirty opened it and peered out vacantly.

"Hi, I'm Terry Caulified. I think we're expected."

"Terry Caulfield? Well, I'll be!" Lonnie Pratt stuck out his hand and introduced himself. "It's a real pleasure to meet you. I'm one of the biggest fans you got."

"Beautiful," Caulfield said, taking the hand and nodding at Paulie. "You know Paul Schultz, don't you?"

"Paul Schultz? The genius himself? You know, I *thought* that was him." Pratt had obviously picked up a little salesmanship from Carl Clinger. "Well, well, well . . . you all come on in and lemme get you a drink and introduce you around."

"What was all that goddamn noise a minute ago?" Paulie asked.

"Oh, you know how it is when home folks get together," Pratt said vaguely. He stepped aside and ushered them into a small entrance hall, led them past an opened bedroom door, past another closed door just as a toilet flushed, and into the dimly lit living room. A few of the younger people recognized Caulfield immediately, smiled and called out greetings. Several of the older women looked him over appreciatively. The others merely eyed him curiously, thinking they probably should know who he was but were not sure why. Nobody paid Paulie much attention.

"Before you do anything else," Pratt said to Caulfield, "I want you to come over here and meet my fiancée."

Caulfield didn't hear him. He was busy evaluating the women. "I beg your pardon?" he said.

"He said he wants you to meet his old lady," Paulie explained.

"Beautiful," Caulfield said, "but how about a beer first?"

"Sure thing, but don't move away from here now, I want her to meet you. How about you?" he asked Paulie.

"Dynamite," Paulie said dryly. He watched Pratt turn and head for the kitchen, and began looking for someone he might know.

"Excuse me, please." A woman's voice came from behind them.

They stepped aside to let a slender blond woman pass. She was about Paulie's height, dressed in an alluring yellow-silk cocktail dress that matched her hair. She moved away from them with a quiet, almost shy grace. Caulfield stared after her. "You know who that is, don't you?"

"Yeah. I wonder what she's doing here. . . ."

"Probably waiting for me," Caulfield said. "Why don't you introduce us?"

"I don't know her."

"Bullshit."

"No, I just seen her on TV a couple of times is all. We don't hang out in the same circles."

"Schultz—did you see that ass?"

"No. Frankly, I ain't interested in shopping around for a new label right at the moment."

Caulfield stood on tiptoes, his eyes scanned the room. "I don't see Donovan here anywhere, she must be by herself."

"She ain't by herself," Paulie said impatiently, "there must be twenty people here, counting me. Besides, you ain't that fucking stupid."

"Don't try to con me, Schultz, you know goddamn well I'm that stupid."

"C'mon Terry, f'Chrissakes—"

"It's not like I've got a choice," Caulfield said. "I mean, I've *got* to get into her pants. I couldn't live with myself another day if I didn't."

"I never realized you had such a fucking ego problem before."

"Oh yeah, it's a bitch. Most of the time I can't control it, and this is one of those times."

"Here you go," Pratt handed them each a can of Bud. "Sorry I took so long but I got back there and got to talking—"

"No problem, old buddy," Caulfield said.

"C'mon, I want you all to meet Dorothy."

"Hey, listen—you guys go ahead, I'll be there in a minute." Paulie had caught a quick glimpse of Tommy Lee Whitaker and remembering the altercation at the Christmas party, he wanted to take a little time and decide what his next move should be.

He slid further along the wall to get out of Whitaker's line of vision. Somebody gave him a push and he moved over a bit more. He felt a tug at his leg and looked down. He shook his head in disbelief at the sight of the young woman in red sitting on the floor beside him with her legs stretched out in front of her. "Hi, Paulie," she said.

424 •

Paulie was unable to control his anger. "What the fuck are you doing here?"

"Paulie, sit down here," she patted the floor, "I want to talk to you a minute, okay?"

"I'm trying to be a goddamn gentleman, so just leave me alone, Gilda."

"Paulie, at least let me tell you what happened. . . ."

Paulie stared down at her for a few more seconds, then slid down the wall and sat on the floor beside her. "I don't understand you, Gilda," he said in his whiney voice. "I mean, how could you do that to me?"

She took one of his hands in both of hers and placed it in her lap. "Paulie, I know you're mad and you've got every reason to be, but—"

"Don't start conning me, Gilda."

"—I didn't mean to stand you up on purpose. Something came up at the last minute and I tried to call you but your line was busy."

"Something came up, huh? Well, don't tell me, let me guess. I bet it was a . . . a party, right?"

"It's not like it looks. I just, uh, couldn't get out of it."

Paulie suddenly realized that she was still holding his hand and jerked it away. "I'm gonna tell you something, Gilda. You've got a lot of nerve, a lot of fucking nerve, after all the trouble I went through for you!"

"I'm sorry."

"You know what I did—I made dinner reservations for us at Tracton's. I made after-dinner reservations at the Hollywood Roosevelt, and that ain't no cheap place, you know that. I went and got my car washed—"

"I'm sorry, Paulie, I really am."

"—and I even stopped at the drugstore and bought you a fucking Christmas present. Now I'm gonna ask you a question, Gilda, and you give me an honest answer—what kind of bullshit is that?"

"Paulie, all I can say is I'm sorry."

"Well, at least you're sorry," Paulie said. "So what are you doing here, and don't gimme none of that 'something came up' crap."

"Well, it's a long story. . . ."

"That's okay, I ain't going nowhere."

She took his hand in both of hers again. "Can I ask you a question, Paulie?"

"What?"

"What did you get me for Christmas?"

"A Lady Gruen wristwatch with diamonds instead of numbers."

"At the drugstore?"

"They got 'em there."

She squeezed his hand. "What are you going to do with it now, take it back?"

"I already gave it to my mother."

"Oh. How did she like it?"

"She don't believe in Christmas. She thought I was crazy. So what are you gonna do now, just keep sitting here?"

"I don't know. If Jimmy doesn't want to take me home maybe you—" She glanced up over his head. "Hi, Terry!"

"Hey, Gilda, what's happening?" Caulfield said. "Where you been? I tried to call you a couple of times."

"Nowhere," she said. "Have you still got your car?"

"Yeah, I'll call you sometime. Maybe we can go out and get it on." He nudged Paulie with his foot. "C'mon, somebody wants to meet you."

"Aw fuck his old lady," Paulie said, "I'm busy."

"No, not her, Carl Clinger."

"*Clinger?* What's he doing here?"

"I don't know. Why don't you ask him?"

"Okay, I'll be there in a minute. I just wanna get a couple of things straight here."

"C'mon, I think he's getting ready to split."

Paulie sighed and raised an arm and Caulfield yanked him to his feet. They started to walk away.

"Paulie, don't leave without saying good-bye. I may, uh, need a ride home, okay?"

Paulie turned and gave her an angry look. "If I give you a ride, Gilda, it won't be home, you can bet on that."

"I didn't know you knew Gilda?" Caulfield said as they started across the room.

"What do you care?"

"You balled her yet?"

Paulie started to lie, but changed his mind. "Naw. To tell you the truth, she don't turn me on that much."

"You ought to. She gives great head."

Caulfield's words dug a little deeper than Paulie would have expected. He was about to make a retort, when Lonnie Pratt stopped him and introduced him to his fiancée, the dumpy brunette with the big earrings named Dorothy. While the introductions were being made, Tommy Lee stared vacantly at Paulie from the other end of the couch. Paulie nodded a peace offering but Whitaker made no sign of recognition. Introductions completed, Paulie and Caulfield started toward Carl Clinger again. Clinger saw them coming.

"Well now, this has got to be Paul Schultz! How are you, boy? Goddamn, I been looking forward to meetin' you and shakin' your hand personally!"

"How's it going?" Paulie said, extending his own limp hand.

"If it was any better," Clinger said, "I'd have to franchise. The only thing is, I guess I just haven't got over Gino's death yet. I don't mind sayin', Paul, it hit me pretty hard—hit us all pretty hard, I guess. Things won't be the same in our business without him. He was a great man, a great *record* man. But I don't have to tell you that, do I?"

"Well, I'm gonna be honest with you," Paulie said. "I met him a couple of times and he didn't impress me that much."

Paulie's words made Clinger pause in mid-platitude. But he continued to smile as he flipped through his mental file to find a way to bring Paulie around to his way of thinking. The first thing, he understood, was to get Paulie to start agreeing with him, and being the complete salesman that he was, it only took him an instant.

"Lemme tell you why—because you're hard as hell to impress, am I right?"

"Yeah," Paulie admitted. "I don't get impressed too easy."

"I know that," Clinger said, "and that's what makes you a good record man."

"I gotta go along with you on that," Paulie said.

"Goddamn right. But I'm gonna tell you one thing, Paul, you damn sure impressed *him!*"

"Well, he never said nothing. . . ."

"That was just his way, Paul. But he admired the hell out of you, I can say that for a fact, the way you been keeping records on the charts for the last couple of years. Hell, it ain't no goddamn picnic tryin' to make decent records nowadays, 'specially when you gotta deal with kids who don't know shit from shinola."

"It ain't all ice cream and ginger ale, I can tell you that," Paulie said, happy to find somebody in the upper level of ITRC who understood the problems connected with being a successful record producer. "You know what my problem is. My problem is, I'm *too* nice, you know what I mean?"

"Do I know what you mean?" Clinger said. "Hell, I know *exactly* what you mean. Your problem is, you wanna see everybody make it and everybody ain't got what it takes to make it, did I state it right?"

"I couldn't have put it no better," Paulie said.

"Yeah, that can break your goddamn heart sometimes," Clinger clucked his tongue, "but it's all part of the game, part of being a successful executive. Gino knew that and I know that, and that's why I admire you like I do, Paul. Come to think of it, you got a tune out now that's doin' pretty good, ain't you?"

"*Two,*" Paulie corrected.

Buddy Pruitt had been standing off to the side, waiting for Clinger to introduce them. He knew who Paulie was, of course, but being a publisher of country music and not being too familiar with the current pop charts, he had no idea that Paulie was producing so many successful records for ITRC. Now, unable to contain himself any longer, he stuck out his hand and introduced himself.

"A pleasure," Paulie said.

"Nosiree, it's my pleasure," Pruitt corrected, handing Paulie one of his business cards. "I can tell just from listening to you and Carl talk, we gotta get together on some material."

"Right," Paulie said. He stuck the card in his pocket without looking at it, then moved his body around a little so as to exclude Pruitt from the rest of the conversation. "So what do you think's gonna happen now?" he asked Clinger. "I mean, now that Turicotti's gone down the tube?"

"Well—I was in New York for the funeral, of course. Just flew in from there this morning, as a matter of fact. And, Paul, all I can say is, there are gonna be one hell of a lot of changes before it's all over."

"Like what?"

"I don't know if you know it or not, but Gino and me got to be pretty good friends over the last couple of years, ever since they bought my label. Now I'm gonna tell you something, Paul"—Clinger put an arm around Paulie's shoulders and drew him into an imaginary circle of confidence—"but I want you to keep it under your hat, follow me?"

"No problem," Paulie said.

"Shortly before Gino died, we had a long talk. We decided that it was high time to go all out on country music. And starting this coming June, with the new fiscal year, we were all set to expand our Nashville production budget by a half million dollars. Now I don't have to tell you what that would have meant, do I?"

Paulie shook his head. He knew what it would have meant, all right. Had Turicotti lived, starting the middle of next year ITRC would have flooded the airwaves with hillbilly music—which, as far as Paulie was concerned would have been a goddamned shame.

"That's right," Clinger said, "it would have meant a lot more country music being played on major market stations. But that ain't the important thing. The important thing is that country music, what I consider to be the only real true-blue American music, would finally be getting the big-money push it deserves."

"So what do you think's gonna happen now?" Paulie persisted.

"Well, I know what *I'm* gonna do, Paul. I'm gonna keep pushing as hard as I can for that raise in the budget. I want it to go through. I feel I owe it to Gino and I owe it to our company, but most of all I owe it to the future of our business to keep on after it. Nashville is the heart of America and country music is the heart of the record business—"

"That's right, Carl," Pruitt said over Paulie's shoulder.

"—and that brings me up to somethin' I want to talk to you about, Paul."

"What's that?"

"Well, two things. First of all, I'd like to see you come down to Nashville and cut one or two albums with us." Clinger raised his palm before Paulie had a chance to respond. "Now wait a minute—before you say no, I want you to think about a couple of things. First of all, we got new people and new money comin' in there every day. And we got some of the best studios and musicians in the world. And we got the very best songwriters on the face of the earth, ain't no doubt at all about that. Before it's all over we intend to have every big name singer in the business cut at least one album there, that means everybody from Sinatra on down, that's our plan."

"Umm-hmmm," Paulie said, again opening his mouth to speak.

"Now wait a minute—before you say no, listen to this. Suppose, say, you bring in that boy over there"—Clinger nodded toward Terry Caulfield, who was sitting next to Sarah on the floor in the corner by the stereo—"and cut him on a few country tunes with country musicians, ain't no tellin' what might happen. Hell, you could open up a whole new market for him and a whole new ballgame for yourself, too, am I right?"

"Maybe so," Paulie said. "What's the other thing?"

"Paul, the other thing is this. In the next few months there's gonna be a whole lot of politicking goin' on back in New York to see who gets Gino's job. Now I'm gonna tell you the truth, I thought it over and I wouldn't mind having that job at all because I think I'd do right by it."

"I don't have nothing to say about what goes on back there," Paulie said.

"Well, you ain't directly connected with the company because you deal with us as an independent producer, I know that. But you carry a lot of weight in this business, and if I have to call on you farther on up the road I wanna know I can count on you to say and do the right thing. . . ."

Clinger's message was unmistakable, and not only did Paulie understand it clearly, he was also vulnerable to it. His production agreement with ITRC now had less than six months remaining and he was already thinking about forming his own label, which he might want ITRC to distribute for him. And Carl Clinger was not only a strong force within the company now, he was preparing for bigger things, which meant that the time could come when Paulie might find himself sitting across the desk from Clinger discussing a multimillion-dollar deal.

On the other hand, in Paulie's opinion, country music sucked. It had always sucked and there was no indication that it would not continue to suck in the future, so the last thing in the world he wanted to do was take Terry Caulfield or anybody else to Nashville to make some money for those Jew-hating bastards. It was a dilemma. But Paulie was up to it, albeit reluctantly, and so instead of telling Clinger what he could do with Nashville and his shit-kicking buddies, he removed Clinger's arm from around his shoulders and gave the hand attached to it a firm clasp.

"Carl, I'm gonna be completely honest with you," he said, reaching to project sincerity, "I never had a chance to talk like this to nobody in your end of the business before, so quite naturally I didn't know what to expect. But I like you. No, I'm *impressed* by you. You are one of the few men I've talked to up there who really knows what's going on out here. So I'll tell you what I'm gonna do, I'm gonna take a good long look at this thing and get back to you by the first of the year, you know what I mean?"

It was a momentous occasion, one that should have been, if not frozen in time, at least preserved for all the music business hustlers-to-come by a photographer from *Cashbox* magazine. Unfortunately, it did not last very long, for at that moment Barbara Jean Clinger approached them with several coats slung over her arm.

"Let's go, Carl. I can smell dope."

Paulie sniffed the air. She was right. It was the Hollywood street people's way of telling the whiskey-drinking home folks from Nashville that it was time to split.

"Honeybunch, have you met Paul Schultz?"

"How do?" she said brusquely. "C'mon, Carl, let's go. I'm sick of this place and I'm sick of these people. Tommy Lee's passed out on the couch and Millie's got some young boy hemmed up in the dining room, and"—she glanced over her shoulder at Sarah and Terry

Caulfield together on the floor and made an ugly face—"C'mon, Buddy, Mary Ellen's already waiting for us outside in the car."

"Paul, I can't tell you how glad I am that I finally got a chance to meet you and shake your hand personally," Clinger said.

"Same here," Paulie said.

"Maybe we can have lunch or somethin' and go over this thing a little more?"

"Yeah, where are you staying?"

"We're at the Beverly Hilton. We're gonna be there for a week, so call me. I'm serious now, boy, call me."

"Right."

"A pleasure to meet you, Paul," Pruitt paused long enough to pump Paulie's hand a few times. "Merry Christmas to you and get in touch with me now, I'm serious about that. I know I got some tunes you can use."

Paulie watched them leave, including Lonnie Pratt and his fiancée. As he stood there quietly, he caught a glimpse of Terry Caulfield and Sarah Donovan on the floor in the corner behind the stereo. Caulfield was trying to kiss her.

Across the room, Tommy Lee lay on his back on the couch with his mouth open. Further away, in the dining room, he could see Jimmy Britto, the guitar player, nuzzling Millie Michaelson, his hands cupping her buttocks. The pinched-face girl who had been sitting at the dining room table now stood at the stereo, changing records. The quiet sound of Jim Reeves was suddenly replaced by the steady thump-thump of the Chantays. As she reached to dim a lamp, she accidentally tipped over an almost empty half-gallon wine jug.

Paulie left the window and crossed the room to Gilda. She was no longer sitting alone with her back to the wall. She was now lying on the rug with her head on the leg of one of the musicians who had been standing in the kitchen doorway when Paulie arrived. They were sharing a joint. It looked like she would have no trouble getting a ride home.

It was, Paulie decided, time to get the hell out of there.

HOLLYWOOD
DECEMBER 1963

Mark pushed his way through Los Angeles International Airport toward the bank of telephones. He dialed his home number and let it ring. He counted twenty times before he slammed the receiver back in place.

Still no answer!

He showed his claim check to a redcap in the baggage area and, impatiently waving the man aside, snatched his bags from the conveyor belt. Outside, the bright sunlight sent a stab of pain through his eyes. He stood at the curb, blinking and fidgeting, trying to control his anger, wondering where the hell she was.

The cabdriver was full of Christmas hangover and half-completed New Year's resolutions. They were all the way to the San Diego Freeway before Mark could convince him that his first priority was to turn around and keep his eyes on the road.

As he neared the house, Mark could feel his anger being displaced by worry. He was sorry now he hadn't insisted Sarah stay home. Yet, even though he had no use for Millie Michaelson, nor any of Sarah's other Nashville friends, he still had no right to tell Sarah not to see them.

The idea that she might be with another man didn't occur to him. If jealousy had been one of his failings, he never would have married her. He was sure she was trying as hard as she could to be a good wife, and was genuinely excited about the baby's coming. And if she wanted to be with another man, it wouldn't take all night and half the next day. No, something had happened to her—and the closer he got to home, the more sure of it he was.

Her car wasn't in the driveway. Inside, the Christmas-tree lights were still on in the living room, which meant she hadn't expected to be out all night. Her traveling clothes were hung neatly behind the bathroom door, an indication that she had intended to be ready for the drive down to his folks' place.

He decided, before he did anything else, to shower and change clothes. Afterward he made a pot of coffee and went back into the living room and sat on the couch, sipping from his mug and looking at the unopened presents under the tree.

"What am I supposed to do now?" he wondered aloud. "Start calling around, asking if anybody's seen my wife?"

He decided he might as well get the worst of it out of the way, and dialed the Los Angeles county coroner's office.

They put him on hold for five minutes before disconnecting him. He called back. No, she was not there. He hung up, feeling a mixture of relief and guilt. Relief because she hadn't been taken there, guilt because he was angry that he still didn't know where she was.

Now he had to start telephoning. He felt like an idiot.

He dialed Bob Silverstein's number, knowing that he was procrastinating. As he'd expected, there was no answer. He listened for a few rings and slammed the receiver down.

Now the obvious. . . .

But there was no answer from Millie Michaelson's phone, either.

He hadn't eaten since the previous morning, and he could feel his stomach complaining. The doctor had told him to try to keep something in it. He went back to the kitchen and looked through the refrigerator. Nothing in there looked worth the bother of chewing and swallowing, so he poured himself another cup of coffee. Back in the living room, he picked up the leather address book on the telephone stand and thumbed through it, looking for Monique's parents' number. Earlier in the week, when he called Sarah from New York, she had mentioned that Monique had invited her to spend a night there. Maybe Sarah had changed her mind and decided to go, after all. If so, she could have started home late. It was a good two hours' drive from Buena Park to Malibu. Maybe that was it.

Monique's father answered. Monique and Les had gone to Knott's Berry Farm with another couple. No, Sarah had not been there either last night or this morning.

Disgusted, he hung up and began thumbing through the book again, trying to think of someone who might know anything. Maybe there had been an emergency, maybe someone had taken sick and called her. He phoned several girls she was attending classes with. They hadn't heard from her. Neither had Mrs. Lydon, the woman who made Sarah's gowns, a friend of both of theirs. He called everybody he could think of.

Twenty minutes later he was no closer to tracking her down.

After he had called the last number without success, he decided he might as well let his folks know that they would be late. He dialed Palm Springs. When his mother answered, all he could think of to tell her was that Sarah wasn't feeling well.

"Can she come to the phone, dear?" He knew his mother wasn't fishing—that wasn't a part of her nature. She was just trying to be of help if she could.

"No, she's asleep now."

"Have you called the doctor yet?"

"No, I'm sure it's just a touch of the flu. She was throwing up when I got in, so I figured maybe we should wait awhile before we drove all the way down there."

"But you're still coming down tonight, aren't you?"

"Oh, I think so." He tried to sound as offhand as he could. "It's according to how she feels when she wakes up."

"Well, don't come now if she doesn't feel better. You don't want her to miscarry. And if she's vomiting, it could be very dangerous for her."

"I know, Mother, we'll be careful."

"She's not hemorrhaging, is she?"

"Oh, no, nothing like that. I'm sure it's just a touch of the flu."

"Mark"—he could almost see his mother looking at him through the phone—"is there anything I can do?"

"No, don't worry, we're fine. We'll be there as soon as we can."

He disconnected and tried Millie's number again. Still no answer. He sat there frowning, drinking cold coffee, and staring at the Christmas tree. . . .

Theirs was not a marriage made in heaven, he knew that. It was a marriage consecrated upon the nebulous reality of the world they lived in. In another time, she might have spent her life on a small farm, churning butter on the porch, sending her kids down the road to wait for the school bus. In another time, he might have started up a record company in a small town in New Jersey, content to live out his days doing nothing more than the best he could, at whatever he did. But those times were gone, irrevocably and for good. And now, the pursuit of happiness entailed not so much the desire to function as the need for something to believe in.

He couldn't just sit there; he had to go find her.

On the second pass by Millie's house, he thought he saw a light. He parked and walked back. He knocked a few times, listened, but heard nothing inside. He walked to the edge of the porch and scanned the block. No sign of Sarah's car. No sign of any familiar cars. He knocked a few more times and thought about leaving a note, then changed his mind.

He went back to the car and sat trying to decide his next move. There was only one other place he could think of. He had tried to put it out of his mind, because if she had gone there, it meant she had lied to him.

But it was his last hope. If she wasn't at Whitaker's house, he would have to go to the police.

It was getting close to dark when he started up the canyon. He had been there only once, two years before, and he wasn't sure which of the winding roads to take. He made two wrong turns before he found himself approaching the three redwood houses shaped like half-moons.

He saw Sarah's car before he reached the top of the road, parked in the driveway behind Whitaker's Cadillac, its two right wheels resting in a clump of weeds. He could see no lights inside the house. He backed the car around and parked across the road and sat there gathering his courage.

He got out and started for the house. The evening was quiet. The only sound he heard was the wind blowing through the canyon. As he knocked at the door, he felt a surge of anger at Sarah for putting him in this position.

He waited, and when there was no answer, he knew for certain that something was wrong.

He tried the door. It was locked. He shook it harder. It wouldn't budge.

He went back down to the foot of the driveway and looked the area over. There was no way he could try to enter from the rear, the way the house was perched out over the canyon. But there was a window on the near side. His lips formed a wry smile as he pictured himself peering through it and seeing that skinny, dope-headed son of a bitch humping his wife.

He went around to the side of the house. The window was higher than he'd expected. He had to stand on tiptoes to get his eyes above the ledge. It was dark inside, too dark to see anything. He tapped on the window. Silence. He stood there for a few seconds, trying to plan his next move.

His next move, he thought, should probably be to go home and forget it.

He returned to his car and got a lug wrench from the trunk. It was flattened on one end. He could use it to pry the window open.

Some of the wood splintered away as he put his weight on the bar. The catch creaked once, twice, then relinquished with a bang that echoed through the canyon. He waited. There was no answering sound, from inside or out He pushed the window up, hoisted himself through it, and tumbled onto the bedroom floor.

His hand searched the bed in the darkness, half-expecting to touch a cold arm or leg. All it found was disheveled bedclothes. He felt like a fool—like a bit player in one of his father's old movies. He stood up and found the light switch by the door.

The room was empty, the bed unmade, a full ashtray on the nightstand beside it. He looked in the closet. It was also empty.

As he turned around, he caught a glimpse of himself in the mirror above the dresser. His eyes red-rimmed. His hair matted. The skin of his face looked like it had been smeared with yellow paint.

For Christ's sake, why am I here? he asked himself.

He made his way along the small hallway to the living room in the glow of the bedroom light, and turned on the lamp by the stereo.

Dirty glasses were scattered about, ashes on the rug. Whitaker's guitar lay facedown beside the couch, an uncapped, empty half-gallon wine jug beside it.

He went behind the kitchen counter. A loaf of bread had been left open. A package of sandwich meat was on the floor beside the refrigerator. A jar of mayonnaise had tipped over, and most of its contents had spilled into the sink.

He went back down the hall to the bathroom and turned on the light. Through the clutter, he thought he caught a whiff of Sarah's perfume, but realized it was probably his imagination. A hand towel had been balled up and dropped beside the toilet. He went over to it and spread it with his feet. It was caked with dried blood.

The room blurred for an instant, and a wave of nausea overtook him. His knees buckled and he had to put a hand on the wall to steady himself.

The Los Angeles County General Hospital guarded the end of Mission Road like a granite sentinel of despair. To get there, he had to drive through a neighborhood of taco huts, anglicized cantinas, and *pachukos* with ducktail haircuts glaring at him from the windows of chopped-down '57 Chevies.

The women's prison ward was on the third floor. He was directed to a middle-aged Mexican woman dressed in the khaki matron's uniform of the Los Angeles county sheriff's department. She sat behind a cluttered desk at the end of a junction of three corridors. Behind and slightly to her left was a twelve-foot door of steel bars. Her name was Mrs. Gutierrez. Her mouth was firm, but her eyes were kind.

". . . I'm sorry, it is not allowed. You must have a permit."

"But you can tell me why they brought her here, can't you?"

"I can tell you nothing. I do not know why she is here. I have not spoken with her." She saw the look on his face and raised her hands in a gesture of futility. "I'm sorry."

He pointed to the papers on her desk. "Does it say there?"

"I am not supposed to—"

"Please."

She seemed to debate with herself for a moment, then began thumbing through the papers. "Yes, here it is . . . Sarah Donovan, is that right?"

He nodded.

"Let's see . . . taken into custody at two-thirty-five this morning . . . direct to Valley Receiving Hospital . . . brought here at one-thirty this afternoon."

"How bad is she hurt?"

She looked through the papers again. "It is not . . . physical."

"Does it say what she did—what the charges are?"

"I am not supposed to say. She has not been arraigned yet."

"I . . . Please, she's my wife."

For someone who had been raised in the *barrio* of East Los Angeles and who had spent the last eighteen years of her life being cursed and spat upon by a procession of determined losers, most of whom regarded her with an abiding distrust, Felicia Gutierrez had retained an amazing amount of clemency for the human condition. Although much of her adult life had been given to offering palliation to those in trouble, seldom had she seen a human being more stricken than the young *anglo* who now stood before her.

"She will be arraigned Friday morning at ten o'clock at North Hollywood Municipal Court."

"On what charge?"

"As of now, suspicion of felony manslaughter." She saw his face blanch, his mouth begin to move rapidly, forming words she couldn't hear. She was sure he was going to crumble to the floor in front of her. She jumped to her feet and hurried around the desk. "Come! Follow me!" She hurried him down the hall and pushed a door open. "In there!"

He had not heeded the warnings soon enough. Ulcers and high blood pressure, the events of the past weeks—his confrontation with Sam Crockett, Turicotti's death, Max Geary's shocking revelations—had robbed him of his strength, destroyed his resiliency.

And now this . . .

Suspicion of felony manslaughter.

It was more than his mind was willing to absorb. He struggled to control the dizziness. One of the delicate vessels inside his brain, a tiny gristle half the size of a pin, collapsed in protest.

As he stepped inside, a violent pain tore at the back of his head. A sticky-sweet liquid filled his mouth and nose. He stumbled forward and reached for the sink to keep from falling. He gripped its edges, bent over, waiting for his head to clear, then looked up at himself in the mirror. His face and clothes were covered with blood. Immediately, another explosion seared his skull. Through the blur, he saw a fresh stream of blood spurt from his nose and mouth, felt himself gag.

"Mr. Donovan?" Felicia Gutierrez gingerly cracked the door and peeked her head inside. She saw him on his knees, smeared with blood, an arm flung over the sink to keep from toppling over.

She ran to him, knelt, and cradled his head in her arms, oblivious of his blood soaking her uniform. She held him until he stopped shaking, then helped him to his feet and wet a paper towel and dabbed at his face.

"I must call a doctor!"

"No. . . ."

She wet another, tried to wipe some of the blood from his clothes. "Can you walk?"

"Yes, I think so. Just shock . . . shock. . . ."

She placed his arm around her shoulders and helped him through the doorway and down the hall a few steps to a small employees' lounge, where she led him to a cot and gently eased him down.

"Don't move! I must get a doctor!"

She ran back to her desk and hurriedly dialed a number, spoke a few words into the mouthpiece, and ran back down the hall.

He was gone.

He left the freeway at Western Avenue and drove west on Sunset, past the prostitutes working the motels between Western and Bronson. At the stoplight at Van Ness, a girl approached his car. She saw the blood on his clothes and quickly stepped back on the curb.

By the time he reached LaBrea, his mind had cleared enough that he could begin to recognize his surroundings, but the cars and buildings and people around him still seemed to be moving in slow motion. At Crescent Heights, on his left, he saw the brightly lit Christmas tree in the foyer of the Litton Building, and laughed.

He was about to drive past the ITRC Recording Center when he changed his mind and made a sharp right turn from the center lane into the underground parking lot. The cars behind him swerved and slammed on their brakes, but he was not aware of them.

He entered the building through the rear, past the unguarded desk, and took the elevator to the twelfth floor. Only when he was walking down the deserted hallway to his office did he remember why he was there.

He stayed in the shower a long time. He dressed in the clothes he kept there for business meetings and went back to his private office, where he poured himself a half-snifter of brandy. Then he turned off all the lights and sat in the chair behind his desk. He swiveled it around to stare through the parted drapes at the city below him. He sat there until the city was quiet. By then, his headache had begun to subside and the knot in his stomach untie itself.

Slowly, he began to rouse his thoughts. . . .

He did not think about Sarah immediately, but about Max Geary and the things Geary had told him. And as he sat there, he could feel a surge of vigor begin to enter his body, a new strength born not from anger or frustration, but from the simple resolution that:

He could no longer tolerate things as they were. He had endured enough of other people's visions. He would now do whatever he must to make himself and his feelings clearly understood.

Obviously, then, he could not withdraw from his present circumstances to search for a better world, a world that, perhaps, existed only in his own imagination. He must first clean up the mess that surrounded him.

He had no intention of resigning from his job now. To quit was one thing; to be beaten, something entirely different. He would stay with the company and continue to work hard and insist his employees do what he felt was honorable and in the best interests of the business. And if they didn't comply, he would fire them or tear up their contracts. They were dispensable. There were more just like them lined up all over the world, anxious to take their places.

Having made that decision, he now turned his attention to Sarah.

He had either failed her in some way, or whatever she needed was beyond his capacity to give. But he would not desert her. He would be in court Friday morning for her arraignment. He would post her bail and they would leave together. He would take her to the little park in Topanga Canyon and they would sit and discuss their marriage and their child, and their lives—together or apart.

One way or the other, they would have to decide. . . .

That was all he could do for the moment, all he could think about, and so he got to his feet and crossed the darkened office to the door.

Downstairs, instead of going to his car, he walked through the parking lot and stood in the driveway, looking up and down the street, studying the Christmas decorations, and watching the cars crawl by. It began to rain. Slowly at first, then harder. He did not want to go home, so he walked the ten steps east to the small bar next door.

It was empty except for a couple in the booth just inside the door. He took a seat at the bar. The bartender, who was at the other end watching a movie on television, threw him an annoyed look before sauntering over to take his order for brandy.

He was studying the various names on the bottles behind the bar when the door to the ladies' room slammed and a blond girl stepped into the dim light of the hallway. He noticed that she bore a resemblance to Sarah, and wondered if it was just his imagination.

"Hi, Mr. Donovan," she called, coming over to him. "Merry Christmas!"

He nodded at her and returned his attention to the bottles.

"Remember me?"

"Yeah, sure—good to see you again. How've you been?"

"You don't remember me, do you?"

"No."

"Judy—I hitched a ride with you a few months ago from Music City to the unemployment office on Santa Monica, remember?"

"Oh yeah." A hint of a irony crept into his voice. "I wondered whatever happened to you."

"Nothing," she said.

The bartender threw them an angry look for disturbing his movie. "Judy, you'd better get those glasses, huh?"

"Oh, he's such a prick!" she mumbled, leaving to clear the glasses from the booth the couple had just vacated. She was back a minute later. "Hey, listen—I heard what happened. I'm really sorry."

"Yeah, well, that's how it goes." He shrugged.

She took the stool next to him. "He was such a nothing guy, I mean—"

"Judy, you know you're not supposed to sit with the customers!" the bartender snapped.

"Oh, you're such a puker, Kim! Why don't you just watch your movie and shut up!"

The bartender retaliated by turning the volume up. She touched Mark's sleeve. "I mean, I know you're not supposed to say anything bad about the dead, but he was, wasn't he?"

Mark finished cataloging the bottles behind the bar and turned around to face her. "Who?"

"Hey, listen, if you don't want to talk about it, I understand. I mean, that's cool, I don't blame you. . . ."

"I *can't* talk about it," he said. "I don't know what happened yet."

"Well, you know your wife is, uh, I mean . . ."

"Yeah, I just left there. They wouldn't let me talk to her, though, so I still don't know anything about it. I was in New York when it happened."

"Oh."

He tossed his drink down and tapped the bar for a refill.

"One of my girlfriends was there. She said it was a mess, a real bullshit scene. I can tell you the whole story." She touched his sleeve again. "But you probably don't want to hear it from me, huh?"

The bartender set his fresh drink down, snatched the money up, and threw him an annoyed look.

"Why not? I'm going to have to hear it sooner or later anyhow."

"You're a nice guy, you know. I never forgot you. I didn't even know who you were, but I was telling one of my girlfriends about you, and she told me. Then, when you got married, I saw your picture in the paper and everything, and I flipped out. I mean, I didn't know you were so heavy and everything."

He shrugged. "So what did you hear about it?"

"Well . . . I guess he went in the bathroom to use something, and passed out and hit his head and then, when somebody went to use it, they couldn't get in because he was blocking the door."

"Who?"

"Oh, I'm sorry, I forgot you didn't know. Tommy Lee."

"Oh." He had already guessed by now.

"And they pushed it opened and he was lying there unconscious with blood all over the floor from where he fell."

"So why didn't my wife leave with them?"

"Well, she was, uh . . ." She dropped her eyes in embarrassment.

"That's okay," he said quietly, "go ahead."

"Well, I guess they couldn't wake her up. She was in the bedroom with, uh, someone, and she had been drinking and dropping a lot of reds, I heard."

He felt a light thump at the back of his head, and the bottles on the shelf behind the bar began to shake.

"I'm sorry."

"That's okay, it wasn't your fault."

"No, people say they're sorry all the time and don't mean it, but I really *am* sorry. I've been through it. That's some cold shit, man." She impulsively put her arm around his waist and touched her lips to his cheek. "People are so fucked, you know."

He took a slug of his drink. "So then what happened?"

"Well, I guess somebody got scared or something when they got outside, and called the police . . . and, uh, I guess they went up there and found them."

"How many people did they take to jail?"

"Well, Tommy Lee was already dead by then, I guess, so just your wife and Terry."

"Caulfield?"

"Yeah, he's such a puker! God, is he on an ego trip! He rides around in his big Rolls, you know, and he thinks he can have any girl he wants."

"He probably can."

"What about your wife?"

"What about her?"

"Are you going to get a divorce?"

"I don't know."

"What did they charge her with, do you know yet?"

"Felony manslaughter."

"Oh, that sounds more serious than it is. They charge everybody with that who's around somebody who od's."

"Yeah . . . well, I appreciate you telling me." He tossed off the last of his drink and got up to leave.

"If you need some company, I can take off whenever I want. I'm just filling in for the regular girl to make a little extra money. She wanted to spend Christmas with her kids."

"No, I don't think so, but thanks anyhow. I don't feel like . . . like being with anybody right now."

"I think you misunderstood. I didn't mean we should get it on or anything like that, I just thought you might need somebody to ride around with you and talk to, maybe have a cup of coffee somewhere?"

"No, thanks anyway. I don't think I'd make very good company tonight."

"If you change your mind in the next half-hour . . ."

"I'll remember. Take care of yourself."

It was still drizzling when he stepped outside. His stomach felt as if it was melting, and he remembered he hadn't eaten anything since the previous morning. He walked to the curb and leaned against a lamppost and took several deep breaths. The rain felt good on his face.

He heard the radio playing before he saw them, and recognized the record as Paulie Schultz's latest on Terry Caulfield. He had a disgusted look on his face when he turned around.

There were three of them, a tall black boy of about eighteen or nineteen, walking with his arm around a white girl a few years younger, and a long-haired white boy who looked to be somewhere in between. They walked past him a few steps and stopped. He heard them whispering among themselves. The girl turned and approached him.

"Merry Christmas, sir."

He nodded.

"I was wondering—do you have any small change on you?"

He automatically patted his pockets. He had left his change on the bar. He shook his head.

"Anything," she said. "A couple of quarters, maybe?"

"I don't have any." He shrugged. She stared at him, obviously not believing him. She looked even younger from up close.

"Jesus, what a prick!" she said.

He shrugged again and turned away. She went back to her friends and said something. He heard them laughing. A moment later, the black started toward him.

"Hey, man!"

He didn't answer.

"Hey, punk!"

He turned around just as the black reached him. The boy was perhaps an inch taller than he. His hair was combed out into a massive, frizzy halo, and his clothes carried the odor of marijuana. The black regarded him contemptuously.

"You didn't have to talk to my woman like that, punk!"

"Like what?"

"Don't get silly with me, man! I'll kick your white ass all over this street!"

"No, you won't."

"Don't tell me I won't, you pussy motherfu—"

Mark's punch exploded in the boy's face. The force of it knocked him off his feet and sent him skidding across the wet pavement. He hit the building with a thud and slid to the ground, groaning and shaking his head. Mark crossed the sidewalk and stood above him, his face impassive. Then he slowly drew his foot back and kicked the black boy's face as hard as he could. There was a crunch of bone and flesh and the boy lay on his back, his eyes staring sightlessly up at the rain, blood pouring from his face onto the sidewalk.

It was the first deliberately cowardly thing Mark Donovan had ever done, and he waited for the wave of remorse to overtake him. It did not come. He felt nothing. His conscience did not speak. The knowledge made him smile.

"You prejudiced motherfuckerrr!" The girl was all over him,

clawing at his face. He pushed her away. She tried to kick him. "You prejudiced motherfuckerr!"

He pushed her away again. She attacked him again, scratching at his eyes. He pushed her harder.

"Get away from me!"

"You dirty prejudiced chickenshit bastard!"

She searched the ground for something to throw at him. The long-haired white boy advanced as if to attack him. He moved toward the boy. "Take another step, you bastard, I'll break your fucking neck!"

The boy darted away, dropping the transistor radio as his back hit the building. The girl picked it up and flung it at Mark as hard as she could. It hit Mark's shoulder and bounced into the street. The black groaned. The girl ran over and knelt on the pavement beside him.

"Are you okay, Raymond?" she asked anxiously. "Can you get up, baby?"

The black continued to groan. The white boy edged toward them, his eyes darting first to the boy on the ground, then across the sidewalk to be sure that Mark had not moved. The black groaned again and rolled over on his stomach.

"You okay, honey?" the girl asked.

"Try to get up, man," the white boy urged.

The girl glared across the sidewalk at Mark. "You didn't have to kick him!" Tears of hatred filled her eyes. "He's not an animal, you know!"

The black tried to struggle to his feet, the girl tugging at one side, the long-haired boy pulling at the other. A car door slammed. A man ran over to Mark.

"What happened? You okay?"

"None of your goddamned business," Mark said.

"C'mon, Raymond." The white boy's voice held a combination of anxiety and embarrassment. "C'mon, brother, you can make it."

They helped the black to his feet. He stumbled against the building and regained his balance. His face was stained with blood, his clothes torn from where they had scraped the sidewalk. One eye was closed. He peered around vacantly through the other, trying to see where he was.

"I don't blame you," the man mumbled, going back to his car. "Goddamned niggers . . ."

The girl came back to where Mark was standing, to retrieve the radio lying in the gutter by his feet. The record was still playing. But with a muddy sound, as if its grooves were caked with dirt. She examined it closely to see that it wasn't damaged, then raised her hate-filled eyes to meet Mark's gaze.

"You're just like my father!" she screamed.

And spit in his face.

They helped the black down the street, glancing back over their shoulders every few steps to see that Mark had not moved. He hadn't. He was standing there wiping the spit off his face with his sleeve, watching them with mild disinterest, thinking he should probably get something to eat before his stomach started acting up again.

EPILOGUE

Mimicry, though it be imitation, is not flattery, rather ridicule; because the mimic can reproduce the airs of his models and parody their seriousness and self-importance without being pledged to any of their physical or moral commitments.

—Santayana

Soon the rioting would begin, and men would gather in the streets to hurl bricks and bottles and bullets at each other in a simultaneous rejection and affirmation of all that had happened before, while all around them the music would play.

The turmoil would herald the coming of the Kings, brought forth from the womb of the Motherland to reign over the hearts of their loyal and foolish subjects. They would reign for seven years before being strangled by the greed of their consorts, and somewhere between their first strident trumbeats and their last mewling gasps, the music would die.

446 ·